# RAVAGED

More Books by Suzan Harden
(Each series is in suggested reading order)

## Bloodlines

*Blood Magick*
*Zombie Love*
*Zombie Confidential*
*Zombie Wedding*
*Amish, Vamps & Thieves*
*Blood Sacrifice*
*Love, War & a Bulldog*
*Zombie Goddess*
*Ravaged*
*Sacrificed*
*Reality Bites*
*Ghouls in the Grocery Store*
*Resurrected*
*Bloodlines Shorts Anthology*
*Bloodlines: The First Boxed Set*

## Seasons of Magick

*Spring*
*Summer*
*Autumn*
*Winter*
*The Seasons of Magick Anthology*

## Tales of the Twelve

*The Trickster Priestess
and the Demon*

## Justice

*Sword and Sorceress 28*
("Justice")
*Sword and Sorceress 30*
("Diplomacy in the Dark")
*Justice: The Beginning*
*A Question of Balance*
*A Modicum of Truth*
*A Matter of Death*
*A Touch of Mother*
*A Twist of Love*
*A Virtue of Child*
*A Hand of Father*
*A Measure of Knowledge*
*A Hint of Thief*
*A Cup of Conflict*
*A Barrel of Vintner*
*A Sprout of Wild*
*A Glimmer of Light*

## The Justice Thalia Stories

Snowfall
Murder Most Fowl
The Sweetest Poison
A Granddaughter of Mine
Too Many Fish in the Sea

## Crossover Worlds

*Invasion!*

**888-555-HERO**

*Hero De Facto*
*Hero Ad Hoc*
*Hero De Novo*
*A Very Hero Christmas*
*Hero De Jure*
*Hero In Camera*
*Hero Amicus Curiae*
*A Very Hero Wedding*
*A Very Hero New Year*
*Hero Ad Litem*
*Queer Eye for the Super Guy*

**Solar System Services, Inc.**

Alone Is Not Lonely
*Halloween Harvest*
("A Place at the Table")
A Place at the Table

**Millersburg Magick Mysteries**

*Spells and Sleuths*
*Fae and Felonies*
*Magick and Murder*
Feline Navidad

**Soccer Moms
of the Apocalypse**

*Pestilence in Pumpkin Spice*
*Famine in French Vanilla*
*War in White Chocolate*
*Death in Double Mocha*
Demons Run at Halloween

**The Enchanted Bakery**

*Chefs, Shrooms, and Sherry*
*Cakes, Cookies, and Conjuring*

**Miscellaneous**

*Sword and Sorceress 31*
("Pig-Headed")
*Sword and Sorceress 32*
("Unexpected")
*Practical Witches*
*Revenge Served Hot*
*The Yule Switch*
*Chocolate for Dinner*
*Silver Shoes and Pigs' Ears*
Snipe Hunt

For updates, news, and giveaways, join Suzan's mailing list at suzanharden.blogspot.com/p/contact-me.html, or visit her website at www.suzanharden.com. You can also check her out on Facebook @SuzanHardenWriter.

BLOODLINES #7

# SUZAN HARDEN

RAVAGED
(Bloodlines #7)

This is a work of fiction. All characters, organizations and events in this novel are products of the author's imagination and are not to be construed as real. Any resemblance to persons, living or dead, is entirely coincidental.



ISBN: 978-1-938745-66-9

Published by Angry Sheep Publishing LLC
Findlay, Ohio

Cover Design by For the Muse Design
Interior Design by JW Manus

---

AUTHOR'S NOTE: This story takes place three years after the events of *Zombie Goddess*.

# Chapter 1

The scent hit Logan Polk as he straightened with a bag of feed on his shoulder. A lady were. Definitely a lady were.

Wolf. His kind.

His canine libido stirred regardless of his human side, and he sniffed the air, trying to detect her location amid the cold, wet wind of the approaching snow storm. Montana was neutral territory for the various North American weres, but most of them visited in the summer and fall when hunting was good.

Not that the occasional loner didn't find it a good place to relax other times of the year. Or hide.

Like he did.

There. He admitted it like the therapist wanted.

It was fucking embarrassing for an alpha to have been kidnapped and tortured by a bunch of Normals. It was far worse to be treated for PTSD because of the experience.

But the therapy was working. He didn't have the nightmares like he used to. He owed Esther and Aaron a lot for insisting he talk to their daughter Sarah's doctor in Billings. Honestly, if another were had suggested it, he would've ripped their throats out.

But the witches understood. Sarah understood even more because she had been captured and tortured by the same assholes. The nineteen-year-old was talking about going to college next year back in California. She was getting on with her life.

And he was killing time in neutral territory.

*Pussy.*

The internal insult was lost when he spotted the lady were. She approached a bright yellow Jeep. Even if the plates hadn't screamed rental, the color did. Not even Marvin Newlin, the town's librarian/theater operator would be caught dead in anything that bright as his camou-flage-style nail polish attested.

The she-wolf had long brunette hair pulled in a tight ponytail. Legs that went on forever. If only she would turn around . . .

"Dammit, Polk! Get a move on. Ed can't wait all afternoon for you to load his truck."

The other were whirled around at Wade's shout. Mother Wolf bless his boss's bullhorn voice. The stranger was even better looking than his imagination had painted her. A perfectly proportioned rack and a face that would make angels weep.

She frowned when she caught Logan staring at her. Even though he was downwind from her, his unblinking gaze would be unmistakably wolf. Instead of approaching him, either to take him up on his blatant of-fer or to warn him off, she tossed her shopping bags in her Jeep, climbed in and pulled away.

Ed and Wade flanked Logan as she headed down Main Street and out of town. Wade clapped his shoulder. "She's a looker all right."

"Yeah," Ed drawled. "We were all beginning to wonder which way your flag flew. Guess Marvin wins the pool."

Alyson Tribideaux glanced in the rearview mirror. Nothing was be-hind her but the deepening twilight. Of all the things that could have gone wrong on this trip, another werewolf in town was not one she ex-pected. Much less a lone alpha from the bold way he watched her.

Was he yet another beau Papa had steered in her direction? Damn, she knew she should have lied to him about where her next project was taking her.

Please, Mother Wolf. Let the were at the feedstore be the only one around. The last thing she needed was fighting off a bunch of suitors in Tuttle Creek while landing the biggest interview of her career.

The Reverend Fred Haight had taken over the Sunshine Believers three years ago. He moved the controversial group from Los Angeles to a ranch outside of the little Montana town. He was also credited with turning them into productive members of society after some associates had kidnapped American TV actress Jessie Alton, the star of the hit comedy *Buddies.*

For some strange reason, none of the media had run the story, not even the most notorious of the tabloids, *The National Scoop.* He'd brought the incident up first when he answered Alyson's letter and emphasized that he wouldn't cooperate if she only focused on his group's lurid past. When she wrote back, saying she strived to be even-handed about her subjects in her documentary on splinter religions, Haight agreed for the Sunshine Believers to be included, but only once they'd talked in person.

When she asked if they could have a phone conversation instead, he refused politely. He pointed out he didn't trust her enough yet to allow her to have the ranch's private numbers. Given modern trolling techniques, she really couldn't blame him.

So, she had taken a chance, packed up her equipment, and flew to Montana on the slim hope she could sweet-talk him into letting her film while she was here. Her already-tight budget simply couldn't afford another trip. She left a message with Maddy, one of Haight's adherents, at the general store to let him know she was in town as he had instructed. The teenager had been far younger than Alyson had expected, but she promised to deliver the note when she went home after her shift. For now, Alyson had to be patient, something she'd never been good at.

Her real problem on this project may be the alpha wolf getting in her way. This close to winter, she figured she would miss most of the hunting crowd. And he may take her rudeness as a reason to approach her.

Oh, hell. If he was one of Papa's plants, he'd approach her anyway. Maybe it would be best to do her own hunting rather than go back into town when she needed more supplies.

Except she couldn't hunt cherry amaretto ice cream in the wild.

Why couldn't Papa be as forward thinking as John Lannigan, the leader of L.A.'s werewolf pack? According to the grapevine, Lannigan's daughter was his beta.

Not that she wanted to be Papa's second. She wanted love, passion, respect for being herself, not courted because she was the pack princess. She definitely didn't want to be treated like a breeding bitch. She wanted to be swept off her feet by someone who adored her.

*You're being as chickenshit and backwards as you accuse Papa of being. You're the wolf, not Red Riding Hood.*

A flash of tan fur darted in front of her headlights. She slammed on the brakes, and the Jeep's tires screeched as it slid on the asphalt. Thank Mother Wolf, the forecasted snow hadn't arrived yet, or the vehicle would have slammed through the guard rail and rolled end over end into the deep ravine on her right.

The acrid scent of burnt rubber mixed with the wet air as she opened the vehicle's door. A few flakes fluttered to land on the hood of the Jeep and her nose. The wolf had already disappeared into the thick brush on the other side of the road.

She took a deep breath. Werewolf. An unfamiliar pack. The one who had been staring at her back on Main Street? She hadn't been able to detect his scent in town with the wind at her back, coming off the surrounding peaks.

The road meandered around the river and up Mount Tuttle. He could have caught up with her if he knew the area better than she did.

Not if. Since. She'd been in Tuttle Creek long enough to pick up the keys for the rental cabin, buy some supplies, and leave a note with one of Haight's people. Scouting the area should have been her first priority.

But then, she'd been mocked incessantly for being more human than wolf. Never in front of Papa though, and she hadn't been stupid enough to whine to him. Deep down, she knew he felt the same way as those who'd insulted her even if he never said a word.

Still, if it were the werewolf in town who'd been staring at her, there were easier ways to get her attention than running in front of her Jeep. She climbed back into the driver seat, shifted into gear, and hoped she found the rental cabin before dark.

❧❧❧

He watched the vehicle as it disappeared around the bend. The shape-shifter would be strong enough to breed. She wouldn't survive any more than the weaker mammals he had experimented with on the ocean-side of these mountains, but she would live long enough. Easy to capture since she'd brought no one with her. And on this isolated plateau, no one would discover she was missing until he had a score of his kind to prepare the way for his master by killing the usurper.

# Chapter 2

Later that evening, Logan's human ears tried to perk when Sarah Goldstein said, "Did you hear about the film maker renting Roy Cole's cabin?" She passed him the roasted potatoes, a mischievous expression on her heart-shaped face.

Even if his ears didn't actually move, the eyebrows on her parents definitely rose. Aaron's brown eyes gave his daughter a speculative look as he sliced the lamb roast.

However, Esther frowned. "Weren't you complaining about the way people gossip in this town when we first moved here?"

"C'mon, Mom. A film maker is a big deal here even if her movies are documentaries." Sarah scooped a healthy portion of lima beans onto her plate.

It was good to see the young witch eating normally again. Logan shifted his attention from her plate before she noticed. After the starvation they'd both experienced while prisoners of Tyrone Mallory and Selene Antonius, it had taken them a long time to fight the urge to eat sparingly and not hoard food. The assholes had captured Sarah two months before the night he and Alex Stanton, his closest friend outside of the were community besides the Goldsteins, had been abducted.

"Even better—" She shot Logan a sly smile. "The film maker is a lady were."

"And how do you know this?" Aaron frowned at his daughter.

"I was in the general store returning our movie rentals when she was picking up the keys to the Cole cabin," she said primly. "She definitely had a double aura."

"That doesn't mean she's wolf," Aaron said gently.

"She is." Wishing he'd kept his big mouth shut, Logan could feel Aaron and Esther's attention turn to him. Knowing what would come next, he shoveled a huge forkful of potatoes into his mouth.

"Really?" Esther murmured. "By herself? This late in the season?"

"Maybe we should invite her over for coffee." Aaron forked a slice of roast onto his plate before he passed the platter to his wife. "Not a whole lot of supernaturals in Tuttle Creek." He eyed Logan as if daring him to dispute the offer of hospitality.

"Definitely!" Sarah chirped. "I could interview her for my independent study project." Except it wasn't her school assignment gleaming in her eyes.

A lump of concrete would have been easier to swallow than his mouthful of spuds, but Logan managed. His friends' plans needed to be nipped now before someone got hurt.

Before he got hurt.

"Y'all need to stop." His already deep voice had dropped an octave. His skin prickled with the threatening change. "She wants to be left alone." That had been obvious from her bald, dismissive look this afternoon. "And quit acting like a bunch of Yentes. I can't do a mate any good until I get my own shit together."

"Language," Esther admonished.

"Will you stop playing matchmaker?" He deliberately narrowed his eyes and stared at each of the Goldsteins.

Any story, any tale, he could pull out of his own pain, he had used to keep Sarah's hopes up. Until there was nothing but his own stories. He should never have told the girl he'd been in L.A. searching for a mate when he'd been taken. Now, her family had made it their mission to fulfill his search in gratitude for keeping their daughter alive in that hellhole.

Unfortunately, their good intentions had made the last four summers excruciating. The appetite he'd built up through an honest day's work disappeared. He stood, placed his napkin on his chair, and headed for the back door. Maybe a run would clear his head.

Sarah's tremulous voice paused his hand on the knob. "I didn't mean to push so hard."

He looked back at the teen. He forced a smile at the anxiety in her expression and the bitter taste of her scent. Great. His irritation and lack of manners triggered one of her own PTSD attacks. "I know you didn't, sweetie. We both need time to heal. I can't fix you anymore than you can fix me. Remember?"

The echo of their therapist's words eased the panic evident in her posture and the hint of ozone in the room. She nodded though wetness still shimmered in her eyes.

The first snow of the season was already falling when Logan stepped outside. A soft, muffled cold enveloped him along with the flakes and the silence. He exhaled the tension, and the cloud of his breath swirled into the blackness.

Not a good evening for a hunt since any prey would be tucked safely in their burrows and dens against the storm. He scanned the area for any townsfolk over the top of the fence before he stripped off his clothes and boots and set them in the box tucked against the house. Aaron and he had built the storage unit when they first arrived in Tuttle Creek for those nights he needed to let the wolf free.

Skin pricked. Muscles stretched. Bones cracked and reformed.

He shook, from the tip of his snout to the end of his tail. The snow fell faster, huge wet globs now. No, definitely not a good night for a run. But he feared what he might do to his friends if he didn't work off his own rage and hate and terror at the remembered helplessness.

And he'd felt just as inadequate when he saw the lady were and her expression of disdain this afternoon. He should have gone over and done something about it. Yet, he'd been frozen in his tracks and just stared at her. How could any she-wolf want him when he was such a mess? With a leap, he cleared the side yard fence and bounded into the forest.

The next morning dawned crisp and bright compared to the low-hung clouds that had greeted Alyson's arrival to Tuttle Creek. The ground wasn't cold enough yet to keep the thick white blanket from last night, but if she wanted to check for a return message from Haight and hit the town's library before lunch, she'd need a path for her rental. Finding a shovel in the shed behind the cabin, she had already cleared the dirt drive of the soft snow when Mr. Cole arrived on his tractor to plow her out.

The discomfort of a seventy-something Normal thinking he needed to take care of her prompted her invitation to make him breakfast for his trouble. Unfortunately, her offer only pricked his pride further. They compromised at Alyson driving them to the local diner and Mr. Cole buying.

"I don't get why a pretty girl like you is up here by yourself this time of year." His piercing gaze drilled her skull as she tried to concentrate on damp asphalt. If a wolf ran in front of the Jeep again, she wasn't sure she could keep it from tumbling down the mountain when she slammed on her brakes.

"It's my job." She shot him a quick smile.

"Doesn't mean you can't have someone to keep you warm at night." Mr. Cole chuckled. "If I was forty years younger, I'd put my hat in."

"I don't know if I could have handled you forty years ago." She smiled back. It was easy to believe he'd been attractive in his youth. Sure he had a full head of silver-white hair and all his teeth, but his easy charm would have been what garnered the ladies' attention.

Finding a Normal sounded appealing. Someone who knew nothing about the supernatural species, much less cared, but the New Orleans pack would never accept such an arrangement even if she were madly in love.

Except John Lannigan hadn't had a problem when his daughter married a Normal. According to the gossip, Siobhan Lannigan's husband was a detective in the Los Angeles County sheriff's department out in California. A Normal strong enough and brave enough to go head-to-head with an alpha for his woman's hand.

And there she was, daydreaming about romantic nonsense again. She sighed.

"What's wrong, Miss Tribideaux?"

"It's Alyson, Mr. Cole."

"Well, then you need to call me Roy."

"No offense, Roy, but insinuating I need someone makes you sound just like my father."

He chuckled again. "Men and women should look out for each other."

She frowned. "He's just looking to—" Somehow, she managed to bite off the improper string of words she was about to vomit. "I'm an only child, and he wants grandchildren so bad he's driving me crazy."

"Nothing wrong with wanting grandchildren."

*It is when he's setting me up with every Tom, Dick and Hairy in a thousand-mile radius.* Her fingers tightened around the steering wheel.

"I see." Roy seemed determined to fill the silence. "He went too far playing matchmaker?"

"You could say that." She glanced at the older man, but he appeared genuinely concerned. "I think he sent someone after me."

"Like stalking you?" Bushy gray eyebrows climbed his forehead.

"No." She sighed again. "There was a man at the feed mill staring at me when I came out of the grocery last night. About six-two or six-three, sandy brown hair, looked to be in his early thirties." Muscles that didn't strain when he was swinging around hundred-pound feed sacks, but Roy didn't need to hear that tidbit.

"Sounds like Logan Polk." He snickered. "Don't think you've got anything to worry about there. The gossip in town says he isn't partial to women. And plenty of the single gals have tried."

"Oh." Had she misread the look he gave her? "I take it he grew up here?"

"Naw, he's from Texas originally. At least, he has the twang though he doesn't offer much personal information. He moved up here with Doc Goldstein's family nearly four years ago from Los Angeles. He really doesn't say much about his past." Roy's voice lowered to a sad note.

"Something happened in Los Angeles, didn't it?" she said softly.

"Don't know the whole story. Really none of my business." He shook his head. "Scuttlebutt is the Goldsteins' daughter was kidnapped when they were in California. Bad things happened. Real bad. I think Logan was hired by the Goldsteins as a bodyguard, though none of them will say for sure. But damn, if any of the boys in town look at that Sarah Goldstein sideways, Logan is on 'em like white on rice."

"I see." This Logan had to be a rogue. An alpha didn't leave his pack unless he was looking to start a new one. And a gay alpha didn't stand a chance of either taking over a pack or founding one. Mate or abdicate was the rule.

It sucked. It sucked rotten eggs in her opinion. It was the freakin' twenty-first century for the love of Mother Wolf.

"My misunderstanding then," she added.

The incline leveled out, and she shifted out of the lower gear. Mounds of snow clung to the prairie grass, but not a cloud marred the crystal blue vista.

"Now I know what they mean about the big Montana sky," she said.

"Yep." Roy didn't sound smug or condescending, just happy with life. "Supposed to stay clear for the next twenty-four hours according to the Weather Channel. Wait until you see the view tonight from your cabin."

The Last Buffalo Diner was crowded and loud when they entered. The noise died immediately as the clientele watched them. The change was unnerving. It raised the hackles on the back of her neck, but Alyson followed Roy as he plowed past men twice his size and half his age.

He settled into a booth at the rear of the diner, his back against the wall where he could keep an eye on everybody. His choice left her with a decision—either sit next to him so her back was against the wall, too, which her wolf-half silently advocated, or sit across from him like a proper Normal would.

Those glittering eyes caught her hesitation. "I'm not the one you should be worrying about, Alyson." His voice was so low, only a supernatural could hear him.

She tried to appear confused, but she had the impression he saw through her act. Slowly, she slid onto the opposing bench.

A stout, matronly waitress with graying hair in a tight braid appeared beside their table, already pouring coffee into one of the two cups she held. She grinned at Alyson and set the first cup down for Roy. "What can I get you to drink, Miss Tribideaux?"

That the waitress knew who Alyson was sent a trickle of unease through her. Back in New Orleans, she had relative anonymity thanks to the big city population. Here in Tuttle Creek, Montana, population four thousand-three hundred-one, she would stand out.

"Coffee, black, please." It seemed the safest bet. She could feel the eyes of everyone in the diner on her. Besides, the odds of getting a decent café au lait in Montana were about the same as her finding a beignet in the forest.

Conversation resumed around them. Once the waitress set down the second cup and toddled off to take care of another customer, Alyson leaned forward. "I take it I passed the city versus country test."

"Yes, ma'am, you did." Roy grinned as he took off his cap and unwound his muffler.

She shed her coat and gloves before she took a sip. Not as bitter as the chicory mix favored back home, but she still missed milk to mellow the flavor. Little containers of artificial creamer sat in a matching mug at the end of the table. Those would be even worse than plain coffee.

Her attention returned to Roy. "So, who should I be worried about?"

"I hear you're in town to interview the leader of the Sunshine Believers." Roy wrapped his hands around his own mug.

"I take it he's not popular around town."

The old man's frown emphasized the deep lines embedded in his face. "He's never caused any trouble here. Neither have any of his people. There's just something off about him I can't put my finger on."

The waitress came back, her pen poised on her pad. "Your usual, Roy?"

"Yep. Thanks, Lois."

She turned a bright smile on Alyson. "And you, dear?"

"Three eggs, scrambled, with bacon and toast." If Roy hadn't insisted on paying, she'd order her normal breakfast, but she wasn't about to bankrupt the man. Besides, she could always grab a snack back at the cabin later. Like maybe some more ice cream if she could swing by the store before they drove back up the mountain.

Lois tucked her pen behind her ear and grinned. "I like a girl who isn't afraid to eat." She sauntered back to the window behind the counter and called out the order.

Alyson took another sip of her coffee. "So, what do folks around here think of the Reverend Fred Haight?" Might as well get a little background. Most small towns were notoriously closed-mouthed, but then, neither she nor Haight were part of the community.

Neither was this Logan apparently.

She shut down that thought. Even if Roy was right, and the man wasn't a suitor planted by her father, she needed to focus on her job.

Roy shrugged. "Don't think many of them care as long as he doesn't cause trouble. You know about what happened in Los Angeles four or so years back?"

"You mean the kidnapping of Jessie Alton, the actress? The men from the Sunshine Believers who kidnapped her all ended up in prison or high security mental wards. Haight disavowed them." There had been a few things missing in the public police reports, too. Things that made her suspect someone involved in the whole sordid affair regarding the kidnapping was supernatural. Something of this magnitude, especially between Alton and her husband's popularity as entertainment stars, required a joint effort to keep things quiet. Well, relatively quiet.

She'd heard stories about the cooperation between the Lannigan pack, L.A.'s master vampire, and Silver Bear, southern California's resident witch coven. But any time she'd asked Papa about specifics, he'd told her not to worry her pretty little head about political affairs.

Roy bobbed his head. "Yeah. While he did say those men weren't acting on his cult's behalf and the police couldn't tie him to the crimes, it makes me wonder." His fingers drummed the side of his cup. "This is the type of town where no one's perfectly innocent, but as long as you keep your nose clean and don't hurt anyone, no one bothers you."

"You think he was involved in the Alton kidnapping, and he hung his people out to dry?"

Boney shoulders shrugged under his insulated coat. "Don't know. What I do know is there are a lot of pretty young things part of his compound. More women than men if you know what I mean."

The image of Maddy, the red-headed teenage girl at the general store who lived at the Sunshine Believers' ranch, popped into her mind. "Do you think they're brainwashed or abused?"

Again, Roy shrugged. "Don't act like it, but I'm not an expert." He reached over and grasped her hand. "Just be careful when you're around him. I suggest you take someone with you when you drive out to the compound."

She took a deep breath. Underneath the aromas of frying food, the hay-sweet scent of cattle, and the crisp odor of fresh-cut pine, the old man still had the super tart scent of an Arkansas Black apple. But something else crossed her nose, and it wasn't from Roy.

Ginger. Lots of ginger followed by the unmistakable musk of another were. None of which came from the surrounding tables.

She turned around to follow the scents. A tall man with shaggy, graying hair strode toward them. He wore the requisite Tuttle Creek uniform of jeans, boots, and flannel topped off by a heavy coat. A young woman followed him, mid-to-late teens by the look of her. Her dark hair framed a heart-shaped face with shining brown eyes. Her appearance was similar enough to label the man as her father. Witches from the tangy ginger with a fainter hint of ozone.

Behind them stalked the were from the feed mill, dressed like the male witch but with an ugly scowl marring his handsome features. A scowl she recognized from her father and cousins. He was itching to shift and tear someone a new asshole.

And of course, the trio stopped in front of their table.

"Roy, you missed your appointment," the male witch said with a milder version of the were's scowl.

The old man scowled right back and tilted his head in Alyson's direction. "Can't you even use your company manners, Doc?"

"Hello, Roy. You missed your appointment."

"So you tracking down patients now?"

The older witch smiled. "Only when they don't come in for their quarterly A1C testing like they're supposed to."

Roy made introductions. The Goldsteins were rather enthusiastic. The were barely gave her a civil nod.

"Why don't you join us for breakfast since there isn't a free table?" Roy added.

*No, no, no.*

"Sure!" Sarah immediately slid into the booth next to Roy. Her father followed.

Which only left room for Logan to sit next to Alyson.

*Normal establishment, Normal manners*, she reminded herself. She scooted across the cracked vinyl seat to make room. On the other hand, he didn't seem too pleased about the arrangement either.

Alyson took a surreptitious sniff of the man next to her. Yep, he was definitely the were who'd ran in front of her last night, but she wasn't about to confront him in front of so many Normal witnesses.

She wondered if one of the Goldsteins summoned Lois by the way she appeared out of nowhere with extra menus. Alyson bit her lip at a more uncomfortable thought. Maybe she was distracted by the bulk of Logan Polk overwhelming everything around her.

Small town gossip filled the minute or two before Lois appeared with plates for Roy and Alyson balanced on her arm. Once she dropped off the drinks for the rest of their table and took the remaining orders, Doctor Goldstein leaned over and said, "Roy, I want you to stop by the clinic for your blood work after breakfast."

"Can't. Caught a ride into town with Miss Alyson."

The doctor's lower jaw worked for a moment before he said, "Roy, you can't put this off any longer. I can't authorize refills of your insulin until I know what your numbers are. You could be taking too little or too much."

Roy reached for the syrup bottle and deliberately poured a healthy amount over his pancakes in response.

Goldstein turned to her, a please-help-me look in his eyes.

The old man's stubbornness reminded her too much of her mother's situation. She had also insisted nothing was wrong. By the time Alyson had figured out she was lying, Mama was dead.

Alyson cleared her throat. "I was planning on doing some research this morning at the town library. Why don't you take care of your errand at the clinic, and I'll swing by when you're done?" she said brightly.

"Fine, but I want something in return," the old man growled. "Doc, you need to accompany Miss Alyson to the Sunshine Believers' compound. She shouldn't be going up there by her lonesome."

The change in topic obviously caught the doctor off guard, too. "I've got a pretty full schedule today. Maybe Logan can go out to the compound with Miss Tribideaux?" He looked at the man next to her.

Alyson could feel the tension in Logan's body. His attitude was a one-eighty from yesterday's frank appraisal. Maybe she really had misread things like Roy suggested. Maybe his stare yesterday was the normal analysis of an interloper in his perceived territory, even though Montana was supposed to be a neutral zone for the packs.

Panic set in. He didn't want to escort her any more than she wanted him to. Not that she needed a chaperone anyway. "I don't have a definite appointment with Mr. Haight yet, and I'm sure Mr. Polk needs to be at work."

"No worries! It's Logan's day off," Sarah chirped. Her statement earned a glare from the male were.

"Then you're paying the gas money," he muttered.

"Sure." She grinned, pulled out a few bills from her pocket, and slid them across the table. "This should cover it."

Alyson tried not to smile at the girl's antics. There was obviously some kind of rivalry going on between the two. More like the sibling version than anything else. Was Logan getting as much pressure to find a mate as she swas? It must be bad if his witch friends were in on it. Maybe they weren't as plugged into the town grapevine as Roy. Or Logan hadn't come out of the closet with his friends.

Those thoughts actually made her feel sorry for the man sitting next to her.

The rest of the meal passed pleasantly despite the tension in the male were. Sarah carried most of the conversation. She had been taking classes remotely, working on her graphic arts degree, but planned to transfer next year to a bigger school. Questions spilled out of her about cameras, software and anything else she could think of relating to the video arts.

Sarah's enthusiasm didn't hide the worry in Aaron's eyes when his daughter spoke about moving away. Another unspoken something was going on in that regard. His behavior cemented Roy's story something bad had happened to Sarah in the past. The more the teen talked about attending school in California, the more Roy fidgeted in a way that had nothing to do with his third cup of coffee.

Which was just plain weird considering none of them had mentioned any familial relationship between the older man and the Goldsteins. And he definitely didn't smell like a witch.

Part of her was relieved when Logan claimed he had things to do. He laid down a couple of bills and stalked off before Lois made his change. Once everyone else was finished with breakfast and the bills were paid, Alyson walked out with the Goldsteins and her landlord.

Alyson and Roy climbed into her rental, and they followed the Goldsteins' SUV out of the parking lot and down the street. At the edge of town, a low-slung concrete pre-fabricated building huddled on itself against the coming winter that threatened to bury it. The only cheerfulness was the bright red signage on the front, stating "Tuttle Creek Medical Center."

"I could have walked five blocks," Roy grumbled.

"I know you could, but Doctor Goldstein insisted."

"This is taking time out of your business."

"I need to check in at the general store for Haight's response before I head to the library. Besides, you're the one who bargained for my escort." She pulled into a parking space in the cleared lot and cut the engine. "So you need to uphold your end of the deal."

"This is why I like my mountain. No one's hassling me up there."

Alyson popped open her door. "Which is exactly why you need your meds sorted out before the real winter sets in."

Roy climbed out and rounded the Jeep. "You're worse than my wife, God rest her soul."

"And you're as cranky as my father," she shot back. "I'll be back in a bit while you take care of business."

"Fine." He waved a gloved hand in the air and stomped into the clinic. If he didn't have the apple smell of a Normal, she'd claim the old man was a were.

Alyson pivoted and strode down the sidewalk to the general store. No one was inside when she entered except the proprietress, Carol Riesgraf.

She looked up from some paperwork on the counter and grinned. "Hey, Ms. Tribideaux! Got something for you."

"Maddy isn't here?"

Carol shook her head. The silver pixie-cut made her look decades younger than seventy. From the way she spoke on the phone when Alyson had been making arrangements, she and Roy had been classmates decades ago. "She dropped this off on her way to the high school this morning."

The admission sent a frisson of unease through Alyson. "I didn't realize she was that young. What do her parents say about her living on the Sunshine Believers' compound?"

A disgusted look filled Carol's lined features as she handed over a sealed envelope. "From the little she told me, there were some problems with her stepfather and his wandering hands. People whisper all kinds of insinuations about Fred Haight, but I'll give him this. He makes the kids he takes in finish school and get their diplomas."

Alyson accepted the envelope. "Roy says he doesn't get a good vibe from the Sunshine Believers."

"I don't like to gossip." As if to emphasize her point, Carol pursed her lips together.

Alyson tried for a reassuring smile. "All I'm doing is collecting background material. The community in which some of these splinter religions live and work can make or break the group."

Carol stared at her fingers clenched on the counter for a moment. "As long as I've known Roy, he's had a . . . sixth sense if you will. I don't discount his opinions, but—" She looked out the window before returning her gaze to Alyson. "Like I said, Haight makes the underage ones go to school. The handful with jobs in town work their asses off."

"Like Maddy?"

"Yeah." Carol smiled. "I don't ever have a problem with her. She shows up on time, ready to work, and doesn't complain about a thing. Maybe that's the problem."

"What do you mean?"

"Have you ever met a teenager who doesn't complain?" One of Carol's silver eyebrows rose. "My granddaughters bitch. My daughters bitched. Even I bitched when I wanted to listen to Elvis records with my friends rather than do my chores on our ranch."

Curiouser and curiouser as one of Alyson's favorite authors would say. Haight had admitted publicly he wanted to redeem his organization's name. But if he had a way of turning Normal teens into model citizens, he could make a mint.

And Maddy had smelled pretty damn Normal when they met yesterday afternoon.

"Thanks for this," she said and waved.

Once outside the store, she yanked off her glove, slid a fingernail under the flap, and tore open the envelope. Inside was a note with the sharp, printed words she came to expect from Fred Haight. An invitation to lunch tomorrow and an interview to discuss the terms of filming his compound and his followers.

He was sticking to his word he wanted to meet her in person before he granted her access to the entire compound and his people. He could still say no, and she'd be out all of her expenses for this trip.

Given his group's history, she could understand his reluctance to let any stranger observe his people. Still, she was disappointed any real work would be put off for another day. She prayed it really was only one day. Her bank account only had enough funds for a month's stay in Tuttle Creek.

Alyson shoved the note into her hip pocket. It didn't mean she couldn't set up some preliminary interviews with some of the town leaders. And the delay would get both her and Logan out of Sarah's attempt to force them together.

Her trip to the town's library was a little more fruitful. The head librarian, Marvin Newlin, happened to be the mayor's brother. He invited Alyson over for dinner that evening. He also pulled a half-dozen books on the town's history he thought Alyson would find useful. Thank Mother Wolf, she remembered to stuff a reusable canvas grocery bag in her backpack.

"I hear you're going to be filming at Reverend Haight's ranch." Mr. Newlin played with his reading glasses hanging from a pink beaded chain around his neck.

"I hope to. We're meeting tomorrow to discuss the particulars." She needed to dump the books in the backseat of the Jeep before Roy saw them. Otherwise, the old man would insist on carrying them.

"The man actually follows Christ's path. Charity to all." Mr. Newlin beamed. "I'm not a member, mind you. Our great-great-grandfather built the town's first church." He chuckled. "Well, the only church. But the way Rev. Haight takes in those lost souls—" He patted the space above his left breast. "It just fills your heart with love, doesn't it?"

Alyson gave the polite smile she always did when the subject of personal religion came up. "He's done a great many things to turn around his organization. That's one of the reasons I want to interview him."

Unfortunately, her simple answers weren't enough. By the time Alyson extracted herself from the clutches of the librarian, the bright morning sunshine was rapidly melting the snow still laying in yards and flower beds. It also made for a pleasant walk back to the clinic. People nodded and gave friendly waves as she went.

Was that why Haight moved his group here? To create a more positive atmosphere?

Everyone she met so far had good things to say about him and his people. Everyone except Roy. And the old man had nothing to go on but a vague feeling. She'd put more stock in Dr. Goldstein having a suspicion, assuming he was telepathic like a large number of witches were.

She could understand why even witches such as the Goldsteins liked living here. But it didn't answer why an alpha would be so closely attached to non-were supernatural family. Rogues didn't bother forming those kinds of bonds. Unless the Goldsteins were rogues as well. She was so discomfited by Logan's presence she hadn't looked to see if Sarah or Aaron had worn earrings, which she should have to determine their coven membership.

No, the Goldsteins being unaffiliated didn't make sense. Solo witches usually attached themselves to vampire covens out of sheer survival instinct. Or at least, that had been her rare experiences and her cousin Frankie's gossip. Why would any witch serve a rogue alpha?

The two witches sure hadn't acted subservient to Logan or vice versa. In fact, the Goldsteins had been damn friendly to her if they were rogues. Even Logan had given her a token amount of civility despite his irritation with being forced to interact with her. The stories her parents told her said a rogue wolf would kill a pack wolf if he discovered one alone. Logan hadn't done anything besides look at her, or try not to look at her, at breakfast.

*Stop it*, she told herself sternly. *You're not interested in Logan, remember? And he's definitely not interested in you.* Marvin Newlin was more to Logan's taste if Roy's gossip was true. Assuming the poor Normal could survive a night with a gay alpha.

Alyson stepped inside the clinic. No one was sitting in the waiting room, but ginger flooded the air.

A dark-haired woman peered over the reception counter. "Hi! Can I help you?"

"I'm here to pick up Roy Cole if he's done with his appointment."

The woman grinned and stood. "You must be Alyson. I'm Esther. Jill of all trades and Mrs. Dr. Goldstein." She held out her palm.

Alyson couldn't help but laugh along with the woman's infectious enthusiasm as they shook hands. Unlike her daughter's wayward locks, Esther's dark hair was pulled back in a neat bun. The studs in the second piercings on the witch's ears were tiny silver grizzlies while the silver hoops in the first piercings were plain. The bear was the symbol for the

Los Angeles witch coven if Alyson remembered correctly. Plain hoops meant Esther didn't hold an office within the group.

"By the way, thank you for getting Roy in here. Aaron hasn't had a chance to get up the mountain. It's been high school sports check-up season for the past two months." She rolled her eyes.

"I can see him being a stubborn patient." Alyson smiled. The old man obviously gave the doctor lots of headaches.

Esther nodded. "Since we've got him here, Aaron's doing a full work up, so it may be another twenty to thirty minutes." She paused as if she wanted to say more, but she leaned over to check the front door before she continued.

"Come over for dinner tonight." She held up her hands when Alyson opened her mouth. "No pressure, I swear. No other supers live in the area, so it's a treat for us to visit with someone new."

Damn, no matter what she said, refusal would be awkward. "Um, I accepted an invitation to the Newlins tonight." When Esther's expression fell, Alyson quickly said, "Maybe we can get together tomorrow night?"

"Sure." Esther's quick smile turned into an embarrassed expression. "I just wanted to apologize. I heard about what my family did to you and Logan this morning. My daughter really doesn't understand personal limits, especially when it comes to weres even though Logan's lived with us for four years. My husband should have known better though, so I'm sorry for his rudeness."

The apology took Alyson by surprise. She wasn't sure what to say, except she had a way out of the direct awkwardness with Logan.

"Apology accepted. Actually, the escort thing isn't a problem. I'm not going out to the Haight compound today after all. I was hoping I could leave a message for Logan?" Instead of making a definitive statement, she ended the sentence on the quivering high Normal women used, asking permission instead of claiming their power. Dammit, she wanted to bite her own tail.

"I hate to do this to you, but I've got a swarm incoming." Esther nodded at the front of the clinic. Sure enough, one stressed mother with three little ones, all under five and with running noses, struggled to herd her brood past the glass door. As they watched, two more vehicles pulled into the lot. "I won't see him until the clinic closes, and he planned to drive up to the Cole cabin before noon to meet you."

Esther pointed to her right. "The first house past the clinic is our place. The gate's unlocked. Logan should be out back chopping wood. Or that was his plan, and if he is, he won't answer the phone."

Alyson swallowed her urge to grimace. Not her first choice of options, but before she could say no, two men rushed in with a third slung between them. The injured man was white as a sheet, probably because the towels wrapped around his right hand were a brilliant, wet scarlet.

"Esther!" one of the men shouted.

The eggs and bacon in Alyson's stomach lurched at the bloody injury. Why couldn't she handle this kind of sight while she was in human form?

Esther ran around the reception desk. "For the love of all that's holy, Abner! How many times are you going to stick your hand in an auger?"

The injured Abner gave a sickly grin. "Till I lose it?" Esther guided the men through a door that presumably led to the exam rooms.

Alyson backed out of the way and into the mother with the three sick toddlers. "Sorry," she muttered.

"I'm sure it looks worse than it is," the woman replied. "My cousin Abner's always doing something stupid."

The oldest child, a boy, yanked on his mother's coat. "Yah think Abner'll still have his stitches at Thanksgiving," he said between loud sniffs.

"We'll see." She gave Alyson a long-suffering look. "If you don't have kids yet, I strongly suggest putting them off for as long as possible," she whispered.

"Thanks for the advice." Alyson smiled and quickly left the clinic. Once outside, she took deep cleansing breaths of cold, mountain air. It lessened the threatening nausea. She had to be the worst were on the face of the planet for letting the sight of a little blood make her ill.

As she stood on the sidewalk, another pick-up and a mini-van pulled into the clinic's parking lot. Aaron hadn't been joking about having a busy morning, even without Abner's desire for self-mutilation.

Like it or not, she was going to have to face the alpha on her own.

Logan set aside his splitting maul for a moment to strip off his thermal undershirt. Mother Nature was making up for last night's snow with a much warmer day than expected. He tossed the shirt over a branch of the backyard maple, grabbed the maul and was reaching for another log when a flash of movement through a chink in the high wooden fence caught his attention.

Whoever picked their way through the muddy, dormant grass in the front yard was downwind as well. His protective goggles didn't help. He shoved them up, frowned and shaded his eyes.

Alyson Tribideaux. The filmmaker. The very attractive filmmaker who happened to be the New Orleans pack leader's daughter. The one who didn't want to give him the time of day.

And moved across the yard like a wolf afraid to dirty her paws.

Or her six-hundred-dollar boots.

Sarah couldn't have known who she'd been trying to set him up with when she brought up the subject at dinner last night. But he definitely needed to have a long talk with the young witch about knowing the players before manipulating the board.

The lady were disappeared from sight. The gate latch jangled before the gate itself swung open. Her gaze didn't meet his until she reached him. Her expression was reminiscent of an omega trying to bluff her way through an encounter. "Hello."

"Hello." He set the log on end, slid his goggles back into place, and swung the maul. The dry wood split with a satisfying crack. He tried not to laugh when she jumped back.

Her cheeks pinked, and she lifted her chin. "I came over to let you know I won't be needing your services after all."

"My services?" He placed another log on the stump he used as a chopping block.

"Dr. Goldstein volunteered you to escort me to the Sunshine Believers' compound? Anyway—"

He brought the maul down a little harder than necessary. She jumped back again when the two blocks flew apart.

Logan swallowed the grin that threatened to split his face just as easily. "You really shouldn't be out here without steel-toed boots."

She ignored his advice. "As I was saying, my appointment has been delayed until tomorrow so I won't need you this afternoon. Thank you for your assistance." She pivoted smartly and stalked toward the gate.

*What a snob.* Not being interested was one thing. Looking down on him as a servant to be ordered about and dismissed when not needed was another. Not to mention, he'd promised his friend Alex, who happened to be the Augustine Coven's chief enforcer, he'd take a look inside the Sunshine Believers' compound if he ever got the chance. There'd been too many deadly encounters between the cult and the vampires over the last few years to be coincidence. His scouting of the area in wolf form hadn't produced jack.

Well, this was his chance to get into the buildings without resorting to breaking and entering, even if it was with the most conceited wolf on the face of the planet, so he swallowed his pride. "What time tomorrow?" he called.

She paused and turned to face him. "Why?"

He set one of the split pieces on the chopping block before he answered. "Because the currency in this part of the world is favors. I'm supposed to escort you to Haight's place, and that's what I'll do."

"You don't owe me anything."

He swung the maul again. She didn't leave when he split the piece as he half-expected. "Aaron owes you for bringing Old Roy in for his check-up. I owe Aaron for putting me up for the last four years. Ergo, I owe you." Not to mention he and the Goldsteins owed Augustine and his people for getting him and Sarah out of the Mallory Labs torture pit, but he wasn't about to admit that to little Miss Holier-Than-Thou.

She grimaced and folded her arms. "The only reason I was in town this morning is because Roy was angry I cleared the drive before he arrived."

Interesting. She was a total pansy-assed omega. No wonder Tribideaux couldn't find a mate for his daughter.

Logan grinned. "By usurping Roy's duties as host, it's your own fault I have to escort you to Haight's place."

Her arms dropped to her sides, and her mouth opened and closed a couple of times. Finally, she said, "Fine," and turned to leave.

"What time?"

An exasperated growl started low in her throat when she faced him again. "Noon."

"I'll be at your place at eleven."

"I can pick you up here."

Logan liked getting a rise out of her. He gave her a mock frown. "The drive going into the compound is an old logging road. I can guarantee that Mother Wolf-awful banana rental of yours doesn't have the shocks or suspension to handle the terrain, much less the mud from last night's snow. We'll take my Jeep."

"Look, you don't want to be around me, and I know why." A wry smile tugged at her mouth. "Sarah really pushed for you to escort me. I'm sure it's because we're both—" She shrugged. "—you know. I get the impression she's a bit of a spoiled princess, used to getting her way."

"No. She's not." He didn't exactly snap at her, but his anger surprised him as much as it startled her.

Tribideaux canted her head. "Then why was she pushing so hard for us to be together? I mean, Roy already told me you aren't interested in girls."

His lower jaw dropped and he gaped at the bitch. It took him a couple of tries to form words. "Where on earth did he get that idea?"

Alyson dropped her eyes, and her cheeks flushed a deeper pink. "He, uh, just mentioned you don't date women, even though you've had several, um, interested parties in Tuttle Creek."

He dropped the maul and strode across the yard until he was inches from her. She looked up at him with a steady gaze, and he had to give her credit for not backing down. "Do you have any idea what an alpha is?"

Her lips puckered in a sour expression. "Too much of an idea."

Logan ignored her odd look. "It means I need a female of my own kind." *Like you,* but he didn't dare say that. She'd bolt. And if the only thing holding her back from approaching him was Roy's dumbass gossip, then he needed to give her another impression of him.

She held up her hands in a warding off gesture. "Hey, I get how hard being an alpha in the closet must be—"

"'An alpha in the closet'?" She surely wasn't suggesting what he thought she was.

"Look, I'm not getting in the middle of some *Brokeback Mountain* scenario you're hiding because you don't have the balls to come clean with your friends."

The urge to kiss her insinuations away vied against the urge to slap her for the insult. And his mother would be the first one to make him pay for laying a hand on a woman in anger. He shoved up his goggles and decided to try another track.

He folded his arms over his chest and rocked back on his heels. "Is that why your nose is bent out of shape? Because as a pack princess, you can snap your fingers and have any stud you want, and you know you can't have me?"

Her face went from bright pink to deep red. "Maybe I want someone who'll respect me, not use me for his own selfish power play. Someone who respects women. Like—like a Normal."

He snorted. "Ri-i-ight. René Tribideaux will agree to his daughter marrying a Normal over his dead furry body. In fact, he'd kill you before he allowed his family line to be sullied with Normal blood."

Her chin jutted forward. "Not necessarily. The beta of the Los Angeles pack married a Normal."

"Siobhan Lannigan?" He laughed. "Have you ever met her?" When she shook her head, he added, "There's a reason I didn't mate with her, even though our parents tried to push us together ten years ago."

"If you didn't like her, why are you hiding up here in neutral territory, pining over her?" Alyson shot back.

He dropped his arms and deliberately leaned over her. "For a documentarian, you can't keep your facts straight. Am I in Montana because I'm in the closet or because I'm pining over a bitch?"

Her eyes swept over him as she inhaled deeply. "I don't care why you're hiding. I just know you are, which means you're not much of an alpha."

"I'm not hiding up here," he growled.

She lifted an eyebrow.

His skin prickled, and he clenched his fists to keep from losing control. "I'll be at your cabin by eleven tomorrow morning. You'd better be ready to go, pack princess."

"Don't be late," she sneered before she marched in the direction of the front fence line.

"Don't let the gate hit you in the ass!"

She yanked the handle and disappeared from sight. The gate swung sharply, but stopped before gently shutting with a soft click of the latch. At least, she didn't leave him with repairs to do on his day off.

He needed to call Wade about taking tomorrow afternoon as personal time. Wade shouldn't argue too much, especially since Cody Grisham had been begging for more hours.

Logan stomped back to the woodpile. For now, he needed to finish splitting the cord of wood Aaron had delivered earlier in the week. If this winter was anything like the last, they needed to save the generator fuel for the clinic when Tuttle Creek lost power.

He picked up the maul and grabbed another log. Otherwise, he may split the New Orleans pack princess's stubborn head open. Yeah, much better doing some solid work than think about how Alyson Tribideaux's ass looked as she sashayed out of the yard.

# Chapter 3

By the time Alyson stalked back to the clinic, she realized she hadn't confronted Polk about running in front of her Jeep last night. Roy immediately distracted her by insisting on taking her to lunch for making her wait. Or that Doctor Goldstein had made her wait, he'd muttered with a pointed dirty look aimed at the bemused physician, who mouthed, "Thank you," to Alyson as she left with her landlord.

This time, he took her to a bar called the Next to Last Buffalo. Once they were seated in a booth and the waiter had taken their orders, she asked him about the naming conventions for the town's eateries.

He chuckled. "According to the story, Last Buffalo was a cavalryman who'd gone native after the Civil War—"

"You mean the War of Northern Aggression," she said, reaching for her soda as their waiter set the drinks down.

"My story, my names, missy." Roy waggled a finger at her. "Anyway, after the Civil War . . ." He eyed her.

Alyson smiled and kept her mouth shut.

"Alfred Tuttle hired Last Buffalo to help negotiate the land for his town and keep the peace. Later, Last Buffalo married a Chinese woman, who didn't know much English but was fluent in Lakota. Well, no one in town could pronounce her name, so everyone called her Next to Last Buffalo."

"And nobody gave them any grief over—" She cleared her throat.

One of his bushy eyebrows rose. "You mean the miscegenation laws at the time?"

She nodded.

"Naw." Roy leaned back against the booth seat. "Like I said, people here pretty much leave you alone as long as you keep your nose clean."

"Or as long as you're not a favor to be traded," she said bitterly.

"What?"

Alyson relayed her conversation with the shirtless Logan to Roy, though she left out any mention of the shirtless part.

The old man shook his head. "Ain't like him to be rude like that." He leaned his elbows on the Formica tabletop. "Though honestly, him escorting you over to the Haight ranch would be even better than the doc. He's a tough one."

"Even after he failed to protect Sarah Goldstein?"

"I don't think Logan was hired until after she'd been kidnapped." Again, he waggled his index finger at her. "And you shouldn't rely on an old man's gossip."

The waiter delivered their sandwiches, and Roy turned the conversation to her work. But the image of the shirtless Logan Polk teased her libido all the way home.

By the time they returned to Alyson's cabin, most of the snow had melted. After Roy headed up the mountain to his house, she spent a few hours looking through the books the librarian Marvin had pulled for her. She ended up pulling out a pad of sticky notes and jotting down questions to take with her.

Dinner that night with the Newlin brothers turned into a pleasant affair with productive interviews despite the odd and unnerving décor of modern hunter and pink leopard print. What little Marvin didn't know, Mayor Tad filled in.

During a lull in the conversation while Marvin served dessert, Tad asked, "Is someone going with you out to the Haight ranch tomorrow?"

Alyson met his concerned gaze with a bold stare of her own. "Why is everyone so concerned about me going to the Haight ranch by myself? What aren't y'all telling me?"

Tad's expression turned grave. "It's not so much him and his people. At least, the sheriff doesn't think so."

"Then what?"

"A couple of weeks ago up at Last Buffalo Meadow, some hunters stumbled across an elk carcass ripped to shreds with all the meat left there. It's between Old Man Cole's property and the Haight Ranch."

She shrugged. "The town is pretty close to Yellowstone. You sure it's not just a wolf pack or a cougar that wandered away from the park, and these hunters scared off the predator?"

Tad shook his head. "I've been hunting this mountain since I was knee-high. And I did a couple of stints with the Marines. This looked more like someone shoved the poor thing through a broken wood chipper."

"I'm telling you someone's messing with people around here," Marvin said as he set bowls of blueberry pie a la mode in front of Alyson and his brother. He propped his fists on his hips. "Probably some of the local teens. Go on, tell her what the tracks looked like."

Tad's cheeks and ears turned bright red. "Doctor O'Connell was just offering an observation."

Marvin turned to her. "Our resident retired paleontologist says the tracks around the carcass were caused by a velociraptor."

Tad rolled his eyes. "And everyone knows the man grows his own weed."

Marvin shrugged and marched back into the kitchen.

Tad coughed discretely. "I'll clear my meetings tomorrow afternoon and take you up there, Miss Alyson."

"That's all right." She gave the mayor a wry smile. "My landlord conned Logan Polk into acting as my escort."

"Good." Marvin slid into his chair. "That's a nice long ride for you two to get to know each other." He winked at Alyson before taking a bite of his dessert.

"Marvin, we have a guest," Tad hissed.

"It's not my fault that boy needs to get laid before he has a mental breakdown."

His brother gasped. "Really?" He turned to Alyson. "God, I'm so sorry. Please don't put that in your film."

Marvin shook his spoon at his brother. "Well, according to Wade, she's the first one to flick Logan's Bic since he moved here." The librarian leaned closer and laid a hand on her sweater sleeve. "I've been telling these idiots for three years and eight months he doesn't swing my way. Believe me, if he did, I would have snapped him up in a heartbeat. And if you ever see him without a shirt, you'll understand why."

Heat flooded her face at the reminder of her third encounter with the mysterious Logan Polk.

"Oh, girlfriend already has!" Marvin laughed. "Tell me, is his ass as delectable without his jeans as it is with them?"

"I don't know," Alyson mumbled. She shoved a spoonful of blueberries and vanilla ice cream in her mouth.

Because part of her really wanted to find out what Logan's naked ass felt like under her palms.

When Alyson returned to her cabin, the bright blue clock numbers on the kitchenette's microwave reminded her about the time difference between Tuttle Creek and New Orleans. And that she'd forgotten to check in with Aunt Francine today as she had promised.

She ditched her coat before she unsnapped the side pocket on her backpack and pulled out her satellite phone. Papa had complained about her extravagance, but the device had been the best investment next to her digital video camera, her laptop, and the software she used for editing.

It took a few seconds for the call to ring through. A wave of homesickness hit her at Aunt Francine's dulcet, "Evening, *chéri*. What can I do you for?"

"Can you ship me a dozen beignets?" Alyson crossed the rental cabin's living room to the bedroom.

Laughter chimed through the receiver. "If you want sweets, *ma petite*, you need to come home. And you need to call your papa."

Alyson groaned as she flung herself on the platform bed. "I called him last night as soon as I unloaded everything. I'm not a little girl. Why is he so overprotective of me?"

More laughter. "He'll be like this until you find a good wolf to settle down with and raise a basket full of pups. Now, tell me what's wrong." Leave it to Francine to ferret out Alyson's real feelings.

"This is an information call because you will tell me the truth and not blow this out of proportion." Alyson sucked a deep breath and blew it out. "Do you know a wolf by the name of Logan Polk?"

Silence stretched until she thought she lost the signal. "Aunt Francine?"

"You have met this gentleman?"

"Yeah, this morning. My landlord introduced us." She wasn't about to add that Logan sat next to her at breakfast. And she saw him shirtless.

"Are you interested in him, *chéri*?"

Alyson closed her eyes to keep from making a nasty comment. Logan's naked torso and incredible abs danced in her mind. "Why does every conversation with my family have to revolve around me finding a mate?"

"Forgive me. It's just that . . . you know how your father feels about involving you in politics."

"Yes, I do. He's willing to sell me to the highest bidder."

"That's not true, child, and you know it." Francine's breath whistled across the signal. "He could not make your mama happy. He is simply trying to make sure he succeeds with you."

The sadness in her aunt's voice tore at Alyson's heart, and threatened to throw her in the same depressional abyss her mother fell into years ago. Somehow, Alyson dug up a bit of courage. "If he wants me to be happy, then he needs to let me live my life. Now will you please tell me what you know about this Logan person?"

Francine sighed. "All right. He's the son of the San Antonio packmasters."

That's why the name sounded familiar, but she'd been doing her best to ignore any eligible males in the eastern half of the country. "So why didn't Papa throw him at me?"

Her aunt chuckled. "Because your father and George Polk fought for the hand of Emily Shipley, and your father lost."

Alyson couldn't imagine her father losing at anything. She also couldn't imagine him with anyone but Mama either. "But that had to have been decades ago! Papa still holds a grudge?"

"Your father holds on to a lot of things he shouldn't. You especially."

Alyson stared at the caulk and plank ceiling. "So what do you know about Logan? According to my landlord, he's been living here with a witch family for the last four years."

Another sigh filled the receiver. "Oh, *ma petite*, he may be too broken for you to pursue."

"Who said anything about pursuing him?"

Francine chuckled. "I am not your father. Don't think about trying to fool me."

Alyson swallowed her irritation. Her aunt may be her mama's twin, but she took the surrogate mother thing too far. Best to change the subject. "What do you mean 'broken'? Has he gone rogue?"

"Not officially. It . . . he . . . the situation was very ugly."

"He said something about his parents setting him up with Siobhan Lannigan, the Los Angeles pack's beta. Did she fight him for the right to marry her Normal?"

Francine clicked her tongue against her teeth. "From what I heard, it was dislike from the start on both sides. There was no fight. It was a mutual decision. When Logan and Siobhan didn't work out, he visited other packs to court but never found a bitch to his liking. He returned to Los Angeles after sufficient time had passed and asked the packmaster's permission to court other girls there."

Silence fell again which meant Francine was getting to the juicy part of the story. And that silence drove Alyson insane. "So, what happened? Why is he living with a witch family?"

"A few years ago, Selene Antonius, the beta of the Augustine vampires went rogue and tried to usurp her brother. She failed miserably, but her brother was foolish and did not kill her."

Francine sighed. "It would have saved so much heartache if he had. In her search for revenge, she sought a way to allow vampires to walk in daylight, no doubt thinking it would give her an edge over others of her kind. She kidnapped many supernaturals of all types, performed obscene experiments on them. Most didn't live."

Gorge rose at the back of Alyson's throat. "Logan was one of them."

"Yes. When Master Augustine discovered Selene's actions, he had his people kill his sister and rescue the survivors. I heard rumors Polk had traveled to the neutral lands and lived there. Few have had contact with him over the years, and most who claim to have done so like to tell tall tales."

Alyson's eyes stung. Mother Wolf help him. An alpha would be ashamed for allowing himself to be captured. It explained his reticence to talk with her. For him to trust the Goldsteins . . .

"Francine, were there any witches who survived the rogue's experiments?"

"I heard one did. A child."

Mother Wolf help her. Sarah.

Bits and pieces of Roy's story made more sense now. Aaron and Esther Goldstein took Logan in because he was the reason their daughter survived. If he was ignoring the Normal women in town over the last four years, the trauma of his capture and torture had affected him. Sarah probably thought she was helping by setting him up with one of his own kind.

Which, once again, made her wonder about Roy Cole. He was just as guilty of pushing her and Logan together, but she trusted her nose. He was definitely a Normal.

"Anything else you can tell me about him?"

"No, *chéri*. Just . . . please be careful around Logan Polk. Avoid him if you can."

For the first time in the conversation, Alyson laughed. "That may be hard to do. I've already been invited to dinner by the witches. And they finagled him into escorting me out to the Sunshine Believers' ranch tomorrow afternoon."

Francine was silent for a long moment before she said, "Frankie hung out with a witch, too."

Oh, shit! Alyson wanted to sink into the floor. Papa may have rightly expelled Cousin Frankie from the pack, but that didn't mean Francine didn't care about her son. And to not be allowed to bury her only child nearly killed her.

"I-I think this is a different situation."

"Hmmm, it may be, *chéri*," Francine said. "Funny how they both include living sacrifices."

Logan glared at Sarah while he jabbed a steak off the platter. "Why didn't you tell me her name last night?"

"I did!"

"You only told me her first name."

"I couldn't pronounce her last name. She said it too fast, and it was in some weird language. 'Alyson' was the only part I caught." Sarah glared right back.

Normally, he'd be ecstatic seeing the scarred girl stand up for herself, but not this time. Not when it came at his expense with a large political price tag. "First of all, French is not a weird language. Secondly, her father, René Tribideaux, is the packmaster of New Orleans. Third, do you have any idea have much shit would be stirred up if he knew I was within a hundred miles of his daughter?"

For the first time, Aaron looked worried. "I wasn't aware there was a blood feud between the San Antonio and New Orleans packs."

Logan was sure the disgust he felt was reflected on his face. "Not per se. Mainly two alpha males and their super-huge egos."

"What did your father and René get into a snit fit about?" Esther prompted.

He didn't want to go into family history with the Goldsteins, but all three looked at him expectantly. "They fought over my mom."

"Like, literally, fought over your mom?" Sarah's eyes widened.

"Yep." He forked a baked potato onto his plate.

"That's so romantic." She sighed dreamily.

"No, it's not. Especially not with werewolves. One of them should have wound up dead. My dad didn't want to take on the New Orleans pack as well as his own. That's the reason he let Tribideaux live. For us, getting your ass beat and being allowed to trot off with your tail tucked between your legs is not only embarrassing as hell, it makes you a target of every other fucking wolf in the pack."

"Logan," Esther said softly. "Language."

He slammed down his fork. "She needs to understand how the world works."

"You think I don't know?" Sarah yanked up the sleeves of her sweatshirt. Under the dining room chandelier, long white scars glistened along the length of her forearms. Even Aaron and Esther's skills as healers could only do so much on the months-old damage once Augustine's team had pulled the survivors out of that hell hole.

Sarah bared her teeth at Logan. "Tell me again how the world works, Mr. Polk." She shoved back her chair, the pine feet screeching against the oak floor, and she raced from the room. Pounding on the stairs was followed by the slam of her bedroom door.

A lump burned in his throat. It had been a while since he'd screwed up that badly with Sarah. "I'm sorry," he whispered.

Esther laid her hand over his fist. Only then did he realize the tension thrumming through his body. The rapid pulse in his ears.

"She pushed. You pushed back. Which is a switch in both of your behaviors." Esther's smile was sad, weary even. "Dr. Plinkman said we all needed to be patient with each other. I'll take this as a positive sign."

"It's been almost four years," he murmured.

"You can't set a time limit on emotional damage, Logan." Aaron rested his utensils on the side of his plate. "My daughter makes a good point though. Maybe you're not using your parents as an excuse with Ms. Tribideaux, though it is a good reason to keep your distance. However, you've also avoided any were that's passed through Tuttle Creek for the last four summers. Sarah's making plans for school next fall. She's moving on. As much as we love having you here, it's time for you to move on with your life, too."

And as much as Logan hated to admit it, Aaron was right. Hell, even Alyson Tribideaux was right. He was hiding in Tuttle Creek. He had a choice to make. Find a mate and start a new pack.

Or go home to Texas and take a lower-ranked place under his parents because he wasn't about to fight them for pack dominance.

But if he was going to be a fucking gamma, maybe fixing the old feud between the Polks and Tribideauxs was a good place to start.

Alyson jerked awake, unsure of what had roused her. She checked her recharging phone. Three a.m. local time.

She scanned the small bedroom. Nothing. Not even the proverbial mouse.

Flinging the comforter aside, she slid out of the high mattress and padded over to the door. There wasn't any sound in the main part of the cabin.

Hinges squeaked when she pulled on the lever and peered through the opening. Moonlight spilled in silver squares along the rag rugs and hardwood floor. It was still two days before the full moon, but her skin tingled at the sight.

She crossed the living space. Embers glowed dully under the grate, but no burning scent indicating one had escaped through the screen guarding the fireplace.

Outside, the few remaining patches of snow gleamed. But there was nothing—

A shadow shifted near the pines that served as a windbreak on the west side of the cabin. The silhouette of a wolf stepped from behind a trunk, as if it knew she was watching. Branches provided enough gloom that she couldn't make out the coloring.

Was it a wild wolf? Or was it the same were that had darted in front of her Jeep last night? Was it Logan Polk?

Alyson cracked open the front door, and a burst of frigid air blew past her along with the odor of the stranger. From his scent, he was the same wolf who'd nearly caused her accident last night. The same scent of the man who'd sat beside her at breakfast and argued with her as he split logs. The shadow wolf darted to the ridge, then looked over his shoulder, daring her to follow him.

Francine's warning blared in her mind. While the urge to shift and run under the moon with him was tempting, something deep inside her said to listen to her aunt. She closed the door and locked it, waiting to see what he would do.

The wolf stood on the ridge for an hour. Or it could have been merely a second. His tail wagged once before he trotted off and disappeared from sight.

She sagged against the door. Was Francine right? Was Logan Polk so damaged he could only be friendly in his animal form? Had he been spying on her the whole time? She hadn't bothered closing the curtains because she believed she was isolated from everyone up here.

Maybe there was another problem. Maybe the reason she clung to her romantic fantasies was from her own emotional damage. Maybe she was so damaged thanks to her mother and her father's problems she would never be a suitable mate for anyone.

Maybe she was the one who was far too broken for Logan Polk.

# Chapter 5

Logan blinked in surprise as he pulled into the drive of Cole's rental at ten-fifty-eight a.m. The pack princess promptly walked out of her cabin with a couple of bags full of equipment slung over her shoulders.

Or maybe it shouldn't be surprising. She didn't want to give him an excuse to see where she slept, which fit more with her prickly disposition.

Not that he wanted to see it.

*Liar*, said the wolf inside him.

"You want this in the back?" she called the second he braked.

"Yeah." By the time he turned off the ignition and jumped out of his Jeep, she had the rear door open and had wrestled the larger canvas bag inside.

"I could have helped," he grumbled. So much for his effort to mend fences between their packs. A surly cub caught in the throes of puberty had a better disposition.

"I'm used to it." A tentative smile crossed her face while she set the padded laptop bag on top of the canvas one. "I can't afford an assistant yet."

He slammed the back door shut. "Not even a college intern desperate to work for free in the movie business?"

"I'm on the road a lot. There's still travel expenses, room and board to deal with. It's not fair to drag some kid around the country and make her pay her own way." She turned and headed for the passenger door.

Something didn't make sense. He climbed into the Jeep. "Not that it's my business," he started as he buckled his seatbelt. "But didn't your parents set up a trust fund for you?"

One slim dark eyebrow rose. "You're right. It is none of your business." She turned and faced the windshield and sighed. "But since you asked, so many people lost everything in Katrina, not just the pack. I asked Papa to dissolve the trust and use the funds to help rebuild."

"You couldn't have been more than knee-high." He flipped on the ignition.

"Old enough to understand what happens when the levees fail, Mr. Polk."

He almost leaned over to brush his shoulder against hers in comfort. Probably not the best idea considering their conversation yesterday. Instead, he reached for the gearshift. "Were you able to get out?"

"Yes." Her voice carried so much sorrow. "My Aunt Francine led a caravan of the pregnant women and pups to Houston. Papa and the rest of the pack tried to secure our boats and equipment. We still lost three quarters of what the pack owned."

He did a J-turn and headed back down the drive. "I can't imagine rebuilding from that." Sweat trickled down his spine. He hadn't lost anything in his life except his self-respect, and he couldn't even get that back.

"Papa is the heart and soul of the pack. If he believed, then everyone believed."

What he wouldn't give to have someone believe in him like that. He blinked stinging drops out of his eyes.

"You okay?" she asked.

He glanced at her before he turned and checked for oncoming traffic on the main road. "I'm fine," he lied. "Why?"

She pointedly looked at his hands on the steering wheel. His knuckles were white.

Great. Nothing like an anxiety attack in front of her.

Logan forced a smile. "Sorry. Thinking of how our dads would react if they knew we were in the same vehicle." Yeah, that was an excellent excuse. Not that he really believed there would be trouble at the Sunshine Believers' compound. Because if there were, it would be his fault for taking her to the isolated ranch, and René would be justified in ripping out his throat.

What if his friend Alex was right, and the Sunshine Believers were a real threat, even to a werewolf? What kind of alpha would he be to put another were in danger? But he couldn't legally get inside the cult's building without her. Breaking and entering wasn't worth causing trouble with the Normal authorities without some kind of proof.

Alyson laughed. It sounded just as forced as his smile. "Yeah, I heard about what happened between Papa and George. How about we vow never to tell them we met?"

Logan pressed the accelerator and turned left. "Sounds like a smart plan. Even Dad's version about what happened makes them both sound like douchebags."

"You don't think it's romantic fighting for your true love?"

"Romantic? Are you shitting me? It's one thing to fight to protect your lady. It's another to fight over a woman like she's a damn prize."

Alyson said nothing for the longest time. Had he royally pissed her off with his statement?

He glanced at her, but she didn't look angry. "Really? Is that how you want to be treated? Like an object to be fucked and brought out to impress other wolves when you're not popping out pups?"

Still nothing. Her silence wasn't helping the nerves prickling his skin.

The need to fill the void in the Jeep overwhelmed him. "Bet you haven't heard my mom's version of the story."

"And what's that? She resents being an object to fuck." Sharpness tainted her voice. So she was angry after all.

He grinned. "You obviously have not met my mother. She's nobody's object. You do know she's really the San Antonio pack alpha, don't you?"

"You're kidding?"

Another glance. Alyson stared at him with rapt attention.

"Hell, no. She left the Dallas pack for the same reason I left San Antonio. Didn't like the idea of battling the parent to be top wolf."

She laughed. "In other words, you're afraid your mama would whip your ass."

Logan chuckled. "Damn straight, I am. She bluntly told both Dad and René they had a choice. They could each fight her to retain alpha position of their packs. Or they could fight each other for her hand and retain some semblance of dignity. Personally, I think your dad lost on purpose."

Now, Alyson was laughing so hard tears ran down her cheeks. "Kn-knowing Papa, you're probably right." That sent her into another spasm of hilarity before she wiped her face with her sleeves.

They rode in companionable quiet for a few minutes before he asked, "So why does a nice wolf like you buy into the Normal myth of Prince Charming?"

And the tension between them slammed back into place.

"Why does a wolf like you resort to pathetic Normal behavior such as stalking?"

"I beg your pardon?"

"I not only saw you, I smelled you. First, you ran in front of my Jeep the night I arrived. I nearly hit you on the drive up to the cabin. Then you were standing out by the cabin windbreak this morning around three a.m."

He frowned. "I admit I watched you when you picked up groceries at Carol's two days ago. It's a little surprising to scent another were this late in the season, but I wasn't anywhere near your cabin until I picked you up—" He looked at his watch. "Fifteen minutes ago."

"Are there any other weres in the area besides you?"

"No," he ground out.

"So you want me to believe you weren't spying on me?"

Her incredulous tone and her accusations irritated him. "Why would I bother? You were the one yesterday who said I had plenty of women after me."

"I was only repeating what Roy had told me." She crossed her arms.

"So you're a gossip, too?" he shot back.

"Shut up. Just shut up," she snapped.

"Happy to oblige," he growled.

Only a tomb would have been quieter than the inside of his Jeep for the rest of their forty-minute drive.

Alyson was never more glad to arrive at her destination in her life. The nerve of that man! Maybe she was too human, but her nose worked just fine. She could tell the difference between a were and a regular wolf. And she damn well knew a were smelled the same regardless of which form he wore.

She rolled down the window of Logan's Jeep, letting in the damp, moldy odor of decaying leaves. The gate to the ranch stood open. Brown remnants of high meadow grass rustled between tiny mounds of snow, but no guards could be seen, much less heard or smelled. Wire fencing was strung between chest-high wooden posts along the drive with occasional neon bright ten-foot poles.

Breaking her oath to never talk to Logan Polk again, she asked, "What are the orange poles for?"

"They're guides for the plow and snowmobiles so the drivers don't accidently run into the fence posts," he said, guiding his Jeep through the open gate. "Last thing you want is cattle and horses escaping in the middle of a blizzard."

She looked at the orange poles again as the Jeep drove past them. They had to be twelve feet tall. She couldn't imagine drifts that deep. Snow in New Orleans was a truly rare event. Something to be celebrated as the city shuts down to enjoy the moment. Another pang of homesickness went through her.

They rolled up to a massive one-story log cabin at the end of the driveway. Similar, slightly smaller buildings spread out from the main one. It resembled a rustic ski lodge.

Or a dude ranch. She wasn't quite sure which effect the Sunshine Believers were going for. According to the information she'd dug up, only the main building had been on the property when Haight's organization bought the ranch.

"Do we just go inside?" Logan said as he cut the engine.

"It's polite to knock," she said.

He gave her an odd look as he yanked the key from its slot, and she realized her words had come out sharper than she intended. Except she'd meant them to be cutting, hadn't she? The bastard had lied about spying on her, hadn't he?

An attractive brunette burst out of the front door of the lodge, waving. "Ms. Tribideaux?"

Alyson leaned out the window. "Yes?" She took a surreptitious sniff of the woman. Golden delicious. Normal. But something seemed off, and she couldn't figure out what.

The woman smiled. "I'm Sharon Tyson, Reverend Haight's assistant. You're a bit early. I can show you around while he finishes his current meeting." She shifted to peer at Logan. "Will you be back in two hours, or would you prefer I call you when Ms. Tribideaux is ready to leave?"

Before Alyson could stop him, he'd jumped out of the Jeep. He rounded the vehicle and, well, he didn't push Reverend Haight's assistant out of the way, but she scurried back at the scowl on his face when he opened the passenger door.

"Where would you like your camera equipment set up, Ms. Tribideaux?" he said.

She slid out of the Jeep as well. Logan seemed determined to repay this favor by proxy he owed her. But it wasn't just his attitude that set her nerves in edge.

The silence of the ranch bothered her. There wouldn't be many insects above ground with the current temperature, but there should have been birdsong from the surrounding forest and meadow. For the first time, she was glad of his company.

She waved at the grouchy were. "Sharon, this is my college intern, Logan Polk." Alyson smiled sweetly at his frowning visage. No question about it. He didn't like being treated as the unpaid help he'd suggested she get. "Just take the equipment bags in with us. I still have to get Reverend Haight's signature before we start filming."

She slung her backpack over her shoulder before she turned back to Sharon. "I hope you don't mind. If our meeting goes as well as I expect, I want to get a jumpstart on my work today."

"Oh, um . . ." Sharon's flummoxed expression would be funny under normal circumstances.

Alyson struggled to keep her own expression nonchalant. It wouldn't do to piss off the woman. She knew how much power the so-called secretaries and personal assistants really wielded in most organizations.

"I think just carrying it in will be fine." Sharon shot Logan a worried look. "I'm not sure how the reverend will feel about having an extra guest."

A quick change of subject was needed. "As I told him in our letter exchange, I have no intention of painting the Sunshine Believers in a bad light." Alyson swept her hand in the air to indicate the ranch. "I find what he's done here quite admirable. I think people need to see what good leadership can do for any organization, not just a religious sect."

Sharon brightened at the compliment. "That would be so great. I wasn't a member when things went bad all those years ago." She lowered her voice. "I heard the stories though. The members of the church at the time were so relieved when those men were caught before they hurt the woman they'd kidnapped in L.A. Human sacrifice is not what we're about." A shudder ran through her.

Alyson went for the gracious, socialite smile she'd practiced for years. "Why don't you show us where we can stow our gear? I'd love to see what all you've built here."

It must have worked. Sharon beamed and said, "Right this way."

Alyson swallowed her irritation when Logan made a point of carrying the equipment bags. She couldn't afford to replace anything if he broke something. But it wasn't worth the pissing contest in front of Sharon after the rocky beginning with Reverend Haight's assistant.

The interior of the main cabin wasn't anything like Alyson expected. Humidity weighed down the air. Instead of the blue-collar American, wild west, or native tribal designs she'd seen all over town, the lodge's great room resembled a Paleozoic museum.

Petrified wood had been carved into various pieces of furniture. Huge potted palms hugged alcoves and corners. Rather than the head of a local large-hooved herbivore hanging over the fireplace, the outline of an eight-point sun had been carved into the stones. Hammered gold filled in the grooves.

Underneath the sun, what seemed to be a skeleton of a tiny dinosaur perched on the mantel, some carnivorous variety from its jagged teeth and prominent ripping talons on each of its limbs. The relic was posed in such a way it almost appeared alive and ready to pounce on its next victim.

Alyson took a closer look. Instead of the requisite four limbs, the skeleton had eight. She waved to indicate the figure. "Was this a particular species native to Montana?"

Nervous laughter burbled from Sharon. "No. Our symbol used to be an eight-legged lizard over a star. After the problems in L.A. and the negative connotation reptilian species have in America, Reverend Haight decided to simplify the emblem." She pointed at the gold design. "Now, it's just the eight-point star."

"But the skeleton?" Alyson raised an eyebrow.

More nervous laughter. "One of the teens was fooling around with fossils and animal bones. Reverend Haight thought it was cute, so he put it up on the mantel."

The ashy smell of fear wafted from Sharon. But fear of what? Being judged for having bones in a worship space? Many shamanistic religions as well as the Catholic Church held bones as religious objects.

Or was it fear of bringing Child Protection Services down on the compound? Anything in U.S. society that wasn't WASP-ish was immediately suspect in a large swath of the country.

Or was it as simple as fearing her boss's temper? What if Fred Haight's views weren't as far removed from his jailed compatriots' opinions as he wanted the outside world to believe?

Whatever it was, Alyson knew if she pushed, the assistant would clam up. Best to give it time, wait until the members of the Sunshine Believers trusted her.

Sharon led them to what she called a coat closet. The space was the size of the cabin Alyson rented from Roy.

Once their gear was stowed and coats hung, Sharon led them around the main building. The place was more like a spa than a religious center. Massage rooms, a sauna, and meditation spaces were interconnected by a brook diverted through the building. The water feature even had tadpoles and tiny fish swimming in it.

While Sharon kept her manner upbeat and cheerful, she kept shooting nervous glances in Logan's direction. Maybe the woman subconsciously picked up on his alpha dominance though he took pains to remain in the background as they toured the facility.

Sharon swept into a large room with a series of tables with white cotton cloths covering them. "This is our communal dining area. We serve a completely vegan diet, and we grow a majority of our food."

"Vegan?" Disbelief twisted Logan's brow.

Sharon tilted her chin in a defiant manner at his question. "It's a healthier lifestyle and much better for the environment."

Alyson took a deep breath, as much to test Logan's doubt as to prepare to smooth over Sharon's ruffled feathers. She caught the faintest odor of Normal blood. Underneath it was a whiff of something else familiar that she often detected in conjunction with the coppery scent. A combination she only smelled when Papa returned from a meeting with the vampire representative of New Orleans. "Is that sandalwood I'm smelling?"

"Yes, it is. We burn incense during services." Sharon's expression became alarmed. "You're not allergic, are you?"

"Oh, no. It just reminds me of—" Alyson caught herself. "Someone I know back in Louisiana wears a lot of sandalwood cologne." She forced a chuckle.

A soft chime rang, and Sharon jumped. "That's Reverend Haight. Wait here please, and I'll let him know you've arrived." She darted out the door.

"We need to get you out of here," Logan murmured.

"Why?" Alyson crossed her arms.

"Can't you smell it?" He looked at her as if she'd lost her mind. "Neither scent is from a tree."

She rolled her eyes. "Has it occurred to you there's a simpler explanation? As in one of the women here is having her period? And you can't be sure it isn't incense and not—" She glanced around herself. "The other thing." If he didn't say "vampire", she wasn't about to either.

His jaw muscles clenched so hard they stood out in sharp relief under his skin. "You can't tell me you think she's acting in an ordinary manner."

Sharon's behavior bothered her more than she wanted admit to Logan, but she didn't want to give him the satisfaction of being right either. "Maybe if you'd stop glowering at her like the big, bad wolf, she wouldn't be so nervous around us."

"I don't think I'm the one she's afraid of." He glowered more.

"Has it occurred to you that if something is going on here, she's more likely to open up to me?" Alyson said softly. "Without you being so . . . intense?"

Slowly, his shoulders relaxed before he inclined his head. "You're right. I get a little . . ." A mix of ash and sour cream tainted the air, overpowering the blood and sandalwood. His anxiety had to be incredible.

And his admission made her feel a little sympathetic. If even half of what Aunt Francine had insinuated last night were true, Alyson understood Logan's jumpiness at the sandalwood odor. "Weird about *them*?" She gave him the slightest of smiles. "I totally understand."

"What's that supposed to mean?" he growled.

Mother Wolf, she'd really stepped into it, hadn't she? But there really wasn't a point in lying. He knew who she was, and he might as well know she knew who he was.

Alyson let her arms drop to her sides, and lowered her voice even more. "All I mean is I'd be nervous, too, if I were the only one of our people who survived Selene Antonius's little shop of horrors."

His nostrils flared, and his fists clenched. For a moment, she feared she'd made the wrong choice. If he lost control here in a compound of Normals, they were both in deep shit.

Instead of sprouting fur, he closed his eyes and quietly counted, "Ich, nie, san, shi . . ." When he reached what she assumed was ten, his shoulders had relaxed and his skin had smoothed.

His eyes slowly opened. "You know."

"Yeah," she admitted. "I'm sorry for questioning you. But you'd know long before now if there are any of *them* were living in the vicinity of Tuttle Creek, which is why I didn't want to jump to conclusions when I smelled the sandalwood and blood."

He shook his head. "You're right. There aren't any of them nearby." He leaned closer to her ear and murmured, "Closest vamps I know of are a couple living in Billings."

She cocked her head. "Literally two?"

He grinned. "No, literally a couple. Ever hear of Toni Wells?"

"The romance writer?" Alyson stopped short of gushing over her favorite author. "I've heard of her," she said coolly.

"Joni and Thomas Wellington."

She snapped her fingers. "So that's why their Ancient Nights Convention is held up here in the middle of winter."

"No, you're not a fan at all," he drawled.

For once, she didn't get angry at his teasing. In fact, she kind of liked it.

Fury ripped through Marcus Giovanni as he watched the video feed from the Sunshine Believers' dining room. If it weren't the middle of the day, he'd charge up there, rip off the wolf's head himself, and ship it to Alex Stanton.

Or maybe he should ship Polk's left hand to that asshole.

He held up his arm and stared at the stump. Not even the V-virus's vaunted healing power could replace a missing limb when it had been cut off by the weapon of a god. Not when he'd left his hand behind, his blood coating the pebbles and soaking into the desert sand. Not when the choice had been his hand or his life.

Maybe daylight was a good thing. It kept him from doing anything stupid like revealing his continued existence. Augustine and the rest of his minions must have assumed he died in the Nazca desert. Let them continue to believe so until it was too late.

No, he needed to lay aside his personal desires and stick to the plan. He wasn't going to make the same impatient mistakes his grandmother and the lizard demons had made.

His phone buzzed. He thumbed the "Answer" icon. "Yes."

"Why is the male werewolf with the filmmaker?" Haight sounded curious.

Not who was he, but why. "Maybe word got out about your little stunt in Seattle." As much as it burned Marcus to say it, he added, "Leave this one alone."

"Why?"

Marcus wanted to yell in exasperation, but Haight didn't think like he did. The idiot was too worried about short-term results. Which was ironic considering how many thousands of years Haight and his siblings had been waiting for this opportunity.

"He's here to protect the female," Marcus said. "She's a pack princess from Rousseau's territory, but she's in Augustine's now. Something happens to her, and you're going to have more trouble on top of you than you know what to do with."

"And why would I be afraid of some vampires?"

As if Marcus didn't already know how Haight regarded him. "You know what happened in Peru."

Faint static was the only sound for almost a minute. "You and your people need to stay where you are until she leaves."

"I wasn't planning on coming out until after sunset," Marcus muttered sourly.

"No, stay there until she's finished filming."

Haight's statement confounded him. "You're really going to allow her access to the entire compound?"

"No, just most of it. When she presents a lovely view of our church, it will attract more lost souls. Fresh human blood will quench your thirst far better than the occasional elk, wouldn't it? Not to mention some additional spawn for our cause."

Despite himself, Marcus's mouth began to water. "Yes, it would."

"Stay where you are. We don't want the weres scenting you or your people. My daughter will be there shortly with a new recruit for you." The signal abruptly cut out.

Marcus leaned back in his chair. Now, why was Haight so damn interested in the Tribideaux bitch?

He didn't realize he spoke aloud until Rivers said, "Probably because he wants to use her for breeding. I would."

Marcus turned to find his progeny staring at the picture of Alyson Tribideaux on the screen with raw lust, the mug of blood that was lunch forgotten in his hand.

"It'd be even better doing her with Polk tied down and watching," Rivers continued.

Marcus glared at the other vampire. "You will do nothing."

Rivers shook his head. "Why are you taking orders from that bozo?"

"Because there's too few of us to make Augustine Coven pay for what they've done," Marcus snapped.

"It's not like they're going to waltz up here on their own," Rivers grumbled before he slammed down the mug of blood and stomped out of the control room.

Marcus rubbed his chin. No, Augustine wouldn't come to Montana without a damn good reason. He leaned closer to the screen. Polk bent and whispered in Tribideaux's ear.

Maybe there was a way to pick off his uncle's minions a few at a time. Certainly, they'd come if one of their own called for help.

And Marcus knew exactly who Polk would call first.

# Chapter 6

"I'm so sorry for making you wait, Miss Tribideaux."

Alyson turned at the friendly greeting. Several things struck her as she examined Frederick Rogers Haight. Medium height, average build, common brown hair with a smattering of grey threaded through, and mediocre brown eyes framed by non-descript steel wire-rims. They all added up to someone who would normally blend in with the crowd if it weren't for his bright smile and jovial attitude.

"That's quite all right, Reverend Haight. Sharon has been taking good care of us." She took a deep breath as she shook his proffered hand. The crisp scent of a red delicious. Well, that killed any theory about him being a super.

The assistant froze for a moment, but Haight's chuckle seemed to relax her. "I'm not sure what I'd do without her. Honestly, she's the one who keeps this place running."

Sharon blushed, and the lightest hint of roses came from her direction. Alyson had to clamp down on her own emotions to keep from revealing the assistant's secret. Sharon had a crush on her boss. No wonder she worried excessively over the reverend's possible displeasure. No doubt she wanted to impress him enough that he took notice of her as more than a capable assistant.

Haight scratched the back of his head. "This place will be filling up pretty soon, and I believe we need to talk a bit before we hammer out the final details. If you don't mind retiring to my office for lunch, Sharon will make sure your intern is fed."

Alyson relaxed slightly. Maybe this would be easier than she thought.

Until Logan inserted himself between her and the sect leader. "Where Miss Tribideaux goes, I go."

Haight frowned. "Just what are you insinuating, young man?"

"Logan!" Alyson glared at him before she turned back with what she hoped was the right amount of sincerity in her expression. "I'm so sorry, Reverend—"

"I think you know exactly what I'm stating," Logan growled. "Starting with Hollywood and leading to Peru."

Sharon clapped her hand over her mouth.

Instead of the fury Alyson half-expected, Haight shook his head sadly. "Our mission is to find lost souls and show them the light. Those men you refer to in California weren't doing our Lord's work, son. They did terrible things. They were caught. They were punished."

"What about the ones who escaped to Peru?"

Alyson blinked. She'd only discovered the incident with the actress. There were others?

"We certainly don't condone the brutal murders of those other two women in Los Angeles. It is my understanding the United States government asked to extradite our former members who allegedly committed the crimes. However, Peruvian law enforcement has yet to apprehend them." Haight exhaled noisily. "And before you ask your next question, I'll give you the same answer I gave the FBI. No, I have not been in contact with them. I would most definitely turn them over to the proper authorities if I knew where they were in Peru. However, I sincerely doubt they would dare show their faces here."

"Because you'd punish them?"

Haight's heated gaze could have melted steel. "Because one of the women they are accused of murdering was our order's prophet."

Alyson retrieved the bag with her laptop and printer out of the coat closet before Haight led her to his private office. Logan obviously wasn't happy about the arrangement, but he kept his mouth shut as she walked away. Once Haight closed the office door, she held up her hand.

"Before we go any further, I want to apologize for Logan's behavior."

"My dear, if I got upset at every accusation thrown our way, I would have given myself a brain aneurysm years ago." He held out a chair for her at a tiny table on the other side of the room from his desk. The wide window showed a panoramic view of the valley below with the town of Tuttle Creek nestled by its namesake. She took the proffered seat and studied his private space.

The museum metaphor carried over into his office. Another prehistoric fossil embedded in sandstone adorned the wall behind his desk chair. It was a smaller version of the dinosaur on the mantel in the receiving area, but with the appropriate four limbs. A bookcase overflowed with tomes on Paleozoic archeology. Framed fossilized footprints from millions of years ago hung on the opposite wall.

When he took the seat across from her, she continued, "I want you to know I have no intentions of dredging up dirt. You're one of several groups I'm filming—"

Haight held up his hands. "Stop right there." He leaned forward, his elbows on the table. "A documentary should give an unflinching portrayal, shouldn't it?"

His candor threw her off the speech she'd mentally rehearsed. "Yes, it should."

"Then you need to include our problems as well." His expression turned grim. "I'm not happy about the terrible acts performed by some of our former members, but they happened. If you ignore it, your integrity will be called into question, Miss Tribideaux. If I ignore it, the odds are something similar could occur again."

He removed his glasses and rubbed his eyes before he laid his spectacles on the table and returned his attention to her. "All I ask is that you don't sensationalize those terrible things the way the news people have. Please stick to the facts." His earnest look was so endearing. He reminded her of the parish priest back home.

"You mentioned one of your own was a victim," she said softly.

He nodded. "Her name was Jane Chevrette. Before we go forward with this project . . ." He stared out the window for a moment. "She was . . . very important to me. I won't ask you to remove all reference of her, but please don't mention her gift. People already don't think much of us. I don't want her name disparaged."

She hesitated. "May I ask a few questions off the record?"

"Testing me?" One graying eyebrow rose, but his smile was more self-deprecating than annoyed.

Alyson inhaled. Grief spiced his scent, but there was no hint of deception. "No. I want us both to be comfortable about this project, but it sounds like Ms. Chevrette was more than a colleague."

He played with his frames as he stared out the window overlooking the valley. "Yes, she was much more to me than just a fellow in faith." When he turned back to Alyson, she could describe the glint in his eyes as murderous. "If I could wreak vengeance on the people who killed her, I would," he said.

Logan's earlier words chilled her. "Did you go to Peru?"

He blinked and sighed before he replaced his glasses. "No, but I did make some enquiries through non-government channels. The people responsible for my Jane's death are no longer in that country, and I cannot . . . reach them at the moment."

"If you know where they are, why don't you call the FBI?"

The slightest smiles curved his lips. "May I ask you a question in turn, Ms. Tribideaux?"

"Of course."

"When a werewolf is killed in a dominance fight, do you report the death to the Normal authorities?"

Her lungs refused to work. "I-I don't know what you're talking about."

He waved a hand. "This is off the record, isn't it?"

She nodded slowly. The old fear of discovery continued to punch her in the gut, making it difficult to breathe.

"Did you really think I'd let a stranger onto this property without learning everything about her?"

What should she do? Laugh it off? Run? And how the hell had he discovered her secret?

What Haight had said about his lover, girlfriend or whatever this Jane was to him being the group's prophet finally registered in Alyson's brain. "Ms. Chevrette wasn't Normal, was she?"

The reverend's smile was sad. He leaned his elbows on the table as he regarded Alyson. "No. She wasn't. And yes, I do know about your world. You have nothing to fear from me. Part of conventional seminary training is learning to keep your parishioners secrets as long as they are not a danger to themselves or to someone else. I have no problem extending the same courtesy to a business partner."

"Let me get this straight. You're asking me to not out Jane as a supernatural and in return, you won't out me as one?"

Haight chuckled. "When you put it that way, it sounds more like blackmail than a negotiation."

If her father were here, he'd kill Haight outright because he knew the truth about them. While the reverend's offer did sound like blackmail, she could understand him wanting to protect someone he cared about. Alyson nodded. "Your terms are acceptable, Reverend."

"As long as that particular term isn't in the contract."

Alyson rested her own elbows on the table. "And how do you propose to enforce that particular clause if it's not in the contract?"

"I guess we'll just have to trust one another," he said.

She considered his statement for a moment. The clause really couldn't be in a contract that another Normal might see. But the thought of following pack protocol made her stomach rebel. And if she did follow protocol, exactly how would she get out of the ranch alive? Not to mention, who had Haight already told her secret to?

"I guess so." She reached down and pulled her laptop out of its bag. "I have my standard contract. If you want any additional changes—"

"Let's get some food before we start. No sense continuing our negotiations on an empty stomach."

As if she were waiting for a cue, Sharon entered with a tray. She set the two salads and bowls of strawberries before them, along with glasses and a pitcher of ice tea.

"Ring me if you need anything else." She bounced out the door, obviously in a much better mood. Alyson wondered how much her improved demeanor was due to Logan.

And immediately squished the thought faster than a summer mosquito.

"I'll need releases from the member of the Sunshine Believers I film."

"That won't be a problem. Most of our folks have agreed, but there's a few that have said they don't want to be a part of your project. I know you'll respect their wishes." Haight reached over and patted her hand, a fatherly gesture. "I trust you to do the right thing."

She relaxed a bit and unwrapped the napkin from the silverware. Maybe her anxiety had nothing to do with this project and everything to do with the werewolf on the other side of the door.

Logan watched the rest of the diners as he poked at the rabbit food before him. Occasionally, one of the group would look his way before muttering to the person next to him or her.

"Lunch isn't to your liking?" Sharon's expression no longer had the fretfulness it had when he and Alyson first arrived.

He smiled. Or tried to. The motion felt unnatural and stiff after the last four years.

*It didn't earlier when you were talking to the pretty were,* the voice in the back of his mind reminded. The voice that was beginning to sound more and more like his therapist.

"I'm more of a meat and potatoes kind of guy," he murmured politely.

Sharon frowned. "I can have the kitchen fry a soy burger for you."

"No, thanks. I appreciate the thought though." He laid his fork aside. "You said you recently joined the Sunshine Believers. When was that?"

"It will be two years next month." She took a sip of her tea. "I can honestly say Fred Haight saved my life."

"How so?" He didn't have to feign curiosity. The attitudes here reminded him of pack mentality. A tight-knit group with a healthy suspicion of an outsider.

She blushed, a hard one compared to earlier. The woman obviously adored her boss. Even a Normal could get that without detecting the rose undertone to her scent. "I became addicted to painkillers after a car accident. My sister dragged me to rehab twice. It didn't help."

Sharon stared at the dead garden outside of their window. "He found me in Cheyenne, homeless, trading sex for oxycontin. I'm not proud of myself. If it weren't for Reverend Haight, I'd be dead or worse. I can't really explain how he did it. He used mainly talk therapy, which never worked before when I was in rehab, but he cured me."

She faced Logan again. "I'm clean. He gave me a decent job. A purpose."

He inclined his head toward the rest of the dining room. "What about everyone else?"

She smiled. "Everybody has their own story. None are the same. Some were adrift spiritually. Some lost their homes in the last economic downturn and had nowhere else they could go. Some were addicts like me or had other problems with the law."

"He sounds like a saint."

Sharon's expression sharpened. "He's a good man, but he's just a man. I know what the people in Tuttle Creek say about him, but they don't bother to get to know any of us either."

"Actually, all I've heard and seen are good things."

Her eyes widened and she blinked. "Oh. Like what?"

Suspicion ran deep in this woman. But then, it had taken the folks in Tuttle Creek a little time to accept the Goldsteins and him as well.

"I work with Avery at the feed mill. He's the hardest worker there. Always on time for his shift. Always polite. You don't see that much in kids these days." Logan reached for a roll from the nearby bread basket. "Carol at the general store says the same thing about Maddy. And she's quite pleased Haight insists Maddy, Avery, and the other kids get their high school diplomas."

Pink spread across Sharon's cheeks again. This time, the scent of sourdough spilled from her, as if she were as fresh-baked as the roll in his hand. "I didn't realize you—"

"Knew a couple of y'all?" He grinned. "Now who's makin' assumptions?"

Her laugh was self-deprecating. "I apologize for my attitude. I guess I'm used to being looked down on or my decisions questioned. It didn't occur to me I was doing the same thing."

He shrugged. "It happens to all of us at times."

Sharon leaned closer and said in a conspiratorial whisper, "You're not really her intern, are you?"

"The man who came with you isn't really your intern, is he?" Haight stared at Alyson with an unblinking gaze.

She hesitated for a moment. She didn't want to damage her relationship with the reverend. Not after they'd hammered out the contract and he'd signed it. "I'm afraid half the town insisted someone escort me to your ranch."

He shook his head and poked at his strawberries. "After all this time, they're still afraid."

"I don't think it's you so much as me." She took a nervous sip of her tea. "I'm the stranger. Worse, I'm a tenderfoot. They're afraid I'll get myself eaten."

"Eaten?" His eyes widened.

"Mayor Newlin and the sheriff think there's a large wild predator a little too close to town."

"A wild predator?" Concern flashed across Haight's mien. "This is the first I heard of any incident."

She shrugged and waved an airy hand. "Some hunters found a dead elk torn up in a mountain meadow. If Logan hadn't driven me here, the mayor or Doctor Goldstein were going to." She smiled. "If I didn't know better, I'd say my father hired them all to keep an eye on me. Honestly, I think the town officials were trying to scare me."

Her statement only increased the furrows of worry on the reverend's forehead. "Because you were meeting with me?"

"More like trying to scare the big city girl." Alyson laughed. "Which is ridiculous considering New Orleans is surrounded by gators."

Haight chuckled as well. "So your father protects you from these gators?"

"No, he tries to keep away far more dangerous predators." She leaned closer and mock whispered, "Men."

Logan smiled at Sharon. "You found me out."

"A lie's not a way to make a good impression." Despite her admonition, she returned his smile.

"You know what it's like with the tourists. They come up here, unprepared, and they think it's a zoo or amusement park." He rolled his eyes and leaned back. "Remember those hikers that got caught in the snowstorm last spring and died of hypothermia?"

She nodded.

He jabbed a thumb in the direction Haight had escorted Alyson. "It's the beginning of winter, and she's up here with a designer coat, six hundred-dollar boots, and no chains for her tires." He shrugged. "She's staying in Old Roy Cole's rental cabin, so he asked me to keep an eye on her. Last thing we need is for some rich bitch to drive her pansy-assed rental off the side of the mountain."

"So why the lie?"

"Probably to preserve her dignity by pretending she's in charge." He shrugged again. "I don't really give a shit what she says." He leaned forward and rested his arms on the table. "I prefer a real woman to some city slicker any day."

Red flooded Sharon's face. "I-I'm flattered, but . . ." She took a large drink of her tea.

"That's okay." He smiled. "I didn't realize you and the reverend—"

"No!" Her outburst drew the attention of the remaining diners. "I mean, um, there isn't anything between him and me."

Logan straightened. "I didn't mean to upset you. You're a very attractive woman. I had to ask."

Her blush deepened. "Well, that's, um, very flattering, Mr. Polk—"

"It's Logan," he corrected gently.

"Logan." She cleared her throat, but wouldn't meet his eyes. "Like I said it's flattering, but I'm still working on my sobriety. It's best if I don't get involved with anyone." Her gaze flicked to him and back down to her hands. "I hope you understand."

"I do." The problem was he really did. In his case, it wasn't drugs, but his damn anxiety attacks. "Again, I apologize for making you uncomfortable. That's the last thing I wanted to do."

She scooted back her chair and stood. "If you're finished eating, why don't we go find the reverend and Ms. Tribideaux?"

Logan rose as well and laid his napkin on his chair. "That's a good idea."

Amusement filled Reverend Haight's face. "If I had a daughter as beautiful as you, protecting her would be a full-time job."

Alyson laughed to cover her discomfort. Why the hell was she bringing up such a personal subject with this man? But talking to him felt so comfortable, like she had known him all her life.

"Well, the other side is he wants to see me married, so he's been parading a ton of associates' sons through our house. But I'm not ready to settle down. My career is just starting to take off."

Haight poured more ice tea into her glass. "And you want to establish your reputation before having a family."

"Yes." She took another drink. "It's not that I don't want family . . ."

"I agree with you." He lifted his own glass. "Sow your wild oats before you have children to worry about. Here's to finding yourself before finding a mate."

She raised her own glass and clinked it against his. "To finding ourselves." She took a sip before she waved her hand to indicate the compound. "Is this sanctuary about finding *yourself*?"

He chuckled. "No, I'm well past my . . . oats stage." His expression turned somber. "This is about protecting my family, and the Sunshine Believers are my family." He took another sip of his tea. "There's a dynamic that some family units have and others don't. It makes the difference of whether the unit can remain together after a family tragedy.

"I know most of the public doesn't believe this, but the things that happened, the terrible crimes some of our membership committed, had the same effect on our organization as it does when a member of a nuclear family unit does those same types of acts. And the same questions go through our heads. Why didn't we see it? What could we have done differently?"

He took a deep breath and blew it out. "The best I can do is give my people some space to deal with those questions, even as I still struggle with them."

"Would you mind if I ask about Jane and what kind of role she played?"

A sad smile appeared on Haight's face. "Jane had the gift of foresight. I know most people would think she was a scam artist, but . . . too many things she saw came true for me not to believe her."

Alyson pushed condensation down the side of her glass as she considered her next question. "If Jane was precognitive—"

"Why didn't she foresee the problems?" His smile turned wry. "In the case of the actress, she did. She warned the men not to do something stupid, and they assured her they wouldn't. Unfortunately, she believed she carried more influence over them than she did. By the time, we learned they had gone through with their plans, well . . ."

He shrugged. "The authorities arrived at our property before Jane and I did. They rescued the woman, and I was questioned about the matter."

Alyson frowned. "Why wasn't Jane questioned?"

"I told her to take our car and leave. There was no sense in both of us ending up in jail." Haight shrugged again. "She was the real leader of the Sunshine Believers after the disaster of that actress's kidnapping. Or she was until she was murdered."

"Was her gift the reason for she was killed?"

"I believe it was. The extremists knew Jane would go to the police if she learned they planned additional crimes." A tentative smile crossed his lips. "I'm sure you find the whole story ridiculous."

"Reverend," she said as she reached over and covered his hand with hers. "Like I said, I'm from New Orleans, the American voodoo capital. I've seen enough strange things in life to know there's more to the universe than we poor mortals understand."

He smiled widened. "I know that as well, Alyson."

A shiver ran up her spine, and she tried to release his hand as quickly as she could without obviously jerking her own away. The echo of Roy's warning yesterday morning ran through her mind. Her inner wolf said there was something off about Fred Haight. Something neither her human side nor her canine side could lay a paw on.

# Chapter 7

Logan swallowed his irritation about getting turned into Alyson Tribideaux's personal pack mule. Or maybe the irritation stemmed from how great her ass looked in her jeans as she bent over her tripod while she set up a shot of the main building. "Since you've drafted a film intern for free, are you saving your money for Morgan Freeman to narrate this documentary?"

She glanced up at him. "What?"

He stared up at the overcast sky. This morning's beautiful sunshine was long gone, and low gray clouds scudded across his view. They insinuated more snow on the way. "Morgan Freeman. He's played God before."

She looked at him and grinned. "I hear James Earl Jones is cheaper."

"You really think Haight would sign off on you using Darth Vader to do the voice-over about his compound?"

She laughed. "You're right. Actually, I don't worry about hiring the voice work until I edit the film and write the narrative." She turned back to the viewfinder.

"Don't you have some idea of what would work?"

"If you mean, will I use Frank Oz as Miss Piggy for the vocals, then yes, I know what definitely won't work." She made a few adjustments, and the camera emitted a high-pitched electronic whine as it recorded. The pitch was so high most Normals didn't hear it.

"So you do have someone in mind?"

She laughed again and straightened. "If I didn't know better, I'd say you were trying to pitch your talent."

"Dream on, Miss Director."

She looked at him with real curiosity. "So are you just going to throw feed bags around for the rest of your life?"

He stared at the surrounding forest. The subject of what he used to do before his abduction didn't sit well with most weres. But why did he care what she thought?

He shrugged. "I don't really know yet. After Vietnam and college, I did the computer start-up thing three times. Sold each of the companies for a profit. I'm not sure what I want to try next."

She cocked her head. "Vietnam? I-I didn't realize you were that old."

"Does that bother you?"

"N-No." She quickly turned back to the viewfinder, though the digital camera was working just fine.

For some reason, her discomfort sent a tickle of amusement through him. He crossed his arms. "Got something against middle-aged men?"

"No. Now, shush. I'm working."

Before he could continue teasing Alyson, Sharon appeared over the little ridge in the field with a cardboard drink carrier. From the way she huffed and puffed, she'd hiked around the compound in order to stay outside of Alyson's camera shot. "Thought . . . you might . . . need some coffee."

Logan grabbed the carrier before she dropped it. "Thank you."

"Sorry." Sharon bent over and rested her hands on her knees. "I'm still working to get back in shape. Believe it or not, I used to run cross-country."

Alyson sniffed. "Oh, my goodness! Is that really café au lait?" She acted like an addict herself with the way she stared at the lidded disposable cups.

"Good nose." Sharon grinned and straightened. "I doubt if mine is as excellent as the ones in New Orleans, but they get me through the afternoon."

Logan handed Alyson a cup, and she took a sip. Her ecstatic expression made him wish he was the cause, not a cup of milk and coffee.

"This is incredible, Sharon!"

Haight's assistant blushed. She seemed to do that a lot. "I'll have some ready for you in the morning."

Logan frowned. "About tomorrow morning, I can't get the time off two days in a row."

Alyson shot him an arch look. On the other hand, a hint of dismay shone in Sharon's eyes. Great, now he had two women upset with him.

"And what makes you think I need your help, Mr. Polk?" the were said sharply.

He suppressed the urge to bark back. "You need someone for the set up. Otherwise, it's going to take you twice as long to unwind all your cords." He pointed at Sharon. "She's got her own job to do, as does every-one else who lives here."

Alyson crossed her arms. "So what are you suggesting?"

He was really beginning to hate her stance. It made him want to tackle her and prove who was alpha. "What about Sarah Goldstein? She can use the experience for her independent study project. You would have your unpaid intern while you're in Tuttle Creek without worrying about her room, board, and travel expenses."

"I'll be the judge of who I need—"

The instant the words left her mouth, a gust of wind seized the camera tripod. Logan caught it before the tripod and the very expensive video camera hit the ground.

"This is why you need a real assistant." He grinned.

She grimaced. "We'll talk about it on the way back to my cabin."

Two hours later, alarm bells rang in Alyson's head when Logan took the turn for the town instead of the road up the mountain. "Where the hell do you think you're going?"

He didn't even bother to look at her. "You accepted Esther's invitation to dinner, remember? And you need to talk to Sarah about her working as your assistant for the next week."

"We said we would discuss it on the ride back to my cabin," she ground out.

"No, you said that, not me." He flashed her a grin. "But we are talking about it on the ride back to Tuttle Creek."

"And why can't we pick up my vehicle?"

His musky scent turned into the sharp tang of wood smoke. "Did you notice the change in weather while you were getting your outdoor shots?"

She shifted uncomfortably in her seat. "It was getting cloudy. So what?"

"First of all, there's another snow storm coming in. This time, it's going to stick for the rest of the winter. Second, we lost four hikers this year because they were too dumbassed to come back down the mountain when the weather soured." He shot a glare at her. "Third, the snow will start before dinner's over, and that pansy-assed banana of yours with its lack of snow tires or chains won't be able to climb back up the mountain."

She made a low growl in the back of her throat, but he ignored her challenge. Her father would be the first to tell her she was damn lucky that Logan didn't accept.

That thought made her feel worse. She swiveled her head to stare out the passenger window.

Why did Logan Polk make her feel so incompetent? Of course she had checked the weather report this morning. She'd actually planned to use the incoming storm to gracefully bow out of the Goldstein's invitation.

Alyson wasn't aware she'd made another sound until he said, "What was that? I have trouble translating wolf when I'm not one."

She turned slowly to glare at him and his shit-eating grin. Aunt Francine was right. She should have kept her distance from this man. "It means you're as controlling as my father, and that isn't a compliment," she snapped.

Logan took a deep breath. Good to know she was irritating him as much as he was irritating her. "Considering some of the damn fool things you've done in the two days I've known you, René probably has a full-time job trying to keep you from killing yourself."

Alyson clasped her gloved hands together and stared out the windshield. Her old grief tainted the air as memories of finding her mother filled her mind.

"You know your father loves you. He's just trying to protect you," Logan said softly.

His half-assed attempt at a non-apology was the last thing she needed to hear. "I guess you middle-aged men know everything." Her reply was as bitter as the scent she emitted, the scent she couldn't suppress.

"More than some snot-nosed pup."

She stared at him. Anger shoved the past out of the way. "Is that what you think of me?"

He took another deep breath. His exasperated sigh reminded her of Papa whenever she rejected one of the suitors he presented. "I think your father didn't do you any favors by overprotecting you. You're making . . . errors of judgment regarding the people and environment around you."

Now he was deliberately attempting to piss her off. "My first instinct was to stay away from you, so my judgment is just fine!"

"Forget I said anything then," he snapped.

"I will, rabbit-bait," she shot back. And Mother Wolf help her, she'd never talk to him again.

Logan bit his tongue to keep from returning her insult. He was going to get through tonight's meal without losing his temper. He owed the witches that much. He knew Esther meant well by inviting the snot-nosed bitch to dinner. And dammit, he wasn't going to be the one who broke the peace of the Goldstein home. But for the love of Mother Wolf, this girl could be an idiot.

Her silence stretched until they reached the valley floor when he couldn't take it anymore. "If things are that bad at home and you don't want to stay in New Orleans, you can always join another pack."

Alyson remained silent.

"Look, if we don't pretend to be civil to each other during dinner, the Goldsteins, especially Sarah, will drive you insane trying to *fix* the problem."

She snorted. "Why should I be nice to you? You see me as either a stuck-up, spoiled pack princess or an omega to be kicked around and raped by the rest of the males."

What the hell had he stepped in? Worse, what the hell was going on in New Orleans? "I don't understand what you're talking about."

"Oh, that's right. I'm also too stupid to understand pack politics. Any other insults you want to add to your list, Mr. Polk?" she finished with a heaping serving of sarcasm.

"I get it. You're pissed Auntie Francine replaced your mom in your daddy's affections." He immediately regretted the words. Obviously, something was itching under her skin, but lashing back like this wasn't going to help him find out what it was.

"How dare you." Her voice was low-pitched, dangerous. Whenever his own mother sounded like that, someone was about to lose some fur.

If they were lucky. Mom had been known take flesh if someone really pissed her off.

Logan tapped the steering wheel with his thumbs in an effort to rein in his temper before he said, "You're the one who's made it clear she hates being a wolf. And I'm getting tired of you treating me like your own personal omega." This time, the grin he flashed wasn't well-meant, and he made sure to show all his teeth. "I bite back."

"You're right."

That simple admission startled him. "About what?"

"My feelings regarding the pack." Her sniff sounded suspiciously like she was trying not to let tears fall. "I'm too much like my mother."

"What do you mean? From what I know, Minuette was everything a packmaster could ask for in a mate."

"And she hated every minute of it. So much so she killed herself."

That bit of news hit Logan in the gut. She couldn't be serious. But her surreptitious swipe of her face said Alyson was deadly serious.

"I'm sorry. I heard she died in a car accident."

"That's the story everyone was told." Her scent switched from bitter grief to the sulfur and brimstone of anger. "Aunt Francine did what she had to in order to protect me."

"I'm still sorry you had to go through that."

She did a one-shoulder shrug. "Let's drop it."

He'd never heard of a werewolf actually committing suicide. Just how bad was life with René Tribideaux that his wife would rather kill herself than live with him? Especially if Alyson was as young as she was when Minuette died.

It wasn't like he hadn't thought about killing himself at a couple of points during his imprisonment, but that was before his captors had placed Sarah in the cage with him. The old memories triggered his own anxiety, and he forced his fingers to unclench around the steering wheel. The itch of fur along his skin faded as he counted each deep breath he took.

But his anxiety wasn't the real problem. Alyson Tribideaux was rapidly becoming his own personal itch he didn't dare scratch. He wasn't about to give her the advantage by letting her know that, but it didn't mean he had to be a total asshole.

The eleventh deep breath didn't do a damn thing to clear his head. Worse, it filled his brain with too many ideas regarding her. How the hell was he going to survive dinner?

# Chapter 8

How the hell would she survive dinner? Alyson gritted her teeth. Logan Polk was acting like every male werewolf she'd ever met. She was a damned possession, nothing more. If Fred Haight hadn't signed her contract, she would have given up on adding the Sunshine Believers to her documentary, tossed her gear into her rental Jeep, and left Tuttle Creek for good. Then she wouldn't have to deal with the infuriating man next to her ever again.

When Logan cut the engine in the Goldsteins' drive, she couldn't climb out of his Jeep fast enough, but he wouldn't give her any space. He escorted her to the front door, close but not touching, as if he were afraid she would shift and run.

Sarah flung open the front door before Logan could reach for the knob. "About time you two got here." Her curly hair was pulled into a loose braid, and her earrings were clearly visible.

Doctor Goldstein's voice came from further inside the house. "Manners, Sarah!"

The teen made a face. "Why don't you come in, Alyson?"

"Ms. Tribideaux," Logan corrected.

*Acting like a jerk to me is one thing. He doesn't need to beat down on a kid.* She smiled at the girl. "Alyson is fine."

Sarah stepped out of the way, smiled in return, and bowed. "Please come in, Alyson." The girl straightened. "Apparently, I'm not the only member of the family with bad manners." She shot an undecipherable look at Logan.

Interesting that the witches considered him family. Alyson couldn't imagine most wolves bonding with other supernaturals to that extent.

After hanging up their coats, Sarah led Alyson into the kitchen. Esther was working on the food while Aaron set the table. Their greetings were friendly, their contact held to the simple Normal gesture of shaking hands.

After the emotionally intense conversation with Logan in a confined space, the Goldsteins were a welcome psychological relief. As were the delicious aromas of roast beef, noodles, and mashed potatoes. She hated to admit the food was welcome after the lunch of salad and fruit with Haight.

The Goldsteins kept up an easy chatter about Tuttle Creek and its citizens over the meal. Alyson responded with her own questions about the area. Logan remained silent through dinner.

"There's something I need to ask you, Sarah—"

The girl squealed. "Yes!"

"I haven't even asked—"

"Are you joking? Of course, I'll be your intern. I've seen all your films!"

Alyson blinked. Sarah's enthusiasm was a bit disconcerting. "How did you know what I was going to ask?"

The older Goldsteins shot the girl pointed looks.

Her neck and ears turned beet red. "I, um, I'm sorry. I didn't mean to read your mind."

Of course. Most witches were telepathic, or so Alyson had heard. She cleared her throat. "It's okay, but you need to be careful around Normals. Anyway, as I started to say I can't pay you—"

"That's fine." Sarah waved her fork and knife enthusiastically. "Look, I can't get this type of experience in Tuttle Creek, so I'm definitely not saying no to you."

Alyson turned to Aaron and Esther. "Are you sure this is okay with you two?"

"Uh, excuse me," Sarah said, jabbing her fork in Alyson's direction. "I am nineteen you know. A legal adult even by Normal standards. Not to mention, I can use the experience for my independent study project. And it'll look good when I attend UCLA next fall."

"Of course, it's fine with us," Esther said. However, worry sat in her husband's eyes.

Alyson injected as much reassurance into her voice as she could. "I appreciate the help. It'll just be for a few days."

Aaron finally nodded. "All right, but you're coming over to dinner every night for putting up with our daughter."

"Da-a-ad!" Sarah wailed.

But what really unnerved Alyson about the whole conversation was Logan. He had been the one to suggest Sarah accompany her to the Haight ranch this afternoon. Yet, he hadn't said a word about the matter through the meal.

Had he called the Goldsteins while Alyson had been in her meeting with the reverend? If so, then why clear the matter of Sarah with her when he fully intended to force the issue anyway? He clearly wasn't interested in mating, had been insulting the entire day, and lied about spying on her.

Werewolves didn't play games, so what in Mother Wolf's name was he doing?

He prowled around the building and its fence. The curtains were drawn, but her scent lay thick about the front door of the witches' house despite the falling snow. As the daughter of an alpha werewolf, she would be strong. Very strong. Maybe even strong enough to bear him more than one offspring.

Now was not the time to draw her out. Not with the witches and the male were so close. Yes, he could destroy them, but it would attract too much attention. It would not do for the hatchling ape god to learn of his new nest. Not yet.

No, there would be a better time to take the shapeshifter and make her his. He needed to be patient. Besides, the other females needed tending. Especially the ripe halfling.

He sauntered into the woods behind the witches' residence, shifted back to his true form and headed for the nest.

# Chapter 9

*They chased Alyson under an ebony night sky. No moon. Not even any stars to light her way.*

*She raced through a strange forest. It wasn't the humid swamps and bayous of Louisiana. It wasn't home, but some place else terrible and familiar at the same time.*

*Air froze delicate lung tissues with every harsh breath. Razor-sharp ice cut into her bare human feet every time she stepped through the crusted snow, leaving a crimson trail any Normal could follow.*

*More chittering and howls from behind her. Closer. The monsters were gaining.*

*A triumphant cry from her left. Brilliant feathers capped the bright scales of her two-legged pursuer. Too many teeth filled its wide snout.*

*Instinct recognized the hunting behavior of a pack. She dropped and rolled to her right. The creature charging from that direction flew over her prone body and crashed into its packmate.*

*Alyson scrambled upright on numb feet and fled.*

*The cries of her pursuers' frustration bounced among the scrub pines and exposed granite. This wasn't home. Her pack wouldn't come to rescue her. She'd run away from Papa and his parade of eligible wolves. Now, she was alone and far too vulnerable.*

*Where to go? There was nothing out here but trees and rocks and crunchy settled snow.*

*And that snow was growing deeper. She couldn't see her feet, much less feel them. Heat filled her hands, nose and ears. This was bad. Very bad.*

*Fur would be better than skin against this deep freeze. Four paws would spread her weight more evenly over the crust. She needed to shift to survive.*

*But the familiar itchy tingles wouldn't come. The raw terror racing through her normally triggered her change. But now . . .*

*Now, she was nothing but vulnerable human flesh, unable to fight with such dull teeth and flimsy claws.*

*So she ran.*

*A gap in the trees opened, and she tumbled down the incline before she realized the river was there. A river she hadn't heard because it was nearly frozen over. A muffled burble came from the narrow dark ribbon between the glittering ice that framed the banks.*

*Until the mild sound was interrupted by her body smashing through the surface.*

*The shock of frigid water blasted the air out of her lungs. The current immediately dragged her down, under the solid sheet. Dark waves tumbled and tossed her body against the rocks. No hint which way was up.*

*Her lungs burned with the need for oxygen. Just when the urge to inhale threatened to overwhelm her, the river spit her into the night again.*

*More jagged ice sliced her fingers and palms as the water tried to swallow her again. She pulled herself onto the frozen shore, gasping for air. Surely, the side trip down the river had helped her evade the monsters.*

*She rolled over on her back, exhaustion making even that simple task nearly impossible, and closed her eyes for a moment. Something tickled her neck. A feather.*

*Her lids popped open in time to see the enormous talon slash across her abdomen.*

Alyson jerked upright, her heart pounding and a scream on the verge of her lips. In her nightmares, she had kicked off her covers. No wonder she was freezing. She pulled them back over her, but the instant she lay her head on her pillow, the same edgy feeling of someone being in the cabin crawled up her spine like it had last night.

She tossed back the comforter once again. When her toes hit the floor, the cold reminded her of the snow and ice in her nightmare. Was Logan out there waiting for her again? She crept over to the bedroom door and peeked through the crack.

Brilliant moonlight spilled around the edges of the curtains. After last night and Logan's refusal to admit he'd been out there, she didn't need more of his Peeping Tom bullshit.

She examined the room illuminated by the clock on the microwave. There was still nothing inside the cabin. She padded over to the window and pushed back the edge of the curtain.

The new blanket of snow glistened under the nearly full moon. A few clouds still blew across the sky, but the storm was over.

And the dark silhouette of a wolf stood beneath the largest pine of the windbreak. Once again, as if he knew she was watching, he paced a few steps closer while still staying in the shadow of the pines.

She was oh-so-tired of his games. He hadn't spoken during dinner at the Goldsteins' home, and had barely said a word to her on the drive to her cabin. He acted alternatively possessive and aloof. Human bullshit, not wolf. Damaged, just like Aunt Francine had said.

They stared at each other for a long time before Alyson released the curtain and padded back to bed.

Alyson was serving both her and Roy coffee when the forest green Jeep pulled into the cleared drive. Her heart threatened to choke her until Sarah's tall, lanky form climbed out of the driver's side.

The girl stomped off the clinging snow before entering the cabin. "Good morning, everyone."

"Need a cup?" Alyson held up the pot.

Sarah grimaced. "No, thanks. Not much of a coffee drinker."

Alyson replaced the pot on the maker's warmer. After the weirdness of the last couple of nights, she decided to take the plunge. "Do either of you know anything about a lone wolf roaming the area?"

Sarah froze for an instant in taking off her coat. Her eyes widened and her head jerked toward Roy. Of course, the girl would be concerned about Alyson's breach, especially since it involved her friend.

Roy didn't notice the byplay between the women, or he choose to ignore it. He set down his cup. "You mean a big tawny fellow? I've seen him a few times over the last couple of years. Funny thing is I haven't seen him with any other wolves."

Trying to maintain an innocent air, Alyson sat down with her coffee at the tiny kitchenette table across from the old man. "Is that normal?"

Roy shook his head sadly. "Not for wolves. I hope he finds a mate soon." He eyed Alyson. "Lone wolves don't survive out here for long. They need a pack."

To Alyson's relief, the rest of the day went rather smoothly. Sarah didn't bring up the subject of Logan, and she was a sharp student, eager to learn the idiosyncrasies of documentary filming. In fact, the young witch had packed them a lunch so they could work without taking too much of a break. Reverend Haight's assistant, Sharon checked on them periodically, but otherwise left them alone.

Once Alyson had finished the establishing shots, she jumped into the one-on-one interviews. Unfortunately, Haight bowed out of her session with him in the sect's chapel, claiming he needed to prepare for a new member.

The five interviews she fit in the rest of the day took place in the workshops or dorms of the compound. All the stories were very similar. Folks down on their luck from various addictions, mental issues, or simply the economic crash had found themselves at rock bottom when Fred Haight came into their lives. The odd thing was none of the members she spoke with had been with the Sunshine Believers longer than four years.

The sun was setting when Alyson and Sarah carried the equipment back to the Jeep with Sharon accompanying them. The teen pointed to one building that sat apart from the rest of the structures. It had one door and no windows. "What's that place?"

Sharon smiled. "It's used for individuals to commune with God."

"Like a sweat lodge or a monastery?" Sarah asked.

Her question drew laughter from Haight's assistant. "You could say so. Sometimes, all the incense, meditation, and fellowship in the world isn't enough to find your connection with the Almighty."

"None of the people I've spoken with so far have been with the Sunshine Believers before the group moved up here to Montana," Alyson said. "Are there any of the older members I may speak with?"

Sharon's expression turned hard. "Yes, there are some folks who were members during the troubles in California. They're the ones who declined to talk with you, Ms. Tribideaux."

That would put a crimp in the story line she planned for the film. "May I ask why?"

Sharon stopped walking and turned to face Alyson fully. "You need to understand something. The members from before our move to Montana were as much victims of the criminals in Los Angeles as the women they kidnapped or killed. Fred—"

Hot pink flooded her cheeks, and the scent of roses coming off Sharon was nearly overwhelming. "Reverend Haight was at a symposium when the actress was kidnapped. By the time he returned, the arrests had been made and everything, including the church's land, seized."

That was odd. Haight had said he'd gone to the Los Angeles compound shortly before the arrests. And that he encouraged Jane to flee, rather than be caught herself. Had he lied to the new members of his congregation to protect himself or cover up something else?

Sharon didn't seem to notice Alyson's hesitation. "He did what he could to help the remaining people find shelter, but Los Angeles is so damn expensive. He was in Seattle, scouting for a new facility, when the murders happened a few months later. It's like the bastards were deliberately trying to ruin everything he worked for any time he was out of town," she finished fiercely.

Or had Sharon changed the story herself? How much of the woman's feelings for the Sunshine Believers' current leader colored her perception of him? However, now wasn't the time for any questions that might be taken as confrontational. Alyson held up her hand. "I wasn't making any accusations. I was hoping to present a before-and-after picture to show how far your organization has come thanks to Reverend Haight."

Sharon's defensiveness deflated, and her shoulders slumped. "I'm sorry. I—" She sucked in a deep breath. "I blame it on hormones."

"Hormones?" Alyson looked askance.

"That time of the month," Sharon said sheepishly.

"It's okay. After all the rumors regarding the Sunshine Believers, I'm surprised y'all even allowed me to film." Alyson smiled. But her gut said the other woman was lying. Well, maybe not about hormones affecting her mood. Alyson would have sworn she detected the faintest hints of honey and citrus under Sharon's apple-sweet odor.

"Thanks for understanding." Sharon smiled shyly in return, and the three of them resumed their walk to the Jeep.

"Why do you think Sharon was lying about being pregnant?"

Alyson stared at Sarah, but the girl kept her eyes glued on the road. "Wh-what makes you say that?"

"Come on." Sarah shot her a disgusted look before returning her attention to her driving. "I live with a were. I know you guys can smell the chemical changes in the body."

"Yes, but how did you know?"

"Double aura." Sarah frowned. "You do know we can see auras, don't you?"

"No, I didn't." Alyson's laugh was self-deprecating. "We don't hang out with witches much in New Orleans. In fact, you keep your distance from any Laveau member unless you want to be hexed." Or maybe that was another of Papa's overprotective half-truths.

However, the conversation resurrected memories of Frankie and his demise at the hands of a necromancer. Sure, the New Orleans coven had expelled David Head for resurrecting his own mother, but that hadn't stopped him from sacrificing her cousin for an obscene purpose. Not even Papa could hide all the rumors about Head using Frankie's death to summon an entire cemetery to attack a supernatural wedding three years ago.

She shuddered. Maybe Papa had been right about excluding her from pack leadership after all. She wouldn't have had the stomach to deal with Frankie's atrocious deeds, much less his murderer's.

Sarah made a noncommittal noise. "The Laveau Coven has its reasons for being the way they are." She held up a hand. "Not saying I agree with their methods, but they definitely have their reasons." She tightened her grip on the wheel before she asked, "What does a pregnant person smell like to you?"

Alyson shrugged. "It doesn't change the fundamental scent of a woman. There's a citrusy overtone to their odor. The scent gradually gets stronger until she delivers. So what do you mean by a double-aura?"

Sarah grinned, probably ecstatic because she knew something an older person didn't. "There's a white light surrounding the general area of the womb. Think of it as a white polka-dot in the middle of a solid-color picture."

"Does the polka-dot change size?"

"Not really, but it does darken to a pastel during the course of the pregnancy." Sarah turned into the cabin's drive. "Sure you don't want to come into town for dinner? Mom and Dad will be disappointed. And you know I can put a choke chain on Logan to keep him in line for you."

Alyson laughed at the image as the teen braked in front of the rental cabin. "No, thanks though. I need to do some research in the local history books Marvin gave me. Not to mention all the food I bought and haven't touched yet." She retrieved the two smaller bags she'd taken today from behind her seat and climbed out of the vehicle.

"Okay, see you in the morning!" Sarah waved before she executed the same J-turn Logan had yesterday and disappeared down the drive.

Alyson took a deep breath of crystal-cold air, and last night's nightmare punched her full force. Maybe she should have accepted Sarah's invitation for dinner.

No, not tonight. Not with the full moon. And not being this close to a strange wolf. She needed to be well away from the cabin before Logan showed up here again.

For the second time in her life, she truly feared the upcoming full moon.

# Chapter 10

Muscles shifted and rearranged. Bones snapped and reformed. Skin itched as fur sprouted. Logan lifted his snout and breathed in the crisp night air. The full moon with the first real snow of winter lent an exhilaration to the change.

He rose and shook himself before he launched his body over the fence. Four feet raced through the white blanket in the direction of Old Man Cole's rental cabin.

Alyson was alone. Despite her accusations, he hadn't come near her except on two feet. If there was another werewolf in the area, he needed to make sure she was all right. The chance that she wasn't made him run even faster.

Instinct had taken over. Four paws dug in and pivoted as the rabbit darted in another direction. Alyson's mouth watered at the thought of fresh meat. And rabbit was so much better than 'coon or possum.

The rabbit zagged to the right, and claws gripped the turf under the snow to correct her course. Guilt and disgust with herself would come tomorrow. Now, power surged through her muscles at the smell of the tiny creature's fear. All she had to do was—

Jaws snapped, killing the rabbit's squeal as abruptly as its life.

Alyson trotted to a secluded spot between the roots of an ancient gnarled evergreen. She settled down to enjoy her meal.

Despite what she'd told Sarah earlier, none of the food at her cabin had sounded appetizing when she returned. Nerves at the impending change kept her pacing in the living room until sunset. Not even cherry amaretto ice cream could distract her on these nights.

She made quick work of the rabbit. Digging a hole for the broken bones and burying them took a moment's effort. She rubbed her muzzle in the snow and licked it clean.

With the edge off her hunger, it was time to run. Her easy lope shifted to a full-out race across the moonlit forest.

Logan approached the cabin from the driveway. It was the human thing to do, but after Alyson's crazy accusation of him spying on her, he didn't want to give the wrong impression.

Her scent permeated the banana-colored Jeep and the front door, which stood ajar. Now that was odd. Why would she leave the door open instead of shifting back to human form to use the lever when she returned tomorrow morning?

He nosed the door wider and barked to announce his presence. No sound. No banked fire. Nothing.

Unease tingled through the fur on his spine. This was strange territory for her. He knew she hadn't had time to scout the area before tonight. Granted, he should have called her and offered to take her someplace safe to shift and run. But he'd been afraid she'd take his offer the wrong way, which would destroy what little civility that still lay between them.

He moved stealthily through the cabin keeping to the walls. Breathing evenly to take in everything besides Alyson. Coffee. Sarah. Roy.

And himself?

He hadn't been inside the cabin. Alyson's clothing had to have carried his scent. Which made sense for her coat over the back of a chair, but not here near the bedroom. He crept closer and poked his head through the doorway.

The scent was fresh. And definitely his own.

And Alyson had accused him of watching her.

Logan whirled and raced for the main door of the cabin. Something was horribly wrong and his gorgeous filmmaker was at the center of it.

# Chapter 11

Alyson bounced across the mountain meadow. She'd never had the chance to play in snow before as a wolf. Her enjoyment was short-lived, assassinated the moment something brushed her ear. She yipped, only to realize it was an owl.

So the bird was irritated by another predator in his field, probably because she'd inadvertently driven away his own dinner. He silently banked and made another pass at her. Alyson ducked, whirled, and raced after her rival.

He banked again. She ran, but he apparently had grown tired of the game. With a few flaps of his wings to gain altitude, he disappeared behind the tree tops.

Alyson slid to a halt and panted. Time to head back to the cabin. She didn't relish the thought of waking up on the mountain, naked and half-frozen, when she shifted back to human form in the morning.

She turned to find another wolf standing at the opposite edge of the meadow. His physical stance matched that of Logan's, and the wolf had the same tawny coat Roy had described. The creature wagged its tail and gave her a canine grin.

But there were far too many teeth in his muzzle for either a regular wolf or a were. Her breath hitched in her chest.

It had the same smile as her nightmare monsters.

She turned tail and *ran.*

Logan followed both the tracks and the two scents, panic in his heart. He couldn't catch his breath, and he stopped. *No, can't let an attack happen now.*

He didn't have time to go back down the mountain. The scent that resembled his was starting to change. No longer only oil-based canine, but some dry undertone of reptile musk, and it followed Alyson's. The trails led toward Last Buffalo Meadow where the destroyed elk carcass had been found. Logan poured on the speed.

Alyson turned her left shoulder an instant before she slammed into the wire field fencing. Thank Mother Wolf, it wasn't barbed. Because of the angle, she bounced to the right. Claws scrabbled for traction, and she took off again.

And right into a chest-high drift. Like in her dream, she floundered through the deep snow. The only difference was she was better equipped to fight than her dream self had been.

A much heavier body slammed her down into the drift. She twisted and snapped. The weight on top of her disappeared, and she struggled from the snow.

The scent of the thing chasing her had changed. It no longer pretended to smell like Logan, even though it still wore a wolf form.

Sort of. Its teeth were far too numerous and far too sharp. Its snout reminded her of the velociraptor skeleton on the mantel of the main house at the Sunshine Believers' ranch.

Instinct told Alyson to dodge to her left. Ice powder flew in all directions when the creature's pounce missed. She raced for the tree line.

Her cabin. She needed to get back to her cabin. Her satellite phone was sitting in the living room.

She'd only managed a couple of lengths when the creature landed on top of her and slammed her face-first into the snow. Agony seared through her. Behind her as it forced itself on her. She struggled or tried to. But nothing stopped the pain.

A howl of fury and terror ripped from her throat. The worst part was no one could hear her.

Logan's ears perked at the cry of a wolf in distress close by. Alyson.

He raced in the direction of the Haight compound's fence line. He made out two dark shapes, the bottom one crying. With a running leap, he crashed into the one on top.

His snap barely missed the other wolf's throat. They rolled, each of them scrabbling for purchase on the other. Alyson's attacker broke free and whirled to face him, teeth gleaming in the moonlight.

Logan bared his own fangs. Whatever this thing was, it sure wasn't a normal wolf, much less a were. Too many razor-sharp teeth protruded from its muzzle.

He steeled himself. Everything had a vulnerable spot. He just had to find this thing's before its jaw locked on his own throat.

The harsh buzz of a snowmobile cut across the meadow. Who the hell would be out this time of night? But he didn't dare take his attention off the other . . . whatever the hell it was.

The non-wolf glanced in the direction of the approaching vehicle. It made a spitting sound before it pivoted and ran. The urge to pursue the creature forced Logan a few steps after it.

Alyson.

He turned back to her. Blood. Mother Wolf! There was so much blood. She was barely conscious, but she whimpered softly.

The snowmobile engine cut off several yards away. Logan looked up and set himself between her and the new person. Or maybe not so new. He recognized the scent.

Roy Cole climbed off the machine and pushed up his snow goggles. "How bad is Alyson hurt?"

Logan cocked his head. His ears had to be deceiving him.

The older man huffed out a frosty cloud. "Logan, I know damn well you can understand me. How bad is she?"

He glanced back at her and stepped aside. Roy carefully approached, keeping his attention fixed on Logan. The old man knelt beside Alyson and ran his gloved fingers over her.

"Shit, she's going into shock," Roy muttered. He looked at Logan. "I know it's the full moon, but can you change back? I can't hold her and drive at the same time, and we've got to get her to Doc Goldstein."

Logan had never tried turning back on these nights before, but Roy was right. Alyson couldn't stay out here, and she'd be even more vulnerable when she shifted back to human form at sunrise.

He concentrated. Mother Wolf, it hurt as he forced his bones and muscles back into their other configuration. Cold seeped through his skin as he lay panting in the snow. He climbed carefully to his feet.

"How'd you know?" He took a deep breath. No, Old Roy still smelled like a Normal. But then, the creature that had attacked Alyson had smelled like a were.

More specifically it smelled exactly like him.

Shit. Everything clicked in his brain. That thing had been disguising itself as him. Probably to lure Alyson and—

His mind shut off that train of thought. Last thing he needed was a panic attack right now. Alyson definitely couldn't afford him having a panic attack right now. Her life depended on him keeping his shit together.

"I'll explain me once we get her taken care of." Roy trod back to the snowmobile and retrieved a blanket from the emergency bag attached to the back. Together, they bundled the injured were, and Logan lifted her. Her canine form felt far too light.

He climbed on the snowmobile behind Roy, cradling Alyson in his arms while his knees and calves pressed against the cold vinyl and even more freezing metal. The old man gunned the engine, and they headed down the mountain.

The Goldsteins met them at the clinic when they pulled up to the back door. Good thing they'd heard his mental yell. Logan could feel Sarah's scowl long before he saw her face.

"And you wonder why I stay up on full moon nights," she snapped.

He ignored her and followed Aaron into one of the exam rooms.

"Honey, grab the portable x-ray machine," the doctor said as Logan laid the unconscious Alyson on the table.

Esther darted off in another direction.

"Sarah, why don't you make everyone some coffee?"

"No." The teen's voice was low, almost a were's growl. "Alyson needs another woman in here."

"Sarah," he said softly.

"Dad, you're going to have to do a rape kit." She swiped angrily at a tear that had escaped while she stroked the fur on Alyson's head and neck. "She needs someone here who understands."

Aaron quickly wiped away his stricken expression and got to work.

Logan clenched his fists against the physical pain of maintaining his human form. The ache in his hands was a welcome distraction.

Esther bustled in, pushing the x-ray machine in front of her. "Logan. Roy. We love you both, but get out."

Logan opened his mouth to protest, but the old man grabbed his arm. "She's right. There's stuff they gotta do, and it would feel like another violation if Alyson wakes up and we're still here. Especially you in your birthday suit."

Rage hit Logan hard. He looked at the werewolf on the exam table. It was the basement of Mallory Labs all over again.

"No, it isn't," Sarah and Roy said at the same time.

"Tell me when she wakes up," Logan said.

"We will," Aaron replied softly.

Roy tugged Logan's arm, and he followed the old man to the clinic's break room. It was a little more than a typical employee area. The Goldsteins kept a full kitchen, plus a recliner and a futon for the times they needed to spend the night with a patient.

The old man started a pot of coffee while Logan grabbed a spare pair of sweats Aaron kept in the closet.

"Change back," Roy said.

"What?" Logan stared at the old man.

"Your pain maintaining your human form right now feels like someone scraping a cheese grater along my brain. Change back to wolf. We'll both feel better."

Logan's eyes narrowed. "How did you know?"

"You change. I'll get me a cup of joe, and explain everything to you."

As much as Logan hated to admit it, Roy was right. He tossed the sweats back in the closet, took a deep breath, and let the shift wash over him.

He blinked and looked up at Roy.

"Feels better, doesn't it?" the old man said.

Logan nodded.

Roy chuckled as he poured coffee into a mug. "Told ya. I'll take the La-Z-Boy. You'll fit better on that half-assed couch."

Logan trotted over to the futon, jumped up and laid down.

Roy took off his snow suit and laid it over one of the matching aluminum and plastic chairs before he settled into the recliner with his mug. "I'm what's called an empath. We read emotions." He waved a hand. "We aren't separate from Normals like witches and weres. At least not yet. But that's why I stay up on the mountain by myself most of the time. As I've gotten older, it's been harder for me to shut out other people's shit."

He took a sip of coffee. "Lemme ask you something. Does someone smell the same to you whether they're in human or animal form?"

Logan nodded.

"Emotions are like that for me. I've seen and felt you several times on full moon nights, but I know you regardless of what form you're in because you always feel the same." Roy blew out a deep breath. "I felt Alyson's panic and your worry tonight. That's how I knew something was wrong up in the meadow. Do you know what the hell that thing was that attacked her?"

Logan shook his head.

"It may have looked like you, but it sure as hell didn't feel like you. Is it like any supernatural you've ever known or heard of?"

Again, Logan shook his head.

"That's what I was afraid of." Roy took a long drink of his coffee. "Don't go out hunting that thing by yourself."

Logan snorted and laid his head on his paws. He wasn't stupid enough to tangle with some unknown creature. He needed information, but he needed rest first. When that thing came back, and instinct said it would, he would be ready.

# Chapter 12

The smell bothered Alyson first. Nothing worse than the antiseptic odor of medical facilities. The pain in her soul reminded her of the night her mother died.

She blinked her eyes open. Bright sunshine filtered through blinds. She lay in a hospital bed. Something had happened last night.

The rush of memories matched the ache between her legs. She slapped her hands over her mouth to muffle her cry.

Esther started in the chair next to her bed. "Hey, you're awake." She stood and held up her hands. "Alyson, you're at the clinic. You're safe. Do you understand?"

She swallowed hard to get her heart out of her throat and back where it belonged. Her head throbbed to her rapid pulse. "How-how . . ."

"Roy and Logan brought you in." Esther sucked in a deep breath. "I'm going to call Aaron. He needs to check you. Do you think you can let him? I'll be right here with you the whole time. Or Sarah can be here if you want."

Numbness settled over her. The doctor was a witch. Aaron wasn't that thing that attacked her. She could handle this.

Alyson wrapped her arms around herself. She was naked. "Umm . . ."

"I've got a gown right here." Esther's smile could only be described as tremulous. It was like the witch channeled all of Alyson's fear and anxiety away from her so she wouldn't feel it. "I didn't think putting it on you while you were still in wolf form was a good idea."

"Probably not." Alyson frowned as some of Esther's words made it past her stupor. "Wait. Did you say Roy brought me in?"

Esther nodded. "He knows about all of us. Apparently, he has for some time. So seeing you in your wolf form didn't freak him out if that's what you're worried about."

"But the rules about exposing ourselves . . ." Alyson gestured helplessly. Haight already knew. Now, Roy. This situation was one more thing out of her control.

"He's not telling anyone. He promised." Esther shrugged. "Besides, if he's known about us and Logan for four years, he hasn't said a peep to a single person in town. And we'd know by now if he had. Frankly, if it weren't for Roy and his snowmobile, you'd still be up on the mountain."

Esther started to rise, but Alyson clamped a hand around her wrist. "Don't ever let Logan out of your sight. Don't be alone with him. Ever. The-the—"

Her lungs wouldn't work. She couldn't inhale. Her own fingers scratched at her throat. She was suffocated under the weight of the monster that had attacked her.

"Alyson, breathe into—" Esther's voice cried out.

Awayawayawayaway. She needed to get away. She fell out of bed, scrambling on all fours, nails scraping tile, running from danger.

Searching desperately for a hiding place. Knowing if the monster found her again it would do terrible things.

Runningrunningrunninghidinghidinghiding.

Until she found a scent. A taste. Someone familiar. Someone . . . safe. Another wolf joined them. She clung to them, and they rubbed their heads against hers until she could breathe again.

"It's okay, sweetie," Sarah crooned over and over again.

Alyson blinked wetness from her eyes. She was under the bed. Still in the clinic. Still naked, but human again. With Sarah on one side and Logan on the other. Both of them held her. And Sarah kept repeating her words.

"What happened?" she whispered.

"That was a . . . flashback," Sarah said. "I've had them. They're not fun."

"Oh." Her throat was sore as if she'd been screaming. Or howling. "Why are we under the bed?"

"That's where you went when you couldn't get the door open," Sarah said. "You shifted trying to run away."

Embarrassment drove away the ebbing panic. "Maybe we should get out from under the bed," Alyson whispered.

"Good idea," Logan said. "This tile isn't comfortable, but if you're not ready, we can put some blankets down here. Especially for later."

"It'll happen again?" Alyson said.

"It might," he admitted.

"Then some blankets would be nice." She didn't move, though her stomach gurgled.

"I can get you some food if you want to stay here," Sarah offered.

"No." Alyson wiggled her toes and fingers. Her stomach gurgled again, and she was pretty sure it was from hunger, not the nausea at the back of her throat. "I think I'm ready."

Sarah scooted out first, and that's when Alyson noticed the extra pairs of legs in the room. She looked at Logan.

"It's Aaron and Roy," he said softly. "We all came running when we heard the commotion in your room. Esther was afraid you'd hurt yourself."

Alyson wanted to sink through the floor. It was bad enough Logan and the witches had witnessed her breakdown. But a Normal?

"I'll head down to The Last Buffalo, and get us all some breakfast," Roy said. One pair of extra legs walked out of the door.

She sucked air deep into her lungs, but she couldn't make her arms and legs move.

"We can stay here a little longer," Logan whispered.

"No." She released her pent-up breath. The mental numbness was back. "No, I can't let it win." She slid out from under the bed and climbed to her feet.

To find Aaron pressing a towel against Esther's arm while holding up the limb. A towel with brilliant scarlet spots.

"See?" the doctor said to his wife. "She's out. Now will you please let me stitch up that arm?"

"Mother Wolf!" Alyson swore and clutched her hands to her chest. "Esther, I'm so sorry. I didn't mean . . ." Her vision blurred at the injuries she inflicted on the witch.

"I know you didn't." Esther smiled, a rueful expression. "It was my own damn fault. I know better." She glanced at Logan before returning her attention to Alyson. "Is it okay if Logan and Sarah stay in here with you while we take care of this?" She inclined her head toward her arm.

Alyson nodded. "Yes." She swallowed hard. "I'm sorry." Things could have gone so much worse with Esther than some slashes that needed stitches. Guilt filtered through her mental cocoon. She could have killed Esther in her panic attack.

Stitches?

"Wait," she called. The Goldsteins paused at the door. "Why can't you heal yourself?"

Aaron and Esther exchanged looks before turning their attention back to her.

Esther shrugged. "No sense wasting the energy over something so minor."

The witch was lying. Alyson could smell it, but she said nothing as Aaron guided his wife from the room. The Goldsteins didn't want to upset her, but it made no sense.

Once they were gone, Sarah held up a medical gown. "How about you put something on before Roy comes back with our breakfast?"

Alyson nodded again and took the proffered covering. "Is your mom going to be okay?"

"Just a couple of deep slashes on her forearm." Sarah laughed and glanced at Logan like her mother had. "She deserves a few stitches. Like she said, she knows better."

Aunt Francine's story flared in Alyson's brain. Of course, Logan and Sarah had known what to do during her episode. They'd experienced the same thing.

"Um, I'm going to get those extra blankets. I'll be right back." The girl whirled and left the room in a rush.

"Is she okay?" Alyson pulled on the gown. It was better to focus on someone else than herself.

"What were you thinking about just now?" Logan carefully avoided watching her dress.

Heat flooded her face. "I, um . . ."

"Witches are telepaths," he reminded her.

"I know that," she snapped.

His focus switched from the door through which Sarah fled and back to her. He cocked an eyebrow. "We're not your enemy, Alyson."

She held the back flaps of the gown together as she sat on the bed. The flimsy hospital wear shielded her vulnerability. "Like I said before, my aunt Francine told me about what had happened to you with Selene Antonius. Sarah is the one witch survivor, isn't she?"

"Oh." He rocked back on his heels, and his face turned as red as hers felt. Only now did she realize his feet were bare. The gray sweats didn't suit him as well as boots and jeans. "Knowing the gossip hounds, there's not many packs who don't know what happened." His hands twitched as if he didn't know what to do with them. "But, yeah, Sarah's the only witch."

Alyson bunched folds of the thin gown in her fists. "I'm sorry about the cracks I made about you hiding here in Montana. I didn't know you were the only were survivor until I asked Francine about you later that night. I didn't understand until—"

Air hitched in her lungs again. Suddenly, he was sitting beside her, holding her. "Take it easy. One slow breath at a time. In. Out."

As much as she hated to admit it, Logan being there kept some of the irrational fear at bay. Except it wasn't so irrational. That thing had hurt her. Had-had—

"In. Out," he repeated the mantra over and over like Sarah had repeated hers under the bed. His voice faded, and Alyson realized they were breathing in unison.

She looked up at him. "What am I going to do? I can't go back like this. The pack already thinks I'm too human."

"Then you have a choice." He brushed her hair away from her face. "You make them accept you as you are, or you find another pack who will."

"Is that why you really left your pack?"

He smiled, the first real smile she'd seen on him. "Like I told you, I left

San Antonio long before the shit in Los Angeles. I wasn't willing to fight my parents for control of the pack."

"I'm not Siobhan Lannigan."

His smile faded. "Why do you keep bringing her up?"

"I . . ." Alyson stared down at her fists. Her knuckles were as white as Logan's had been, wrapped around the Jeep's steering wheel two days ago. "I admire her. She's so strong. She fought for what she wanted. No one considers me that capable."

He squeezed her shoulders. "You built a career outside of your pack's business interests. That sounds pretty capable to me."

"I can't even defend myself," she whispered. "I just ran. I should have fought. Should have ripped out its throat—"

"Alyson, listen to me."

She looked up at him.

"That thing has been stalking you since you got here," he said. "You said it ran in front of your Jeep the first night you arrived."

"Yes," she said. "And-and it was outside my cabin the next two nights. I thought it was you. It smelled like *you*."

"I know." Logan grimaced. "When it couldn't lure you away, it waited until the one night it knew it could get you alone." His mien turned fierce. "I promise you won't be alone again."

His expression should have scared her, but for the first time in her life, she actually felt protected.

Alyson ripped through the three western omelets and biscuits Roy had brought back for her. Thank Mother Wolf, Aaron let her eat. After last night's attack, she surprised herself with her healthy appetite.

What came next was much harder.

Team Goldstein kicked Logan and Roy out of her room to do a second exam.

Aaron sat beside her. "Your discomfort is probably just your nerve endings still playing catch-up with your natural healing abilities. Most of my effort last night was helping you out of your state of shock."

"Shock?" She blinked.

"Yes." He removed his reading glasses and rubbed the bridge of his nose. "It can happen with severe emotional or mental trauma as well as physical trauma. Your blood pressure dropped to dangerous levels. Unfortunately, you were in your wolf form last night when Logan and Roy brought you down from the mountain. I could only do so much. They don't exactly teach wolf anatomy at UCLA so I had to wing it."

"That's because we don't get sick like witches or Normals," Alyson said.

"But you do suffer life-threatening physical injuries," Aaron said softly.

Guilt flooded through her, threatening the omelets in her stomach to make a reappearance. She stared at Esther. "You had to suffer through stitches because of me?"

"We don't waste our talents on minor injuries." Esther's scowl wasn't as threatening or reassuring as Logan's. "And Aaron and I always keep one of us in reserve."

Alyson looked at Sarah, who shook her head. "I didn't inherit Dad and Mom's healing abilities." The teen shrugged. "Everyone expected it, but I ended up with fire abilities instead."

"I-I'm sorry." Wetness blurred her vision.

"Stop apologizing," Aaron said. "And I really do need to double-check things. The closest doctors are in Billings, and all of them are Normal. We can't risk you shifting in front of them."

"I can stay here with you," Sarah said. "If you want. Or if you want Logan—"

"No." Alyson realized how sharp that sounded. "I know you're suggesting him because he's another were, but after what happened earlier—" She shot an apologetic look at Esther. "—Sarah's a better choice for holding my hand."

The teen grinned. "All right, but if you squeeze my hand too tight and break any of my bones, I'm gonna hex you."

Alyson managed to get through Aaron's exam before the next panic attack broke the surface of her numbness. Once again, she ended up under the bed with Logan and Sarah.

This time, she was still in wolf form when the flashback ended. She lay there in the shreds of her medical gown, panting.

Logan poked his head out without releasing her. "She'll be okay for now. Go run your tests."

Alyson couldn't stop the whine at the back of her throat. Her comforting numbness was fractured. The wolf inside her whispered she needed to kill her attacker. Otherwise, how the hell was she ever going to be able to return to New Orleans in this damaged state?

When Aaron returned a couple of hours later, Alyson was dressed in a new medical gown. Roy entertained Logan, Sarah and her with his tale of a misadventure during his and his late wife's honeymoon involving a recalcitrant mule and the Grand Canyon. But the look on the doctor's face immediately killed the mood in the room.

"I need everyone to leave for a moment," Aaron said.

"No." Alyson shook her head. Logan and Sarah's fingers automatically twined with hers. She softened her abruptness. "Please, Aaron, I need all of them to stay."

"Alyson," the doctor said softly. "This could be—"

"Could be what?" She trembled, but the reassuring touches helped keep the waking nightmare at bay. "Worse than what happened to me last night?"

"Fine." He nodded his head, though reluctantly. "I have to ask you again about the last time you had consensual sex."

Heat blazed on her face. Maybe she had been too hasty, especially with Logan here. She cleared her throat. "It's been two years." Four months and three days, but she really didn't want to get into her vacation fling in Barbados with a werepanther she'd met. Not in front of Logan.

But all he did was squeeze her hand.

Aaron didn't appear uncomfortable. In fact, he looked more worried than ever.

Esther came into the room, pushing another machine in front of her. "I've cancelled the day's schedule, but Mrs. Olsen brought in Danny. He may have strep."

The doctor nodded. "Let's take care of this first."

"Wh-what do we need to take care of?" Alyson asked.

"I want to take an ultrasound of your abdomen to confirm one of this morning's tests." He eyed her. "You sure you want everyone here?"

"If I have another . . . incident, Logan and Sarah will need to be here anyway." She tried to smile. "Roy's going to know whether he's in the room or not."

"True." The old man nodded.

Alyson shrugged. "And just in case I shift, you'll want someone here to make sure I don't escape unless you really want the Olsen family wondering why an abnormally large wolf is running through your office."

"All right," Aaron said.

Alyson laid back against the bed, keeping a tight grip on Sarah and Logan as Esther lowered the bed. She folded down the blanket and rearranged Alyson's gown so the expanse between her breasts and her bikini line showed, while the doctor flipped on the machine and squirted a clear gel on the paddle.

Alyson swallowed hard. Any idiot could have figured out what Aaron suspected. While she would have preferred Aunt Francine to be holding her hand, somehow dealing with this would be easier without her or Papa.

There was nothing on the ultrasound machine's screen at first except static. But as Aaron glided the paddle over her skin, a familiar *thump, thump* sounded through the speakers.

"How can there be a heartbeat already?" she whispered.

"There shouldn't," Aaron answered. "Let's see if I can get a better picture—"

Only the thrum of the heartbeat sounded in the room as the image resolved. An image awfully familiar to the fossil on the wall behind Fred Haight's desk at the Sunshine Believers' compound. The figure was curled in a fetal position. Same tiny sharp teeth. Same prominent ripping talons on its limbs. Same long tail.

What the hell had impregnated her?

# Chapter 13

Logan stared at the screen. The embryo couldn't be what it looked like. Not to mention the timing. Mother Wolf, she'd been attacked less than twelve hours ago. Alyson's hand trembled beneath his, but she wasn't huddled under the bed again.

Yet.

Even Aaron looked stunned. He set aside the paddle and rose. "Let me take care of Danny Olsen before we discuss the next step."

Esther grabbed some paper towels and wiped the excess gel off Alyson's abdomen. Sarah jumped up, released her hold on Alyson, and started cleaning the paddle.

Logan looked at Alyson. "You okay?"

"I'm not sure." She closed her eyes, breathed slowly and deeply, and mouthed numbers in sequence. When she reached ten, she opened her eyes. "What language do you count in when you're trying to keep control?"

He gave her a rueful smile. "Japanese. I have to think about each number. I can't rattle them off like I do in English or Spanish."

"What? No French?" She was avoiding the subject of what they'd seen on the ultrasound machine's screen. He couldn't blame her one little bit.

Hell, he wanted to shift and hunt down the bastard who did this to her. Especially since it had disguised itself as him to get close to her. Now, he'd never have a chance of developing a relationship with Alyson Tribideaux.

But he would damn sure help her get revenge.

A half hour later, Aaron returned and repeated the ultrasound. For the second one, Sarah assisted her father while Esther stayed at her reception desk and kept any potential patients at bay.

"This is odd," Aaron murmured, staring at the screen.

"What?" Logan and Alyson said at the same time.

"It's grown three centimeters since the last scan."

Logan tried to squelch his own unease. Aaron hadn't sounded this upset since the night Augustine and his people rescued Sarah from Mallory Labs.

"Can you get it out of me now?" Alyson said.

The embryo twitched at the same time Roy shouted, "No!" The old man held up his hands. "I don't know how, but it can understand us." He stared at Aaron. "If you try a D&C now, that thing will rip through her internal organs trying to get away from you."

"It'll do that if I try to deliver it," Alyson said. "Dinosaurs were hatched from eggs."

"She's right," Sarah added. "That looks like a velociraptor. According to Doctor O'Connell, those big talons were used to gut their prey."

"Mother Wolf!" Logan ran his free hand over his jaw. "That explains the elk found up in Last Buffalo Meadow. But how could a dinosaur exist here and now, much less shapeshift?"

"Let's worry about one thing at a time. I want to try something else." Aaron rose and waggled his fingers. "Ready for a little magick?"

Alyson nodded.

The doctor flipped off the lights and cracked his knuckles. He approached her bed, stood with his palms a few inches above her still naked abdomen, and closed his eyes. Ozone tainted the air.

A flash and a sharp *crack* erupted from Alyson. Aaron flew backward and slammed into the drywall.

"Dad!" Sarah shrieked and rushed to her father as he crumpled to the tile.

The second discharge didn't hit Logan as hard, but he yanked his hand out of Alyson's. Everything below his elbow went numb after the initial pain.

A third blast sent Roy tumbling backward over his chair. He crashed hard on the floor.

However, Alyson seemed totally unaffected.

Logan knelt by Roy's side. The old man grunted in pain as Logan helped him upright.

"You okay?"

"No," Roy muttered. "I landed pretty hard on my side. Hurts to breathe like the dickens."

Sarah helped her father to his feet, and he straightened his skewed glasses. "Alyson, I'm sorry. I have no idea what else to do."

She stared at her belly as if she expected the creature growing inside her to erupt any moment.

Sarah caught Logan's eye. She moved to Roy, gently wrapped her arm around him, and guided him from the room.

Logan returned to Alyson's bedside. "Sweetheart?" He grabbed her hand with the one of his that still had feeling. They needed more help than three witches, an empath, and a were with PTSD. "I have an idea. Do you trust me?"

She looked up at him. Alyson wasn't injured, but she may have been in shock again from the dazed look on her face. She stared at him for a moment before she nodded.

"I'll be right back. You're going to be okay. I promise." He kissed her forehead, strode out of her room, and headed for Aaron's office.

For the witch to admit he was out of his league scared the shit out of Logan. And he prayed he hadn't just lied to Alyson. His gut, and the damn ugly teeth and claws of the embryo, said that the thing gestating inside of Alyson would rip her to shreds when it came out. And that gut feeling had been there before Roy's warning or the ultrasound's pictures.

Now that he was technically on his own, he couldn't call his parents for help. Not that they wouldn't fly to Montana in a heartbeat, but he'd be constantly challenged by other alphas for the rest of his life if he did. But his parents wouldn't know how to handle this situation any more than he did.

That left one person he knew he could rely on.

The feeling in his zapped hand started to return by the time he sat in Aaron's office chair. He lifted the receiver and punched in the number.

Alex Stanton answered on the first ring. "What's up, cowboy?"

"Sorry to wake you, but your doctor friend, Bebe Zachary, the one that helped pull us out of that laboratory hellhole we were in?"

Alex's joviality died faster than a mayfly. "Yeah?"

"Does she make house calls?"

Standing outside in the snow with his cell phone an hour later didn't make any sense, but if it meant saving Alyson's life, then he'd do it. The wait gave him a chance to change clothes at the house.

Flakes brushed Logan's face as he walked a few steps away from the clinic's delivery entrance. The awning blocked most of the latest snowfall.

"Okay, I'm at the back of the building. I've got deep shadow, and there's no one around."

"We've got a lock. We're on our way now," Alex confirmed.

A soft puff of displaced air sent flakes whirling away from a spot a yard in front of him. Alex appeared with two women, both of whom he recognized. The taller blonde was attractive in her own way, but too skinny for his taste.

Now, Doctor Zachary had the curves he preferred, even if she barely came up chest-high on him. But making a pass at the witch wasn't worth getting his head ripped off by her two thousand-year-old master vampire boyfriend.

"That wasn't as bad as you claim, Alex," Doctor Zachary said. A few errant flakes collected in her dark curls.

"That's because his father-in-law deliberately gives him a rough ride, trying to make him yak." The blonde grinned. "Hey, Logan." She waggled her fingers. "Long time, no see."

"Sam." He inclined his head. "Not since Alex's wedding." It had been the one and only time he'd left Montana in the last four years. He'd survived the trip thanks to the ton of antianxiety meds Aaron had given him.

Actually, he, Alex and Sarah owed both women. Bebe had provided medical care to the survivors.

But Samantha Ridgeway had been the one who escaped Antonius and Mallory's little basement of horrors and brought back the cavalry before she fast-talked Mallory's daughter Sierra into releasing the surviving prisoners. Except she didn't have the sharp stainless steel odor he remembered from their brief encounters. Instead she smelled like fresh venison that had been buried three days to tenderize and . . . Twinkies?

Ignoring the strange combination, he said, "I'm sorry I have to ask you for help again. If I didn't say thanks then, I appreciate what you did for us. Especially getting Sarah out of there. I definitely owe you folks."

"De nada." Sam waved a hand. A dark expression crossed her face. "You two weren't the only ones they held down there."

He didn't want to look the proverbial gift horse in the mouth, but their sudden appearance bothered the hell out of him. "How'd you three do that? I thought only the fae could move through Otherwhere safely."

Bebe shrugged. "So can gods."

Sam smirked. "And I happened to be the deity on call when you contacted Alex."

Logan cocked his head and inhaled again. "So you're a zombie goddess now?"

"Something like that. Comes in handy for fast transportation."

He shook his head. Her odd admission would explain the slight decay odor, but not the Twinkie smell. Not even Esther's secret stash of the snack cakes had such an overwhelming odor. But the witch's supply was also wrapped in nearly airtight plastic.

The doctor looked up at Sam. "Well, I'd rather have you schlepping me all over creation. I don't need Ares pinching my ass while I'm dealing with a pregnant were."

"Can we please focus on the problem in front of us, ladies?" Alex said irritably.

Logan chuckled. If neither he nor Alex's maker couldn't talk him out of marrying a daughter of the Greek god of war, then he deserved what he got. On the other hand, Bebe had brought the arrogant Olympian to his knees from what he'd heard. The woman knew her drugs.

But he was forgetting his company manners. While the cold didn't affect him and Alex, or seem to bother Sam, Bebe was a California girl and definitely shivering. "Not that I don't appreciate the conversation, y'all, but let's get inside. We've got a patient for you."

It only took a moment for everyone to hang up their coats in the staff room before he led them back to the space allocated to Alyson. Sarah still sat by her side, holding her hand.

Sam interrupted the introductions and immediately inserted herself between her friends and Alyson. "Stay," she ordered them.

"I dare you to try that with a were," Bebe teased, but she and Alex stayed put when Sam shot her a dirty look.

Logan glanced at Alex, who gave a slight shake of his head. Whatever Sam was doing, they needed to stay out of her way.

The zombie or goddess or whatever the hell Sam classified herself as these days waved Sarah over with Logan and circled the bed, her sniffing reminiscent of a wolf. She paused when she reached Alyson's extended abdomen a second time.

Sam looked at the group standing by the door. Her own scent wasn't quite ashy fear, as if she were more concerned about Alyson than herself. "Confirmed. She's pregnant with a demon, just like the ladies in Seattle."

# Chapter 14

"What ladies in Seattle?" Alyson demanded. She looked at each person in turn, but only Sarah appeared as confused as she felt.

"Shit," the vampire muttered.

"Are you absolutely sure?" Logan asked.

"What ladies in Seattle?" Alyson repeated. As if making the same demand, the thing inside her moved.

From their eye twitches, Logan's friends were discussing her with him telepathically. Alyson pushed up from the bed and glared at them. "So help me, if someone doesn't give me an answer, I'm shifting, and I'll take a bite out of all of your asses!" Anger was so much better than hiding under the bed with strangers in her room.

The tall blonde turned to her. "You know about what happened to Logan and Sarah, correct?"

Alyson nodded.

"I'm Sam. The assholes who kidnapped them also snatched me. I used to be Normal." She looked at the paneled ceiling for a moment as if trying to find the right words. When her gaze met Alyson's again, Sam's blue eyes had a silvery sheen. "I'm the end result of their experiments. They accidentally created a god."

*I've got a velociraptor in my uterus, so why should I be surprised by her revelation?* Alyson sucked in a deep breath. "I get the impression there's more to this story than you being a reverse-image Frankenstein's monster."

"Whenever a new pantheon comes into existence, it weakens the barriers between this universe and the universe where the first god the humans worshipped banished the dinosaur gods."

Alyson stared at the woman. The numbness of her soul was probably a good thing. Otherwise, she'd want to run away from the crazy blond chick. "So-o-o-o what you're saying is I'm going to give birth to a dinosaur god?"

Sam shook her head. "You were raped by a dino demon."

"Only a dino demon?" Alyson licked her lips. "I guess that's better than a dinosaur god."

The numbness ruptured, but it wasn't terror that poured out. An odd sound burbled from her throat. It grew and grew until she was laughing so hard tears rolled down her face.

Everyone stared at as if she were insane. Maybe she was. It wasn't everyday her life was turned into some horror B-movie. To top it off, as a werewolf, she should be the monster, not the damsel in distress.

"Oh come on! This is fucking hysterical!" She waved her hands and laughed more until once again, she couldn't catch her breath.

Somehow, Doctor Zachary found a brown paper bag and held it around Alyson's mouth and nose. "You're hyperventilating, Ms. Tribideaux. I need you to take nice, even breaths so you don't trigger premature labor."

"What happens if I do?" Her voice sounded loud and indistinct in her ears with the bag over her mouth and nose.

"We want to control the removal of the fetus."

"You mean you don't want it to rip its way out of my womb." Alyson grew woozy at the thought. Or maybe it was too much carbon dioxide. She pushed the doctor's hands and the bag away from her face.

Doctor Zachary pursed her lips before she said, "No. I don't. Neither do you."

"But Doctor Goldstein and Roy said the fetus couldn't be removed or it would do exactly that," Alyson said. Without the hysterical laughter, the all-too-familiar panic rushed into the empty space. The last time she was this terrified was when she found Mama. Except the woman who gave birth to her was long gone by the time she discovered the body.

She started breathing hard again, but Doctor Zachary's touch reminded her she was still here and alive.

Alyson turned to Logan. "You promised to watch out for me."

He crossed to the hospital-style bed, grabbed her other hand and held it tight. "I am. I will. That's the reason I called for Doctor Zachary. She's mated to the Augustine Coven's master."

"Whoa!" Doctor Zachary held up her hands. "I am not mated to any-one."

"Puh-lease." Sam rolled her eyes. "You two mate like bunnies in heat."

"Excuse me," the doctor said primly. "I don't do it in *your* hallway and *your* library and *your* garage—"

Alyson giggled. She recognized the two women teased each other to lighten the mood, but their behavior raised more questions than it answered. "But how do you do it without getting infected?"

Doctor Zachary turned to Logan, who shrugged and said, "Alyson is the New Orleans' pack princess—"

"Excuse me?" She glared him.

He paused, a mix of humor and apology in his expression. "Sorry. Packmaster's daughter. Her mother passed away some time ago, and her father—"

"Keeps her as ignorant as possible? What a douche." Sam scowled. "Some witches have developed a natural immunity to the V-virus over the years. Bebe here is one of them."

The thing inside of Alyson twitched again. It felt larger than before.

Logan gestured toward the vampire. "That there is Alex Stanton, a fellow San Antonian and the chief enforcer for the Augustine Coven."

"Ma'am." The vampire nodded politely.

At the footsteps behind him, Logan glanced over his shoulder and squeezed her hand, but Alyson recognized the ginger scent.

Aaron grimaced as he strode into the exam room. "Got Roy settled at our place. Just some bruised ribs. Esther's watching him." He caught sight of Doctor Zachary and held out his hand. "Bebe. It's been a while." He frowned and added, "I see you haven't managed to totally cut ties with White Rose yet."

She shook Aaron's outstretched palm. "Technicality. I'm only the heir until Alice pops out a rugrat. And let's skip the coven gossip for now." She pointed at Sam who circled the room again, still sniffing like a prison warden's bloodhound. "I don't know if you remember Sam Ridgeway."

Sam crossed and shook Aaron's hand. Alyson frowned. The slight twitch in her abdomen turned into a dull ache, which seemed to follow the movements of the tall woman.

"We owe you our daughter's life, Ms. Ridgeway," Aaron said.

"Definitely," Sarah piped in and turned to Alyson. "She's the one that escaped and brought back help."

Sam smiled. "Actually, it was my husband who arranged for the cavalry. He'd been looking for Alex and Logan here for a while. I just pointed him to the right psychotic basement nerds."

The so-called goddess paced over to Sarah and laid a hand on the teen's shoulder. The ache in Alyson's belly followed her once again.

"Sweetie, I think it's best if you go home with your dad," Sam said.

"No." The girl's attitude was fierce. "You have—"

Pain erupted on Alyson's left side, and she cried out. Her abdomen bulged beneath the medical gown. She clenched her teeth and squeezed Logan's hand.

"What's wrong?" Logan asked.

"Don't know." She couldn't seem to catch her breath once again, but this wasn't a severe anxiety attack. It felt like something was kicking her lungs. "The pain seems to follow her." She managed to point in Sam's direction.

"Oh, shit," the blonde muttered.

"Out! Now!" Doctor Zachary ordered.

Sam disappeared from view, and there was a muffled pop of displaced air. The pain immediately subsided. Alyson relaxed and took slow, deep breaths to Logan's whispered count in her ear.

"Wow!" Sarah turned to stare at her father. "She can teleport!"

Aaron looked at Logan.

He shrugged and said, "Zombie goddess."

Alyson rubbed her side, and the bulge settled back in the middle of her abdomen. Thank Mother Wolf, the pain was subsiding. "Just keep her away from me. I think this thing wants to kill her, and it's going to take me out in the process."

A jingle came from Doctor Zachary's jacket pocket. She pulled out a phone and thumbed a control. "Hey." A pause. "Yeah, the fetus settled as soon as you left." Another pause. "Let's try putting you on speaker." She jabbed at her phone screen.

"Can you hear me now?" Sam's voice had a faint echo.

Doctor Zachary looked at Alyson and lifted a questioning eyebrow.

She rested her free palm over the bulge. No movement. Not even a twitch. She nodded to the doctor. "I think we're good."

"Where are you?" Logan asked.

"The lobby. I think we've got our game plan for getting that fucking thing out of her. Use me as bait. The demon will make a beeline for me once it leaves Alyson's body." Sam sounded too damn enthusiastic about her idea.

"Whoa!" Alyson jerked out of Logan's grip and waved both hands franticly. "I am *not* volunteering to be an extra in the next *Alien* movie!"

"No." Bebe said. "Aaron and I will perform a C-section on you. Sam is the bait. She'll teleport into the room the instant we cut through your uterus. We'll need a third witch to cast a circle to keep the demon from escaping once Sam's in the room. Logan and Alex will backup Sam in killing this thing."

Alyson grabbed Logan's hand with both of hers. "I can't do this." Terror prickled her skin. Deep down, she knew they needed to get the demon out before it killed her, but hair sprouted along her arms, and claws emerged on her fingers.

He leaned close and nuzzle her neck. "Deep breaths, sweetheart. I get you're having a panic attack, but you can*not* wolf out right now."

She did as he said. His scent, so clean, so familiar, helped. "I'm so scared," she whispered.

Sarah joined her on the other side and stroked Alyson's hair. "It's okay. We all are."

Tears trickled down Alyson's face. "Oh, honey. Please go home. You're just a kid. You have your whole life ahead of you."

Sarah raised her chin a bit. "You think this is scary? Bitch, please. If Sam and Bebe can save Logan's hairy ass, then they can save yours."

"Besides," Aaron added dryly. "Two witch doctors are better than one."

Bebe groaned at his atrocious joke, but Sam's laughter erupted from the phone speaker. "You're my kind of supernatural, Doctor Goldstein."

Alyson sought Logan's gaze, needing his reassurance. For all her complaining, she never realized how much she emotionally depended on her pack.

He squeezed her hands between his. "Listen to me. I trust these ladies with my life. I already have."

More tears filmed her eyes. Back home she would have been mocked for being human, but here, for the first time, she really felt these people had her back.

"Is there any way we could do a D&C?" Aaron said. "I don't like the idea of cutting for the sake of cutting."

"We can't." Bebe shook her head. "Dino demon blood is poisonous to all of us, Normal and supernatural alike. It would kill her faster than the fetus clawing its way out."

Aaron turned to his daughter. "Sarah, I want you to go home. Now."

"No." Sarah crossed her arms. "Mom has the medical training. She needs to look after Roy."

"Then I'll cast—" Aaron started.

"No, I need you helping me with Alyson," Bebe said. "That demon may do something to her as it exits, and I'm a surgeon, not a healer. Neither of us can spare the concentration." She turned to the young witch. "How's your shielding spells and circles?"

Sarah gave one firm nod. "My best skills after I was kidnapped in Los Angeles."

Bebe smiled at the girl. "Heaven forbid, if the demon kills Sam, Alex, and Logan, it's up to you to keep it inside the room." Her expression sobered. "No matter what. Sarah, this thing *cannot* get out. It'll be hungry. Innocents will die."

Sarah lifted her chin. "I won't let you down, Doctor Zachary."

Her determination made Alyson smile. She just wished there was something she could do.

"Survive, Alyson," Sam said through the phone speaker. "What you can do is survive. Then we'll hunt down the bastard who did this to you."

# Chapter 15

Logan took Sam over to the Goldsteins' house to load up on meat to carry back to the clinic while the doctors prepped for Alyson's surgery. The lady were would need a lot more protein since Aaron had pretty much drained his power keeping her alive last night. Esther watched with amusement as they raided her kitchen.

"How's Old Roy doing?" he asked as he filled a reusable shopping bag with hard-boiled eggs and leftover lamb and chicken.

"Asleep finally." She shook her head. "He was lucky it was only some bruised ribs." Her humor evaporated. "I don't want Sarah in the clinic when you deal with the demon."

Logan resisted the urge to sigh. Of course, she knew. She'd probably been listening to the conversation with Alex and his friends through Aaron.

Sam paused in packing sodas, crackers, and bread. "She's a tough booger. I told you that four years ago."

"She's not your daughter," Esther snapped. "You haven't dealt with—"

"What makes you think I haven't dealt with PTSD like Logan and your daughter?" Sam said softly. "Because I was only in that hellhole three days and not six months like Sarah? She got out alive, Mrs. Goldstein. I didn't even manage that." Sam maintained a fairly neutral expression, but Esther couldn't meet the zombie goddess's glowing silver eyes.

Logan waited to see what Sam would do. Her glow was similar to the neon flare of an upset vampire, but different enough to trigger a tingle under his skin. He clamped down on his own unease. Alyson wouldn't listen to him at the clinic if he didn't keep his own emotions in check.

Sam glanced in the bag she'd packed. "If I'd known we'd be dealing with these bastards, I would have stocked up on Twinkies," she muttered.

Logan turned to the witch. "Cough 'em up, Esther."

"What?" She stared at him in feigned surprise.

He crossed his arms. "Cough 'em up, or I'll tell Sarah where your secret stash is."

"You . . ." If looks could kill, he'd be one fricasseed wolf. In the end, she produced the industrial-sized box of crème-filled vanilla sponge cake treats.

"Thank you, Esther. I'll pay you back." Sam crossed her heart before she turned to Logan. "The demon baby will do its damnedest to hurt me. If Alex and Bebe are down and I hulk-out on you, unwrap these and cram them in my face as fast as you can."

He was afraid to ask, but any and all information was critical right now. "Hulk-out on me?"

"Yeah, but supposedly, I turn silver instead of green."

"What do you mean 'supposedly'?"

"I'm not exactly in my right mind when it happens, so I'm going by what everyone else tells me. You're not going to mistake what's happening to me for anything else."

That didn't reassure him very much, but he decided silence was a wiser move.

The snow fell thick and fast as he and Sam walked back to the clinic.

"If that thing's blood is poisonous, I can't shift, can I?" he asked.

"It doesn't matter if you shift or not." She glanced at him. "Don't let its blood touch you in any form you take. It's some kind of super acid. If you get any in your mouth, it'll kill you faster than your biology, or even the V-virus, can stitch you back together."

"Is it poisonous to you?"

"Don't know." She grimaced. "I don't plan on testing it today, either."

"Hey, Logan!" Marvin Newlin waved at them from the opposite side of the street before he jogged across the pavement.

"Shit," he muttered. He forced a smile. "What's up?"

"Is everything okay with Doc Goldstein? The clinic's never closed." However, the town librarian's attention was fully on the woman standing next to Logan.

"Just a crazy day. Esther accidentally sliced herself bad enough to need stitches. Then Danny Olsen came in with strep, and the doc's worried about contamination." He lifted the bags in his arms slightly. "We're taking over enough groceries to tide him past the infectious period. Aaron's insisting on staying at the clinic until he's sure he's clean or cured."

"And who's your friend?" Marvin fluttered his eyelashes, showing off his glittery pink eye shadow in the process.

Logan tamped down his irritation at the delay. "This is Sam."

"Of course, she is." Marvin probably thought his smile was demure, but it came across as campy. "Have you seen Ms. Tribideaux?"

"Not in the last five minutes," Logan said.

"She didn't go out to the Sunshine Believers' compound this morning by herself, did she?" Marvin placed a dramatic hand on his pink and purple plaid jacket. "Tad will have a fit if she does."

"Sarah's been going out with her." Logan pursed his lips. "I just hope that girl hasn't given everyone at the ranch strep throat, too."

"Well—" Marvin placed a well-manicured hand on Logan's sleeve. "When you see Sarah tonight, have her pass along a message for me. I found another book on local history Ms. Tribideaux will find useful. Tah!" The librarian jogged back across the street.

Logan turned to Sam. "You realize he's probably headed for The Last Buffalo to tell everyone about you."

"What the hell is The Last Buffalo?"

"The local diner," he said as they continued to the clinic.

Sam snorted. "Tell everyone I work for *The National Scoop*. That usually keeps small town assholes away from me."

Logan chuckled. "I forgot you worked for the gossip rag Caesar owns."

"Used to," she muttered. "About the time I lose control, eat Ryan Reynolds, and another tabloid nabs pictures of it, we're all in trouble."

"There is that little problem," he agreed.

When they entered the clinic, Logan took Sam's bag, and she settled in Esther's comfortable office chair. He walked to the break room and stowed the contents in the refrigerator and cupboards before he headed back to Alyson's room.

"How's everything going?" he murmured to Alex.

"They're going to do it in here," the vampire answered. "It's the biggest room besides the waiting area, and we don't need the whole town to see this."

Sarah chalked out symbols in the corners of the floor and on the walls. "Almost done." She looked over at Bebe. "You sure I can't use blood?"

The doctor shook her head. "I wouldn't recommend it at this point. These things use sacrificial blood magick to tear through the dimensional barriers. Alyson's life is already at risk. I don't want to give them more ammunition. If you don't think you can hold the circle by yourself without amping through blood, I need to know now, Sarah."

Aaron shot his daughter a worried look. His expression seemed to strengthen the girl's resolve. "I can hold it."

Alex leaned closer to Logan. "Whatever you do, don't—"

"Bite it," Logan finished. "Sam already gave me the lecture." He frowned. "Are you going to be okay? We don't have any non-human blood stocked here."

A wry smile tilted his friend's mouth. "Fed before we came, and I don't need as much these days. I told you what happened in Peru."

"I just hope you're right about Sam. We don't have any god weapons handy to kill the demon."

Alex chuckled. "What do you think Sam is?"

"All right," Bebe said. "Is everyone ready?"

"Logan?"

At Alyson's plaintive cry, he was at her side. "I'm right here, sweetheart." He took her hand and stroked her hair.

"Good." She had a glazed look in her eyes. "Didn't want you to miss the show." She giggled. "The sedative Bebe gave me is really good. You should have one." She probably didn't realize they had strapped her to the portable operating table they had replaced the bed with.

Logan glanced at both doctors. "How'd you manage that?"

The corner of Bebe's mouth quirked. "I've been keeping vampires out of my head for years. I can keep out one demon." Her mien turned serious. "It's just a sedative. We couldn't give her a general without that thing knowing, and I'm not cutting into someone without some kind of painkiller."

The doctor's gaze swept over the people in the room again. "Everyone ready?"

Logan followed her track. Sarah crouched next to her silver chalk marks on the floor. Aaron and Bebe, wearing surgical scrubs and gloves, and masks, stood on each side of Alyson, who sang softly to herself in French. Alex stood as far back as he could and still remain within Sarah's shield when she activated it.

Which left Sam plenty of room to teleport in.

*Sam?* He could feel her presence in the back of his mind.

*Just give the word.*

From the looks on Alex and the witches' faces, they'd heard the zombie goddess, too. He nodded. "Do it."

Bebe said something he thought was in Hebrew when she reached for the scalpel. Aaron muttered a spell under his breath. Ozone filled the little room.

The demon fetus bulged under Alyson's skin, away from where Bebe was cutting. Bile rose in Logan's throat. If it started clawing its way into her chest—

*Sam!*

The blonde popped into the room, except her jeans and t-shirt were gone. Black pants and a calf-length black coat with a Mandarin-style collar covered her.

"No!" Bebe shouted at the same time Alyson screamed and passed out.

A blood-covered nightmare exploded out of Alyson's body. It gave a high-pitched squeal before it leaped for Sam's face, scarlet talons extended.

# Chapter 16

The ozone level rose, and red energy sparkled in Logan's peripheral vision, which meant Sarah had done her job. Sam swatted the gore-covered lizard demon into the magickal shield. The newborn demon let out another high-pitched scream, and the scent of cooked flesh joined the ozone.

The lizard landed on the tile, jumped to its feet and raced for Sarah. Alex's diving slide intercepted it. Talons slashed at the vampire's eyes, and he let out a stream of curses that would have rivaled Mom's bad language if it weren't for the lisp from his extended fangs.

The damned thing squirmed out of Alex's grasp and leapt over him. Sarah raised a hand. The lizard shot across the room and slammed into the shield again. Its skin popped and sizzled like bacon in a frying pain before it landed on the floor.

Logan's skin prickled. It was all he could do not to shift. If he did, instinct would take over. And if he bit the demon, he'd be dead.

Injuries didn't seem to affect this demon lizard thing. It scampered across the tile wickedly fast and crawled up inside Sam's coat.

She cursed in every single one of George Carlin's forbidden words while she ripped off her outer garment, revealing a black t-shirt. Her leg glowed silver through her shredded pants and equally shredded skin. She snatched the lizard by its tail. It swung itself up and chomped on her forearm. She yelled, but didn't let go of it.

The lizard tried a different tactic. It released Sam's arm and did a jerky twist. Its tail snapped off its body. Black blood sprayed over Sam's face and chest, and she screamed. The demon dropped to the floor once again, and ran for the incapacitated Alex.

Sam collapsed to her knees, and the tail fell from her grasp. Black blood oozed from the stump, and an acrid chemical odor came from the dissolving linoleum. If the ichor dissolved plastic, what the hell was it doing to the zombie goddess?

Sarah raised her hand to protect Alex, but the lizard dived toward the operating table instead. It was too damn fast for Logan to reach it in time.

"Bebe! Aaron! Incoming!" he shouted. He tried not to think about what could happen if the demon lizard got blood on one of the doctors.

Bebe dropped her hand and light flashed behind Alyson's unconscious body. With another squeal and a puff of smoke, the blackened lizard skidded out from under the table and across the floor. It reoriented itself and ran for Sam. And her exposed skin was starting to glow silver.

A desperate idea lodged in Logan's brain since the stupid critter had been totally ignoring him. "Sam, let the demon on you."

She didn't answer. She was too busy choking. It answered his question about whether the demon's blood was poisonous to her, too. The zombie goddess crumpled to the floor, desperately trying to breathe.

The lizard jumped on her back. Logan leapt, struggling to stay in human form. His fingers circled the lizard's neck. He could see the blood-coated creature's surprise and panic at its miscalculation in its slitted pupils.

Talons raked at his wrist as he landed on his shoulder and rolled to a crouch. With a quick twist, he snapped its neck. Its body went limp, and he tossed it aside.

Logan rose and went to Sam. The zombie goddess's eyes and skin glowed with a hard metallic silver, and her lips pulled back in a grimace. Even her hair shone gold. She hadn't been joking about turning a different color. She panted, but she wasn't struggling to breathe anymore. Nor was there any evidence of demon blood on her.

"Sarah, drop the shield," he ordered. The girl did so, and he turned back to Sam. "Let's get you some food, lady."

She growled low in her chest, but she was in no condition to resist when he hooked his arms under her shoulders and hauled her upright.

"Alex?" he called over his shoulder.

"Give me a minute," the vampire said.

Logan slung one of Sam's arms over his shoulder and turned with her to face his friend. "Were you bit?"

"No." Alex pushed himself upright. "It scratched out my eyes, but I'll live. It just won't be pleasant for a few minutes."

Sam snapped at Logan's face. Luckily, she had enough poison blood in her she was too slow to actually bite him. "Whoa, girl! Let's find you some Twinkies."

He tried not to think about the doctors as they feverishly worked on the pale form laying on the operating table. If Aaron and Bebe couldn't save Alyson, there was going to be hell to dish out, and not just from the New Orleans pack.

Logan had fed the entire industrial-size box of snack cakes and four raw T-bones to Sam before Sarah helped Alex into the break room. He didn't look much better than the zombie goddess.

"You sure you don't need blood?" Logan asked. "You look like shit."

"You try having an extra-dimensional demon dig out your eyeballs and claw your face off, then we'll talk," Alex said. "And yeah, I'll need blood, but not this minute."

"You were the one who said those things were poisonous to supernaturals." Logan reached into the refrigerator. He pulled out a wedge of Swiss and handed it to Sam before he retrieved two beers, from the six-pack Roy had brought over this morning during his breakfast run, and popped the caps.

The zombie goddess hadn't spoken yet, but she had stopped growling. Nor did she bother slicing the cheese. She simply started gnawing on the pound chunk.

"They are," Alex said as he accepted a bottle. His eyeballs had returned to normal but his eyelids and the skin around the sockets were still shredded.

"Sam, I get." Logan waved his beer in her direction, but she ignored him in favor of the open bag of Cheetos Sarah dropped in front of her. "But why are you still alive?"

"Well," Alex drawled. "First of all, I didn't get any of that black crap on me. Second, after drinking Mama Pacha's blood, I could walk in sunlight for three days. Since then, the effect has been a lower hunger and faster healing."

Logan took a swig from his bottle. "So if you drink Sam's blood—"

"Can't." Alex shook his head. "She's a death goddess. Hers definitely would kill me."

Sarah sidled past Logan and pulled a cup of yogurt out of the refrigerator. "So Sam, what's with the Neo look?"

The zombie goddess's eyes and skin no longer glowed silver, and she finished chewing the last bit of Swiss. "I don't know. Probably some weird-ass subconscious shit." She sighed. "Or my latent pre-teen crush on Keanu Reeves." She paused to cram some Cheetos in her mouth and chew. "It could be worse. I could be wearing blood-soaked shifts or a belt of skulls."

Logan took a good look at her. Her Katy Perry t-shirt and blue jeans were back, but they showed the same damage as the black t-shirt and pants she'd had on in Alyson's room. She wasn't as invulnerable as she or Alex liked to think, but he wasn't about to point that out to them, though he did wonder what had happened to the black coat. Was it still lying on the floor of Alyson's room?

Alyson. He didn't want to think about that damn demon ripping its way out of her. It was his fault. He had called for Sam too soon.

When the back door opened, all four of them jumped to their feet. But it was Esther who walked into the break room, unzipping her coat. She already wore scrubs underneath her winter wear.

"Aaron said he and Doctor Zachary needed some help." Her gaze drifted over each of them, but mainly focused on her daughter.

"Chill, Mom," Sarah said. "They kept the dino demon away from me."

"Good, but I need you to go back to the house now."

"Mo-o-o-o-o-om!"

Esther crossed to her daughter and cupped her cheek. "You proved yourself, honey, but your father needs me on the medical side. Roy's at our place, he's a Normal despite his gift, and he's seen this thing that attacked Alyson. He's alone and defenseless at the moment, and as I said, you proved you have the strongest shields, except for Doctor Zachary."

"Doctor Zachary?" Sarah appeared and smelled more perplexed than offended. "She's not even a healer."

Logan glanced at Alex, and they both chuckled.

"Don't underestimate her, Sarah," Logan said. "She may be the heir to White Rose, but she's also the granddaughter of your own high priestess. Bebe Zachary took out the witches plotting against her in her own co-ven, plus the rogue were and vampire allies of the rebels."

"Don't leave out the gods she's taken down a notch," Sam added.

Both Sarah and Esther looked over at the goddess, who had finished the bag of Cheetos and was now ploughing through her second package of raw hotdogs. While the teen stared with fascination, Esther turned a shade of green.

"It wasn't me," she mumbled around a mouthful of processed meat and pointed at Alex. "She stabbed his father-in-law Ares in the ass with sedatives." She swallowed and reached for the box of crackers.

Sarah leaned over and whacked Logan hard in the bicep. "You bas-tard! You could have taken me to the wedding and introduced me to a real live god!"

"Hey!" Sam glared at the girl. "I'm not exactly chopped liver here."

"On that note, I need to get back to our patient," Esther said, and she strode out the door.

Sarah's attention turned back to Sam, and she shook her head. "I don't get it. You really didn't do anything to the baby monster."

"Excuse me?" Cracker crumbs flew from Sam's mouth.

"She took a shitload of poison in the face that would have killed all of us damn near instantly," Logan growled. "Now get over to the house and shield it like your mama told you to."

Without a word, Sarah jumped up, snatched her coat off its peg, and charged out of the break room. Two seconds later, the back door of the clinic slammed hard enough he could feel the vibration through the soles of his boots.

"By the way—" Sam swallowed the half of a Pop-Tart in her mouth. "—where's the lizard carcass?"

"Ah, fuck." Logan set his bottle on the counter. "It's still in Alyson's room." He tried not to picture her laying on the bed. Or the blood-soaked surgical drapes as Aaron and Bebe tried to repair the damage to her from the demon tearing through the partial incision. If he charged in there now, he'd only get in the witches' way. "I'll retrieve it when we get the all-clear from Aaron."

Sam regarded the ancient refrigerator. "Think there's enough room in that to preserve the body for a little while?"

Logan frowned. "You've probably cleared enough space though the chest freezer at the house would have more room. Why?"

Alex stared at her like she'd lost her mind. "What are you planning?"

Her grin could only be described as pure evil. "I want to see if I can bring that thing back to life."

# Chapter 17

Consciousness came back to Alyson in fits and spurts. The pain in her gut had dulled somewhat since the monster had torn its way through her flesh. Everything after that was pretty hazy. The taste of ozone. People shouting and the snapping of bones. The smell of sandalwood and blood.

More ozone and ginger surrounded her, but it was the warm touch on her wrist that gave her the courage to face reality. A tiny part of her hoped it was Logan next to her.

She opened her eyes to find Doctor Zachary holding her wrist. The doctor's dark curls were pinned up, and Alyson could make out the intricate silver roses in her upper piercings. Doctor Zachary looked at the wall clock.

"It's still beating," Alyson said, though her voice sounded slurred.

"Yes, it is." The doctor smiled. "You gave us a bit of a scare."

Alyson rubbed her abdomen. Her fingers found the ridge of scar tissue just above her pelvic line. "Why do I still hurt? Couldn't Aaron heal me? Did he run out of juice?"

"He and Esther did what they could." Doctor Zachary inhaled deeply. "Part of the pain is from the initial trauma. Your brain still hasn't fully processed the fact that the damage the nerves reported is no longer there. The other part is post-partum contractions. Since you had an accelerated pregnancy, your uterus is reacting accordingly." Another deep breath. "There's something else . . ."

Alyson groaned. After everything that had happened over the last few hours, nothing the witch could tell her could be any worse. "For the love of Mother Wolf, just spit it out."

"The dino demon shredded your left ovary beyond the Goldsteins ability to heal it." Doctor Zachary bit her upper lip before she continued.

"I had to remove it. You'll still be able to get pregnant, but it may take some patience."

Of all the emotions Alyson would have expected at such news, relief was not it.

"Alyson?" The doctor squeezed her hand. "Do you want me to get Esther?"

"No, thank you." Alyson smiled. Papa couldn't pressure her to find a mate if she couldn't have pups. Maybe she owed the bastard who had raped her. Something feral rose in her. Yeah, she owed him a slow, painful death.

"Alyson?" the doctor repeated.

"Sorry," Alyson murmured. "Y'all killed it, right? The demon growing inside of me?"

A frown drew Doctor Zachary's fine, dark brows together. "Yes. For now."

Shivers traveled down Alyson's back. "What do you mean 'for now'?"

"If you feel up to it, we'll get you dressed and some food in you." The doctor's frown deepened. "As the injured party in this matter, you should be involved in the war council."

Thankfully, the doctors let Alyson lay in the hospital bed and eat cold lamb roast and leftover chicken plus the two dozen reheated breakfast burritos from the Last Buffalo while the supernaturals dragged extra chairs into her room. Surprisingly, they let Sarah and Roy join them. And it comforted Alyson that Logan not only sat the closest to her, but his shoulder brushed her elbow as well.

Once everyone was settled, she waved a grease-coated hand for attention.

"Before y'all get started, can I please ask some questions?" She wiped her mouth and her hands with the flimsy paper napkins the diner had provided as she spoke. "I'm not trying to pry, but it seems I'm in the same mess as the rest of you now."

"Me, too," Roy added. "Questions, I mean. After Alyson's done, of course."

When the rest of the supernaturals nodded, she turned to Logan. "What exactly was Selene Antonius and her Normal partner trying to accomplish with kidnapping all those people? Because it seems to me that all of this is connected."

"What do you mean?" Alex asked. His eyes glowed a soft blue, and his sandalwood scent overwhelmed everyone else's odor.

She tested the feeling against logic and frowned at the vampire. "From what little gossip my father missed censoring and things that Logan and Sarah have said, a lot of this . . . demon weirdness started around the same time as the supernatural kidnappings in Los Angeles."

Alex nodded. "You are totally correct, Ms. Tribideaux."

"So what was the point of the kidnappings?"

Logan looked at her. "Testing our limits to see what each of our types could do and how we did it." He cleared his throat. "They were trying to separate the best aspects from the worst."

"And there was a bit of sadistic torture involved," Sarah added. The brimstone and ginger scent of her fury managed to override Alex's for a moment.

"Those motherfuckers," Sam muttered. She scrubbed her eyes for a moment, as if trying to erase something she had seen in Sarah's mind. "Alex, if we ever get our hands on Heckyll and Jeckyll, those bastards are mine."

"Heckyll and Jeckyll?" Logan asked.

"Rivers and Stone. Mallory's pet goons," Alex said.

"Oh, them." Logan flashed a nasty grin at Sam. "I'll give you what's left."

Alyson had seen that same look before. It was the expression Frankie had before he killed that Normal, the incident that had gotten him exiled from the pack. And she had no doubt Logan meant what he said.

She laid a hand on his shoulder. "Leave them for the International Council." Her comment set off a round of laughter from the newcomers.

Logan didn't laugh, but he turned his wolfish grin toward her. "They're

Normals. If this were ordinary circumstances, we couldn't touch 'em. But the I.C. already sanctioned Augustine's enforcers to hunt down any survivors of Antonius and Mallory's people. And they have leave to recruit whomever they wish for additional assistance."

Which meant as a lone alpha, Logan didn't need a packmaster's permission to go after these bastards.

Alyson took a slow deep breath. What if she joined Logan? Papa would be furious, but she had no doubt the wolf beside her would teach her everything she needed to know to hunt down her attacker.

"Can you please explain to me what you mean by picking out our best and worst traits?" She glanced at Sarah. "Without the extraneous details of their testing."

Logan's nostrils flared, checking her scent. Her determination to understand must have registered with him. "They mixed the best of all our DNA together, programmed microscopic robots called nanites to rewrite a person's DNA based on the mix, and pumped the nanites into a human test subject." He jabbed a thumb in the zombie goddess's direction. "Sam."

Alyson turned to the blonde. "What did these nanites do to you? You smell like . . . tenderized meat and Twinkies."

Sam sighed. "Well, that's better than the stainless steel odor I gave off during the first year of my death. To answer your question, they are rewriting my old human DNA into god DNA."

"Excuse me?" Alyson blinked. The woman could not possibly be serious.

"I know what you're thinking, and no, I'm not boasting." Sam crossed her arms. "It's been confirmed by several sources." She inclined her head toward the vampire. "Alex's father-in-law even volunteered a sample for Bebe to compare to mine."

Alyson's attention darted from the vampire to the zombie goddess and back. "Father-in-law?"

"Ares of Olympus," Alex said dryly.

Sarah glared at Sam. "He would have been more useful today."

"What am I?" Sam glared at the teen. "Lizard leftovers?"

"Actually, yes." Sarah smirked. "You stood there and let yourself get sprayed with blood. A were had to save your ass, so color me not impressed."

Maybe it was the lingering effects of the sedative Bebe had given her, but Alyson was having trouble keeping up with the conversation. Steel? Steel was made of iron. The sidhe were as sensitive to iron as vampires and weres were to silver.

The mega-watt lightbulb went off as all disparate puzzle pieces slipped into place. She stared at Sam. "You're the superweapon the fairies have a price on, aren't you?" That was one bit of gossip not even Papa could stop. Several in the pack thought it was worth invading Lannigan territory to collect the bounty.

"Yeah, but I think we got a truce in place." Sam grinned. "At least, Morrigan threatened to wipe them all out of existence if they didn't lay off me."

"Morrigan?" Alyson squeaked. "The Celtic goddess?"

"Yeah, but don't ever play poker with her." Sam turned serious. "She cheats."

Too much information. Alyson licked her dry lips to buy a little time to compose herself. "So what exactly are these dinosaur demons? Why are they fixated on you?"

Sam regarded at her. "Maybe it would be best to get you home to your family."

"No! Th-this thing didn't threaten your life," she snarled. "I damn well will have full knowledge of what that thing is that raped me and what it planted inside of me."

"You're wrong. It didn't care if it hurt you or not. It tore its way out of your uterus for the express purpose of killing me." Sam's scowl relaxed a bit, but her expression was no less serious. "Look, I know you're scared. I've been somebody's plaything and it sucks. But—"

"No 'but's!" Alyson slashed her hand through the air. "I will not be treated like a pack princess! My father's been doing that my entire life."

She sucked in a deep breath. Yelling the were way wasn't going to get her anywhere. Neither was being the helpless bitch her father tried to turn her into. She opted for professional calmness.

"I can tell by your expression and what you're not saying that you've run into this type of thing before. Something that can disguise itself so thoroughly we can't smell through it."

"Yeah," Sam said softly. "This is something that can trick gods a hell of a lot older than me. I don't want to make things worse by involving you people." Her gaze swept the entire group, including Bebe and Alex.

"Facing our fears makes us stronger," Sarah said.

Sam's frown deepened. "You get that from a fortune cookie, kid?"

"From my therapist," Sarah said primly.

"Holy . . . me, you have no idea how much I hate shrinks," Sam mumbled.

"So you're saying you didn't have nightmares after our vacation in Mallory's basement?" Logan asked. "Because even I did. Which means you're a lot more human than you like to pretend, so cough up the answer to the lady's questions. If you don't, I will."

Warmth tingled through Alyson's body. Now, why did him defending her feel better than Sarah standing up for her?

Unfortunately, it sounded like Logan came with a load of baggage she couldn't begin to understand. Mother Wolf knew she couldn't deal with his problems on top of her own. She didn't have the strength.

And to find that strength, she needed to shred the bastard who had hurt her.

Sam looked at Alex and Bebe, and once again, irritation prickled Alyson's nerves because they were talking about her in front of her. Their telepathic conversation ended with Sam sighing. "All right. This is crazier than any lameass cable movie, but don't say I didn't warn you."

"Anyway—" Sam sucked in and blew out a deep breath. "Alex and his wife Phil killed two of the three known dino demons—"

"We had a little help," the vampire said dryly.

Sam rolled her eyes. "We think these dino demons were left over from the last attempted dinosaur god incursion into our universe. Like I said, two were killed down in Peru, but the third one escaped. This was about three and a half years ago."

"Peru?" Alyson wanted to scream. Her blanket bunched in her fists. "About the time members of the Sunshine Believers were accused of murdering two women in Los Angeles?"

"Yeah." Sam's expression turned somber. "Four months later, a University of Washington historical team stumbled across a nest in Underground Seattle. Near as we can figure, the surviving asshole impregnated fourteen Normal women. Neither the women nor the baby demons survived the births."

She inhaled deeply and appeared distinctly uncomfortable. "We speculated that he'd try with . . . hardier stock."

"You mean supernaturals," Alyson said.

"Yeah," the so-called goddess said. "We've been hunting the bastard, but this is the first time he's poked his head out since Seattle. Didn't your packmaster warn you?"

"No." Alyson pursed her lips. Papa's desire to protect her had put her in much worse danger than he originally feared.

A silvery sheen appeared in Sam's eyes. "In addition to informing the I.C., the supernatural leaders in Los Angeles, including the Summer Queen and her consort, sent word out to every coven, pack, and mound around the world."

"It doesn't mean the leaders spread the word within their groups," Alyson said wryly. But something else bothered her besides her father's archaic sensibilities. "What are these dinosaur gods exactly?" She released the blanket and waved both hands. "Why do they care about us?"

" 'Care' is not the right word," Alex said. "As far as they are concerned, we're the usurpers of their planet. The first human god banished them long ago because they were weak. They'd lost most of their power because their worshippers started dying out sixty-five million years ago. When a certain type of deity is born or created—"

"Specifically, a death god," Sam inserted.

Alex shot her a dirty look at the interruption before he continued. "Near as we can figure the initial power of the new human god creates some kind of resonance that weakens the barrier between where the dinosaur gods now exist and our dimension."

"Like a mini big bang," Alyson said. Their story sounded like something out of a sci-fi movie, except—

She rubbed her sore abdomen before she met Sam's gaze. "So that's the connection. You were altered by Antonius and Mallory's experiments to such an extent you became a god, and your rebirth, creation, or whatever we want to call it, is a small breech in the dike."

Sam sighed. "Yes."

"This dinosaur demon wants to breed more of his kind to expand the breech."

Sam nodded. "The paradox of the situation is I'm the only one who can plug the hole my existence has made. If the demons can kill me before I plug it, well . . ." She shrugged.

"And why aren't you plugging it?"

Sam grinned. "According to the other human-based death gods, I have to use the corpse of the dino god."

Alyson's breath caught. Thoughts chased each other in her mind. Dino god. Dinosaur god. Dinosaur fossils. The bizarre fossilized skeleton with eight limbs on display at the Sunshine Believers.

She wiped her hands down her face. "Mother Wolf, I am so stupid. Haight and his people worship the dinosaur gods, and I waltzed right into the demon's den."

# Chapter 18

Alyson wanted to kick herself. Her attitude was nearly as bad as Papa's. As much as she despised her animal side, she arrogantly believed it would protect her from anything. Except this time, it made her an attractive target for beings that wanted to destroy the entire planet.

She looked around the room. None of the group seemed surprised. "The rest of you already knew?"

Esther cocked her head. "We belong to Silver Bear, so yes, we were informed as Sam said."

Alex nodded. "For Augustine Coven, it's a little more personal. One of the dino demons murdered a long-time employee of my wife, then posed as the girl, a Normal named Jane Chevrette—"

"Oh, shit." Alyson covered her mouth. Until she realized what a human gesture she'd made, and she dropped them to her lap. "That bastard admitted the Sunshine Believers killed her. He tried to tell me she was the group's prophet, and the others murdered her to stop her from turning them over to the police."

"The bastards lie damn well, don't they?" Alex scowled. "We didn't discover Jane's murder until Lizard Girl—"

"Lizard Girl?" Esther frowned at the vampire.

Alex shrugged. "We didn't know what else to call her at the time, and the nickname kind of stuck. Anyway, she fled to Peru with a powerful artifact she'd stolen from my wife's shop. While there, she had members of the Sunshine Believers and Selene's surviving rogue vampires working with her, along with her brothers. Not all of the cult's members were involved, so we weren't sure if the survivors of the skirmish had retreated here."

"Maybe that was the original plan." Roy spoke up for the first time. "But Logan and the Goldsteins arrived here in town first. Why would

Haight and his people come here after they failed to sacrifice your father-in-law?"

Alex stared at the Normal. "How do you know that?"

Sam and Bebe both tensed. Fur prickled along Alyson's skin at their reaction. She glanced at Logan. He was in the same straits.

Roy shrugged. "Kill me if you think I'm your demon. At least, I won't have to listen to Doc Goldstein nagging about my blood sugars anymore."

Sam was the first to relax. "You're an empath like my friend Agnes."

"Yep." The old man nodded. "My guess is Haight and his group are in Tuttle Creek for the same reason I am. A bit of isolation from both the supernaturals and the Normals." He looked over at Logan. "That's the reason I've seen you near my place, isn't it? You've been checking 'em out on the full moons. Did you see anything suspicious over the last four years?"

Logan shook his head. "No. Alex asked me to keep an eye on 'em. We knew if these lizard demons can disguise their scent, their essence, from a god, I wouldn't be able to detect them. It didn't mean I couldn't use my other senses. Look or listen for something unusual."

Anger threaded through Alyson at the other were's admission. "You used me to get into the compound."

He looked up at her. Determination mixed with regret in his eyes. "I meant what I said about protecting you. But no, I wasn't going to pass up a chance to sniff around the ranch either."

Aaron cleared his throat. "I wouldn't get too upset, Alyson. You weren't the only one played." The witch's gaze travelled from Logan to Roy before landing on Alex. "I have no idea what you're talking about. Would you mind telling us what we've gotten ourselves into?"

Alex told them what Alyson strongly suspected was the abbreviated version of the murders in Beverly Hills and Los Angeles three years ago. He and his wife had followed the trail of the woman who had murdered the girl working for his wife to Peru, only to find themselves in a huge mess that had nothing to do with what they thought was a forged Incan artifact.

"Are we sure Haight is the third demon that escaped y'all in Nazca?" Alyson asked.

Alex pursed his lips. "No, we aren't. Hell, we're not even sure he's a dino demon. He may only be a front. And there may be other demons still alive besides the one that escaped us."

Alyson rubbed her temples. "All this is giving me a headache."

"Welcome to the club," Sam said.

Alyson leaned a little closer to Logan, his warmth comforting despite her irritation with him at using her to access the compound. "If Haight is your dino demon, why would he have only Normals at his compound? If he's trying to breed an army, he needs more supernaturals than just me. The only scent, other than Normal, Logan and I picked up at the compound was sandalwood. Frankly, Sharon, his assistant could have told us the truth, and it really was incense. Not to mention, how would he get a female vampire pregnant? They—" Realizing what almost came out of her mouth, she glanced at Alex.

"You mean we're sterile because of the V-virus?" A wry smile curved his mouth. "It's not like I don't already know." He shrugged. "Maybe after Peru, the survivors did come here. Quietly, in ones or twos so the townspeople wouldn't notice. It makes sense. The entire state is neutral territory for the weres, the closest members of Augustine are in Billings, and the nearest witch coven is in Denver."

"People around here would damn sure notice if vampires were drinking," Logan said.

"None of the people I met at the compound had unusual auras," Sarah volunteered.

"Except we didn't see the older members who refused to speak to me," Alyson added.

"Shit," Logan muttered. "Sharon said they were in that meditation building, and it didn't have any windows. We got lucky."

Alyson shook her head. "No, we got sunshine." She turned to Roy. "My first morning here, you said Haight went out of his way not to cause trouble or attract attention. If he has vampires here, they wouldn't hunt anywhere near Tuttle Creek."

The old man nodded. "That mutilated elk was the first indication something was up. Maybe this demon needed something from it in order to mate. And Haight and his people were the only ones who knew Alyson was on her way here, other than Carol and me."

Aaron blew out a harsh breath. "We're going to need more help if we're dealing with rogues on top of a dinosaur demon."

"No," Alex and Sam said at the same time. They looked at each other, frowning.

"You go first," Sam said.

"We've got a goddess, a vamp, two weres, and three witches," he said.

"Four witches," Sarah corrected.

"And an empath," Roy added.

Alex grinned. "And an empath who knows this area as well, if not better, than our opponents. If we bring in more supernaturals, there's a bigger chance of something going wrong and the local Normals learning the truth about us."

"Not that I disagree with your assessment," Bebe spoke for the first time. "But you're the only enforcer here."

Alyson could feel the vibration of Logan's subvocal growl, but only Alex and Sam looked at him.

"It's not like the rest of us are helpless, Doctor," Logan said.

Sarah scowled at Bebe as well. "And if these are the same assholes that kidnapped me, I want in."

Aaron and Esther stared at each other, obviously discussing Sarah and the situation between themselves. Finally, they faced the rest of the group. Neither of them looked very happy about their decision.

"If Sarah's in, we are, too," Esther said.

"So what was your reason?" Alex asked Sam.

Her grin sent a shiver up Alyson's spine.

"I can still be the bait." Sam winked a glowing silver eye at Sarah. "If I'm not in an enclosed space and worrying about everyone else, Sabrina here can see what I can really do when I cut loose."

# Chapter 19

Logan shook his head. "We're making a big assumption Haight is our culprit. Not to mention, how exactly are we going to flush this Lizard Boy out without tipping our hand too soon?" While he agreed with Sam and Alex about not bringing in more people, he didn't want Alyson or Sarah in the middle of this mess.

But he was a smart enough wolf not to open his big mouth about keeping the two women safe. Not unless he wanted to get bitten or fire-balled.

"What if Sarah and I simply go back to the compound tomorrow?" Alyson said.

Logan stared at her. So much for even wanting to keep them safe. "That's not a good idea."

"Why? Because I can't possibly scout the compound." She looked like she wanted to bite him, but more the rip-out-his-throat than a playful nip. "We have the advantage if this demon and his rogues think their se-cret is intact. Not to mention—" Alyson's eyes widened, and she covered her mouth. Her gesture didn't muffle the obscenity she said. Her hands dropped back to her lap. "I was supposed to be there this morning, but I didn't call them."

"Don't worry," Sarah said. "I did."

Alyson's eyelids did a very slow blink. Logan already had a good sense of how important her professionalism was to her. Add in her southern manners, and she was probably more mortified by her slip than the idea of the demon getting his claws on her again. Or she was using etiquette as a shield from her own emotions.

Logan swallowed his grimace. On second thought, that was far more likely. He'd done similar things over the last four years.

Alyson cleared her throat. "What story did you give Sharon for us not showing up this morning?"

"I said you had food poisoning," Sarah said.

Alyson shrugged. "Good. It would be totally reasonable for us to show up tomorrow."

"No," Alex said. "If we let you go in by yourselves, and something goes wrong, they could kill you before we could get to you."

"You're underestimating us," Sarah scoffed.

The vampire flashed his fangs. "If it were just the renegades, I'd agree. You've only seen what a baby demon can do. The full-grown variety will be tough for even Sam to handle."

"Hey!" Sam said.

"It's true, and you know it," Alex shot back. "The reason I'm still alive is because she wanted Phil, and I wasn't worth the time it took to kill me. Right now, we're making a huge assumption there's only one of the full-grown variety hiding in the Sunshine Believers' compound. We need the intel first."

"And that's why it has to be Sarah and me," Alyson said quietly. "You need a scout, and sending in anyone else will tip off your demon."

"I'm the last person to be super-cautious—" Sam's words prompted a round of snickers from Bebe and Alex.

Logan couldn't keep from grinning either. He'd heard about a number of her antics through his parents and Alex. Mom had taken a shine to the zombie goddess. In fact, she'd even suggested that Logan consider courting the woman. While Sam had a lot of sass, she simply wasn't his taste.

He looked up at the were who had become his acquired flavor. But that was assuming she'd ever look at any man after what was done to her. "What if I went with you instead? It wouldn't be the first time I've gone with you to the compound. We could say you had the stomach flu after all, and now Sarah has it."

"Hey!" Sarah exclaimed.

Logan ignored the teen's protest. "Alex and Sam would Hear my shout if things go sour and 'port in the cavalry."

Surprisingly, Alyson nodded. "That could work."

"Traitor!" Sarah glared at them as if they had actually stabbed her in the back.

"No." Alyson held up her hand. "Logan goes with me tomorrow. We case the compound, then we can plan for a better use of your talents the next day."

That seemed to mollify the teenager. She crossed her arms and said, "You'd better use my talents."

"What can I do to help?" Roy asked.

Sam glanced at Logan before she turned to the empath. "I understand you knew what the baby lizard demon was feeling when it was still inside Alyson."

"Yep," he said. "And it blasted me for it."

She tilted her head. "Think you could do it again for me if I shield you?"

Roy glanced at the Goldsteins for a moment. "But Esther said it's dead. Logan broke its neck."

Unlike the shit-eating grin Sam had earlier when she came up with her plan, her expression was somber. "He did. I'm going to try to bring it back to question it."

Roy leaned away from her. "That ain't natural, girl."

"Neither am I," she said. "But we can't let anyone go into that compound totally blind, no matter who's paired up with Alyson. It's too risky. We need to know how many of these dino demons we're dealing with and how many vamps they may be hiding up there."

Sam scrubbed her eyes before she continued. "Then there's the civilians. I don't know how many Normals are in on the demon's plan, and how many are innocent dupes. Not to mention, the citizens of Tuttle Creek could be used as hostages. If we try to evacuate the town, Big Daddy Lizard is going to know something's up. We need a plan that will keep all of them out of harm's way."

Alex shook his head. "I hate to say it, Sam, but we might have to consider any Normals at the compound a lost cause."

"That ain't right either," Roy said. "Those folks were looking for hope and a purpose. It ain't their fault they got taken in by a demon."

"That's why we need to question the baby." Sam's voice was soft. From her scent, she wasn't happy about the situation either. "If you have an idea about how to get the intel or the innocents out of the compound without getting someone killed or letting the demon that attacked Alyson get away, I'll take it."

The old man was silent for what seemed like forever.

Logan leaned forward. "Roy, we need your help. You'll know if the baby demon is lying. If Alex or the witches try to read its mind, its ghost could possess them and kill all of us before we knew what was happening."

"I know, I know." The old man rubbed his jaw. "Raising the dead though—" His head rose, and he stared at Logan. "It don't seem godly."

"Depends on which one of us you're talking about," Sam quipped.

"Can you walk into a church?" Roy snapped.

"Yes," she said, all joking gone. "I've also been in a mosque, a Jewish temple, a Sikh temple, and a fae circle grove. And that's just the funerals I've attended in the last week." She held her hand up. "And before you get your tighty-whities in a twist, it was all by invitation of my counterparts."

The old man cocked his head. "Your counterparts?"

Sam shrugged. "You know, like the Angel of Death and Morrigan."

"Why would they do that?" Roy asked, an incredulous expression adding wrinkles to his craggy face.

"So I can get an idea of how to deal with the dead. Showing by example. Consider it an internship. We're all in the same business. The death gods don't have quite the rivalries their pantheons may have."

That was a lot of new information. Logan shot a look at Alex, who gave a slight shake of his head. So, it wasn't just him out of the loop.

"All right. I'll do it," Roy said. "I won't like it, but I'll do it."

"Thank you," Alyson said. "We need all the help we can get if we're going to stop this demon from hurting anyone else."

"What do you need from the rest of us, Sam?" Logan said.

She turned to Sarah. "Think you can do another shield?"

"How big?" the teen asked.

"A much smaller one. The size of a large indoor dog kennel would be good."

"No problem." Sarah grinned.

Sam faced the medical personnel. "Any of you doctors have a scalpel you don't mind losing? It'll have to be destroyed when I'm done."

"I've got a couple still in their wrappers," Bebe volunteered.

"Wait a minute." Esther's eyes were huge, and ashy fear rolled off of her. "You're not sacrificing anything on our property. I will not condone blood magick!"

"It's my own blood I'm using," Sam said. "And it's not exactly magick. My blood can resurrect the dead." She blew out a deep breath. "Or kill the living."

"Wait a minute." Aaron cocked his head. "That thing bit you while Bebe and I were patching up Alyson. If your blood can kill, it should have died then."

"In theory, yeah." Sam nodded. "I think it knew better than to drink my blood." She held out her right arm. "Can you see all those teeth marks?"

"Barely," Aaron replied.

Logan frowned. His eyesight was perfect, and Sam's skin looked flawless to him. It must be something that only the witches' Second Sight could detect.

"The baby's teeth were hollow, similar to a rattler," she said. "And they're designed to be shed like a shark's. The broken teeth left in my skin acted like plugs so it didn't get any of my blood in its mouth. If it did, whatever random blood cells of mine that may have been on its enamel from the teeth it retained wasn't enough to affect the baby demon." She lowered her arm.

"Hold on," Alex interjected. "Whenever something alive drinks your blood, it explodes. The baby couldn't have ingested your blood."

Sam and Bebe exchanged a slightly guilty look that sent Logan's skin tingling and itching.

The lady doctor cleared her throat. "That was the old result based on the nanites' defense programming. As Sam's DNA has changed, so have the affects of her blood. We've . . . been running experiments with mosquitoes."

Sam plucked at a loose thread where her jeans had been ripped, not bothering to, or not daring to, meet anyone's gaze. "It's not the nanites killing the bugs now as a self-defense mechanism. It's definitely the chemical and magickal composition of my blood."

"Nanites?" Sarah frowned. "That would make you some kind of a cyborg, not a god."

Sam looked up and shook her head. "The nanites are what's rewriting my DNA. Have been for almost four years now. Ares was kind enough to give Bebe samples of his blood for comparison. My DNA is looking more and more like his."

She grimaced. "Every time I get a handle on what those damn robots are doing to me, the rules change. But right now, I'm still pretty sure I can resurrect the baby demon."

Logan leaned forward. "So we have two problems. One, your blood may have no effect on the demon and may not resurrect it for us to question."

Alex nodded. "That scenario simply leaves us in the same position we already are in. What's the other problem?"

Logan stared at Sam. "If you resurrect this thing, how do we kill it again after we question it?"

Everyone looked expectantly at Sam.

She shrugged. "I give it my blood again."

"You've never tried it before," Roy accused. "Resurrecting, then killing the same creature?"

"No," she mumbled. "No, not even with the mosquitoes."

Logan stood. "Then we need to try this with a guinea pig first."

Alyson grabbed his hand. "You can't volunteer!"

Her concern sent a bolt straight to his heart. He brought her hand to his lips and kissed her soft skin before he grinned at her. "Wasn't planning on it, *chéri*."

He didn't relish torturing an innocent creature, but they needed to know if Sam's crazy scheme would work before trying it on the dead demon. Otherwise, they could make matters far worse than they already were. He turned to the goddess. "Would a rabbit do?"

She grimaced. "It's as good as anything."

Everyone else in the room looked on the verge of puking, even Alex.

Delicate fingers squeezed his hand, and he met Alyson's gaze. Surprisingly, she didn't appear sick at the thought. In fact, she pushed back the blanket covering her legs. "With the snow, you're going to need help flushing one out."

"You're still recovering," he protested.

"Who else knows how to find a rabbit burrow? Plus I have experience capturing them alive." She tilted her chin, as if daring him to argue with her, and jabbed a finger in Sam's direction. "She's not even sure if it was her blood or you snapping the neck that killed the damn demon. We're going to have to go through the entire cycle to be sure, which means we need at least two rabbits."

"You just had your guts ripped up by that thing," he ground out between clenched teeth.

"Which is why I'm going to be part of this." Her pupils and irises shifted from human to canine, and a sheen of fur sprouted along her bare skin.

He turned to Aaron and Bebe, silently pleading with them for help.

"Let her do this, Logan," Sam said as she also stood. "You know what the need for revenge is like."

And that was the entire problem. The itch to do something, anything, when you were unable to stop others from being hurt, to stop others from hurting you, was overwhelming. As much as he wanted to keep Alyson safe, he knew that wasn't what she needed. Reluctantly, he nodded.

Sarah jumped to her feet. "I'm going with you guys."

"You most certainly are not—" Esther started, but Aaron grabbed his wife's arm. She glared at him. "You can't be serious!"

"It'll be good practice for her shielding spells," Bebe said. With a somber gaze, she looked at Sarah. "We need to hide this experiment from the adult demon just like we will have to shield the baby demon's resurrection—" Esther opened her mouth, and Bebe held up a hand to stop the nurse before Bebe continued. "Assuming we end up doing so. But be careful. Witch magick doesn't play nice with Sam's talents, and vice versa, just like if you were dealing with a fae."

Sarah charged for the door. "Let me get my coat."

"Whoa, there, John Wayne." Sam grabbed the teen's shoulder as she passed and brought her to an abrupt halt. "Let the weres hunt first. Once they have a couple of rabbits, we'll pop over to their location."

"But won't the demon know if you're teleporting all over the place?" Aaron asked.

Alex stood. "According to our sources, the demons either can't tell, or they don't get enough warning." He eyed Logan. "And luckily those assholes can't 'port either. But if we're doing this, we need to get moving before he learns Sam's in town through conventional means."

Logan snorted. "Too late for that. The queen of gossip in Tuttle Creek already knows. He saw Sam with me earlier today."

"That means we need to move faster than we originally thought." A frown followed Alex's words. "Who was it? Maybe Bebe and I can head off the town gossip." He turned to Bebe. "Can you whip up more of that memory potion you and Caesar used at Anthony's restaurant a few years ago?"

Someone banged on the front door. Everyone in the room stared at each other, frozen like proverbial deer in headlights. The banging started up again.

"There's a Normal girl at the front door," Sam said.

Aaron stood and faced Logan. "What's the story you gave Marvin?"

"You were exposed to Danny Olsen's strep throat, and you were staying at the clinic until you were sure you were clean."

Aaron nodded curtly. "I'll be right back."

Logan deliberately eavesdropped on the good doctor. From their various expressions, he was sure the rest of the supernaturals were as well. He took pity on Roy and relayed the gist of the conversation.

"It's Maddy from the general store. She's asking about Alyson." Logan looked at her.

The female were shrugged. "She was my first personal contact here."

Sam frowned at the next exchange. "Oh shit. That girl is too smart for her own good."

"Maddy's asking why Alyson isn't at your rental cabin," Logan paraphrased for Roy.

From the twitching of Alex, Sam and the witches' eyes, there was a major debate going on about what story Aaron should use.

"He's telling her that Alyson's here. He thought her vomiting was food poisoning at first, but now he knows it's strep, and Maddy needs to go home before she's infected." Logan looked at Bebe. "What about that memory potion you were talking about?"

Bebe's sharp shake of her head sent her dark curls flying. "Not enough time to mix it up. This may be innocent, or . . ." She, Alex, and Sam exchanged worried looks.

"You can't really think Maddy is the demon?" Alyson said.

Alex grimaced. "Lizard Girl had my wife's assistant manager down pat for a minimum of two weeks, and Jane was a Normal. I really doubt the demons' shape-shifting is limited by gender or species."

"Impersonating a runaway she killed may have been the easiest way for her to slip into the compound without any outsiders knowing," Sam added.

Aaron stalked back into the room and yanked down the surgical mask he'd been wearing. Quick thinking on his part before he'd answered the front door.

"I think the memory potion is a bust," he said as he sat down with a weary groan. "Marvin's already announced Alyson's health issues at the general store."

"Then we need to question the baby demon," Sam said. "We have to assume everyone at the compound will know when Maddy gets home. Unless we . . ." She looked at Alex as her voice trailed off.

"You are not killing her to keep her quiet," Alyson said sharply. "And you're damn sure not killing her without proof she's in league with this demon of yours. We'll get the rabbits for you to experiment on, then you can do your voodoo."

Logan nodded sharply. "We'd better get going." To his surprise, Alyson's hand still held his. "You sure about this?"

She nodded. "Where's a safe place to shift?"

"Come on. I'll show you."

She hopped off the bed, and he pretended not to notice her wince at the jolt to her body. She followed him with a determined step through the clinic and out the back door. The woman by his side was no longer the spoiled pack princess. No, this was a bitch any alpha would appreciate.

But they needed to survive the next couple of days before he could even think about pursuing those thoughts. And even then, she may not want him, considering what the bastard demon had done to her while looking like Logan.

*One problem at a time*, he told himself. Except problems were gathering faster than snow drifts in a Montana blizzard.

# Chapter 20

Alyson tried to hide her nervousness as Logan led her through the snow toward the Goldsteins' backyard. The sun was already low in the sky. The shadows hid them from the street when the buildings didn't. The initial shock of the attack and her injuries was wearing off, and she wanted to hide in those shadows.

*No, call it what it was*, she told herself. *I was raped and impregnated by a demon.*

New rage throbbed along with her pulse in her gut. The fresh scars ached, and both doctors were right. She should be in bed, recovering from the physical trauma.

But if she tried to sleep now, she wouldn't truly get any rest. Not with the nightmares she'd no doubt have. Is that what Mother Wolf had been trying to tell her a couple of nights ago in the dream where she was chased by monsters? That she was in danger?

Last night, she'd been so busy rebelling against a father hundreds of miles away she hadn't paid attention to her surroundings, much less who or what was in them. A stupid pup mistake. And look where it had gotten her.

Icicles hung from the edges of the Goldsteins' roof. She halted at the graphic reminder of her attacker's teeth. Frigid air hitched in her throat.

"Alyson?" Logan must have smelled the change in her mood. He watched her, but didn't try to touch her. "Alyson, you still with me?"

She clutched her stomach for a moment before she could catch her breath. "Nothing that taking down this demon won't fix." She pushed past him and unlatched the gate.

His scent flooded her. Despite everything that had happened, her body reacted to the close proximity to an alpha. A sob escaped from her throat before she could stop it.

He laid his hand over her mittened one that still clung to the gate handle to keep herself upright. "Alyson, I can handle this. Why don't you—"

"No," she growled and fiercely swiped at the hot tears that had escaped. "No, I'm hunting tonight."

"All right, but we're taking this easy." He held up his free hand when she started to protest. "Roy's in no condition to ride a snowmobile to our rescue tonight if you rip yourself open out there." He gestured toward the valley.

He was right. She owed the old man as much as she owed Logan and the witches.

"Fine."

"Leave the gate partially open so you can slip through," he added. "I don't want you tearing new holes in your abdomen, trying to jump the fence."

"Anything else," she spat out.

His eyes narrowed. "I'm not your enemy, Tribideaux, but I'll do whatever you need me to do to bring this asshole down. He's yours."

His declaration broke through the miasma of her anger. No one had ever stood up for her like this before, much less stated she had the right to the killing blow. And somehow she knew he'd hold his friends to the same promise he'd just made to her.

She nodded. "Thank you."

Yesterday, she would have question her emotional ability to kill anyone. Today . . .

Today, she wanted to watch the light die in her rapist's eyes.

Logan strode toward a utility box nestled against the house. "Leave your clothes on the left and shoes on the right. Aaron and I water-proofed the clothing side and varmint-proofed the entire chest. They'll be safe here until we come back." He was already stripping as he spoke.

And Logan's bare skin set off a war inside her. Whatever attraction she may have had over the last couple of days was clawed at by last night's terror.

He glanced at her. His expression wasn't sympathetic. More like understanding. "I'll wait for you on the other side of the fence by the tree line." He stowed his jeans, sweatshirt, and boots.

Thankfully, he didn't look at her as he fell to all fours. When his change completed, he shook out his beige coat.

A beige coat that was too familiar. It had been chasing her, pinning her, forcing—

*It wasn't Logan last night.*

If he noticed the knife edge of her panic, he didn't acknowledge it. With a reassuring *woof* over his shoulder, he launched himself over the back fence.

Alyson released her white-knuckled hold on the gate latch and hugged herself. Everything had changed. Her emotions jumbled and tangled over everything that had happened in the last twenty-four hours. Papa, loving, overprotective Papa, hadn't protected her from the world after all.

And she couldn't blame him because she made the choice to come here. He was right after all. She couldn't protect herself.

The rage surged inside her again. Maybe she hadn't been able to stop what had happened, but she could make damn sure the demon didn't rape another innocent woman.

She stripped off her clothes and tossed them into the box along with her damp, borrowed shoes. Less than twenty-four hours after the full moon, her wolf still tugged at her. She took a deep breath of chill air, and the change swept over her, a gentle tide compared to the pain from her attack and the attempted C-section.

Heeding Logan's warning, she didn't try to jump the six-foot high boards. She slipped through the opening in the gate and rounded the exterior of the fence. Since the Goldsteins house was near the end of the street, it wasn't a far jog to where the tree line curved around the valley. Another furry body waited for her.

For a split second, she hesitated at his scent. Images and terror froze her in place. Logan had been out of her sight for a minute.

Long enough the demon could have taken his place.

Shadows shifted beneath the trees, and Alyson jumped back. The shadows resolved into a tall woman with the vanilla-sweet scent of Twinkies and the slight stench of decay.

Sam stepped into the ambient streetlight, dressed once again in her black coat and slacks. No tears showed in the clothing. "He's Logan. I promise, Alyson." She brushed a hand across the were's fur. "I'll be listening for you."

Logan trotted over, licked Alyson's nose and nuzzled her neck. The gentle reassurance of an alpha, encouraging a packmate that she was safe.

If he could survive unimaginable horrors in a Normal and vampire's torture chamber, she could survive this. Alyson butted her shoulder against his. He set off at an easy lope parallel to the timber line surrounding the valley, and she followed.

Two rabbits quivered in the snow. It took all of Logan's willpower to rein in his wolf side at the tempting odor. Alyson didn't seem to have the same problem. If one of the rabbits tried to make a break for freedom, she simply paw-slapped it back to the center of the circle of packed snow.

*Sam!*

Displaced air made a soft *pop*. Like earlier at the tree line, the zombie goddess was dressed in her long black coat with its mandarin collar, slacks, and boots. Sarah still wore the same clothes as before with the addition of her hat, gloves, and insulated parka. The teleportation and Sam's clothing weren't the odd things though.

It was the rabbits bowing to the goddess.

After she inclined her head to them, both fuzzy gray creatures made squeaking sounds. Sam answered with the same *wheek, wheek* noise.

Alyson cocked her head, and Sarah had a confused expression. It was a relief to know he wasn't the only one flabbergasted by this turn of events.

Movement flashed in his peripheral vision. Logan backed two steps and circled as he took in the change of their situation.

Rabbits. Hundreds of the long-eared critters surrounded them. A larger rabbit, easily twice the size of any of the bucks, hopped toward the two Logan and Alyson had caught.

Sarah raised her hands, unintelligible words on her lips when Sam grabbed her wrists and yanked them down.

"Don't do anything." Sam's scowl turned to the weres. "None of you do a damn thing."

The huge rabbit balanced on his hind legs. Sam matched the slight inclination of its head. Once again, an obvious conversation took place, but for the life of him, Logan couldn't understand a thing. Most talking in his wolf form dealt with body language, but this sounded like a very specific tongue. Especially when Super Bunny waved a paw in his direction.

Finally, the bigger rabbit lowered his forepaws to the ground. The emotions on Sam's face looked like a mix of anger and embarrassment.

She blew out a deep breath that left a white cloud hanging in front of her face for a second or two. The temperature had dipped now the sun had set though the western sky still glowed a muted gold. "Here's the deal. Mastisapa's people are willing to act as our sacrifice if I guarantee they go to my new paradise."

"What are you talking about?" Sarah's attention flicked from Sam to the huge rabbit and back.

This needed a real discussion, not half-assed telepathy. Logan forced his human skin to the surface and stood upright. "Can you even offer them that, Sam?"

"Oh, for the love of—" She covered her eyes with both hands. "There are things I don't need to see right now."

Warmth spread across his bare legs. Logan looked down. His jeans covered his lower half.

"Did I do it right?" Sam asked without moving her fingers.

"Depends on what you mean by 'right.'" Sarah giggled. "But yeah, you covered the interesting bits."

A huffing noise came from Alyson, the equivalent of wolf laughter. The horde of rabbits surrounding them chittered.

"Good." Sam lowered her hands.

"Really? You put pants on me?" Logan stared at the woman. "You're married! It's not like you haven't seen—"

Sam made a chopping motion with her right hand. "And I'm married to a guy born in Tudor England who pretends to himself that he's my first lover even though he's telepathic. So excuse me for wanting to avoid a stupid marital spat over me seeing—" Her cheeks flamed bright pink. "—your assets."

Sarah's giggles turned to outright laughter. Alyson continued huffing. Even the large rabbit Sam called Mastisapa chirped.

Logan swallowed his own humor at the goddess's embarrassment. "Surely, you've been around weres?"

"My secretary is a 'coyote so back off," Sam snapped. "What did you need to discuss that you had to be in human form to do it?"

He rubbed the back of his neck. "Can you actually offer the rabbits Paradise?"

She waved a hand at the rabbits. "Like I told Mastisapa, I haven't created an afterlife place yet." She sighed. "They said they are willing to wait."

"But we can't wait!" Sarah threw her hands into the air. "With this demon attacking—"

"They know about the demon." Sam's quiet voice interrupted the teen's threatening tantrum more than shouting back at her would. "They're in the same danger of annihilation as we are if the demon succeeds in his plan."

Logan folded his arms. "Out with it, Sam. All of it."

The goddess plucked at her coat and stared at the snow beneath her feet. "The rabbits would rather sacrifice their lives to me if it helps to prevent the apocalypse rather than be eaten by you and Alyson."

Fur receded from the other were's form, and bones cracked until Alyson stood upright as well. "Maybe we need to reconsider our plan." She looked down at the two smaller rabbits at her feet. "And no, I'm not saying that because I'm hungry and you smell very tasty. The damn demon tried to use me to do its dirty work." Alyson's eyes met Logan's. "It's wrong to do the same thing to someone else."

Mastisapa squeaked some more rabbit language at Sam.

"He says it's their choice, not yours, Alyson," she translated.

Alyson slashed her hand through the air. "That still doesn't make it right. It's no different than what—"

One of the smaller rabbits she'd flushed out whistled sharply and thumped its hind leg three times.

A wry smile crossed Sam's face. "Do you really want me to translate that for you?"

Alyson sighed. "No, I got the gist of it. I just don't like this."

Logan didn't really like the whole situation either. Rabbits were something to be caught and eaten. When they talked back to you and they weren't werebunnies . . .

He rubbed the back of his neck. "The big guy's right. It is their choice as long as they understand exactly what Sam and I will do to them and the consequences."

"All right, then we're back to our original plan." Sam sat in the snow. She and the super-sized rabbit she called Mastisapa talked for a moment before he turned to the circle of his people and *wheak*ed at them. They all hopped back several feet, but retained their positions.

"Is that big enough for you to cast a shield circle?" the goddess said to Sarah.

The girl nodded. She pulled a sea shell and salt shaker with a lid from her parka pocket. "Alyson, you might want to join the rest of the rabbits."

"Why?" she growled.

"Sarah, Sam, and I need to be inside the protective circle," Logan said, "if we're going to replicate what happened to the dino demon back at the clinic. You didn't interfere the last time. If you're outside the circle, you won't be tempted to do something."

"I didn't interfere because I was barely conscious after that damn thing ripped its way out of me," she snapped.

"Alyson—" he started, but Sam reached up and tugged on his hand.

Thankfully, the lady were stopped arguing. Fur sprouted from her skin, muscles shifted and bones reformed once again. She trotted to the circle of rabbits. They parted, giving her a place beside them. She sat primly, ears perked, as she watched.

Mastisapa nuzzled the two rabbits beside him before he hopped over to sit next to Alyson.

Logan clenched his fists at the urge to return to wolf form. He'd been on two legs when he snapped the dino demon's neck. Like they had discussed earlier, they needed to replicate the conditions as exactly as they could with the rabbits before they attempted to resurrect the demon corpse.

Sam nodded to Sarah. The witch circled them, tramping out a line and sprinkling salt behind her before she sat in the snow as well, a yard behind and to the left of Sam so she could see the events. Her position would leave the three of them and the two sacrificial rabbits within her magickal shield. He counted silently to three before ozone flooded his sinuses.

The goddess pushed up the left sleeve of her coat, exposing skin barely a shade darker than the snow. Part of him wondered if she had been simply one of those Beverly Hills women who eschewed the tanning salon, or if the whiteness was a result of her transformation by the nanites.

Sam said something to the rabbits. The doe tentatively hopped forward, and she sank her teeth into the goddess's forearm. Sam winced as the doe jerked away, taking a hunk of flesh with her.

The rabbit screamed and dropped to her side, convulsions wracking her tiny body. Bloody foam covered her muzzle. After a final kick of her hind leg, she lay still. The sickly-sweet smell of death filled the witch's circle.

Logan looked at Sam's forearm. Except for a smear of scarlet on the surrounding skin, her wound was gone.

"At least she didn't explode," Sam said. However, tears rolled down her cheeks as she picked up the rabbit's body and cradled it in her lap. Good to know she wasn't taking the animal's self-sacrifice lightly.

"Alex mentioned that." Logan ran a hand over his chin. "That had to have been messy."

"It was metallic dust, not blood and guts," she muttered. "Worst case scenario was pneumonia from irritation to the lungs from breathing the crap. Now, for step two." She fished in her pocket and produced one of Bebe's scalpels. She pulled the steel from its wrapper and drew a blade across her left wrist.

Crimson welled along the cut, and she held her wrist over the dead rabbit's open mouth. Only four drops fell before the wound sealed itself.

Logan had counted to ten when Sarah said, "You sure that's enough?"

"I'm guessing on dosage here," Sam said quietly. "These aren't exactly laboratory-controlled conditions. It usually took a minute or two for the mosquitos to revive, and they are a hell of a lot smaller."

Raw curiosity prickled Logan's skin as much as the scent of ozone and trepidation over Sam and Bebe's experiments. "How'd you get your blood into them?"

"Very tiny needles." Sam swiped at the wetness on her cheeks again.

Night had totally fallen, and the moon would be rising in another hour or so. The itching along his skin would increase until he couldn't resist the change. He glanced at the buck who looked back nervously. Maybe the rabbit could sense the nearing shift.

"Not yet," Logan said.

The rabbit cocked his head. Sam translated, and he relaxed a bit.

Sarah's sharp inhale alerted Logan. He watched the lump of fur in Sam's lap. The dead doe's ear twitched. She stretched so far she tumbled over the goddess's calves and into the snow, which seemed to wake up the critter. She jumped up and shook herself before looking around.

The faint odor of decay still lay within the circle, but Logan couldn't tell if it came from the resurrected rabbit or Sam. The buck tentatively hopped closer to the doe and sniffed. The doe's nose wiggled as well. They circled each other a few times before the buck chirped at Sam.

"Wow," Sarah said. "I've never seen anything like that."

"That's a good thing," Logan said sharply. "We don't need more necromancers raising the dead."

"No, I mean—" The witch shook her head. "I forgot you can't See what I can when you're in human form. The rabbit's soul literally got sucked back into her body." She turned to Sam. "Does that happen to the mosquitoes, too?"

The goddess stiffened, her expression slightly guilty. "Yes."

"That is so awesome!" Sarah said. "I've always been taught it's impossible to put a soul back into its body once the cords have been cut."

Sam sighed. "Normally, you're right. That's the reason a ghost possession goes wrong. An unconnected soul inside doesn't stop the body from rotting. But this . . ." She shrugged.

"Before we get too excited about reconnected souls, we need to try part three," Logan said quietly.

The goddess nodded. She held her arm out once more. The doe asked a question, and Sam answered.

The doe bit her again with the same results as before.

The bizarre part this time was after the rabbit stopped kicking. Sam picked up an invisible . . . something next to the corpse. Logan frowned as she tucked whatever it was into an inner coat pocket.

"Was that the rabbit's soul?" he asked.

"Yes." She looked at him with such remorse he was afraid she'd start crying again. So she wasn't the cool, heartless bitch she pretended to be. Her gaze dropped to the other rabbit. "It's your turn."

The buck hopped over to him and looked up, the rabbit's black eyes unafraid. Logan swallowed hard and scooped the animal into his palm. It was one thing chasing them down for food. It was another when one offered itself up to help save the world.

"Thank you," Logan whispered as he rubbed the buck's head. A quick twist of the fragile neck, and the rabbit exhaled its last breath.

Logan handed the body to Sam, who cradled it in her lap as she had the doe and carefully aligned his broken bones. With a slash of the scalpel along her wrist, four crimson drops fell into the buck's mouth.

This time the wait seemed longer than the last. Logan rubbed his arms. The need to shift was on the point of unbearable, but what if Sam and Sarah needed him in human form? Or maybe the need to run had more to do with breaking all the natural laws he'd lived with his entire life. He glanced at Alyson, but she calmly sat with the rest of the rabbits, watching this whole scenario play out.

Finally, the dead buck sneezed, sat up, and shook himself. He stared at Sam and said something in rabbit language. For the third time, the goddess held out her arm.

The buck's death by blood was just as brutal as both of the doe's deaths. Once again, Sam tucked the rabbit's soul into her pocket.

"Are they going to be okay in your coat?" Sarah asked. Her voice was timid, no longer displaying the brash confidence of earlier.

"They will be. I promise," Sam said.

Logan looked at Sarah. The teen was trembling. "They volunteered," he reminded her.

"I know." She drew a shaky breath. "I'm reminding myself of that. Do you need the shield anymore, Sam?"

"No."

The smell of ozone faded. Sam placed the used scalpel into her other pocket before she gathered the corpses of the rabbits gently in her arms. "Does your dad and mom have a sacred spot where we can burn the bodies?"

Sarah considered the question for a moment. "Mom will throw a fit if we do it at the house. I'd ask Roy if we can use his place."

Mastisapa approached Sam and spoke in his rabbit language, and she answered. Whatever they said must have satisfied them both. The circle of rabbits broke up, and they raced across the snow.

To her credit, Alyson resisted the urge to chase them. Instead, she padded over and nudged Logan's jean-clad thigh.

The moon peeked over the east end of Tuttle Valley. He couldn't stay human much longer. "Alyson and I need to run for a bit. Will you make sure Sarah's okay?" He thought he concerns to Sam. Flashbacks and nightmares were a bitch, and he would have a rough time sleeping himself after what he witnessed today.

*Of course.* Out loud, she said, "Sure. Yell if you run into trouble."

"We will. One more thing." He tugged at his waistband and smiled. "The jeans."

Cold air whistled past his suddenly bare legs. The change swept over him faster than it ever had before, but he'd never delayed this long on the three nights of the full moon. He stretched and shook out his fur.

Alyson nudged his shoulder before she charged across the field, not chasing anything but the sparkle of moonlight on the snow.

Logan yipped and ran after her.

<h1 style="text-align:center">Chapter 21</h1>

Logan spotted Bebe waiting for them by the rear door of the clinic. The faintest hint of light edged the eastern end of Tuttle Valley. With a paw, he pointed toward the Goldsteins' backyard. She must have understood his message because she nodded and went back inside the clinic.

Once he and Alyson slipped through the gate, she immediately shifted to human form and strode to the box with their clothes. "You think your friends will let us take a nap before they try their cockamamie plan?" The huge dark circles under her eyes stood out against her pale skin.

Guilt washed over him as he resumed human form. It hadn't been thirty-six hours since she had been attacked, much less their desperate attempt to get the baby demon out of her. Of course, she needed some rest. Hell, he usually spent a day sleeping after the three nights of the full moon.

"'Cockamamie'? That's a little old-fashioned, even for me." He grinned when she stuck her tongue out at him. Despite her trauma and obvious exhaustion, their run seemed to have brought back her sassiness.

"I'm sure they will," he said as he caught his Texas A&M sweatshirt she tossed at him. "Sarah's the one who needs to be fresh. She expended a lot of energy on her shields yesterday that Pop-Tarts and cola can't compensate for."

Even Alyson's throaty chuckle sounded weary. "I remember having that kind of energy when I was a pup."

The tension along Logan's neck and shoulders eased. He half-expected she'd blame him for the attack. *Call it what it was. Alyson was raped.*

Maybe they'd both needed last night's run. No hunting. No flirtation. Just concentrating on the rhythm of four paws and the inhalation of frosty air. Time with someone who understood the contentment of racing under the stars.

The back door of the house edged open, allowing the scent of bacon, coffee, and nutmeg to slip through. Aaron poked his head through the narrow aperture. "Breakfast is hot if you two want to eat before you get some sleep." He didn't wait for an answer. The door eased closed behind him.

"I could use some food," Alyson. Her words were immediately followed by a huge gurgle from her stomach. Her cheeks pinked.

Her flushed look sent improper thoughts through Logan's brain. Of the myriad ways he wanted bring out that flush. It triggered new rage at the demon for ruining what could have potentially been a good thing with Alyson.

"Then let's get some before Sam eats Aaron and Esther out of house and home."

Alyson couldn't stop staring at Alex while she and Logan ate. He sipped coffee while he worked on his laptop. His eyes met hers over the lid. "Is there something I can help you with, Ms. Tribideaux?"

Heat rushed through her face, but she wasn't sure if it were her unintentional rudeness or her embarrassment at being caught.

She cleared her throat. "My apologies, Mr. Stanton. I just never . . . um, my papa never . . ."

One of his blond eyebrows rose. "Met a vampire, much less had one at the breakfast table?"

She stared at her plate. "Yes, sir."

"Oh, for the love of Mother Wolf, don't 'sir' him." Logan rolled his eyes. "He's insufferable as it is. Want some French toast?"

Alyson peeked between her lashes as she accepted the platter, but Alex ignored the other were, his expression openly curious. "Your father's the packmaster of New Orleans. Surely, you've met some members of the Rousseau Coven?"

She shook her head. "Papa doesn't trust anyone outside of the pack.

While I've met a handful of witches from Baton Rouge and Beaumont, I've never met anyone from the Laveau Coven either."

Alex snorted. "No one wants to deal with Laveau, not even other witches."

Aaron coughed, but Esther smirked at the vampire's comment.

"But contrary to the Bela Lugosi and Christopher Lee movies, we don't shun modern conveniences," Alex said. He looked up and tapped the rim of his cup. "Especially not decent coffee that doesn't have an inch of grounds in the bottom of the cup." He cocked his head. "I take that back. I know one vampire who does, but she was Amish when she was Normal."

"Actually, I was wondering about drinking coffee," Alyson said. "I thought you could only consume blood."

Sam strode into the kitchen in shorts and a t-shirt, her hair wrapped in a towel. The sweet smell of citrus and fresh water followed her. "Everyone needs caffeine," she declared before she headed straight for the coffee maker and poured herself a mug of the dark liquid. After the first sip, she rolled her eyes and groaned. "Holy me, that's even better than the shower. Thanks, Esther."

The witch raised her cup in salute. "You replaced my Twinkie stash. We're even."

Alyson stared at Sam. " 'Holy me'?"

"Who does a deity call on?" Sam leaned against the counter and took another long drink of her coffee.

Alyson opened her mouth and realized the odd logic of the zombie goddess's question. "Point taken, but what happens if you say another deity's name?"

"They might show up, which is not necessarily a good thing." Sam grabbed a piece of French toast and bit off a hunk. "Anyway, to answer your original question, as long as there's not too many solids suspended in the liquid, vampires can drink it. Coffee, wine, tea are okay. Milk is pushing it," she said around her mouthful.

"Holy Sam!" Alex muttered. Everyone in the kitchen turned and stared at the vampire.

"Not funny, asshole," Sam growled.

He looked up from his computer. "I think I just found some of the money Selene stole from the coven."

"What money?" Aaron asked.

Alex glared at the laptop screen. "When Selene tried to usurp Caesar six years ago, we discovered she'd been embezzling for centuries. To top that off, she cleared out the bank accounts of our casino in Las Vegas. We're talking over a couple billion dollars in today's terms. I think I just found part of it."

Logan slid his chair closer to Alex's, and Sam stalked around the table so she could see the laptop screen, too.

"What makes you sure it's your coven's money?" Alyson asked. She scooped some more scrambled eggs onto her plate.

"When we lost the trail through the banks in Switzerland and the Cayman Islands, Logan helped us create a series of algorithms to search for the funds." Alex looked up and shrugged. "You can't move that much money without leaving some kind of a trail. We followed a chunk to Mallory Labs, but Furry and I were kidnapped before we could do anything about it."

Logan scratched at his chin. "Yeah, snatching us only made Caesar and Duncan look at Mallory more closely." He chuckled. "If Selene knew about our traces, she wouldn't have bothered keeping us alive."

"Yeah, well, the bitch didn't know as much as she liked to think," Sam muttered.

"And I've been too busy looking for direct links, I didn't think of indirect links," Alex grumbled. He pointed at his screen.

Logan looked at Alyson. "What was your impression of Sharon Tyson?"

Alyson jerked. "Crap! I need to call her about Sarah and me not coming out to the ranch until this afternoon."

He frowned. "That didn't exactly answer my question."

"I never smelled any deception on her part if that's what you mean." She shrugged. "But I didn't with Haight or anybody else at the compound either."

Sam reached across the table and grabbed another piece of French toast. "Let me guess. That huge chunk of change is in this Sharon's name?"

"Yeah." Alex's eyes shone a neon blue. "Sharon Tyson has five different accounts scattered in five different countries. Close to ten billion total."

"So either Sharon's partnered with Giovanni—" Logan started.

"Or a shapeshifting demon is pretending to be her to hide the money for Giovanni," Alex finished.

Sam snorted. "Or they could have simply used her personal information when she became Haight's secretary to create the accounts."

Alyson sucked in a deep breath. This was too much information for her to process. "Who the hell is Giovanni?"

"He took over the rogues who broke away from Augustine after his grandmother's death." Alex continued staring at his laptop screen.

Logan glanced at Alex before he faced Alyson. "I also don't think it's a good idea for you two to go out to the compound today after all."

She stiffened. "Just a damn minute! We discussed this yesterday—"

"It's got nothing to do with your or Sarah's abilities," Alex said. "Even with immediate treatment, strep throat doesn't go away overnight. Even the Normals would be suspicious of that."

"Hold up," Sam mumbled around a mouthful of French toast. "Problem with her story. Weres don't get sick."

Alex and Logan looked at each other, then at the zombie goddess.

"And you couldn't point this out last night," Alex said dryly.

Sam shrugged. "If you wanted super genius help, you should have brought Tiffany."

Logan shook his head. "It would only matter if a Normal knows she's a were. The demon can't say anything without revealing who he's impersonating."

"Oh, shit. We've got a bigger problem." Alyson buried her face in her hands. Why hadn't she remembered her first in-person conversation with Haight yesterday when it mattered? Like when Aaron was giving a cover story for her last night?

Wood scraped against wood. "It's okay, sweetheart," Logan murmured. His shoulder rubbed against hers.

She dropped her hands. "Haight knows I'm a werewolf."

Everyone in the room froze.

"How?" Logan asked.

"He admitted it during our lunch the first day. He said he researched me." She swallowed hard. "He also said Jane Chevrette was a supernatural, and if I exposed her talent for precognition, he would expose my secret."

Alex's eyes bore into hers. "And you didn't think to do a background check on Jane before admitting you're a were?"

"I wanted the interview with him so bad I wasn't thinking straight." Alyson sagged. "I planned to check out his story when I got back to New Orleans. It's just that—"

The neon glow of the vampire's eyes grew brighter. "Of all the goddamn stupid—"

"Stop it, Alex," Sam snapped. She turned to Alyson. "Don't listen to him. Fake Jane played with him, just like Haight did with you, but I think we have our confirmation Haight is Lizard Boy. These fuckers have had millions of years to perfect their scams. It's not your fault."

Alyson shook her head. "No, it only means he knows what I am. He could have told someone else without realizing the other person is a demon." Her heart sank. "Like Sharon."

"That kills Plan A." Logan wrapped an arm around Alyson's shoulders and hugged her. "What's Plan B?"

As much as she needed the reassurance of his touch, Alyson shrugged off his arm and waved her hands. "I thought we needed to get out there today in order to scout the place. If Haight questions me, I can blame my missed days on the full moon. Like y'all just said, Sharon can't reveal her suspicions without exposing herself."

"Maybe." The glow in Alex's eyes had faded, and he rubbed his chin.

"No, there's no point in a scouting mission if everyone's too tired to do it right," Logan said. "If you and Sarah miss something vital—"

"I'd be more worried *you'd* miss something," Alex murmured before he took a sip of coffee.

Logan huffed. "I'm not the one who decided to be a white knight that night."

"You weren't that far behind—"

"If y'all could stop sniping at each, maybe you could tell me what story you want me to tell Sharon when I call," Alyson said. "She hasn't given me any funny looks, so if she's really a Normal, then Haight hasn't told her what I am."

Alex shook his head. "Or she could be the demon and got all excited when Haight told her a female were was coming to the ranch."

Aaron pushed back his plate. "If this thing's supposed to be a dinosaur demon from another dimension, Sam only knows—"

An outraged expression appeared on the goddess's face. "Hey!"

Aaron continued without batting an eye. "—what microscopic bugs it brought with it." He turned to Alyson. "Be honest with them. Tell them I have no idea what you allegedly contracted two days ago. It's entirely possible our demon will think you had a miscarriage."

Esther handed her a phone. "Since you're supposed to be quarantined with Aaron, use this phone. It's registered to the clinic, so our official business name will show up on their caller ID."

A wave of nausea caught Alyson. Did Sharon know what was hiding at the Sunshine Believers' ranch, or was she an innocent dupe? What if she was actually the demon that had attacked her? Everything she thought she knew about the world had been torn apart by this trip to Tuttle Creek.

Realizing she hadn't really answered Logan's question about Haight's assistant as she took the phone, Alyson looked at her fellow wolf. "Going back to your question about Sharon, I don't trust anyone at this point."

The corner of his mouth quirked. "Smart lady."

She dialed the number, trying not to let her hands shake. The number rang once. Twice.

"Reverend Fred Haight's office, Sharon speaking."

She deliberately hoarsened her voice. "Sharon, it's Alyson Tribideaux."

"Alyson!" The woman positively gushed. "Sarah Goldstein called yesterday. How are you feeling?"

"A lot better, thank you." Alyson shredded her paper napkin. She'd been fooling herself to think she could go back out to that ranch.

"She said it was food poisoning?"

Alyson sucked in a deep breath. "I almost wish it had been. Unfortunately, the vomiting was only the start of my symptoms."

Sharon make *tsk*ing noises. "Maddy said Doctor Goldstein had been exposed to strep and closed the clinic yesterday."

Logan grabbed Alex's legal pad and pen, scribbled something, and held it up for her to read. *He didn't want to spread it. You don't have it.*

"Yeah, he was exposed. He didn't want to spread it around town," Alyson said. Logan wrote some more and held the pad up again. She read the name. "The doctor said some kid named Danny Olsen came in yesterday morning. The Goldsteins spent yesterday scrubbing down the clinic. Apparently, I'm a medical enigma though. He tested me for strep, and that's not what I have. He's not sure what it is. Has anyone at the ranch been vomiting, have a sore throat, unusual abdominal pain, anything like that?" *Pregnant with demon babies?*

"No, no. Nothing like that." Sharon paused. "Are you sure you're okay?"

"Yeah, I will be. It was probably something I caught on the plane to Billings. I was worried I may have passed it on to you or Reverend Haight." Alyson chuckled weakly. "Not the best impression I wanted to make with y'all."

"No, no, we're fine here. We were just worried about you when I took some soup up to Old Man Cole's cabin, and you weren't there."

This conversation was becoming painful in more ways than one. "I'm glad you don't have this. The doctor was keeping me here for an IV with antibiotics since I couldn't keep anything down. Since I'm recovering, he says with another day of rest and meds, I should be as good as new. Can we move our interview schedule to tomorrow?"

"Of course," Sharon said. "Don't fret about it."

Alyson gritted her teeth. "And please tell Reverend Haight I sincerely apologize for screwing up his calendar."

"Really, sweetie, don't worry about it. I assure you he understands." They ended the call, and Alyson's stomach threatened to heave her breakfast.

Esther reached over and grabbed her hand. "Breathe deep."

Alyson did as she was told. The faintest hint of ozone filled the air, and her nausea dissipated.

"Another one," Esther ordered.

Alyson took another cleansing breath. "Thanks." She smiled. "I feel better now." She realized everyone in the kitchen was watching her. Judging her.

"No, we're not," Esther said quietly. "If anything, they know exactly what you're going through." She inclined her head toward Logan, Alex, and Sam before she released Alyson's hand.

The goddess walked over and clasped Alyson's shoulder. "You're going to have nightmares about this for a while. If you don't have anyone to talk to, just yell my name really loud. I'll be there in a flash."

Logan scowled at Sam's words. "Pack takes care of pack."

Alyson shivered and her skin prickled at Papa's words coming out of Logan's mouth. What happened to everything he had said yesterday?

"Down, boy," Sam said. A subtle vibration thrummed through the floor. "I don't plan on making a major lifestyle change."

What the hell was going on between the two of them? A slight whiff of sourness drifted past her nose. Why would Logan be jealous of Sam offering her help?

Logan stared at the goddess for a long moment. "You know what I mean."

"Then don't make me get Emily." Alyson could hear the threat in Sam's voice.

The tension broke at Logan's incredulous expression. "You'd tattle on me to my mom?"

"Would you prefer I tattle to a certain Celtic goddess of the wolfish persuasion?" Sam said archly.

Logan's jaw dropped. "You couldn't."

"You really want to bet your life on that?"

It was all Alyson could do to stifle a giggle. Seeing the alpha nonplussed was the highlight of her week.

On the other hand, Alex didn't bother to hide his chuckle. "Don't ever play poker with her, *mi amigo*. She will call your bluff every time."

Logan's jaw clenched. Alyson could almost see him weighing the various scenarios if he tried to take on Sam. In the end, he inclined his head without taking his eyes off the goddess. "I apologize, ma'am."

"You're a lot smarter than John Lannigan. And you do need to give your mom a call. She worries about you," Sam added.

Logan obviously wasn't sure how to handle the backhanded compliment.

"I meant what I said." Sam squeezed Alyson's shoulder again before she released it. The goddess refilled her coffee and left the kitchen with her steaming mug.

Logan crossed his arms. "I can't believe Mom wanted me to court that woman."

Alex rose and stretched. "Because she knows you need someone to keep you in line." He winked at Alyson as he rounded the table for his own refill.

"What is that supposed to mean?" The pitch of Logan's voice dropped dangerously.

"Don't pull that were shit with me." In comparison, Alex's tone was mild, amused even. "I've known you too long, boy."

"Boy?" Logan's outrage filled the kitchen.

"Since I rode with your grandpappy in the Rangers, yes. Boy." Alex drawled out the last word.

Alyson got the impression the vampire was teasing Logan for her benefit. Things had become too tense between the alpha's bullshit and her own guilt at breaking the cardinal rule of all supernaturals. Alex's technique was working, too. Her skin no longer prickled with her wolf's urge to flee.

She yawned before she said, "I wonder if I can get Sam to teleport me to my cabin so I can sleep while you two destroy Esther and Aaron's house."

"No!"

She jumped at the emphatic word from the four people still present.

"We don't know what the demon's plan is," Alex added.

Her chin tilted. "Sounds like he plans to rape a bunch of supernaturals so he has an army to take out the human gods, Sam in particular."

"You're staying here and getting some sleep," Esther said. "Use mine and Aaron's bed. I've already put on clean sheets."

"I'd really like a shower and clean underwear," Alyson muttered.

"You're more than welcome to use our bathroom," Esther said. "Aaron's going to relieve Bebe and open the clinic while the rest of you grab naps. Sam and I will go up the mountain and retrieve your belongings and some things for Roy."

Alex crossed back to his laptop and tucked it under his arm. "And I'm going to hide in the Goldsteins' basement until sundown, and steal back the money the rogues stole from my master. Get some rest while you can, Alyson. Things will get crazy once Sam resurrects the baby demon."

"Thanks," Alyson said dryly. "That's just the image I need in my head before I go to sleep." She shoved her plate away, her third helping of eggs no longer appetizing.

After Alex closed the basement door behind him, Esther pushed away from the table and stood as well. "Let me get you some clean towels, and I'll check your healed injuries."

Alyson rose and followed the witch. She half-expected Logan to say something arrogant and alpha, but he remained silent as she left the kitchen.

And between the end of the full moon and the ache in her abdomen, she would have bitten him if he had.

One shower and an hour later, Alyson rolled over in the Goldsteins' bed for the umpteenth time. Running all night should have exhausted her, but every time she closed her eyes, the demon who looked like Logan with too many teeth invaded her thoughts. To top it off, her abdomen still ached despite the morphine Esther had given her. Sometimes, supernatural physiology sucked.

She kicked back the covers and got out of bed. A trip to the bathroom only reminded her of the trauma done to her body. She ran her fingers along the scar tissue, from the knife-straight ridge of the scalpel to the jagged tear where the demon had ripped the rest of its way out. She hadn't thought much about pups. The right wolf hadn't come along. But now . . .

Now she felt like damaged goods. If she couldn't protect herself, how the hell would she be able to defend her children?

Aunt Francine had told her to stay away from Logan. Funny how the demon disguised itself to look and smell just like him as a wolf. It knew her deepest desire before it delivered a nightmare version. Despite Logan's arrogant alpha attitude, he wouldn't hurt her. Not like this.

Finishing her business, she washed her hands. No sense trying to sleep. She left the bathroom, strode through the bedroom, and stopped at the door. What could she do?

Everyone else still in the house was probably asleep. It wouldn't help the story she'd told Sharon if Alyson were seen traipsing around Tuttle Creek. Maybe Esther could find something for her to do at the clinic.

Or maybe Sam might be awake. How much did a goddess sleep anyway?

Slipping out of Aaron and Esther's room, Alyson headed for the stairs. Strong ginger said Sarah was in the next room. And if his apple-scent didn't give him away, Roy's snores echoing through the oak-paneled door on the opposite side of the hall would have.

Passing the second bathroom, Alyson stopped in front of the last bedroom. Musk filled her head, a scent that said home and family. Despite her silent admonition to herself, she knocked softly on Logan's door.

He opened it in the space of a breath. Red and black plaid flannel covered his lower half. "What's wrong?"

She drew a shaky breath. "I'm having trouble sleeping."

A faint smile quirked his lips. "Yeah, I hoped for a long time Bebe or

Aaron would develop something that works on us." He stepped out of the way, leaving the decision up to her.

She entered his room. The area wasn't messy like her cousin's sleeping space. His clothes from earlier were neatly folded on a chair. What looked like a state-of-the-art gaming computer sat on his desk. It was the large bookshelf that surprised her.

Crossing to the huge oak piece, she looked at the titles. Computer language manuals and advanced artificial intelligence volumes filled all the shelves.

Alyson looked at Logan. "You're such a paradox. Why are you working at the mill?"

He shrugged. "It fills the time and wears me out so I don't think too much. If you want to talk, mind if I close the door so we don't wake Sarah and Roy?"

The wash of relief that he left the decision to her made it easier. "Go ahead. I just . . ." She faltered, trying to sort out her jumbled emotions.

"Need someone else in the room," he said as he shut the door. "I understand. Sarah and I did that a lot after we—" He raked a hand through his hair, searching for the right words. "After we were rescued."

Logan waved at his rumpled covers. "You take the bed." He stalked to the mattress, knelt and yanked out a medium-sized box. "Just give me a couple of minutes to set up the air mattress."

Alyson watched as he unrolled the plastic and fabric device. "Aaron probably didn't take Sarah sleeping in your room too well, huh?"

"Actually, it was Esther, and she royally objected to us being in the same bed. But it was easier if I was in wolf form for Sarah." He paused and looked at her. "She was raped, too, when we were prisoners."

His form blurred and her throat burned. "She's just a kid," she whispered. She blinked to clear the threatening tears.

"Yeah." He plugged the pump into the wall socket. The machine hummed, and the plastic crackled as it inflated. "But the thing was I needed her just as much as she needed me. No one else . . . understood. Aaron and Esther tried, but—"

"Alex and Sam . . ." Alyson tried to relax her hands when her nails punctured her palms. If she had Sam's abilities, she'd go after her attacker. Rip him from limb to limb. The violence of her thoughts should have frightened her. It had when other 'wolves displayed such attitudes and behaviors. But now, it seemed almost logical.

"Had the support of their coven." Logan flipped off the air pump and unplugged it. "The Goldsteins didn't walk away from Silver Bear. They just needed the space to heal. Aaron and Esther as much as their daughter because they blamed themselves for what happened though it wasn't their fault. Being up here around Normals took a lot of pressure off them."

"What about you?"

Logan grimaced. "An alpha can't show weakness."

He stood and walked over to the chair where his clothes were and grabbed the blanket draped over the back. "Let's get what sleep we can before Sam tries her resurrection stunt. Want to toss me a pillow?"

Again, leaving the choice up to her. He'd made a point of placing the air mattress so it wasn't between her and the door. Alyson swallowed hard. She really hadn't given him enough credit.

She handed him a pillow as he crossed back to the air mattress. Plastic squeaked and air hissed a little under the weight of his huge frame until he settled.

Alyson climbed into his bed and pulled the covers to her chin. His scent coated everything. With a start, she realized she needed more. But would he be willing to give only what she needed?

"Logan?" she whispered.

"Yeah?"

"Would you be willing to sleep with me as a wolf? Just sleep."

He propped himself on his elbows and looked at her. "Are you sure that's what you want?"

Alyson nodded. "Aunt Francine did the same thing for me after my—" She swallowed hard again. The damn lump in her throat wouldn't go away. "After my mother hung herself."

"All right," he said. "Close your eyes."

She did. It wasn't like they hadn't seen each other naked already. But it helped he understood what she was experiencing.

Material rustled, then tendons and bones popped and cracked. A heavy weight landed beside her on the bed.

She opened her eyes. Huge golden ones stared back at her. The panic attack she half-expected at seeing him in wolf form didn't come. Maybe the run had helped more than she realized. "Thank you," she whispered.

He stretched out on his side, his back to her. She rolled on her side as well, snuggled against his fur, and wrapped her arm around his chest. The steady beat of his heart and the sweet smell of canine finally lolled her to sleep.

*Logan?*

The voice inside his head jerked him out of the nightmare he'd been having. "Yeah?"

*It's late afternoon. Sam's ready to try her damn fool stunt. Thought you might like to sit in.* Alex sounded concerned. Far more concerned than he had when they devised the plan earlier. *We're already at the clinic.*

Alyson stirred beside him. "Time to get up? Oh!"

Logan looked at her, then at himself. He was in human form. "Shit!" He yanked the covers up to his waist. He hadn't lost control of his shift in the last couple of years, but he wasn't sure she'd believe him.

*What's wrong?* Alex's alarm didn't help.

"Get out of my head. We'll be over in a couple of minutes."

"I'm not—" Realization dawned on Alyson's face. "Oh, sorry. You were talking to someone else."

"Alex says they're ready to resurrect the demon." At the flicker of unease in her eyes, he added, "You can stay here and get some more sleep if you want."

"No." She didn't look happy, but from the set of her jaw, she would argue if he tried to order her not to come. "We need all the information we can get. Let me get some clothes." She flung back the covers and practically ran from the room.

He just wished he knew if it was his human nudity or the prospect of questioning a zombie demon that bothered her the most.

# Chapter 22

Logan retrieved the corpse from the house's chest freezer. The sun was well behind the mountains when he and Alyson trudged through the snow to the clinic. A sharp, wet edge to the wind said another storm was on its way.

He set the rock-solid body down in the middle of the exam room Aaron had originally used for Alyson. He suppressed a shudder, not from the cold but from the corpse's strange scent. It was definitely not natural.

Logan stepped back and crossed his arms over his chest as he watched everyone else prepare. Aaron and Esther had already moved the smaller equipment out of the exam room, which left Alex and Sam to do the heavy lifting of the bed and non-mobile furniture.

When they finished clearing the room, Sarah drew a circle around the corpse with a piece of silvered chalk while Bebe laid a trail of salt in a much wider circle around the teen and the body. They traded the canister for the stick and repeated their circles. The witches weren't taking any chances.

Once they were finished, Sam stepped into the inner circle, careful not to disturb the chalk or the salt lines. Somehow, her sweatshirt and jeans were gone, and the black coat, pants and boots cloaked her again without her changing her clothes. She sat next to the frozen corpse.

Sarah knelt between the two circles, facing Sam. "Exactly how are you planning to question that thing if its mouth is frozen?"

The goddess shrugged. "I'll warm its head. I've picked up enough elemental magick from Bebe and Ares that I can manage a little heat spell."

Esther shuddered. "I'm still not sure we should be doing this."

"It worked last night," Alyson said.

"For the love of Moses!" Roy snapped. "All of you need to get a grip on your emotions or get the hell out of the clinic. I can't help Sam if you're all freaking out about her performing necromancy. That thing wants her dead, and she's the only calm one in the bunch of ya."

Sam laughed. "Really? So what do you pick up from me?"

"You're peaceful to be around." A bemused smile crossed Roy's face. "There's something there, but I can't quite reach it. Like trying to catch a trout and having it wiggle through your fingers. But it's not wrong."

Her smile was grateful and sad all at once. "Thank you. I think you're the first person who's said that. Everyone else calls me unnatural. Even the supes."

"What do we supes say?" Alex asked as he carried in Aaron's office chair. The doctors' consensus had been it would be easier on Roy's still-healing ribs. According to Esther, the old man had thrown a fit when she tried to heal him earlier. Apparently, he told the witch to save her strength for someone who really needed it.

In some pretty colorful terms.

Logan chuckled. "That we don't consider Sam 'natural' because she smells like a cross between Twinkies, a three-day dead whitetail, and Esther's Revere Ware pans."

Alex set down the chair well clear of the silver and salt rings. "No, we don't consider you edible, which isn't necessarily a bad thing." He grinned at the goddess. "Every species has their defense mechanism. Yours is not smelling like food."

Sam's chin jutted forward. "Twinkies are food."

"No," the vampire said. "They're sugar, hydrogenated vegetable oil, and BHT. None of which can keep anyone alive for an extended period of time."

"Shut up, Stanton," she muttered, but she didn't sound upset about the vampire's teasing. "Let's just get this done."

Alyson took her position by the covered window, and Logan took his by the closed door. There was no point in locking the damn thing. If the resurrected demon managed to get through Sarah's and Bebe's shields, killed Sam and took out the rest of their little team, a standard-issue door lock wasn't going to stop it.

"Everyone ready?" Alex asked.

After the murmured assents, Sarah flicked her fingers and muttered under her breath. Bebe's casting wasn't as dramatic, but definitely as effective. Nothing else happened that Logan could see, but ozone burned his nose and made his eyes water.

As she had last night, Sam pulled a scalpel package out of her pocket. She drew the blade across her wrist and let a few drops fall into the corpse's partially open mouth. However, this thing wouldn't simply shake itself and have a conversation as the rabbits had last night.

*Mother Wolf, please let them be right that the frozen body would inhibit any attacks the demon planned.*

Sam cupped the corpse's head, her fingers spread to cover the maximum amount of skull surface. The filmy eye closest to Logan blinked, and he nearly sprouted fur. Resurrecting bunnies was one thing. This went beyond normal.

The demon hissed.

Sam smirked. "Really? That's the best insult you can come up with?"

It said something else.

Sam's eyes narrowed. "In my language. If you're going to threaten the people in this room, do it so they can understand you."

"You will all feed my lord when he comes," the demon hissed.

"And what about you? What are you little minions eating?"

"You."

It jerked in an attempt to lunge at Sam. It slipped between her palms and hit the tile floor. Momentum spun its frozen body in slow circles. Logan couldn't stop his chuckle when the demon realized it couldn't move and started cursing in his own language again.

Sam reached out and caught the stump of its tail on the third revolution and pushed it back to face her again. "Where's your daddy keeping his breeding stock?"

A queer sound came out of it. Logan finally realized it was laughing at them.

"Kill me," it said. "I am not afraid of death. I will not tell you anything."

"Do you realize you're already dead?" Sam leaned closer. "While you may not recognize me, and you may not be afraid of me yet, you will be. I can torture you and bring you back over and over again until you tell me what I want to know."

"I know what you are, abomination," the demon spat. "And it doesn't matter. I will tell you nothing."

"Where is your lord breaking into this world?"

Silence.

"When is he planning to come through the dimensional crack?"

Silence.

"How many of the elder demons remain in this plane besides your father?"

Silence.

Something wasn't right. Logan examined the circles. Checked Sarah and Bebe. Everything looked right. He never pretended to be the smartest man in the room, but something was definitely off. It went beyond the dino demon's lack of cooperation.

His eyes met Roy's.

"Sam!" the old man called.

"What?" she snapped.

"It's up to something—"

With a horrendous *crack*, the demon's body snapped in half. Tentacles shot out through the fissures and flexed, shattering the frozen sections of the corpse. One tentacle whipped out and wrapped itself around Sam's neck. Others snatched the bits of frozen phalanges with talons and slashed at the struggling goddess.

Gray wisps floated out of Sam's coat, and resolved into the two ghost rabbits. They nipped and scratched at the tentacles, but they barely made a dent in the demon.

From the look on Sarah's face, Logan realized what she was about to do. "Don't drop—"

Too late. She scuffed her salt and silver chalk circle. The inner shield fell.

The demon didn't hesitate. It seized the teen by the throat. Her face went from pink to purple as she fought to breathe.

"Bebe?" Alex shouted.

The witch winced as the demon beat against her shield with its unoccupied tentacles. "Blood!"

A horrified expression crossed Esther's face. "No!"

Aaron seized his wife and pulled her away from the battle. Even Roy scrambled out of his chair and joined them in the corner.

"On it!" Logan took off for the lab. Alyson followed. He skidded around the corner and charged toward the special refrigerator unit.

"Does it matter what type?" Alyson asked.

"No." He checked the labels. "But no sense depleting the rarer blood types." He snatched three of the bags labelled as type "O" and shoved them into her hands. "Take these to Alex. He'll tell you what to do."

Her eyes widened. "Where are you going?"

He slammed the fridge door shut and pushed her back toward the hall. "I need a tool. Be right back."

Once outside, Logan ran at full speed. It didn't matter if anyone in town saw him. If they didn't contain this demon, everyone in Tuttle Creek could die.

He vaulted over the Goldsteins' backyard fence and raced for the actual tool box. With his ax firmly in his grip, he ran back to the clinic.

Inside, Alex and Alyson finished pouring blood from the bags in a circle around Bebe and her salt and silver chalk circle when he entered the room.

"I'll grab Sam—" Alex started.

*No! Leave me in here. Get Sarah and Bebe clear so I can kill it without killing them, too!* Sam's nails were longer, sharper and a totally different color than they were at the beginning of this asinine episode. As fast as she lopped off demon tentacles with her silvery talons, more waving green-gray appendages sprouted from the demon's body, and the determined monster kept her pinned against the shield on the opposite side of the circle as Sarah.

Logan met Alex's gaze. From the grim set of the vampire's mouth, he didn't like the plan.

"I'll pull Bebe out. Can you two free Sarah?" Alex said.

Logan looked at Alyson. "I'll cut. You grab. Don't smear the blood circle."

She gave a sharp nod and straddled the crimson line.

He lifted the ax. "On one," he said. "Three, two, one."

At the last syllable, Bebe dropped her shield. Alyson snagged Sarah by the waist and leapt backward, drawing the tentacle around the teen's neck taut. Logan swung his ax.

Black blood spurted and sizzled against his exposed face and arms. He'd spilled hydrochloric acid on himself once, but the demon blood burned a million times worse. Someone yanked him away from the flailing tentacle, Alyson from the musky scent.

"Clear!" At Alex's shout, a black diamond shield sprang from the blood circle. Bebe jerked her hand back as if she been burned by the blood as well, but she was well out of the splatter perimeter.

Logan blinked, but no, he hadn't gotten demon blood in his eyes. He could actually see the magickal half-circle. Vague shapes struggled inside, but he couldn't make out details.

Alyson unwrapped the writhing tentacle from Sarah's neck and tossed it aside. It continued flailing where it landed. Black blood still oozed from the cut, and the acrid odor of melting linoleum filled the air.

Bebe muttered something under her breath. A fireball flew from her fingertips and enveloped the appendage. Before the fire alarm had time to activate, it turned to ash amid the warped sections of tile it had touched.

Something screamed inside of the translucent shield, a high-pitched metal-on-bone sound that nothing human could have made. White light flashed followed by blast furnace heat. Both were gone the moment the heat registered against Logan's burned skin.

So was the shield.

Sam and the ghost rabbits sat in the middle of several inches of ash. She started coughing, which turned to dry heaves, and she doubled-over. Liquid metallic gold dripped from her ears. One of the ghost rabbits gently nudged her knee while the other hopped over to Sarah.

"Sam?" Alex knelt by her side. "You okay?"

"No." She belched. The odors of sulfur, rotten meat, and snake filled the room. "The bastard stuck a tentacle down my throat to suffocate me. I need to vomit, but nothing's coming out." She straightened and rubbed her chest. "I must have incinerated the part inside me when I blasted it."

"How do you feel?" the vampire asked.

Sam's expression shifted from disgust to sheer surprise. "Full. For the first time since I died, I feel full." She looked at Alex. "That sounds incredibly gross out loud."

He cocked his head. "There's something dripping from your earlobes."

The goddess reached up and dabbed at the substance. "Aw, shit. I just accidentally melted the earrings I borrowed from Tiffany."

Alex chuckled. "Your sister-in-law is going to kill you."

"Tell me something I don't know," Sam said sourly.

"Stop it, Alyson." Sarah's voice drew Logan's attention to the women on the floor beside him. The teen pushed the kneeling were's hands away from her, sat up, and rubbed her neck. "I'm going to have the hickeys from hell, but I'm fine."

"Let me be the judge of that." Aaron crossed the room and crouched beside his daughter to examine her injuries. Sarah suffered through it with an eyeroll, which seemed to relieve Alyson.

She rose and stood beside Logan, touching an unburnt section of his arm with her shoulder, needing the reassurance from an alpha that everything was indeed all right.

And it was until Esther spat, "You used blood magick." The emotion on the witch's face was a combination of disgust and horror as she pointed to Bebe.

"Technically, I didn't, but I sleep with a vampire and can belch the Hebrew alphabet," Bebe said. "Any other of my bad habits you'd like to discuss?"

"You asked for the blood, and she did use it!" Esther jabbed her finger in Sam's direction. "It's immoral and you know it!"

"No one was sacrificed," Sam said. Another loud burp released more obnoxious smells. She rubbed her chest some more. "They were technically voluntary donations, and for me, a blood circle is far stronger than anything else I could use." She climbed to her feet and tried to brush the ash from her jeans. Her weird clothes had disappeared once again.

Esther's hand rose as if she were about to cast a spell.

Alyson stepped between the two women. "Stop it, Esther! She saved your daughter's life."

"You and Logan saved her—"

Logan went to Alyson's side and faced the enraged witch. "Which we wouldn't have had to do if Sarah hadn't broken her circle."

"Hey!" the teen croaked.

"He's right, kid." Sam sounded tired as she stepped to Logan's other side to eyeball Sarah. "What part of not-breaking-your-shield-no-matter-what did you not understand?"

The teen batted her dad's hands away and climbed to her feet. "But it was going to kill you!"

Sam crossed her arms. "It didn't matter. I'm already dead, Sarah."

"I want you out!" Esther's shrill scream pierced eardrums. "Out of this clinic and out of this town!"

Logan shook his head. "What do you think's going to happen if Sam leaves? Or did you not notice what was done to Alyson? What do you think the demon's daddy will do if it gets its claws on Sarah?"

"It'll follow her," Esther spat, pointing to Sam.

In the nearly four years he'd spent with the Goldsteins, he'd seen Esther joyful, frightened, and pissed as hell, but she'd never been out-and-out illogical. "So why has it stayed here in Tuttle Creek all this time instead of heading to Vegas?"

The witch's mouth open and closed a couple of times before she finally said, "Blood magick is forbidden."

"To witches," Bebe said quietly. "And for a reason. Sam's not one of us."

Esther glared at the lady doctor. "You've done it before." A statement, not a question.

"Yes." Bebe lifted her chin. "My own, in self-defense when an eclectic my cousin hired was trying to kill me. I won't apologize for that."

"And you were going to do it now."

Bebe folded her arms as well. "To save your daughter from a demon. And as Sam said, the blood was freely given."

"For medical—"

"Stop it!" Logan slashed his hand through the air. "Enough, Esther! All bets were off when the rogues that kidnapped me and your daughter aligned themselves with those things." He jabbed a finger at the pile of ash. "If you have a problem, then report it to your high priestess."

As he expected, her outrage disappeared. Coven politics had never been Esther's strong suit.

She shot a nervous glance at Bebe. "Maybe I . . . overreacted."

"Really?" He cocked his head. "It wouldn't possibly have anything to do with Bebe being Ziva's granddaughter, or were you planning to hold the blood magick over Ziva's head during the next election?"

Esther's jaw dropped, and her cheeks burned bright red.

By then, Aaron had stood as well, and he also stared at his wife. "I really hope that's not what you were planning to do, honey."

Her husband's accusation seemed to shake Esther out of her indignation. "I would never—"

"Then either call Ziva now, or shut the fuck up while we figure out our next move," Sam said.

"One question, first." Bebe gestured at Sam, then the pile of ash. "Did you see anything unusual when you killed the demon?"

Sam frowned. "No, but I—" She crouched and traced her fingers through the fine gray particles. "I had a face full of ash so I couldn't have seen the hooks or teeth or whatever they are. But there's no dimensional scarring here either."

"Dimensional scarring?" Logan asked.

Sam sat back on her haunches. "There're marks on our penthouse balcony in Las Vegas and on the pavement in front of the Augustine mansion in Brentwood. They're like . . . wounds on reality. In both cases, Bebe Saw something reach through and tear apart the souls of the dead. In Vegas, it was an eclectic witch who worked for Selene Antonius, but the two men in California were Normal."

She stood. "And we know the guys in California were members of the Sunshine Believers."

"What about the women and fetal corpses y'all found in Seattle?" Logan pointed at the ash pile. "Was there this . . . dimensional scarring?"

"No." Sam shook her head for emphasis. "All of the women were reported as missing. None of them had any connection to the Sunshine Believers."

Alex stepped closer to Sam. "Unfortunately, only gods can see the scarring. Ares said he didn't see similar scarring in Nazca because the area had been sealed from invasion by the Incan god of death centuries before. It's looking more and more like Selene's eclectic who tried to kill Bebe in Vegas was connected to the Sunshine Believers somehow."

"This is a demon death without any accompanying human deaths." Bebe hugged herself. "It's not a good comparison." Logan felt sorry for the petite witch. Whatever she had witnessed years ago still haunted her.

"Actually, it is." Alex nudged Sam with his elbow. "This confirms our half-baked theory, but I still don't get why the Old Ones only consume the souls of the human worshippers."

The goddess grimaced. "Because they need servants, and wouldn't you trust your own kind instead of the damn dirty apes who took over your planet?" Sam turned to Logan. "How late is that diner of yours open? We're both going to need some food while the doctors take a look at your face and arms."

"This doesn't excuse using blood magick," Esther spat.

"Drop it, honey," Aaron said. When she opened her mouth, his eyes narrowed. "I mean it. We have bigger problems than a little blood magick."

Roy shuffled between Esther and Alyson. "Last Buffalo is open until eleven. Um, just to make sure I didn't have a stroke during all the excitement, does anyone else see ghost rabbits hopping around the room?"

# *Chapter 23*

Alyson pulled into the diner's parking lot and cut the engine of Logan's Jeep. She had been a little surprised he'd insisted she be the one to drive while he stayed at the clinic, especially since the first flakes of the next promised storm floated through the air, but it was a good thing he stayed behind. A shudder racked her body at the memory of the awful burns on his face and lower arms despite werewolf accelerated healing.

And he needed more food for that healing to kick into the next gear.

"You okay?" Sam looked concerned under the glow from the diner's neon sign. "I knew Bebe should have looked you over before we left."

"I'm more worried about Logan," Alyson sheepishly admitted. "I managed not to get demon blood on me or Sarah during the fight."

"You did good back there." Sam smiled. "You're definitely not the hothouse flower you pretend to be. Besides, once you two are healed and you've had some time to process, things will get back to normal in the bedroom department—"

Heat rushed through Alyson's skin.

Sam's smile faltered. "Ah, shit. I stuck my size tens in my mouth, didn't I? I'm sorry."

"We're not mated." Alyson wanted to wince at her prim school teacher tone. She sounded just like Mom and Aunt Francine.

Sam exhaled loudly. "Again, I'm sorry for poking my nose where it didn't belong, but—" She looked down at her lap for a moment before she met Alyson's gaze once again. "Logan's a good guy, he's a friend, and he does like you. A lot. Please don't break his heart."

Alyson stared out the windshield. Was that why he agreed to let her sleep in his bed this afternoon? So he had a chance to seduce her?

No, she was second-guessing herself and him again. Logan had been embarrassed over his unconscious shift this morning, the male were equivalent of a wet dream, especially in an alpha. She'd been the one who insisted he lay in the bed with her after her own freak-out.

It had been totally different when he slept with Sarah. He looked at the teen as a little sister, but Alyson had known damn well he was attracted to her when she pushed him into sleeping in the bed with her.

"I was starting to like him, too, but—" Her fingers tightened around the steering wheel. "Things happened, and . . ."

"There's nothing for you to feel guilty about, Alyson."

She jerked and stared at the woman beside her. She still couldn't quite wrap her head around what Logan said Sam was, even after what she'd seen the blonde do. "Did you read my mind?"

"No." Sam tapped the side of her nose. "My snout is as good as any were's, and right now, you reek." She shook her head. "If anything, you're with a group of people who collectively understand what you're going through."

"D-did they do to you what they did to Sarah?"

It felt like time stopped around the Jeep. Outside the windshield, glittering snowflakes hung in mid-air. Even the twilight seemed to pause for breath.

"No," Sam said quietly. "They only killed me." Her own guilt shivered in her low voice and tainted the air in the cab.

"I'm sorry." Alyson wrapped her arms around herself. "I shouldn't have asked."

"No, you have every right." Sam released a deep breath and stared at the diner. That exhalation jumpstarted time again. Flakes landed on the Jeep hood and melted. "In fact, you have every right to blame me. I should have done more to hunt down the bastard after what happened in Seattle—" She rubbed her eyes.

"You're right. It is your fault for not tracking down this demon." When a shocked Sam stared at Alyson, she added, "But unless you can time travel, there's nothing any of us can do about that. The question is what are we going to do to fix it."

The goddess slowly nodded. "Okay, first we pick up the food, then we brainstorm while we eat. There's got to be a way to set me up as bait to draw him out."

They climbed out of the Jeep. Alyson steeled herself against the potential hubbub as they walked to the front door, except the Last Buffalo Diner was nearly empty when they went inside. Lois took their order and warned them it could take a bit.

"Roger started cleaning up the back," the waitress added. "With the weather folks saying tonight's storm could hit blizzard conditions, everyone's staying home. I'll bring some coffee and pie out while you gals are waiting. Good to see you feeling better, Ms. Tribideaux." She winked before she headed for the counter, yelling their order as she went.

Sam frowned. "I thought gossip traveled fast in Los Angeles."

Alyson chuckled. "I haven't been here a week, and I can tell you these people are tight."

"We gotta be." Lois set down two ceramic mugs and filled them. "We depend on each other. A lot more than you folks on the coast give us credit for." She eyed Sam while she placed the little pitcher of cream on the table.

Thankfully, the only two other people in the diner waved for their check. Otherwise, Lois would be lucky to only find herself at the receiving end of a goddess's tongue lashing.

"Geez," Sam muttered once the waitress stalked off. "It's not like I asked for a triple mocha." She ripped open a packet of sugar and dumped the contents into her mug.

"Every community has its own personality," Alyson said. She added some cream before she blew on the surface of her coffee and took a sip.

Sam continued pouring packets of sugar into her coffee. At ten, she poured some cream into her mug and stirred the mixture.

Alyson propped her elbow on the table and her chin on her palm as she watched. "How do you not get sick on that much sugar?"

Sam gulped down half her coffee before she answered. "Right now, I'm trying to get the taste of this afternoon's barbeque out of my mouth." She belched and made a face. "Excuse me."

A whiff of sweet coffee and burnt demon stained the air. Alyson clinched her fist to keep from waving her hand in front of her nose, Mama's lecture on rudeness in the back of her mind.

Sam winced. "Sorry. Maybe you should have left me at the clinic."

Alyson checked, but the party at the other booth had left and Lois talked with the fry cook as she plated today's pie special. Her attention returned to Sam. "It's better that you came with me. Esther . . ."

"You have no idea why she freaked out, do you?" Sam asked.

"Not really." Alyson grimaced. Yet again, Papa keeping her in the dark about the other supernaturals may have put her in danger.

Sam glanced over her shoulder at the Normals in the diner. When she looked back at Alyson, she lowered her voice. "Witches have a major taboo against blood magick. Using life force in a spell amps up the power. A witch can do some pretty awful shit if they sacrifice, which is the reason for the prohibition. In theory, your own blood or volunteered blood is okay, but some witches think even that crosses the line."

Alyson sighed. "Let me guess. Esther's one of them, even though we did what we had to in order to destroy the demon. Is that why Bebe lied to her?"

Sam squirmed in her seat. "Damn you weres and your noses."

Lois set the slices of apple pie in front of them.

"Thanks." Alyson smiled at the waitress until she was out of hearing range before she glared at Sam. "Well?"

"She didn't lie. Exactly."

"Has she sacrificed an animal or a person?" Alyson lifted her mug.

"No. She did, um, use my blood one time to take out some zombies."

Alyson set the warm ceramic right back down without taking a drink. "Zombies?"

"Yeah." Sam rolled her eyes and cut into her slice. Steam from the apple filling shimmered and faded. "Everybody told me they weren't real, too, until they showed up at my sister-in-law's bachelorette party."

Alyson took a drink of her coffee. Definitely TMI from the goddess. But she would have been prepared for this level of weirdness if Papa and Aunt Francine had been straight with her, and not their overprotective selves. She was more in danger of the depression that claimed her mother than in danger from other supernaturals.

And dinosaur demons from another dimension didn't count.

She set down her mug again. "Your blood had to have given Bebe's magick a major jolt compared to a regular person's."

"Not really," Sam said around a mouthful of pie. "This happened a couple of months after I died, so I was still closer to being human than what I am now. Not to mention, Bebe's pretty powerful in her own right. She only took what was already smeared on my face from cuts on my cheeks. But it was necessary, and at the time, we didn't know what I was becoming."

Alyson shoved her plate toward Sam. "Go ahead and eat mine. This conversation is destroying my appetite."

The goddess paused in her chewing. "What did I say or do wrong?"

"It's not you. It's—" Alyson glanced out the window. The snow fell thicker. "Old family shit." She looked back at Sam and tapped the edge of the plate. "Seriously, the pie's yours. I need some protein, not sugar."

"Thank you." Sam stacked the plate on her empty one and dug into the second piece. "You're saving a life."

"Pie isn't saving—"

"I 'old a widdle whide wie," she mumbled before she swallowed the bite of apple and crust. "It's not just the taste of burnt tentacle. Sugar keeps the hunger under control."

"So I wouldn't like you when you're hungry?" Alyson knew the pop culture joke sucked, but it kept the tears at bay.

Sam poked at the remaining pie before she faced Alyson. "If I don't eat, constantly, I'll make the demon look like Sunday brunch at Café De-Monde." She shoveled more apple pie into her mouth.

Alyson shifted uncomfortably in her seat. When she was twelve, she'd been unable to control her shifts. What she was had scared the shit out of her, even though she'd known what was coming. But here she was, blaming everyone else for their lack of control when deep down, she blamed herself for being the demon's victim.

Maybe it was time to take some of her own damn control back.

"We need to take the fight to the ranch," she said quietly. "We can't put the people in town at risk."

Sam's right eyebrow rose. "Tonight?"

"Will the demon be expecting it?"

The goddess took another bite of apple pie and chewed slowly. "We still don't know how many other demons they may have up there."

Lois waved and placed their sacks on the counter.

"Finish your pie," Alyson said. She slid out of the booth and stood. "We need to plan a reconnaissance mission after all."

Logan tried to sit still on the examination table in a different room of the clinic while Bebe treated his chemical burns. While he'd rather have the healer, Aaron had been preoccupied with dragging Esther away from the scene of the alleged crime. She was still ranting about the blood magick.

Never in a million years would he have believed Esther was that anal, but he suspected her anger had more to do with the danger to Sarah than Bebe and Sam using blood magick. The Goldsteins should have been furious with him for backing their daughter's decision, not screaming at his guests who had saved Sarah and Alyson's lives.

"Ouch!" Logan glared at the petite doctor as she dabbed some kind of cream over what was left of his skin on the top of his right forearm. "I swear you're a sadist, Zachary."

"And alpha wolves are always the biggest babies," she calmly replied.

"It would help if I could get some more food." He looked longingly at the tray Sarah had brought from the house. No more mozzarella sticks or potato skins remained. Neither did more beef jerky sticks appeared amidst the wrappers Alex was gathering and tossing in the trash.

"The girls will be back soon," the vampire said.

"Not soon enough," Logan grumbled.

"Quit bitching," Alex snapped. Even the doctor looked at him with a raised eyebrow.

Logan wanted to kick himself. While he was wallowing in self-pity for putting Sarah in danger, Alex had been shoveling out his own barn of shame.

Logan glanced at the doctor, but she shrugged and resumed slathering her concoction over his burns. "It's not your fault, Alex," he said.

The vampire slammed down the wastebasket filled with cellophane. "We should have pursued him back in Peru. Esther has every right to be pissed because we don't clean up our own damn messes."

Bebe whirled to face Alex and jammed her fists on her hips. "If you're going to blame someone, blame me. I'm the one who convinced Caesar not to kill his sister when she showed her true colors."

"Stop it, you two!" Logan glared at both of them. "I'm bitching as a coping mechanism. My shrink will be the first one to tell you that."

Both the witch and the vampire looked at him with surprised expressions, but the irritation crawling under his skin spurred his mouth to continue running. "But all this self-blame and recriminations will get us nowhere. We've got to find this thing and put it down along with any other babies it has conceived."

The door eased open. Delicious odors preceded Sarah's head poking around the corner. "Is it safe to come in?"

"Yeah." Logan smirked. "I'll keep 'em on short leashes."

"Well, you folks weren't quite as loud as Mom and Dad." She kicked the door open, revealing another baking sheet filled with French bread pizzas. "The first two roasts will be done in twenty minutes." She crossed the room and set the tray on the spot Alex had cleared on the counter.

"Is your mom calm yet?" Logan asked as she handed him a piece with extra pepperoni and cheese along with a napkin.

"Nope." Sarah shook her head. "Which is why Roy is trying to talk some sense into her and Dad's cleaning up the mess in the other exam room."

"I'll go help," Alex said. A slight breeze blew through the room at his speed in leaving. Logan half expected the door slam. Instead, it closed with a quiet *snick*.

He shook his head and whistled before he bit into the bread.

"You've never seen him this upset, have you?" Sarah asked.

"Nope," he said around the mouthful of chewy dough and tangy sauce. He eyed Bebe as he swallowed. "How'd you talk Augustine into not killing his twin? A conversation with a master his age is like speaking to a mountain. Alex didn't tell me all the details."

Her jaw shifted, and she was silent for so long he didn't think she would answer him. Finally, she exhaled. "She'd just killed their brother Ptolemy because he tried to protect me. Caesar . . ." Her voice faltered, and moisture filmed her eyes. "His eyes turned scarlet. Have you ever seen a vampire in the throes of a blood rage?"

He shook his head.

"I have," she said quietly. "If he had killed her that night, he wouldn't have stopped killing." She sighed. "And he wouldn't have been able to live with the shame of murdering a member of his biological family even if she did deserve it. I thought I was saving him. Saving his sanity. All I did was get a lot of people killed, just in a multitude of other ways."

The tears she'd held in finally escaped.

Sarah rounded the exam table and pulled the weeping doctor into her arms. "It's not your fault. You tried to do the right thing."

"She's right, Bebe," Logan added. "Selene made her own choices. Just like Giovanni did by joining with these dinosaur demons. And I'll say it again. Blame doesn't fucking matter anymore. We need to find a way to take these bastards down before anyone else dies."

The savory odor of beef hit him an instant before Alyson's sweet southern accent. "That's just what I was telling Sam at Last Buffalo's." Alyson walked in with two full plastic bags in each hand.

The zombie goddess was similarly loaded down with the addition of a plastic cooler. She frowned as she took in the scene. "Bebe? Was Esther rude again?"

The doctor gave a weak laugh. "No, and I'm fine. I let the stress get to me."

Sam didn't say anything, but her expression remained concerned.

Alyson held up her bags. "Why don't we take the burgers to the break room so we're not trashing the one usable exam room?" She looked at the tray of French bread pizza slices remaining on the tray, then at Logan.

He shrugged. "I'll bring them."

Sam sniffed at the air. "Any of cheesy bacon potato skins left?"

Logan grinned sheepishly. "You're a little too late."

"Greedy," she muttered, rolling her eyes. She pivoted and headed down the hallway. "Alex! I brought you blood!"

Logan hopped off the exam table and grabbed the tray before following Alyson. "Thanks for making the protein run."

She glanced over her shoulder, a wry smile curving her lips. "Caring for an injured packmate is one of the few things my family taught me."

Alex and Aaron came out of the bigger exam room. The vampire yanked off the surgical mask he wore. "We'll wash up and meet you in the break room."

"You two okay?" Logan asked.

Aaron slid his mask down from his nose and mouth. "Yeah. We didn't want to chance breathing the demon dust after what its body fluids did to your skin."

Logan nodded, and he and Alyson continued down the hall. "We should take some burgers and slaw over to Esther and Roy," he whispered to her.

"I'll do it," she whispered back.

Sam looked up when they entered the break room and whispered, "You don't have to take a bullet for me, Alyson."

Logan laughed.

And immediately stopped at the inferno that burned across his right cheek.

"You." Sam pointed at him, then at a chair. "Sit. Eat."

"Would you like me to roll over and beg?" He wanted to scowl at her, but his face hurt too much. "Play dead?"

"You already look like you're playing dead," the goddess sniped back. She pulled out most of the contents in one of the bags and placed the various wrapped burgers, onion rings, and pie slices on the table. "I'll be right back." She grabbed the bag and winked out of the room.

Shaking his head, Logan sat on the chair Sam had indicated. "I'm never going to get used to that."

"Tell me about it." Alyson took the seat next to him and slid over three of the burgers. "She went to Las Vegas and back while I was driving to the clinic after we left Last Buffalo. Freaked the shit out of me." She glanced at him while she unwrapped a sandwich. "You sure Esther won't hex Sam?"

Logan wanted to laugh, but between his pain and her naiveté, he swallowed the humor. "If Esther tried, she'd end up blowing up herself, Roy, and the house."

A frown marred Alyson's features. "Blow up the house? You mean Sam would, right?"

"Shit, your family really kept you in the dark, didn't they?" More irritation crawled along his nerves with the first twitches of an itch, and he couldn't scratch. "It's a wonder you haven't gotten yourself killed out of ignorance."

"Excuse me?"

"I'm insulting your parents, not pissed at you." He ripped the first hamburger into small chunks. "Different types of magick can interact violently. If you have a witch and a fae throw spells at each other, it's more likely to kill the respective casters. From what I understand, deity power acts under a similar principle, but the deity is more likely to survive the magickal backlash. And Mother Wolf help any innocent were or Normal who's in the way if the magick users get that stupid."

"What if a witch attacks another witch?"

He shrugged. "No different than a were challenge. Whoever's smarter, faster—"

"Stronger," she said sourly before taking a bite of her burger.

"More determined," he finished. "There's a reason my mom's the alpha in San Antonio. It isn't always about size and strength."

"Says the huge alpha werewolf." But there was a glint of humor in her eyes.

"Who was smart enough to avoid the demon blood spatter?"

Sam flashed back into the room. "And who's not healing because he isn't eating?" She looked at Alyson while she grabbed the cooler. "Have you told him about your idea?"

Alyson swallowed. "Not yet. We're waiting for Aaron and Alex to clean up. I didn't want to repeat myself fifty times."

"Understandable." Sam crossed to the fridge and shoved the cooler inside.

Logan flicked his attention between the two women while he popped the tiny bites into his mouth as fast as he could chew. The motion of his jaw stretched his skin painfully, but there was no way around the problem. Well, there was a way. However, his gut said Aaron and Esther would need every bit of their healing gifts before this whole mess was over. No sense wasting that power on some burnt skin that would heal by itself in the next few hours. Faster if he could take a proper bite of meat.

The goddess grabbed another chair at the table and plowed through a half dozen double bacon cheeseburgers before the men entered the room, followed by Sarah and Bebe.

Alex eyed Sam. "I didn't hear an explosion."

She grinned. "Esther thought about it for a couple of seconds until Roy pointed out the blast radius would take out the entire town. Also, I swung by Las Vegas and picked up some dinner for you."

"Thanks," the vampire said and headed for the fridge.

"Sorry, Sam," Logan said. "I didn't realize she'd go that apeshit over using donated blood."

"Don't sweat it." The goddess turned to Alyson. "Floor's yours."

Pink tinged her cheeks when all eyes turned to her. "Well, uh, Sam and I were talking at the diner." She sucked in a deep breath. "We should go to the Sunshine Believers' ranch tonight, find the demon, and kill it."

"That sounds more like revenge," Aaron said. "Besides we're not sure who the demon is in its Normal form."

"It's Haight. It's got to be."

"Why?" Alex leaned against the counter while the microwave hummed beside him.

"Something Roy said my first morning here. Haight went out of his way to make sure his people did not cause trouble." She dragged a fry through her ketchup. "Every other alternative religion I've met with has had some problems with the locals. They range from snubs and insults to violent personal acts and property destruction on both the local and the alternatives' sides." She shrugged. "It's just human nature. But according to Mayor Newlin and everyone else I've talked to, the Sunshine Believers have had no problems since they moved to Tuttle Creek." She threw down the fry. "I guess I wanted to believe they had changed for the better."

Logan rested his hand on her arm. "There's nothing wrong with looking at the good side of things."

"But Alyson has a point," Sam said. "The Sunshine Believers had similar issues in Los Angeles. They ranged from local kids trespassing on the Believers' property to a Believer knifing one of the neighbors who complained about the noise level."

"How do you know?" Sarah asked.

"I witnessed Jessie Alton's kidnapping by the Sunshine Believers four years ago," Sam said. "I did the research on them for a follow-up story that was nixed by my editor."

The ding of the microwave punctuated Alex's laugh. "Damn, I'd forgotten what a pain in the ass you were back then."

"Pain in the ass?" Logan looked at Sam before returning his attention to Alex. "I seem to recall us sitting in someone's basement four years ago."

"This was before. Sam had a nose for supernatural shit back when she was a Normal." Alex grinned at the goddess as he pulled out his mug of blood. "She drove a good chunk of the Augustine enforcers crazy, but Ralph said he needed her."

"Wait a minute!" Sam glared at him. "Was I getting cover stories as bribes to keep me from the juicy stuff?"

Alex shrugged. "Can't vouch for O'Malley's incentives, but I do know you got too close to outing David Head as a witch back in the day."

"Thanks for the self-esteem boost." She glared at the vampire as she crammed an onion ring in her mouth.

Alyson cleared her throat. "The other thing I've noticed is the lack of fear in his followers."

"What do you mean?" Bebe examined the different pies before she took a slice of cherry.

"A lot of times, a splinter religious group has a fear of the outside world, or a fear of its own members' disproval—"

"They're a cult," Sam grumbled. "Let's call a spade a spade."

"That's just it." Her stomach growling, Alyson seized a couple more burgers. Despite Aaron and Esther's efforts, her body must be still dealing with the trauma from the baby demon.

As if in response to his thought, Logan's face itched like crazy. He reached for his cheek, only to have Sam slap his hand down.

"No scratching," Bebe ordered.

Alyson continued as if she hadn't been interrupted. "The Sunshine Believers interact normally with the townspeople, as if they consider themselves part of Tuttle Creek along with the non-members. And for the most part, everyone likes them. Carol at the general store couldn't say enough good things about Maddy. Wade at the feed mill did the same for the boy who works there—"

"And when Alyson and I were at the ranch, they let us talk to everybody!" Sarah interjected. "Except the people in the windowless cabin!"

"I've had my people reviewing missing persons reports for the last four years," Alex said. "So far, there's no links to Haight or anyone else at the compound."

"What if the people aren't missing?" Alyson said.

"What are you saying?" The vampire frowned.

And when Alex frowned hard enough lines appeared on his unaging, immaculate forehead, Logan knew he wasn't going to like what he was about to hear.

"I really do think the primary demon is Haight." Alyson laid down her burger. "The entire compound could be his offspring, and maybe the reason no one's been reported missing is because the baby demons have already taken their place."

# Chapter 24

Alyson held her breath. The urge to squirm in her chair was overwhelming with everyone staring at her.

"And you want us to go in there tonight?" Logan tossed the burger he'd been eating onto its wrapper. "When the entire compound may be full of these demons?"

"Well, we did say we wanted to keep the number of supers involved to a minimum," Alex said dryly.

Alyson glared at Logan. "You yourself said that besides you and the three Goldsteins, the closest supernaturals were the Wellingtons in Billings."

"And they are . . . ?" Sam prompted around a mouthful of hamburger and pickles.

"Vampires," Alex said. "Relatively quiet. Pay their taxes. Have never caused any trouble since they joined Augustine Coven a little over a century ago."

"Unless the demons have kidnapped Joni Wellington and done the impossible by impregnating her, what other supernaturals could they have used?" Alyson waited for Logan to contradict her. "More likely, Haight may have sired a girl from a single rogue supernatural and used that child to breed more demons."

"Eeeew." Sarah stared at Alyson, then her half-eaten container of coleslaw. She set the plastic container on the table. "Watching incest on *Game of Thrones* is bad enough."

Alyson shrugged. "Keeping it in the family is the only way I know of to keep his breeding attempts quiet."

Bebe nodded thoughtfully. "And maybe the reason he attacked you was to speed up the process. By the time René reported you missing, it would be too late."

"Alyson's probably right about a female rogue being used." Logan looked at her. "Any supernatural who came to town during the last couple of tourist seasons was with a group, and they left with their group."

"What about those hikers you mentioned?" Alyson asked.

"The ones who died in last spring's freak snowstorm?"

She nodded.

Logan frowned. "They were the only ones reported lost, and their bodies, their very Normal bodies I might add, were accounted for. You're the only solo female super who's come to Tuttle Creek since we moved here."

Alyson shrugged. "And I planned on being here for a month." Bebe was right. She literally set herself up to be attacked. No pack nearby. No one she really knew or could depend on in Tuttle Creek.

Oh, hell. Even if her pack were here in Montana, they were sorely outmatched by the dinosaur demon.

"You can count on us to be your pack for now," Sam mumbled around an onion ring. "How often do you call your family when you're on the road?"

Alyson frowned, not following the goddess's logic. "Why?"

Sam waved her hand, obviously forgetting she held a cheeseburger. Logan stifled a chuckle when a pickle flew out. With his vampire reflexes, Alex used the trashcan to intercept the slice before it hit the floor.

"Well, to use me and my brother as examples—" She swallowed her mouthful of protein. "When we're working on a big story, we don't talk to anybody for days—" Another wave of the cheeseburger. "Or weeks at a time. Do you work that way? Was your pack expecting contact from you before you left Tuttle Creek next month?"

Alyson made a disgusted face. "I wish I could have that much time alone. If I don't call either Papa or Aunt Francine every day or two—" Her eyes widened. "Mother Wolf! I haven't called either of them since the second night I was here."

"Will your pack show up to look for you?" Logan asked. The last thing he wanted, the last thing they needed, was trouble with René Tribideaux.

Alyson looked at the ceiling, giving his question serious consideration. Her gaze settled on him, and she frowned. "He might. I told Francine I'd met you."

Logan groaned. "This is not good."

Alex chuckled. "Only for you."

Sarah looked around the group. "Someone want to explain to me what the hell is going on."

"Later," Bebe said. She laid a hand on Alyson's arm. "If you don't want to talk to them yet, you don't have to. A lot has happened to you over the last two days."

"If I don't, they may show up." Her fingers tapped a rapid rhythm on the tabletop. "I'll call Papa. Francine will hear it in my voice that something's wrong." She glanced at the wall clock. "And with the time difference, I should do it now."

When she pushed away from the table, Sarah followed.

"I think I can walk over to your house and get my phone by myself," Alyson said dryly. Good grief. Now, she had babysitters in Montana, too. But a little quirk of fear reminded her it was dark outside. With the current snow, not even the moon shone to reveal danger.

Sarah cocked her head. "Under normal circumstances, I'd agree with you whole-heartedly. But these aren't normal circumstances, and none of us should be anywhere alone for the time being." She glanced at Logan. "Not if these things can look like any of us."

He nodded, but it was more like approval that the teen was using her head.

After a moment's hesitation, Alyson said, "Okay."

Logan cocked his head and watched Alyson sashay out of the break room. She really didn't realize the sensuality she naturally exuded. Nor did she argue or fuss over Sarah's suggestion.

He shook his head, amazed at her reasonableness. "Maybe there's some hope for that woman after all."

Bebe and Sam exchanged looks before Sam reached over and smacked the back of his head.

He rubbed the spot on his skull. "Ouch! What was that for?"

"For acting like an idiot," Bebe said.

"And staring at her ass behind her back," Sam growled.

He looked at Alex and Aaron, expecting some support.

"Sorry, man. You're on your own." Alex walked over to the sink and started rinsing his cup.

Aaron merely shook his head, grabbed Sarah's discarded coleslaw, and began eating it.

Maybe it was best to face whatever the women thought he'd done wrong. "How'd I act like an idiot?"

"You need to keep your emotions in check around her," Sam snapped. "After what she's been through, she needs some time to deal. I could feel your emotions. What do you think is going to happen if she smells your attraction?"

"Really?" Bebe leaned back in her chair. "I would have gone with his mistake of not escorting her back to Goldsteins' house."

Logan wasn't sure if the itch he felt was his healing skin or his over-loading brain. He clenched his fists to keep from doing anything stupid. "So one of you thinks I should give her more space, and the other thinks I'm not close enough. Any other tidbits of relationship advice you two want to share?"

Bebe acquired greater interest in her burger. Sam murmured, "Fine. We'll stay out of it."

"Good." He started ripping apart another burger, wishing to Mother Wolf the sandwich was the dino demon who had assaulted Alyson.

## *Chapter 25*

*Maybe there's some hope for that woman after all.* Logan's words still burned Alyson's ears even after she'd settled on Sarah's bed and punched the numbers to call Papa. She'd been thinking of the teenager being vulnerable outside, which was why she hadn't argued. But obviously, he still thought of her as a pack princess.

Of course, he did. She hadn't fought off her attacker. Her vision blurred.

Papa's phone rang once. Twice. She swiped her eyes and took a deep breath.

"Alyson?"

For the first time in her life, she heard hesitation in his voice. "Hi, Papa."

"Are you all right?" The hoarse question made her sit up straight.

"I'm fine. I'm . . . sorry I haven't called the last couple of days."

"You've been spending time with Polk." His words were more accusation than statement. So Aunt Francine had told him about Logan anyway.

This snippiness? This she could deal with much easier than everything with the dinosaur demons and their plots.

"Yes, I have," she snapped. "I've been spending a lot of time with all the supernaturals up here in Tuttle Creek. Witches, vampires, and—" She hesitated about what to call Sam, but it wasn't like the problems between her and the fae were that big of a secret. "—a goddess. By the way, thank you very much for the lack of education. I'm lucky these people are nice. I've stuck my foot in my mouth plenty due to your desire to keep me ignorant."

There was a sharp intake of breath at the other end of the line. "I did no such thing! I taught you what you needed to know to be a good mate!"

"A good mate?" She laughed, a harsh, bitter sound. "You're all worried about Logan Polk ravishing me, but guess what? He's not interested. He thinks I'm a dumbass bitch who couldn't find her own tail."

The soft padding of Papa pacing his office stopped. "Did he insult you? I'll challenge him—"

"You will do no such thing," she hissed. "The problem is he's right. This is the twenty-first century, Papa, not the eighteenth."

"Alyson?" His conciliatory tone grated along her already raw nerves. "Why don't you come home? We can discuss the situation. If you want a bigger role in pack leadership . . ."

She rubbed her lower abdomen. While the pain had faded with appropriate food, her scar felt tight and itchy. Part of her wanted to run home. Away from the pain. Away from the terror. But deep down, her wolf needed to see the destruction of the demons.

Even more, she wanted the respect of Logan and his friends. The earlier insult had hurt, but not as much as a total dismissal of her efforts would have.

"What I need is some time to figure out what I want, Papa," she said softly. "Alone. I may not call you or Aunt Francine for a couple of weeks while I do that."

"What am I supposed to do without an heir?"

She winced at the plaintive whine in his voice. Tears formed at the realization she didn't truly respect her own father.

And she'd never be able to follow him again.

Alyson swallowed the large lump forming in her throat. "Etienne has always been a good beta to you. Ask his advice. You know he'll be honest with you."

"Well, uh, then, give your aunt a call when you're settled. She misses you." Another hesitation. "We both do."

"I love you, Papa."

"We love you, too."

She thumbed the "End" button. To her surprise, the expected flood of tears didn't come. Maybe because she'd finally gotten what she had always wanted. Her freedom. She forced her fingers from her itchy, freshly healed skin. The price for her freedom had been steep.

Maybe too damn steep if one of her new friends died in the coming battle.

At the soft knock, she yelled, "Come in!"

Sarah poked her head into her room. "You okay?"

"Yeah." It was an effort to smile, but she did so for the teen. "Nothing that hadn't needed to happen for a long time."

"Mom's slicing the roasts," Sarah said. "Thought you might want some." She made a face. "Roy's got her calmed down enough that the group's reconvening here. They've got a tentative plan."

"Let me guess," Alyson said dryly. "It involves you and me babysitting Roy."

"Nope." The girl grinned. "That job is going to the Normals."

Centuries ago, one of the International Council's first laws had been that supernaturals were not to knowingly reveal their existence to the Normals. Considering the number of subsections outlining exceptions to that very law, Logan had always thought it was a bullshit rule. Marvin Newlin proved him right.

Sort of. While the librarian's delight that people even more different than him lived so close, his questions were snapping everyone's last nerve.

"Why can't everyone just pour salt in front of our doors and windows like the hunters do on *Supernatural*?" The librarian waved a manicured hand. Tonight's nail color was a glittery olive green.

"Because this isn't a fucking TV show, and these aren't Christian demons," Sam snapped.

"Well, actually, he's right about that part. We do use salt circles, Sam." Bebe bit her lower lip, probably in an effort not to laugh.

"Whatever!" Sam threw her hands in the air.

Carol leaned forward in her chair. "Can we spread road salt around whatever building we use?"

"Absolutely," Aaron said. "But it'll probably kill the grass."

"What about using the city truck to spread it?" Tad looked absolutely serious. "Will that affect your spell? Does it have to be a perfect circle?"

Bebe let loose her laughter. "Yes, no, and as perfect as possible."

Marvin waved a manicured hand. "But if they aren't the demons we learned about in Sunday school, what are they? How do we kill them?"

"Dinosaur demons are ancient, pissed-off primal entities," Alex said. Since his promotion to Augustine's chief enforcer, he'd been acting more and more like his predecessor, Duncan St. James. It was a little creepy. "Our only saving grace is that the last one has been interbreeding with humans, which means the younger ones can be killed by conventional means."

"And the daddy demon?" Tad asked. The mayor's skin tone matched his brother's nail color, but without the glitter.

"He's our problem." Sam's index finger circled to indicate the supernatural contingent.

"The high school gym would fit the town's population, but how are we going to get everyone there?" Carol asked. The proprietor of the general store frowned. "Especially with a storm like tonight's?"

"We tell them the truth," Logan said. Everyone turned to stare at him.

He shrugged. "Well, as much of it as we can. We have a serial killer wanted in the United States and Peru sighted in the area. A special team's been sent in to track him down."

Tad groaned and buried his face in his hands.

Marvin shook his head. "Sweetheart, that's just asking for trouble. Every man, woman and child in Tuttle Creek will want to haul out their semi-automatics and join the hunt."

Logan held up his hands. "I'm open to other suggestions."

"I hate to say it, but I think Logan's right." Carol held up her hand when Marvin opened his mouth. "That also means we have armed guards at all the entrances into the high school, the folks with the coolest heads in a crisis. Everyone knows Roy and the Goldsteins. We just make sure they also know the rest of you by sight so we don't have any accidents."

"That actually sounds pretty good." Logan scratched at his healed cheek, and Sam slapped his hand again. Rather than getting mad at the goddess, he glared at the diminutive lady doctor. "Dammit, Bebe. Have the balls to tell me to stop scratching, instead of having Sam hit me."

The witch grinned. "I didn't have to tell her anything."

Tad lifted his head. "What do these critters look like when they're not in human form?"

Logan cleared his throat. "They, uh, look like velociraptors."

"Like Steven Spielberg velociraptors?" Marvin stared at Logan.

"Yeah."

Carol shook her head. "So Doc O'Connell wasn't joking about those being dinosaur tracks in the snow up at the meadow?"

"No, he wasn't, but these things can shapeshift into anything else they want," Logan said. "The daddy demon made himself look like me to get close to Alyson."

"So how are we supposed to know who's really our neighbor?" Tad asked.

Marvin waved glittery fingers. "We mark everyone. I still have metallic-toned Sharpies we used for signs from the elementary book festival." He grinned at Sarah. "We can do those stylized 'T's on the backs of everyone's hands."

The girl nodded enthusiastically. "And we still have the ash from the demon we—" She glanced at the goddess. "Well, Sam incinerated. I've got a spell that could act as a demon detector."

"Something else to remember," Bebe interjected. "We have rogue supernaturals that have joined forces with the demons. So it won't be just demons who may come after us."

"Us?" Tad's thick black eyebrows drew together to form a single line across his forehead. "You're not going with Logan after the daddy demon?"

"Sam, Logan, Alyson and I will check out the Sunshine Believers' ranch. The witches and Roy will stay here and help guard the town." Alex met each person's gaze. "Any complaints are fine, but I want an alternative plan if you need to bitch."

The mayor straightened, and the smoky scent of his irritation drifted through the Goldsteins' living room. "Who made you boss?"

"I'm the most experienced lawman you have in town right now." Alex's eyes glowed neon blue and his fangs extended. "If you don't want our help—"

"Yes, we do!" Carol shot Tad an ugly look. "Some people let their dicks get in the way."

"Alex, honey, your dick can get in my way any time." Marvin's remark poked a hole in the building tension, and almost everyone laughed.

"I think my wife would have something to say about that," Alex said. He grinned and the neon glow faded from his irises.

Sam stood. Her clothes melted and reformed into her familiar calf-length coat. "I'll retrieve some more appropriate ammo from our safe. Then the rabbits and I will patrol the outskirts of town until you get everybody at the high school." Air popped when it rushed into the space she had been standing.

"Rabbits?" Tad's eyes met Logan's. "Was she talking about wererabbits?"

He grinned. "No. She's a death goddess, and these are her ghost bunnies, but I highly recommend you never call them 'bunnies' in their presence."

"Ghost bunnies, huh?" Tad rubbed his lower jaw. "Maybe I shouldn't have had that second Coors after dinner."

# Chapter 26

Alyson trotted beside Sam. She was pretty sure the goddess was going at a slow clip for her sake. Sam sure as hell wasn't affected by the heavy snow or fierce winds. In fact, flakes seemed to whirl past her.

On the other hand, Alyson had to shake the accumulation off her back and head every few hundred feet despite the heavy cover of the Aspen pines.

Sam had teleported them only part way to the compound. Not even she wanted to risk a jump directly into the Sunshine Believers' territory. Not without scouting how many demons there were.

Instinct said lizards wouldn't be out on a night like this. Neither would birds, rabbits, or even the normal wolves who roamed up from Yellowstone. This was the type of night where only monsters tread.

Another shudder rippled through her that had nothing to do with the cold or the snow or the wind.

Sam looked over her shoulder. "Am I going too fast for you?"

Alyson shook her head. Something tickled the inside of her brain.

*You sure? We can stop for a breather.* Sam's voice, but the goddess's lips didn't move.

Alyson stopped in mid-stride. How the hell was she supposed to respond?

*Just think at me.* Sam's teeth gleamed in the shadows. *Sorry, I've gotten used to talking to the Los Angeles 'wolves telepathically. I forgot how little the eastern packs and covens work together.*

*It's weird,* Alyson admitted. *If you could extend your shield or aura or whatever you call it so it's around me, too, I'd appreciate it.*

Sam's gaze turned inward for a moment. The abrupt silence after the howling wind left Alyson's ears ringing. She shook herself to rid her coat of the remaining snow.

"Is that better?"

*Yes, thank you.*

The rest of their trip could have been a walk in Jackson Square. Now that she wasn't ducking her head against the wind, she realized Sam wasn't breaking through the surface of the snow. A woman of her height and build without snowshoes should be floundering through knee-deep drifts.

Like Alyson was even though she was on four feet.

One more thing Papa declined to inform her of.

The trees thinned out as they neared the compound. Alyson followed Sam as a precaution, but how anyone could see through this storm was beyond her.

They approached the windowless building at the rear of the compound, and Sam held up a hand. Alyson dropped to her belly and crawled closer to get a better look.

Maybe it was the blizzard raging around them, but she couldn't spot any lights from the dorms or main facility. Had the compound lost power?

*I don't think so.* Sam indicated the power lines going into the building in front of them. *I can still feel electricity pulsing in the wires.*

*The plan is still you kicking in the door?*

*Yep. Remember, no biting. Ready?*

Alyson nodded. Adrenaline crackled along her nerves.

They ran. Sam's flying kick took out not just the door, but the door-jamb and a few concrete blocks as well. She landed in a crouch.

Alyson skidded to a stop beside her. The place reeked of sandalwood and blood. It was completely empty except for the pile of Normal corpses in the middle of the building.

She edged forward and sniffed. They hadn't been dead long. She jumped back when she recognized the first face.

"Who was she?" Sam whispered.

*One of the Sunshine Believers. Her name was Erin. She was the third person I interviewed here. She lost her job, her home, and her kids.* Disbelief drowned out the adrenaline rush. Alyson's gaze swept the pale, still faces. *They are all Sunshine Believers.*

"Shit," Sam muttered. "We're too late."

*Where are all the lights?* Logan asked. *Even with such an intense storm, we should have a glimpse of lights through the windows.* Sam had dropped Alex and him southwest of the compound while the ladies approached from the opposite direction. He glanced toward the valley below where streetlamps twinkled through the driving snow. *Town hasn't lost power yet, and the transformer for this side of the mountain comes through their substation.*

*Something's not right.* Alex's mental voice held an edge of concern. *I'm not picking up anyone. Not even animals.*

With the storm at Logan's back, he couldn't pick up any scents either. *No animals. They don't have livestock. They're vegan.*

He felt rather than heard Alex's grunt over the howling wind. *So are cows*, came the vampire's grim reply. *What about pets?*

A chill ran through Logan that had nothing to do with the howling wind and driving snow. *I don't recall seeing any.*

*Let's go.*

His words launched some awful thoughts in Logan's head. What if the Normal folks here were nothing more than a demon's first food?

With no cover from the tree line to the main building, they had no choice but to run for it. His paws pounded against frozen soil and dead grass, the wind having scoured the field bare of snow.

For now anyway.

They reached the front doors. One hung at and awkward angle by its top hinge. The wind slammed the broken left door into its partner over and over again. The sharp metallic scent of blood puffed out of the building with each bang of the wood. There wasn't any other sounds coming from inside.

Alex drew the firearm he had concealed under his coat. *On three.*

*No.* Logan shook his head. *How many times do I have to tell you I'm a lower target profile than you?*

Blue eyes gleamed in the dark. *Fine, but don't blame me if you're gutted by those raptor claws.*

Logan let his wolf part take control. When a sharp gust seized the broken door, he slipped through the gap. The wood slammed extra hard behind him. Dim illumination shone farther in the building. No flickering and the lack of smoke indicated it was artificial.

He crept past the foyer and coat closet, staying close to the wall. Broken shards from the mirror and a decorative vase littered the hardwood floor. Drops of dark blood stained everything. A little tickle in the back of his mind said Alex was watching through his eyes.

Logan reached the entrance to the fossil room and peered around the corner. The low lighting for museum-style displays was still working, as were the underwater lamps in the diverted creek bed. With nothing to stop the cold from rushing through, the ferns were already wilting and ice had formed on the rocky edges of the artificial waterway. Fish bones lay amid a pool of ichor that dripped into the creek.

A blood trail too large for the dozen or so fish led from the bones through this room before taking a turn down the hallway toward the dining area. Something else came from that direction. The sickly-sweet odor of fresh death.

Air whistled past his ear as Alex joined him. *I've got your back.*

Logan eased across the room, once again staying close to the wall. More debris littered the hallway. A discarded sweater. Torn papers. A broken chair. Dents and holes marred the drywall. The carpet under his feet was damp. He bent closer and sniffed. Creek water and Normal urine.

He edged around the corner. The scene that greeted them was straight out of a modern horror movie. Or from a much older period in supernatural history.

A pile of bodies lay in the middle of the dining room. He trotted closer to the grotesque sight while Alex kept an eye on the other entrances.

Avery stared at Logan with unseeing eyes from the middle of the pile. From the grotesque angle of the kid's neck, he'd probably died instantly.

Logan's gaze swept the other corpses. He recognized a few of the other faces. All of them members of the Sunshine Believers. The head of one woman tilted back, and he peered closer. She had been the one shooting him ugly looks when he had lunch here with Sharon the other day, but it was the fang marks where her carotid artery passed under her skin that sent a worried chill through him.

*Alex? I don't think demons were the only thing they were making up here.*

The vampire joined him. "Shit. Sam!"

Brilliant white light blinded Logan an instant before the percussive shockwave knocked him into the pile of corpses.

# Chapter 27

Sarah winced as more voices joined with Abner Little's protests. The cacophony echoed off the Tuttle Creek High School's gymnasium ceiling. She gave up trying to focus on the spell she'd started to cast. The magick sputtered and died. Even Marvin paused in drawing a "T" on the back of Uma Willis's right hand and stared in the direction of the podium the mayor had placed on risers.

"Dammit, Tad! Yer not tellin' us the whole truth!" The rancher waved his bandaged arm like a banner. "If there's killers running around, then we should be out on four-wheelers and snowmobiles, looking for these bastards!"

"You don't have to worry about a damn serial killer, Abner," someone in the crowd yelled. "You'd flip your snowmobile and do the job yourself."

Most of the townspeople laughed, but more than a few shot worried looks with their family and friends. Everyone quieted down when Roy climbed to his feet and stomped over to Mayor Newlin's podium. As ornery as the old man could be, the people of Tuttle Creek respected him.

"You want the truth, Abner?" Roy's glare swept the crowd before he focused on the rancher again. "You play like you're clumsy as hell, but you've got a death wish. You have since your twin brother died in that flash flood when you were eight."

Abner's jaw dropped. Sarah gasped. A murmur ran through the crowd. Was that Roy's plan? Blackmail the town into staying by telling their secrets?

"If you think getting yourself killed will solve your guilt, it won't," Roy continued. "And what're Tessie, Nora, and your daddy going to do if you succeed? They depend on you. They need you."

Abner's mouth closed, and his ears burned red. Roy's gaze swept the crowd, daring someone to say something.

One of the high school girls raised her hand.

"This ain't a classroom, Paula," Roy snapped. "Spit it out."

"Why's Mr. Newlin and Miss Carol drawing on us like they're bouncers stamping us when we go to a club in Billings?" She looked around the gym. "Everybody knows everybody in town."

"The powder the Goldsteins and their doctor friend are brushing on will glow in the dark if we lose power." The wind rattled the roof as if to emphasis Roy's statement. "That way if someone manages to sneak into the school, the guards can tell, and we don't have to worry 'bout shooting one of our own. Any other questions?"

The crowd remained silent. It was eerie. They couldn't be quiet even during the moment of silence during the Memorial Day observance at the town cemetery.

Sarah exchanged a look with Marvin. The librarian shrugged and resumed drawing on the hand of Mrs. Willis, one of the elementary school teachers. The babble picked up a little bit as people discussed Roy's proclamations. No one seemed to notice his little white lie. The abundance of glitter in Marvin's markers made the "T"s sparkle under the fluorescent lighting, which added a semblance of truth to Roy's words.

Picking up the make-up brush she'd donated to the cause, Sarah brushed a bit more ash on the back of Hannah Willis's hand. She concentrated, and a bit of scarlet magick swirled and sank into pale skin.

The six-year-old smiled shyly. "Thank you. How long will my hand glow in the dark?"

Sarah returned her smile. "Probably just for tonight."

Hannah's expression faltered for a second. "Would you do it again for my birthday next month?"

Sarah leaned close to the little girl. "I bet I can do something even better for your birthday." Her statement triggered a huge smile on Hannah.

Across the basketball court, Carol and Bebe sat at another table borrowed from the high school's lunch room/study hall. The grocery store owner's "T"s didn't have the flourish that Marvin's did, but the fancy lettering wasn't what mattered. The magick did, and even Mom had to agree that the baby demon's ash had come in handy.

Sarah glanced at her parents at the opposite end of the gym from Mayor Newlin's podium. Since Mom's healing abilities weren't as strong as Dad's, she did the spell with the powdery ash in case Dad was needed if they were attacked and ended up with casualties. With the grimace twisting Mom's lips, someone else would think she was upset about being dragged out of her warm bed.

The real problem wasn't three witches casting over four thousand tiny spells. The problem was four thousand-plus spells together would be like flashing the bat signal to whatever prowled the frigid night.

Luckily, Logan's boss, Wade, didn't ask too many questions when Mayor Newlin instructed him on what to do with the town's salt truck. He had given the mayor the side-eye and a shrug, but he did as he was asked.

Sarah cast the detection spell on the last of the Willis family. The floor pads for the wrestling team had been set up in one corner along with sleeping bags to give the littlest kids a place to sleep. Someone dimmed the gym's lights, and a hush fell among the adults and older children.

Sarah rose and stretched before she slung her backpack over her shoulder. "I'll meet you at the student entrance in a bit."

Marvin nodded and collected their things. As she headed toward the principal's office, a group of teens took over the table to play a card game.

The administration offices were the closest to the center of the salt circle Wade laid around the high school. As she passed the building's main entrance, the three guards let the owner of the feed mill owner and Ed McCrory inside and relocked the doors.

"Tell your dad I did just as he told me," Wade said to her as they passed each other.

Sarah saluted. "Will do." They'd find out immediately if he hadn't laid the salt properly across the sidewalks coming in from the three parking lots, but Wade was a straight-shooter. If he said he followed Dad's directions to the letter, then everyone in Tuttle Creek could bank on the fact that he had.

And they were banking on his word.

With their lives.

Sarah sighed as she reached for the handle into the admin offices. Too bad they didn't have enough silver to add an extra layer of protection around the school.

The outer office was terribly quiet. No cheerful clatter of keyboards. The industrial-size scanner/copier stood silent. No constant buzz from the phones. She crossed the room and tried the principal's office door.

It opened easily. Mayor Newlin had been on the ball. She flipped on the lights, eased the door shut and took stock of the area as she dug into her backpack.

The principal's desk would have to work for their makeshift alter. She pulled out four cloth-wrapped bundles and set them on the wood veneer. First, she moved the computer to a long, low filing cabinet. Clearing the paperwork and office supplies off the surface took a matter of seconds. It took a lot more time and man-handling, but she shoved the desk into the middle of the office and aligned it with the compass she retrieved from her backpack.

She unwrapped the small jar candles and placed the appropriate colors at their corresponding cardinal points on the desktop. It wasn't as formal a set up as she preferred, but as her shrink had said, her perfection issues came from trying to regain control of her life again.

A shiver took her at the memory of her captivity years ago. *It's just the pressure of this situation.* But her internal admonishment did nothing to diminish her anxiety. It had been months since she'd thought about her rapists. Just from the tips and tricks she'd picked up from Bebe over the last couple of days, if she had five minutes with those assholes today . . .

Her parents burst into the principal's office. Mom's expression was apprehensive, fretful. Dad appeared far more determined.

Sarah reached for her backpack. "I'm almost ready."

Mom twisted her wedding ring back and forth around her finger. "This isn't right, Aaron."

"Honey, we can't just do nothing—"

Sarah slammed the fingersticks on the table at Dad's placating tone. "Quit whining, Mom."

"Sarah!" Dad stared at her.

Mom gasped.

Sarah glared right back. She clenched her fists to keep her hands from trembling. "Is this what you two did when I was kidnapped? Nothing, but complain. Did you even try to find me?"

Dad stepped between her and Mom. "You're out of line, young lady."

Old anger froze into clarity. "No, Dad, Mom was when she bitched out Bebe and Sam. You're both still trying to make things the way they were before I was kidnapped. When I was all about fluffy rainbow unicorns and shit. In all these years, you haven't taken what our therapist said to heart."

Sarah sucked in a deep breath and forced her fingers to relax. "You can't keep treating me as a child. And Logan and I can't keep hiding up here. I-I thought if I went to school, he'd go back out into the world and find his mate. But now—"

She waved a hand. "Everything got fucked up again. What happened to Alyson is way worse than what was done to me. If we don't do something, bad things are going to happen to the people here. And Mom—" Her mother's tear-filled eyes almost made her heart break. The last thing she wanted was to hurt one of the people she loved most in the world. "We're not going to stop these demons by playing it safe."

Mom's throat convulsed. "I-I know that."

"Do you really, Esther?" Bebe Zachary stood in the doorway, her expression nearly as sad as Mom's. "Because if your heart and soul isn't in this spell, it's going to fail, and your friends and neighbors will die."

Mom took a shuddering breath. "I know that, too, Doctor Zachary."

Sarah circled the desk and pulled Mom into a hard hug. Mom's grip on her was equally tight.

When they released each other, Mom brushed Sarah's hair away from her face like when she was little. "Let's do this before I lose my nerve."

With two water dominant witches and two fire dominant witches, they had a quick discussion of placement. It made sense for Dad to take blue and Mom green, but the last thing Sarah wanted was to annoy a high priestess's heir.

Bebe laughed when Sarah expressed her concern. "You do realize I have to know all the elements because of my position. I'll take air because we want our best shield caster with the element she's most comfortable with."

Curiosity overrode Sarah's awe of the woman. "You almost sound like you don't want to be a high priestess."

"Never did." Bebe summoned a flame and lit her candle. "The only reason I'm White Rose's named heir is because we're still on the hereditary system. But my cousin Alice is dating a very nice accountant from her father's company, so I'm keeping my fingers crossed we have a huppah and a baby soon." She grinned. "Not necessarily in that order."

Mom and Dad lit their candles before he turned off the overhead fluorescents. The light from the four candles gave the dark, windowless room a cheerful glow. Sarah could almost forget why they were doing this.

"Wait." Dad glanced at the fingerstick he'd picked up before he stared at Bebe, his eyebrows drawn together. "Are you sure about this? After what you said about the dinosaur demons using blood magick?"

Bebe sighed and stared at her own fingerstick. "Sacrificial blood magick." Her gaze met each of the Goldsteins in turn. "We're not sacrificing anyone or anything. All we're doing is reinforcing our own spell with our own blood. I wish I could guarantee the results, but I can't. Sam's been talking to all the other death gods, but no two experiences with the Old Ones has been the same."

"What if the other gods are lying to Sam?" Mom asked softly.

Bebe's curls bobbed when she shook her head. "They aren't. They're kind of like Dorothy when the Wicked Witch threatens her in The Wizard of Oz. The death gods will see everything else in the universe die before they do because of what they are. They don't have a reason to lie to one of their own."

"Then let's do this." Sarah picked up her fingerstick and poked her index digit. The sharp pain faded, and blood welled black against white skin under the flames. She inscribed the symbols for protection around her candle on the desk.

A glance said Mom was doing the same while Dad and Bebe waited for her to finish. And leave it to Mom to produce a handful of disposable antibiotic wipes when she was done.

Once they had cleaned up, they joined hands though Bebe had to seriously stretch across the desk as short as she was. Dad led the spell, and Sarah could feel the magick collect around them. Wade had done as he said from the resonance thrown back by the salt crystals surrounding the high school.

When Bebe spoke the last words, their combined energy sped outward from the principal's office. The salt caught, shaped and contained the magick, and the brick, wood and plaster of the building thrummed with power.

Bebe breathed what could have been a sigh of relief. "All right. Two down. Let's get to our positions."

"Have you heard from Alex or Sam?" Mom asked tightly.

Bebe smiled despite Mom's curt words. "They'll yell once they know something definite."

Sarah grabbed her backpack. "Holler if you need me." If those two were going to get into a fight, she didn't want to be around.

"We're not fighting," Mom and Bebe said at the same time.

Sarah waved a hand. "Whatever." Secretly, she was glad she'd thought it loud enough for them to Hear. With their combined spell, it would be hard to keep things private while it was active, but if Mom got her hackles too high, the shield could collapse.

Then the demons would turn the residents of Tuttle Creek into an all-you-can-eat buffet.

Marvin, Wade, and Ed stood at the exit to the student parking lot when she turned down the dark corridor. Snow reflected the ambient light from the safety lamps in the lot through the glass and steel door. The result was illumination brighter than usual at this time of night.

The men were intently discussing something in low voices. As she got closer, she had to bite her lip to keep from laughing at the subject matter.

"I don't get how a man can go that long without getting some ass," Ed said plaintively. "I couldn't last a week—"

Wade elbowed Ed sharply in the ribs when he spotted Sarah. The rancher immediately shut up and shuffled uncomfortably. Marvin handed her duffle to her as she dropped her backpack to the floor.

"I take it they don't want to talk about getting women in bed around the sensitive teen girl," she said dryly.

Marvin grinned. "They're just pissed I won the town betting pool concerning the delectable Mr. Polk's orientation."

Sarah pulled out her compound bow and quiver of arrows and set them aside. "You tried to tell them."

"That I did," the librarian replied smugly.

She reached into the duffel and pulled out a wide-mouth jar full of liquid and a cup-sized sieve.

"What the hell is that stuff?" Ed asked while she unscrewed the cap.

"It's a silver nitrate solution." She pulled her arrows out of the quiver and retrieved the box of latex gloves.

"What the hell is coming after us?" Ed cocked his head to watch her dip the sharp hunting tips into the bluish liquid. "Werewolves?"

"No, the werewolves are on our side," Sarah said.

"You're shitting us." The rancher spat snuff into his empty soda can.

"Not tonight." She shook the excess drops from the arrows into the jar. "Marvin, unload your clip and bathe your bullets." She kicked the box of latex gloves over to him. "Make sure you use the gloves, or your beautifully manicured hands will turn black. Once your reloaded, Wade and Ed can do theirs." She handed the jar and the tiny sieve to Marvin, who set them aside and donned the gloves with record speed.

"So Abner was right." Wade changed places with Marvin by the door. "There's stuff Tad wasn't telling us."

She peeled off her gloves and stuck them in a plastic shopping bag she fished out of her duffel. "He didn't want a panic."

Wade's eyes narrowed, and his nostrils flared. "What's really going on, Sarah?"

She met Marvin's gaze as he swished the sieve with his bullets in the silver nitrate.

"Your man Alex wanted shooters who can keep their head in a crisis." His attention returned to his task. "They need to know."

Sarah sighed. Telling Normals went against everything her parents had ever taught her, but the men needed to know what to shoot at.

"We facing at least one demon." She sucked in a deep breath at the shocked looks on Wade and Ed's faces. "And possibly some rogue vampires."

"Don't we need crosses and holy water and shit like that?" Ed said.

She shook her head. "The only thing the movies got right is a stake through the heart, but I don't recommend getting that close. Shoot them. Silver nitrate won't kill a vampire, but it will slow him down. It's best if you get a heart shot the first time. Otherwise, the only way to kill them is to chop off the head, and frankly, if you're that close, you're dead."

"And this demon?" Wade crossed himself even though there wasn't a parish for miles and he definitely wasn't Catholic.

Sarah shoved the dry arrows back into their quiver and stood, slinging the strap across her chest "Logan, Ms. Tribideaux, and two of Logan's friends are tracking the demon. If he comes back here, let me handle him."

Ed frowned as he accepted the jar from Marvin. "Them arrows of yours aren't going to do shit if those vampires are as fast as they are in the movies, much less a demon." He traded places with Marvin and yanked the clip from his semi-automatic rifle.

"Ed's right." Wade pulled a handgun he had tucked in his waistband. "This will do you better."

"Trust me." She couldn't help smiling. "You don't want me shooting a gun. Logan's been trying to teach me for years. I'm better with a bow, and I've got more than enough fire power at my fingertips. But make sure you dip those bullets, too. Just in case."

The men finished bathing their bullets in the silver nitrate, including their spare clips. Sarah refused to relinquish her spot by the door, much to Ed and Wade's consternation. Thankfully, Marvin backed her up. Her Sight would spot the intruders long before the men's normal eyesight.

Quiet settled even more deeply over the school. The silence before the storm Grandmére would have said.

She wasn't sure how long they waited when light flashed to her right. A series of sharp reports followed by a low rumble set the windows rattling.

"That sounded like an explosion," Marvin muttered. "More than one." He glanced at her, followed by a double-take. "Sarah, your hand."

The stylized "T" he'd drawn, and she'd bespelled, glowed. She looked at Marvin's hand. His mark glowed a faint purple, but the light strengthened the longer she stared. A quick peek showed Ed and Wade's hands glowed as well.

The blasts up the mountain must have been a signal. Shadows emerged from the woods beyond the student parking lot. She shifted her Sight, and her blood froze. Instead of the brick red secondary aura of a mature vampire, spikey hot pink surrounded most of these figures. One silhouette though had an aura as black as Sam's, confirming her modified detection spell, but it didn't bother with a human shape.

And it sure as snow in January wasn't as small as the baby that had ripped its way out of Alyson. Sarah swallowed hard. No, it was easily as tall as her five-six.

"Christ Almighty," Marvin muttered when it got close enough for him to see the lashing tail and odd gait. "You weren't joking."

*Mom. Dad. Bebe. We've got newborn vampires and one dino demon in the student parking lot.*

# Chapter 28

Alyson peered closer at the corpse that had been the vivacious Erin. Glass and plastic were embedded in one of her open eyes.

*Sam, there's a camera—*

She looked over her shoulder at her companion. Sam ran toward her, faster than anything Alyson had ever seen. The zombie goddess scooped her up the same instant Alyson felt the change in air pressure in her ears. Then everything went black, and she was falling. Out of instinct, she flailed, attempting to find some purchase for her paws.

Only to end up with a face full of snow.

She floundered out of the drift, and shook herself. Looking around, she was alone.

And the concrete building she and Sam had been in was nothing more than a pile of rubble and assorted body parts.

Except Sam wasn't here. More explosions thundered across the grounds. The earth and snow shook, knocking her down, and her ears rang.

Air popped. The goddess struggled to keep hold of Logan, who thrashed just as Alyson had. Sam dropped the werewolf in the snow drift, but gently lowered the injured vampire to the ground.

Smoke floated past them. Alyson looked toward the main building. What was left of the complex burned.

She looked up at Sam. *They knew we were coming.*

"No shit, Sherlock." The goddess's eyes glowed so bright they were nearly white.

*Close your eyes!*

"What? Why?"

"Because you'll attract the Abominable Snowman, Rudolph," Alex said dryly.

Sam did as she was told.

Logan scrambled out of the drift and shook himself before he trotted over the vampire. He circled Alex and sniffed the rapidly healing scrapes and burns.

"I'll be fine." He playfully shoved the werewolf away from his face. "And if you keep this up, Alyson will think everyone in town is right about you being in the closet."

Golden eyes focused on her, and she dropped her gaze to the snow. Oh, sweet Mother Wolf, she didn't want to get into this now.

"Alyson's right, Alex," Sam said. She opened her eyes, and they were back to their human blue. "Now's not the time to tease Logan about the town gossip about his sexuality. Someone was watching us. Alyson spotted a web camera inserted in a corpse right before the explosives were detonated. They waited until we were all inside a building."

"Giovanni," Alex growled. He climbed to his feet. Only his clothing showed evidence of how close he'd come to dying along with the former residents of the compound.

Alyson pawed Sam's leg to get her attention, then trotted towards the smoldering remains of the concrete block building. *Can you track the wireless signal from the web cameras?*

The goddess frowned. "Normally, yes, but they were destroyed, and the power lines into the complex went down with the explosions." Her eyes widened. "How many people lived here, Alyson?"

*Sharon said one hundred-twelve. Why?*

Sam tugged on Alyson's fur, urging her to back away from the ruined building. The guys didn't even question Sam. They edged away too though they couldn't possibly see what had spooked the goddess, even through the heavy snowfall.

*Sam? What's going on?* Alyson asked again.

"Sixty souls are being collected. Or what's left of their souls." Sam swallowed hard. "The demon must have tied them to their bodies somehow. Nonbelievers. He used the nonbelievers as food."

"That's not how—" Alex started.

"I know that's not how it works!" The goddess's eyes started glowing again.

Alyson looked at Logan and almost laughed despite the horror of the situation. She was so far out of her depth she automatically turned to the closest alpha. He drew a "V" in the new snow.

Vampires? She'd been sidetracked by the camera forced into Erin's eye socket, but he was right. There definitely hadn't been enough blood for the carnage she'd seen in the former concrete block building. She nodded in affirmation.

*Sam, do demons drink—*

The goddess held up her palm. "Hold it, you two. I can't understand you when you're both yelling in my head at the same time."

Alyson inclined her head to Logan.

Alex frowned. "Fang marks? You're sure?"

The low growl from Logan told the vampire not to question him again.

Alyson stared at the rubble where the concrete building had stood. *What if they weren't guarding vampires here? What if they didn't start making them until a few days ago?* She looked over her shoulder at their little group. *What if they didn't start until the demon attacked me?*

Sam stared at Alex. "I thought it took three days for the virus to complete a Turn."

He stared back at her. "It's like a Normal pregnancy. Three days is the average. It could be shorter or longer."

*What if they started right after Sarah and I packed up for the day last time we were here?*

As one, the four of them whirled toward the valley.

Lights in the town twinkled through the falling, blowing snow. Alyson counted silently to five before those lights disappeared.

Not all the lights. Flashes of orange sparked around the high school.

In her mind, Bebe said, *Guys, I think we found your demon.*

# Chapter 29

Marvin raised his rifle the instant the parking lot and the night lights in the school's main corridor went dark.

"Not yet," Sarah whispered, but the librarian didn't lower his gun.

The emergency generators kicked in, and the corridor was filled with a bloody-colored light. Outside, the vampires spread along the edge of the magickal shield.

"What are they doing?" Ed whispered.

"They can't reach us." Sarah drew an arrow. "Not until they bring down the shield."

"Shield?" Marvin glanced. "You mean, like on *Star Trek*?"

"Not exactly." She smiled. "More like the salt and magick kind."

"That's what I was doing with the town's salt truck?" Wade asked.

She nodded, but kept her eyes on the rogues.

In unison, the baby vamps beat on the barrier. It set her head to thrumming, and she lowered the bow as she tried to fight the mental barrage. The reddish-orange flashes of light didn't help.

"Why isn't the demon doing anything?" Wade asked.

Sarah took a deep breath and focused on the thing that looked like a velociraptor. With one foreclaw, it scratched something on the shield.

*Are you sure the demon is on your side of the school?* Mom asked. *I've got him on this side trying to cast a counter-spell.*

Dad's solid presence filtered through Sarah's mind. *Then we have three.*

*Four,* came Bebe's grim reply. *Goddess, I pray there's not more.*

*Where's Sam and the others?* Good to know Mom had gotten over her aversion to the death goddess after her resurrection of the baby demon.

*On their way.* Bebe sounded perversely amused. *Apparently, Giovanni left an unpleasant surprise for them at the ranch.*

Sarah grinned at the sight of a familiar furry form slipping like a ghost between the trees, downwind from his prey. The tawny wolf stalked the vampires, and the rogues were too busy with their percussive attempt to distract the witches from the demons' counterspell. They didn't notice him.

A series of gunshots echoed through the shield. Ed and Wade raised their own firearms, but she waved them down. "That's Alex taking out rogues at the practice field behind the school."

At the shouts of agony that followed, the rogues seized their pounding and looked around wildly. Logan took advantage of the confusion. His leap toppled a female vampire while his massive jaws snapped her neck. He released her, and her body rolled into a hollow in the snow. Before any of the newborns could react, he darted back into the forest.

A deep bass note sounded, a bell in the bowels of the earth. Bebe had warned them what would happen when a believer in the dinosaur gods died. A female scream ripped through the night. On the plus side, they wouldn't have to worry about ghosts possessing Alex or the weres.

"What the hell was that?" Wade whispered.

"From the large, hairy balls, I'd say he was Logan Polk." Marvin winked at Sarah.

"You always look at animals' balls, Newlin?" Ed asked.

"Just yours," Marvin shot back.

While Wade laughed, Logan downed another vamp by ripping out his throat. The tension didn't leave Sarah. The Normals with her didn't feel the earth throb in pain or the mental cries of the vamps. In addition, whatever the demon was doing to the shield buzzed harshly against her mind. She drew an arrow from her quiver.

The rogues at this end of the high school realized their own problem had nothing to do with guns. Once again, Logan darted into the forest. Several rogues chased after him.

The demon finally noticed the situation. It screamed at the rogues in its odd language, but since newborns had little discipline, only twenty or so resumed beating on the shield.

Sarah could have sworn the demon rolled its eyes before it resumed scratching symbols on their magickal buffer. Blackish-green energy flickered through the barrier, accompanied by a high-pitched screech inside her head.

*I hope you senior citizens have a backup plan because the demons are doing something to the shield.*

*They're draining our power somehow,* Bebe said.

*I said the blood magick was a bad idea.* A mix of sour lemon and ash flavored Mom's bitter statement.

*Then we drop the shield.* Dad's presence was solid and sure through the mental link.

Mom's shock pierced whatever it was the demons were doing. *You can't be serious.*

*Aaron's right.* Bebe's mental voice sounded harsh. *Otherwise, they'll be using our own power against us.*

"Guys," Sarah called over her shoulder. "On my mark, Marvin and I are stepping outside. Wade, Ed, you're our backup. You cannot let anything through this door."

"But your shield—" Marvin started.

"The demons are casting a counterspell. It's not staying up much longer." She left out the part about deliberately bringing down the barrier. Last thing she needed was the Normals freaking out. Especially since they would do that anyway when she started using her powers in front of them.

"Wait a minute." Wade's baritone lowered a full octave. "You didn't tell us there was more than one of them things."

"Yeah, well, we just found out." Sarah winced at a human scream that came from the woods. The only consolation was it couldn't have been Logan. He could fight better as a wolf.

She matched Dad's internal countdown out loud. "Three, two, one!" She shoved the side door open as she released the contaminated shield.

The few vampires, who had been still beating on the barrier, stumbled when the magick suddenly disappeared. A female vamp actually fell to her hands and knees.

When Sarah cleared the doorway, she darted to her left. Most of the vamps still chased Logan through the woods, ignoring the demon screaming in barely comprehensible English. She focused on the confused newborns, and she nocked her arrow.

Gunfire erupted next to her, but she ignored Marvin and focused on her own target. She released the string. The freckle-faced, red-headed vampire, who couldn't have been more than a couple years older than her when he was Turned, stared at the fletching that stuck out of his chest. He took one step before the flesh melted from his face. The rest of his skin, muscle, and organs liquefied, and gravity did the rest. His remaining skeleton wavered a moment before it hit the red stain in the snow.

The ghost of the boy, she couldn't think of him as a dangerous rogue vampire anymore, stared at the remnants of his corporeal body. Power thrummed faster beneath her feet. Crimson hooks burst through the snow and latched onto his ectoplasm, just as Bebe had warned. His scream echoed through Sarah's mind, but there wasn't a damn thing she could do unless she wanted to be devoured by the dinosaur gods, too.

No, not hooks. They were more like the slicing talons of velociraptors. And they shredded the soul of the boy and sank back into the snow with the pieces in less than a blink.

Not realizing the true fate of their companion, two other vamps didn't wait to be shot. They rushed toward Sarah and Marvin, but they were unsure of their new strength and speed.

Sarah threw up a glamour that showed her standing in the same spot as she slid to her right and drew another arrow. The female vamp ran face-first into the wall of the high school. Mortar and red brick cracked and crumbled. Sarah released the string of her bow. She couldn't watch what was about to happen to the female rogue, so she pivoted to keep an eye on the demon and check the remaining vamps. But not seeing didn't mean she could shut out the tortured earth vibrating beneath her boots or the tormented cries of the devoured souls.

She didn't have a target in sight besides the demon. There wasn't much left besides skeletons and red snow. Marvin had taken care of the other rogues. With his marksmanship, she didn't have to worry about a stray bullet hitting Logan.

Marvin swung his rifle behind his back and drew his handgun. The demon screamed. Sarah couldn't be sure whether its irritation was directed at her and the librarian for killing its allies or at the vamps who still chased Logan through the woods.

*One demon down*, Sam reported.

Sarah grinned. Or maybe there was a third reason it was pissed.

The demon's tail lashed, and it growled at them.

"Marvin, catch." Sarah tossed her bow to him and yanked the quiver over her head. "Get inside."

"Maybe you shouldn't be out here without a weapon," he muttered as he grabbed the strap and slung it over his shoulder.

She concentrated. The reassuring tingle of magickal heat crawled from her fingertips to her elbows. "I need something with a little more firepower than conventional weapons for the demon."

Talking about magick in a living room while snacking on coffee and donuts was one thing. Seeing flames flickering along her forearms for the first time was another. Marvin audibly gulped, then whirled and raced for the school doors.

"Fool!" Or at least, that was what it sounded like the demon said. "Your petty magicks—"

Sarah threw, and her fireball exploded in its face. It shrieked in pain and crumpled to the snow. At its scream, rogues who had been chasing Logan poured out of the woods, only to be met with gunfire.

She glanced over her shoulder. Despite Alex's original plan and her words, Marvin stood to her left. He'd exchanged his rifle for Ed's. Peering through the scope, he squeezed off shot after shot, downing the vamps heading in her direction.

Sarah summoned another fireball. The demon rolled to its feet, but its attention was no longer on Sarah, but to her right. She turned. A black fog flowed around the corner of the high school, but from the angry cry of the demon, it wasn't one of its compatriots.

The black cloud coalesced next to the demon, and silver flashed in a downward arc. The demon jumped and lashed out with its feet before it somersaulted to a standing position. More blood sprayed across the snow, and the resolved form of Sam grunted.

"Holy shit," Marvin muttered.

*Logan, go help Alex and Alyson with their vamps. Sarah and I have this guy,* Sam said.

*On it.* Pale fur flashed in the underbrush as the werewolf ran toward the east entrance of the school.

"Marvin! Get inside!" Sarah ordered. "We've got this."

The rapid-fire exchange of blows between Sam and the demon convinced the librarian to listen. Or maybe it was the witchfire flickering along Sarah's arms. Marvin raced for the door.

Sarah faced the fight again. The instant the combatants parted, she threw her fireball at the demon.

The battle turned into a bizarre, deadly three-way dance. Sam would assault the demon physically and with her powers, then withdraw to let Sarah launch her own offensive. It must have been what the goddess and Bebe had done with the demon at the main entrance of the high school.

And the tactic worked because they didn't give the demon a chance to use its magick with the constant physical pummeling. Not when Sarah was literally frying it alive while Sam's silvery knife-edged nails drew its black blood with every strike.

Sarah wasn't sure how long the back-and-forth continued. Her arm ached horribly as she drew back to throw a zillionth fireball when a horrible squeak came from the tattered demon. It wavered for a moment before it tipped over and landed face-first in the disturbed snow. In the chaos, the storm had died to an occasional flake fluttering through the air.

"Finally." Sam groaned between pants. "I was beginning think it wasn't going to die. Burn its corpse."

Sarah tossed her fireball onto the body. A rush of flames licked the air.

Slow clapping came from behind her. She jerked around because the sound couldn't possibly be any of the Normals. Two male vampires stepped out of the woods, and a chill ran through her that had nothing to do with the night's frigid temperatures.

"Well, well, well. If it isn't Heckyll and Jeckyll." Sam folded her arms over her chest. "You survived the massacre at Mallory Labs. However, I don't recall you two being infected when your bosses died that night."

So, what happened to the labs and the people who'd tortured the supernaturals was true. Mom and Dad had refused to tell her what happened after Logan and she had been rescued. But Alex had told Logan, and Logan talked in his sleep when he shifted from wolf to human and back during the worst of his nightmares.

But Rivers and Stone had survived.

"We've been improved, baby. Sorry we didn't get to play with you the first time around. We'll definitely make space in our schedule for you now." Stone's gaze swept down Sam's body in a way that made Sarah shudder. When he'd looked at her like that, when she'd been drugged and naked and trapped in a cell, he'd hurt her. And when he was done, Rivers would take his turn.

Rivers must have picked up her thoughts because his attention switched to her. "Well, looky here, man. Our favorite playmate. Unfortunately, she's filled out a bit. I liked her better when she was softer. More girly."

Sam cocked her head. Sarah wasn't sure what the goddess was looking at. The two vampires' auras were nothing special. Both were ugly, dark gray-green with the brick red overlay of someone who'd contracted the V-virus at least a year ago.

A terrible smile spread across Sam's face. "They're yours, kid. Do whatever you want to them."

Stone chuckled. "That's not the way it's going to work, bitch. First, I'm gonna—" His jaw abruptly snapped shut. Weird sounds came from him.

"Yadda, yadda, yadda. Don't give a flying fuck about the lobster bisque." Sam's eyes started to glow. "I won't hobble you, but I won't let you leave either. You will have a fighting chance against a pissed-off young woman that you gangraped repeatedly for months, but I think she's going to need a lot of closure. And she won't be handicapped this time either."

Sam was insane. There was no other word for it. Sarah glanced around, but there was no one alive nearby, other than the three Normal men watching this drama play out from behind the glass and steel door. Goddess help her, she couldn't even Hear her parents, Bebe, or Alex. There was no fucking way she could take these two.

Sam's arms dropped to her sides, and she took a step back. Her huge grin could only be called maniacal. "Your real problem is that you didn't swear allegiance to the dinosaur god Haight is trying to resurrect. In fact, you have no allegiance to anyone but yourselves. Which means the instant my little witch friend kills you, your souls are mine."

# Chapter 30

Alyson crept on her belly through the underbrush. Sandalwood and ozone permeated the area in front of her. She carefully peered over a fallen log. If she didn't look directly at the magickal shield the witches had raised, she could detect flickers of light rising from the circle of road salt.

Vampires ringed the perimeter marked by the tracks of Wade's truck, their attention focused on the school as they pounded on the witches' shield. In a one-on-one fight, she had no doubt she could take out a bloodsucker, but there were too many for her to fight alone.

Esther touched her mind, a gentle caress. *You just need to distract them, Alyson. Keep them off balance. Let the folks with me do their share.*

She selected a tiny blond woman well away from the demon. After everything that had happened at the clinic, she wasn't sure she could keep it together if she had to take him on. The last thing the people of Tuttle Creek needed was a were having a nervous breakdown in this mess.

One shot rang out, then a series from multiple directions. From the pause in their drumming, the vampires weren't expecting any resistance from the Normals. More likely, they were as uneducated as Papa tried to keep her.

Alyson leapt over the log and charged for her target. Another leap, and her jaws clamped on the vampire's neck. A snap when the vertebra broke. She tumbled with the dead weight, scrambled to her paws, and raced for the forest.

Shouts came from behind her, but she zigzagged, running for the other end of the teacher's parking lot. A vampire darted from behind a tree and grabbed for her. She pivoted toward him and bit his calf. Powerful jaws and sharp teeth ripped through muscles and tendon. The vampire screamed, and collapsed.

Unfortunately, with the vampires' healing factor, he wouldn't stay down from the injury. She whirled and jumped. His second scream cut off as she ripped out his throat.

Branches breaking and people shouting sent her running in another direction. Whoever these vampires were, they definitely weren't the silent deadly hunters Frankie had described when the two of them had been children and he'd been trying to scare her. These creatures trampled through the woods like a bunch of drunk frat boys.

Sam's silent count of taking out the demons helped. Alyson jumped out of the underbrush and nailed a third vampire. His body fell through the snow-covered branches of a huge pine tree, and she ducked beneath them to crush his trachea. One of the dead demons had to be the bastard who'd attacked her, right?

Even though Logan had promised her the kill, it wouldn't break her heart for one of the others to do the deed as long as he never hurt anyone again.

The earth vibrated underneath her paws. Pine needles jumped and skittered along the bare ground. She padded carefully away from the body, back into the snow, and peered through the trees.

Esther was outside of the school, her arms raised. Around her, chunks of asphalt, stones, and dirt erupted from the snow. With the flick of her fingers, the projectiles launched toward the vampires and the demon. Shrieks and screams filled the air along with the scent of blood.

Roots slithered beneath Alyson's paws. She yipped and hopped back like she was one of the rabbits she'd collected for Sam. Woody tendrils wrapped themselves around ankles and legs before climbing to the necks of the vampires. She averted her gaze when Esther popped off the first head using the roots of the surrounding trees.

No wonder Papa said to give the New Orleans Coven a wide berth.

Alyson would have almost smiled if she were in human form, and her stomach wasn't churning from the sight. It seemed the witch had things in hand with protecting the Normals at this end of the building. All she needed to do was pick off the rest of the vampires chasing her.

She loped toward a set of voices. A familiar scent reached her nose, and she skidded to a halt. Logan.

But he wouldn't have broken with their plan unless . . .

*Esther! Sam! Anyone! Where's Logan?*

Esther's mental touch was no longer gentle, more like sharp-edged glass violence. *Sam sent him to help Alex since she's taken care of the rogues at the main entrance and she's assisting Sarah. They'll work their way towards us once they take care of the demon on Aaron's side of the building.*

A tawny wolf rounded the cluster of aspens in front of her. The chill that ran down Alyson's spine had nothing to do with the temperature drop from the storm. This time, she didn't hesitate.

She pivoted and ran like Death itself was after her.

# Chapter 31

Sarah swallowed hard. From the expressions on Rivers and Stone's faces, they didn't believe Sam could do a damn thing to them. So where did that leave her?

*You can take them, kid. Unless you don't want to.* Sam of the glowing silver eyes found all this funny as hell from the tickle in the back of Sarah's head.

*Aren't you supposed to be telling me revenge is wrong, and I'll never be whole if I do this?*

Sam cocked her head as she regarded Sarah. "Have you ever seen the original Star Wars trilogy? It's never a simple moral path. Kenobi and Yoda trained Luke to kill his own father."

"Do we look like Darf Vader?" Rivers lisped. Someone hadn't learned to talk clearly with his fangs extended. But neither of them had made a move, probably because of something Sam was doing to them without them realizing it.

Sarah clenched her fists. Morals weren't the problem. The problem was an ugly part of her deep down inside, a part she'd never even shown her therapist, wanted the revenge Sam offered. The part that dreamed of cutting off bits and burning those bits in front of these horrible, cruel men.

Except now, she had the opportunity to cut off the bits, burn them, and watch them grow back on these assholes now that they were infected with the V-virus.

And Sam was a goddess. Sarah's nails dug into her palms as the thoughts rolled around in her mind. It wasn't like the entity her parents taught her to worship ever gave her such direct choices.

That was the problem. Sam wasn't making her do a damn thing. Sarah swallowed hard. It was her decision.

"What'll happen if Mr. Augustine takes them into custody?" She said the words out loud to see her torturers' reactions. They laughed. The moral part of her, the part she desperately hung onto with her fingernails, was sorely disappointed by their behavior.

The goddess shrugged. "They'll be executed. Given what happened inside Mallory Labs, you might be doing them a kindness. The Romans could be pretty brutal. Caesar's had over two thousand years to hone his techniques."

The snow around Sarah melted from the heat she generated. The energy she kept in check. Dad and Mom taught her to use that power to help, not harm. "No. We're going to do the right thing and deliver them to Mr. Augustine."

Security lights flickered on around them in the parking lot. Someone must have gone to the substation and restored electricity to the town.

That's when Rivers and Stone made the dumbass decision to rush Sam.

Logan darted for the demon's hind leg. The damn nightmare finally realized he'd only been feinting to allow Alex to inflict the real damage. Its tail lashed out so fast he didn't have the chance to change his course. The demon walloped him in the side, and he flew nearly fifty feet until he slammed into the chain-link fence surrounding the high school's baseball diamond.

Of course, all these shenanigans were meant to give Aaron time to cast his spell. It wouldn't be so bad if Logan could catch his breath. How the hell had they gone from one demon to four?

Well, two now.

"Logan! Move it!" Alex roared.

His paws dug into the snow, and he flung himself to his right. A metallic screech rent the night as slashing talons cut through the steel fence.

Blue light sparked in his peripheral vision before Aaron yelled, "Clear!"

Logan gained his footing and raced behind Alex. The snow beneath their feet flowed like a mountain stream.

Or an avalanche.

They slid to a stop next to Cody Grisham, who had been covering them in case more newborn vampires appeared, and turned to watch Aaron. The way his hands waved, the doc looked like he was conducting an invisible orchestra. Snow whirled around the demon, far more intensely than the dying storm could generate. Its shriek of rage could barely be heard over the rumble of the swirling whiteness.

The snow moved faster and faster, compacting as it did. The sound changed from a deep rumble to the ringing of crystal wind chimes.

Flood lights in the baseball field kicked on. They illuminated the scoured earth and the snow spinning like a top next to the diamond's fence. The outside utility faucets gurgled to life. Water ribbons flowed through the air to join the snow.

This time, the tinkling died to be replaced only by the rush of air, and even that faded as the top slowed and stopped. The demon stared at nothing through the solid block of ice, which teetered for a moment before it toppled over.

Alex caught the doctor when he sagged. "You did your job, Aaron. Now, it's my turn." He helped the doctor inside the school where friendly hands pulled Aaron inside. The vampire inclined his head. "You, too, Logan."

Worry filled Logan from snout to tail. Sure, they'd both changed since their abduction, but Alex's somber expression went far beyond a little PTSD. *What are you going to do?*

"What I have to." Alex held the door open. "Now, get inside while I clean up this one. Go see if Esther and Alyson need some help."

Logan entered the school. People he had known for the last four years backed away from him. For the first time in his life, the Normal reaction bothered him. He padded over to Aaron who sat on a plastic and aluminum chair.

"What's he doing?" Aaron murmured.

*I don't know.* Logan looked out the glass and steel door.

Alex popped the clip of his gun and fished something out of his pocket. A bullet.

"By all that's holy," Aaron whispered. "What is that?"

One in the chamber. *What do you mean? What's wrong with the bullet?*

"Whatever it is, it's got more power than anything I've ever Seen." Aaron's fingers dug into Logan's fur. "Anything except for Sam."

Oh, shit. Alex still had one of the bullets the Incan god of death had given him. *Everybody, get down!*

Aaron verbally echoed Logan's mental shout. The doc and the three guards hit the tile floor.

The vampire raised his gun and sighted the demon encased in ice. He said something to the frozen demon Logan couldn't quite make out through the glass and steel door. Alex squeezed the trigger.

The blast rocked the building. Projectiles smashed into the door. Everyone in the hallway covered their heads, but the safety glass held.

*Three down,* Alex said.

Logan trotted back to the door. He could make out the vampire through the cracks. *I think you left out some of the things that happened in Peru, old man.*

Instead of Alex's answer, Esther's voice rang through Logan's head. *Hey, people! The fourth demon just took off after Alyson.*

# Chapter 32

Heart hammering, Sarah launched a fireball at Stone since Rivers was too close to Sam. Stone ducked backward and slid forward on his knees in the snow so her spell passed over his head instead of hitting it. The fireball landed in a bush, but its flames sputtered and fizzled in the melting slush that fell off a branch from the impact.

Rivers launched himself into a diving tackle, but Sam popped out so the vampire landed face-first in the fresh powder. Sarah looked wildly around for the goddess, but she wasn't in sight. Last thing Sarah needed was to accidentally take out her most powerful ally with a wayward spell.

Marvin pounded on the school's doors, but they seemed to be jammed shut. Maybe Sam was trying to keep the Normals safe. Maybe Mom or Dad were having trouble with the demons at their sides of the school and needed her help. Maybe Sarah had earned the goddess's confidence after she proved herself with the baby demon.

Except these two weren't demons from another dimension. They were assholes who relished hurting drugged children. And dammit, she wasn't a child anymore.

She straightened. She *could* do this.

As long as she didn't do anything stupid like dropping her shield again.

Bebe's comment about the other elements before they had set the school shield whispered through Sarah's mind. The older witch had a point. Sarah no longer needed to focus on a single element for a greater working with the others. She could cut loose.

"I'm going to drink your blood, bitch." Stone raced toward her.

She threw up a personal shield. At his supernatural speed, the vampire didn't just bounce off it. He flew back a good twenty feet and slid on his ass in the snow another thirty. She followed up with another fireball.

Rivers jumped to his feet. Her blast of air drove him back. He leaned into the wind she generated, but he couldn't get traction with the snow covering the asphalt parking lot.

Silver was out of the question since the Normals had her arrows. Fire, decapitation or something through the heart were her options. She doubted these two would stand still long enough to incinerate them. All she had out here was snow.

But she didn't have quite Dad's talent with switching between the various states of waters. Fire was much simpler in that regard.

*Sarah, you are such a dumbass.*

When the mountain snow melted in the spring, Tuttle Creek turned into a raging cacophony of power. She grinned at her idea.

Beneath her feet, her magick warmed the asphalt. Water seeped into her boots as she used blasts of frigid night air to keep the vampires away from her. Neither man seemed to have any concept of their full abilities. Had the Augustine rogue Giovanni Turned them and not properly trained them?

"What's the matter, little girl?" Stone sneered. "Use yourself up on the babies and the demon?" He and Rivers circled closer now that the snow they'd been slipping on had melted into several inches of water, and she'd stopped throwing air blasts at them.

Sarah smiled. "No, I'm saving myself for you." She yanked sharply on the threads of magick she'd been weaving into the water. A streamer of liquid sliced through the air.

And through the vampire's neck. His head landed with a splash.

Rivers ducked a split second before the water touched him. He stared at his partner. His disbelieving expression matched the face of the dead man's until the flesh melted from Stone's skeleton.

Neon yellow eyes turned red when Rivers met her gaze, and he charged at her. Sarah threw another water ribbon, pulling the heat back into herself as she did so. The ice pierced Rivers' heart. He stumbled forward a few more steps, enough that the protruding chunk touched her outstretched hand, before skin and muscle slid from his bones.

When someone touched her shoulder, she jumped and pivoted in the same motion.

Sam's expression was neutral. "Feel better?"

Sarah considered the question as she tried to catch her breath and calm her racing heart. "Not really. It's just good to know they won't hurt anyone else."

Mom's voice rang through her head. *Hey, people! The fourth demon just took off after Alyson.* There was a pause, and Sarah could feel the spell Mom launched at an opponent. *I could use a little assistance here. Still have about twenty vamps even with Carol's help.*

Sam grimaced and pointed at the student entrance. "You stay here in case any of them swing around this way."

"But I—"

"Marvin needs some supernatural backup, and you need a breather." Sam winked. "You did more than your share already, kid." With that, she popped out again.

"Dammit," Sarah muttered. "I need to get into shape if I'm going be an enforcer." Yeah, the CGI degree was still a good idea, a fallback when she was older. And Mom and Dad would have a fit when she put in her name with the high priestess. But for the first time, she knew she'd found her true calling.

At Esther's words, Alex's shadow disappeared. Logan growled low in his throat. His idiot best friend forgot he was inside with the Normals.

Logan jumped, hit the crossbar of the door with his front paws, and shoved. The door swung wide and slammed into the brick. The abused safety glass gave up on any semblance of unity and rained to the concrete.

He was already through the opening when the first shard hit. A member of his pack was in trouble, and alpha instinct had taken over. He raced for the north side of the high school.

The teachers' parking lot was riddled with bloody skeletons and scarlet splotches of snow. It looked like Esther and Alyson had already made a dent in their attackers. Sam and Alex were taking care of the rest. Logan pivoted and headed into the forest. Alyson's scent stood out among the vampires' sandalwood.

As did the scent that was his, but not his.

Really? Did the jackass think his trick would work twice? Or was this the demon's way of psychologically torturing Alyson?

Logan paused and sniffed again. A little fear from her, but not the full-blown panic he expected. More . . .

He inhaled deeply. Determination. She had a plan.

What the hell was that she-wolf up to? Paws dug into the fresh powder as he raced in the direction of Alyson and the demon.

# Chapter 33

*Mother Wolf, what was I thinking?*

Alyson's breath whistled in her lungs as she ran. The demon was faster. She was more agile. Nothing that she hadn't already learned the night she had been attacked. It meant she had to be smarter.

So far, he was staying in wolf-form. A reminder of how he'd hurt her. He wanted her to surrender to the terror that gibbered at the back of her mind. If she did, she'd die.

And dammit, she wasn't going to give Logan, much less her father, the satisfaction of knowing she was as weak as they thought she was.

She darted out of the woods and bolted for Roy's pickup. *Please, Mother Wolf, don't let this be the one time he sticks his keys in his pocket.*

In the high school's main parking lot, she maneuvered tightly around parked cars. Daring a peek, she saw only wolf paws. He could have tossed the vehicles aside. Instead, he played cat-and-mouse among the minivans, SUVs, and rusted, battered pickups.

Alyson started her shift two cars before Roy's truck. By the time she reached it, her front appendages were human enough to grasp the door handle and push the release. She quickly climbed in and slammed the door shut.

The vinyl and cloth seat on her bare skin reminded her how low the temperature had dropped during the storm. She locked the doors and snapped down the visor. The ice-cold stainless steel keys and keyring fell into her lap.

*Boom!*

Something slammed the driver's side door, and the truck rocked. She yelped and grabbed the steering wheel.

A scaled head with beady eyes peered into the cab to her left. Lights in the parking lot flickered back to life. They revealed something that looked like a very large, very angry orange and purple gecko.

If he hadn't already attacked her, if she hadn't seen the monster he had impregnated her with, Alyson would have laughed. The giant lizard began muttering something in his own language. His cadence matched the witches' when they cast a spell.

She jammed the key into the ignition and turned it. The starter cranked twice. The engine sputtered and died. A quick glance out the driver side window enforced the distinct impression the demon was internally laughing at her.

Energy pricked her arm hair, and ozone filled the cab. Dammit! The demon was going to finish his spell before she'd get the truck started. In the same motion, she unlocked the door and hit the latch. A hard shove slammed the metal and glass into the demon's face.

A handful of its multitude of teeth broke off, and his head snapped back. She yanked the door shut, but not before a taloned finger curled around the frame. The demon bellowed at his trapped and probably broken digit, though he sounded more furious than in pain.

Alyson turned the key again, and this time the engine roared to life. She jammed the gear into reverse and stomped on the accelerator. The pickup fishtailed to the left in the new snow and slammed into the sedan parked beside it.

The demon squealed the same way Frankie had when one of the pack bitches had kicked him between his legs for daring to cop a feel. But Alyson wasn't going anywhere. The tires spun, kicking a spray of dirty white across the aisle.

*Think, girl! Don't panic.* Snow wasn't that different than mud, and she'd gotten vehicles out of bayou slime before. She let off the gas, shifted into drive, and pressed the pedal a little more gently.

Luckily, Roy had parked facing the grassy strip in front of the wide sidewalk leading to the school. Both metal and demon lizard screeched as the truck scraped the side of the sedan when it inched forward, but Alyson knew the injuries she inflicted would be nothing more than a movie hero flesh wound to the demon.

Once she cleared the other car, she gave the pickup a little more gas and turned toward the exit. The truck swerved back and forth as she tried to stay on the sidewalk, but it gradually gained speed. She swerved right onto the street. The sound of flesh ripping was her only warning.

Fire hit her shoulder and thigh, and she hissed at the pain. The demon's finger tumbled to the floor of the cab. She glanced at the rearview mirror. The demon awkwardly somersaulted in the snow at a ninety degree angle to the road.

Another movement caught her peripheral vision. To her right, a cream-colored wolf raced through the fresh powder. Another look confirmed the demon was definitely behind her. So far, it wasn't getting up.

*Please, Mother Wolf. Please don't let there be five of these monsters.*

Tapping the break nearly sent her into a spin. Her lungs ached when she finally slid to a stop, and she took a deep breath as she flipped the locking mechanism for the passenger door.

Like she had earlier, Logan started his shift as he aimed for the truck. By the time he grabbed the handle, he was nearly human-shaped.

"Go," he growled.

She pressed the accelerator. The pickup fishtailed again as it started, but she quickly regained control.

"Not bad for a southern girl." Logan grinned.

"No different than mud," she murmured.

He sniffed. "What's burning? Why's your left leg curled up on the seat?"

"My skin, and there's a demon finger rolling around on the floorboards." She grimaced as something brushed her right heel, but no pain came.

"What's your plan?" Logan looked over his shoulder. "And whatever it is, you might want to hurry. Our friend's standing up."

"Yeah, I didn't think he'd stay down long. He's the original." She slung the wheel to her left, but the snow was too much for the truck's momentum. The back end swung in a slow one-eighty-degree arc until they were facing a very angry demon.

A demon who wasn't impeded one bit by the snow as it raced toward them.

"Reverse!"

At Logan's shout, Alyson smacked the stalk into the correct gear and pressed the accelerator. The closing demon chose that moment to leap. Maybe Roy's pickup was sentient, and she was tired of the abuse. The tires dug in, and the truck rolled backward just as the mutilated lizard completed his arc. He landed face first on the snow-covered asphalt.

Alyson threw the pickup into drive and gunned the engine. The truck bounced as it rolled over the orange and purple form. She deliberately spun the back tires on the demon for good measure before she turned down a residential street.

"Remind me never to piss you off," Logan breathed when they cleared the mangled form.

"Do we need god powers, or can we simply dismember the bastard?"

"Alex said they needed weapons made by the Incan gods to kill the two dino demons down in Peru."

Dammit, the man was being stingy with his information. "Like what? Or do I simply throw Sam's ghost bunnies at him?"

Logan sucked in a deep breath as he looked behind them. "Bullets made in Uka Pacha and Supay's tumi."

"Uku Pacha?"

"Incan hell."

*Well, crap.* Alyson bit her bottom lip. Weres who followed the old ways didn't believe in a hell. At least not the way the European and Middle Eastern religions did.

She looked at Logan. "Please tell me we don't need a magickal Colt to fire these special bullets."

"No, but—oh, shit." Logan's face went slack for a moment. He shook his head to clear it. "I think Alex used the last bullet he had to kill the baby demon Aaron froze behind the high school."

"That's not very helpful," she bit out.

"Hey! He and Sam are cleaning up your vampires!" Logan shot back.

"I don't want this thing raping more women and breeding more demons!" Her jaw tightened. She'd never yelled at anyone in her life the way she yelled at Logan, but her heart ached worse than the burns on her skin. She'd never bear it if this thing got away.

After a moment of only the sound of their breathing competing with the engine in the cab, he said, "I'm sorry. I don't want it to get away either."

She released the accelerator but didn't touch the brake. This turn was a little more controlled.

Logan cleared his throat. "So where are you going?"

"The hardware shop next door to the mill. Tell Sam and Alex to join us there when they're finished killing the rogues."

# Chapter 34

Logan scanned the area when Alyson pulled into a parking space on the street in front of Sharp's Hardware Shop. Well, slid into the parking space. Luckily, no one was on the street. "Maybe the demon decided the fight wasn't worth it."

Alyson shuddered. "No. I can feel him. He's too determined to take me."

"Feel him?"

She cut the engine and stared at him. "I can't explain it. It's like I've felt him watching me since I arrived at Tuttle Creek. But then—" A self-deprecating chuckle erupted from her. "He invited me here. A naïve little bitch he could use."

Logan grabbed her hand, her fingers icy in his. "Then we make him pay for messing with you."

She nodded slowly.

"Come on then." He released her. They both scrambled out of the truck, and ran for the storefront. The snow reminded him human feet weren't meant for these temperatures. But they couldn't fight this thing as wolves.

Not this time. This time tooth and claw would be more dangerous to them than their opponent.

Logan lifted one of the cement geese Lydia Sharp had dressed in an orange and black cape with a matching cone hat and smashed a window pane on the old-fashioned double doors that secured the store. He reached through carefully and flipped the lock.

"Watch out for the glass," he whispered.

Alyson made a disgusted sound at the back of her throat.

Okay, so he was being overprotective again, but it wasn't because she was a pack princess. And he damn sure wasn't about to waste their precious time apologizing.

He unlatched the second door and leapt over the glass. Alyson did so as well and followed him back to the protective wear section. "Here." He grabbed the smallest pair of coveralls he could find and shoved them into her hands.

Surprisingly, she slipped them on instead of arguing. In fact, while he shrugged on another pair, she found boots for both of them.

He led her back to the welding section. Thankfully, Tuttle Creek was far enough from Billings that Lydia carried more equipment than the typical hardware proprietor. They opted for goggles for their wider range of vision than the full masks.

Alyson eyed him as they donned the thick, elbow-length gloves. "You're not seriously going to drag around acetylene and oxygen?"

He hefted two of the smallest tanks. "Got a better idea? What else is going to keep that blood of his from burning us besides cauterizing whatever we cut off?"

She grimaced. "I'm more worried about what its blood will do if it dissolves a pressurized steel cylinder." She pointed at the wall to their left. "Since they seem more susceptible to cold, what about the fire extinguishers?"

At the tinkle of glass near the front of the store, they both froze.

"Come out, my dear Ms. Tribideaux." The voice rasped as if its vocal cords weren't working quite right. Hell, they may not be after Alyson ground the pickup's tires into the demon.

She eased over to the shelf she'd pointed to and grabbed a couple of the kitchen-sized extinguishers.

"I'll even let your fellow were live," the raspy sing-song continued. "But you definitely owe me for what your friends did to my children."

Logan caught Alyson's attention and pantomimed lips moving. She frowned until she understood his gesture meant she needed draw the demon towards the back of the store. Logan swallowed his own frustration. This whole maneuver would be so much fucking easier if one of them were a telepath.

"I think you owe me for what you did to me," she shouted. Her voice trembled, but she focused on her task. She set down one canister and pulled the tab to fire on the other. She switched and repeated the process.

Logan set his canisters down and prepped them before he reached for an ignitor. He prayed to Mother Wolf that he got everything right. It had been a couple of decades since he'd used anything larger than a circuit-board micro-welder.

"Letting you live in a world that you stole from us is compensation enough," the demon spat. Occasionally, the tip of a purple and orange tail appeared above the shelves, and it was coming closer.

And from his own experience, the tail could be just as dangerous as the monster's teeth or cutting talons.

"We won it fair and square," she shouted back.

Logan ignited the nozzle and quickly turned down the flame to lower the noise. He waved Alyson toward the rest of the extinguishers.

Again, she frowned. No wolf would deliberately allow themselves to be cornered.

A soft click, distinctly toenail on concrete, came from the aisle between them, and understanding dawned on her face as Logan backed a couple of paces, ducked and peered through an empty space in the shelves. He checked the aisle between them. Orange and purple scales headed in their direction.

"Why bother stalking me? Come on! What are you afraid of?" she shouted.

"Definitely not the big bad wolf." The demon made the odd coughing noise that was his laughter. The shelves in front Alyson groaned and tilted, their contents spilling to the concrete floor. The steel shelving landed at a thirty degree angle against the wall. She froze, totally exposed.

The huge head full of teeth poked his head around the corner. The demon's attention was engrossed with her. "Hello, dear Alyson."

Logan turned up the gases. A blue flame shot out a yard and singed the arm the demon threw up to protect his face. Alyson took advantage of the distraction and dived beneath the overturned shelving.

That was the last thing Logan saw before the orange and purple tail whipped between the intervening space between him and the demon. He flew through the air and crashed into the stepladders half-way across the store. Instinct curled his body in a ball as he and the ladders tumbled to the floor.

"Fool!" What looked like a cross between a colorful children's toy and a mangled piece of roadkill stalked toward him. "She's mine!"

The demon wasn't bothering to hide his scent anymore. Logan almost couldn't believe his nose. The musk of desire mixed with the reptilian dry odor. This thing was actually initiating a mating challenge?

And this was one challenge Logan knew he couldn't win. Not against some extra-dimensional dinosaur demon. Not in a straight physical battle no matter what form he took. Hell, the damn thing was healing from the truck abuse as he watched.

He drew his legs in and kicked ladders toward the demon. Wood and metal skidded across the smooth concrete, but the Jurassic Park wannabe leapt on top of the closet shelving unit to avoid the projectiles.

"Come on, big boy." The demon's tail lashed back and forth. "Let's see some fang. I know you want to bite *eeep!*"

His leering grin disappeared, and white mist sprayed from his rear end. No, not from him.

From one of the fire extinguishers. Delicate hands swung the empty canister overhead and brought it down on the demon's foot. He roared.

Logan took advantage of the distraction and scrambled out of the pile of overturned ladders. Alyson threw the empty canister at the demon's head.

He swatted it aside and leapt down. Metal clattering muffled Alyson's aborted squeal.

Logan looked around wildly. He needed a weapon, but the acetylene torch was out of reach. It hissed impotently in the middle of the floor. The concrete beneath it cracked and glowed. The next section contained garden implements, but plastic leaf rakes wouldn't do squat.

His eyes fell on the pitchforks. Better than nothing. And he used to be able to toss them with decent accuracy back on Mom and Dad's ranch when he was a pup. He snatched a couple, leapt over the fallen ladder display, and headed for the spot where the lizard tail lashed.

"Come out of there, Alyson," the demon screeched as he tossed debris behind him. She must have taken refuge under the fallen shelving again. "I might even let your fuzzy boyfriend keep a limb or two."

Logan timed the lashes and tossed the first pitchfork. All four tines penetrated flesh and nailed the appendage to the wooden display rack. The demon shrieked. Black ichor dripped onto the camp extinguishers scattered on the floor around it.

"Alyson! Duck!" Logan dropped the other pitchfork before he twisted and dived down the adjoining aisle.

The first explosion rattled the store. Demon screams rent the air. The second explosion, or maybe the demon, knocked over the shelves next to Logan. He covered his head with his arms as hinges, doorknobs, and locks rained on him.

The shelves started a chain reaction as each successive rack tilted, fell and spilled their contents over the floor. He clamped his palms over his ears at the sheer volume of sound. When it stopped, he dared a peek in the direction he'd come from.

In time to see a series of aerosol paint cans rolling toward the still burning acetylene torch.

Panic filled his throat. "Alyson, run!"

Logan belly-crawled faster than he ever had in his life. He couldn't be sure since his overly-sensitive ears had given up at the first explosion, but from the vibrations in the concrete, something was crawling parallel through the wreckage as fast as he was. He just prayed it was Alyson and not the demon.

The main entrance was in sight when the first can hit the super-heated concrete behind him, and the world turned into a roar of flame.

# Chapter 35

The concussive force of the next series of blasts pushed Alyson along the concrete and pinned her against the cash register. The heat followed. When she dared to open her eyes, flames licked the back half of the store and the ceiling, and they were spreading fast.

She climbed to her feet, a little surprised that she still held the ax she'd found in the debris and had been using to fend off the demon. "Logan!"

Dammit. He would be as deaf as she was from explosions.

And the store was rapidly filling with smoke.

He'd been three aisles from her the last time she saw him, and she was pretty sure he'd been yelling, telling her to get the hell out of the store before something else besides the extinguishers had blown up.

Surely, the blasts had taken care of the demon. He still had plenty of injuries after she'd run over him a few times.

Alyson dropped back down to her hands and knees in order to breathe. She couldn't leave a fellow were behind.

Even if he were an over-protective pain in the ass.

The fire crackled above her, and embers fell from the ceiling. She didn't have much time. A faint, familiar whiff reached her. She touched a human hand. For one brief instant, terror filled her at the thought it might actually be the demon, shape-changed to fool her again.

She tugged the body out of the debris. It sure looked like Logan. Blood trickled from a cut on his forehead. Alex and Sam had said not to bite the demon, that his blood was poisonous.

There was only one chance to get this right. Maybe it was worth her life. She stuck her little finger in the liquid before she sucked on the tip.

Coppery taste hit her tongue, but nothing else happened. It was Logan.

She shoved the handle of the ax in a belt loop on her overalls and took a deep breath of the relatively clean air near the floor. Bigger chunks of burning debris rained from the ceiling. She wrapped an arm under his shoulder and hoisted them both upright. Her lungs ached by the time she half-carried, half-dragged Logan out of the burning store and across the street.

Only when Alyson settled him down onto the snow-covered sidewalk did she realize the wind had died. An occasional flake spiraled through the air with ash and embers from the burning store. When his eyes flickered open, she smiled. "You still alive?"

His eyes widened, and his lips moved, but she couldn't make out a damn thing he said.

"What?"

"Behind you," came his muffled reply, and he pointed.

She turned in time to see the burning figure of the dinosaur demon stagger out of the black smoke pouring from the wide-open doors of the hardware store. He spotted her and limped in their direction. His left arm hung at an odd angle. It brushed the hood of Roy's pickup, and the paint blistered.

How in the name of Mother Wolf was that thing even moving?

Alyson rose and pulled the ax from her belt loop. Logan struggled to his feet beside her. Without a word between them, instinct took over. They parted, angling in opposite directions to keep their prey between them.

Logan didn't have anything to use as a weapon. Alyson backed along the street and prayed he'd get the hint. She was pretty sure Roy's snow shovel was still in the bed of his truck.

The demon ignored Logan in favor of stalking her. Yeah, she really did wish she had the gift of telepathy right now.

"What's the matter, dear Alyson?" the demon rasped. "No pithy remarks?" The flames on his skin flickered and started to die, leaving a blackened, oozing crust.

She kicked off the borrowed steel-toed boots. She needed the maneuverability of her bare feet, and either she'd die and wouldn't need the boots, or she'd retrieve them once the demon was dead.

"I don't talk to prey." She feinted to the right, then darted to the left, her ax already swinging as the tail lashed out. Instead of a *thunk*, his flesh crunched when it parted beneath her blade.

He didn't cry out in pain either. She backpedaled out of range of his equally blackened talons as they passed where her face had been an instant ago. Ducking beneath a second swing of his claws, she chopped at his dangling left arm. It landed on the street with no sound of agony from the demon. Not even a little squeak of discomfort. Snow hissed, whether from the heat or what little blood was left in it, she wasn't sure.

She backpedaled again to give herself room to maneuver. The demon crouched. He could easily reach her when he jumped, so her legs tensed, ready to dive one way or another depending on the shift in his weight.

Logan brought the snow shovel down on the demon's head as the monster launched himself. A resounding *gong* echoed against the buildings on Main Street.

The demon landed hard, but snow cushioned whatever damage may have been inflicted. He rolled over, and the hind leg shot toward Logan, ripping talons extended.

The were jumped back but not fast enough. Heavy cloth ripped, and lines of blood appeared on both of his thighs. But he hadn't been disemboweled, thank Mother Wolf.

*Opportunity*, her other half said. *Prey is down.*

Alyson launched her body, the ax blade aimed to come down on the demon's head.

For something that been run over multiple time, skin burnt to a crisp, and missing a couple of appendages, he was fast. He rolled to his right and used his momentum and remaining arm to gain his feet. The stump of his tail swung around and smacked into her back, thrusting her into Logan. They went down in a tangle of limbs.

Somehow, they each managed to retain their implements and roll apart a split second before the demon landed where they'd lain, slashing talons extended to cut their throats.

Logan's gaze met hers. "Trust me?"

She gave him the barest of nods as the demon whirled to face her.

"Toss me the ax."

A sick feeling filled her stomach. Their lives were on the balance, and he didn't trust her to save them.

"I don't break promises," he said.

He remembered his oath to her. Time seemed to slow to a crawl. The demon advanced toward her. Logan stared at her, his eyes pleading. Deep down, she knew this was the moment that would define their relationship for the rest of their lives.

Define her life no matter how much longer it lasted.

She shuffled to her right, feinted to the left, and jumped to the right again. She tossed the ax, praying she didn't accidentally chop off one of Logan's limbs. He slid the steel shovel in her direction at the same moment.

The demon laughed again before he pivoted to face Logan, who caught the ax. "Still trying to save the damsel, Polk? Didn't work out so great the last time, did it? Or maybe you enjoyed watching me rape the little witch?" His form flowed and shifted into that of a human male, naked and still showing the burns and missing arm.

A slight burst of wind leftover from the earlier snowstorm carried sandalwood. No, not a Normal. A vampire. Someone Logan knew from the shocked look on his face. He backed away from the demon.

Everything Sam and Alex had said that morning in the Goldsteins' kitchen gelled. The dino demons had been involved in the attempted supernatural coups in California from the beginning.

Agony filled Logan's countenance. He continued to back away. The demon stalked right after him. Of course. It didn't consider her a threat.

"I'm sorry," Logan mouthed to her. Except the breeze and his odor said something else.

She was already running when he slid the ax right between the legs of the demon. In its injured state, it wasn't fast enough to grab the wooden handle. She snatched up the ax and was swinging as the demon whirled to face her.

Sharp metal connected with blackened, desiccated skin and continued through flesh and bone. The demon actually looked shocked an instant before its head came off and tumbled across the street. Blood spurted and oozed from the stump instead of spraying like a geyser.

Then her human feet slid in the packed snow. Alyson landed hard on her ass with the demon's body landing on top of her.

# Chapter 36

Logan's heart stopped when the body of the demon reached for Alyson as it toppled over. He ran for her, but she was already kicking her way free of the corpse. At least, he hoped it was a real corpse and wouldn't sprout tentacles like the resurrected baby demon had.

He knelt beside her. The scent of something burning hit his sinuses. A few spots of demon blood had landed on her overalls and were dissolving the fabric. He yanked at her zipper.

"What the fuck!" Alyson raised her hand.

"You can either smack me, or you can let that blood burn you," he growled.

"Shit!" She yanked the zipper down, and together they pulled off the contaminated clothing. She rolled to her feet. Cold pricked her bare skin as they watched the demon blood eat through the thick material, the packed snow, and a good chunk of asphalt.

She shook her head. "I will never complain about the sight of blood again."

"Wow, dinner and a show."

Logan looked up to find Sam nudging Alex. "Can't you do something practical and get her some clothes?" he growled at the goddess. Alyson shivered, but he was pretty sure it was adrenaline overload more than the cold.

Sam's eyes glowed silver, then white. Alyson's own clothing appeared around her, including boots and her coat.

"Bra and everything." Alyson grinned as Logan pulled her upright. "That's a nifty trick."

A horrendous cracking sound drew their collective attention to the hardware store. Or what was left of it. The roof collapsed, shooting ash and smoke all over this block of downtown before the wind caught the black cloud and dragged it down Main Street.

Alex leaned close to Sam. "Don't suppose you can put out the fire before it spreads to the feed mill? The fire department is still holed up at the high school, and a wheat dust explosion would take out the entire town."

Sam's expression didn't change, but the flames licking the sky died. A burnt timber exuded an occasional wisp, but otherwise, nothing indicated the burnt-out hulk had been a raging inferno less than a minute before.

"Logan, was there a reason you set the place on fire?" Alex asked dryly.

"I don't need your shit right now, fang face," Logan answered. "Take a look at the head."

Alex crossed to the head and toed it out of the snowbank it had rolled into. His gasp confirmed everything Logan needed to know.

"How-how—" The vampire swallowed hard. "How could this be Marcus Giovanni?"

"It was trying to mindfuck Logan," Alyson said bitterly. "And it isn't the real Giovanni. The flesh didn't melt when I cut off his head. That's definitely the demon who attacked me."

"Could the real Marcus be dead, and the demon's replaced him?" Sam asked.

"Possible, but I doubt it." Alex rubbed his chin.

"Did we get all the rogues?" Logan asked.

Sam slowly pivoted. "All but three who were at the school. They're running south. Alex thought it was a trap, or an opportunity to get us away from the Normals." She blinked, and her eyes were blue again. "I can See them now that the demons aren't hiding them anymore." She grabbed Alex's hand. They disappeared in a pop of displaced air.

"What now?" Alyson looked up at Logan.

"Now?" He blew out a lungful of air. "Now, we try to deal with the Normals after what happened tonight."

Maddy dropped her binoculars and started for the interloper and her followers, but a hand landed on her shoulder and yanked her backwards. She whipped around and glared at the vampire. "They killed my father, Marcus. My siblings. We can't—"

"We can, and we shall. I'm not risking you. And if your father managed to pull off what he claimed, he'll be with us again in a few months. We need to be patient."

She stalked back to the Jeep on the logging trail. The vampire jogged to keep up. When she reached the vehicle, she yanked open the back door. The rich scent of honey filled the air, overwhelming the woman's apple odor. Despite the gag and handcuffs looped through the restraint in the middle of the floor, Sharon shrank as far away as she could, her eyes wide with fear.

Maddy grinned. She could feel the flesh on her face stretch as her real teeth slipped into place. "Don't worry, Sharon." Watching their prisoner, she patted her flat stomach. "We'll be sisters, pregnant together just like Daddy said. Too bad you probably won't survive the birth, but I promise I'll take good care of our babies." She climbed into the back seat.

Sharon's muffled screams didn't stop until they were well into Idaho.

# Chapter 37

Before leaving the high school, the residents of Tuttle Creek decided to have a town meeting at noon the next day. The idea was to give everyone a chance to go home, get some rest and food, and think about what they wanted their next step to be. Quite simply, too many Normals had learned about the supernaturals for them to make the problem go away through a witch potion or vampire telepathy.

Not to mention, the rest of the world would notice if the residents simply "disappeared".

Even though Alyson wasn't a citizen of the town, Mayor Newlin made a point of inviting her. When she asked him why, he shrugged. "We consider you one of us. That's all."

She'd slept until Logan poked her awake with his cold wet nose. No one said a word about them sharing a bed last night. And she pretended not to notice the antianxiety meds he took before he shifted to wolf form and huddled next to her on the mattress. Drugs and closeness were the only way they could both sleep.

As Alyson ate breakfast with the Goldsteins and Logan, she asked about the Augustine folks.

Logan forked some more French toast onto his plate before he said, "Alex is back in Los Angeles coordinating the seizure of any assets of the Sunshine Believers and Haight. Bebe's leading the CSI team on the retrieval of evidence and bodies. And Sam's ferrying in personnel and supplies. By the way—" He snatched the last piece of bacon Sarah had also been reaching for.

"Hey!" She raised her hand, her fingers in a peculiar pattern. "Goddess help me, give it back or I'll—"

"No hexing at the breakfast table," Aaron ordered.

"Besides, you're not healing," Logan said while he stuffed the slice in his mouth. Sarah flipped him off before she grabbed another piece of French toast.

"You were saying?" Alyson said dryly.

He swallowed and nodded at the same time. "Alex wanted to know if he could have copies of your interviews."

"Why?"

Logan paid careful attention to his food as he smeared butter on his toast. "To help with identifying the bodies."

"Sure." She exhaled. "I can't use them. Not after what happened."

Logan looked at her. "You sure? I know this project was important to you."

"The Sunshine Believers would have been a major career coup, but I had some alternatives lined up in case things on this trip fell through." She gave him what she was sure was a weak smile, but it was the best she could muster after everything that had happened.

At some point, she'd have to go back to New Orleans and talk with Papa and Aunt Francine. Try to repair some of the damage to their relationships. But she no longer thought of Louisiana as her home.

The problem being she was no longer sure what was home. In her desire for independence, she'd gotten exactly what she asked for. Now she understood why Mama called getting your wish granted a curse, not a blessing.

The crowd in the high school gym was quiet compared to last night. Carol and Marvin waved to Alyson and patted the seat between them. For a brief instant she was very thankful she wasn't on the dais with Logan, Roy, and the Goldsteins.

Tad Newlin spoke first about how he was thankful that everyone who'd made it to the high school shelter were fine.

"What about the people that didn't make it?"

Alyson looked over her shoulder to see Abner Little waving his bandaged arm. There was either something personal between him and Mayor Newlin or Abner was what her father would call an ornery cuss.

"As far as we know, just folks up at the Haight ranch were killed." At the murmur that went through the assembly, Tad raised his hands. "Most of you heard the explosions up on the mountain last night." He lowered his hands and gripped the podium pretty tight from his white knuckles. "An investigative team are collecting and identifying the bodies. Ms. Tribideaux volunteered copies of her interviews to help with the identification. This isn't a slam on the sheriff. We just don't have the facilities to handle that many casualties."

His answer seemed to satisfy Abner, who sat back down.

The mayor went on to say that the property damage at the high school was coming out of the town emergency budget. Also, that an anonymous donor had provided money for those with vehicle damage and to rebuild and restock Lydia Sharp's hardware store.

At which point, Lydia, a wiry woman with a blue-black braid that hung past the ass of her jeans, stood up. "No."

"What?" Mayor Tad looked flabbergasted.

"I'm not takin' charity from no one." Lydia folded her arms over her chest. "It'll be a loan."

Logan stood. "It's not a loan," he said loud enough to carry without the microphone. "It's not charity either. It's reparations. It's my fault your store burned to the ground."

Alyson jumped to her feet. "The fire's partly my fault, too. And we owe you for the clothing and ax we took." She shot a look at Logan daring him to contradict her.

"How about you three decide fault and liability between yourselves later?" Tad said. "We got a bit of other business to get through here." Alyson immediately sat down, but Logan and Lydia glared at each other for a moment longer before they did so.

Poor Lydia. Logan's alpha behavior had pricked her pride, even though Alyson knew deep down he meant well. Maybe she could smooth things over between the two after the meeting.

Tad cleared his throat before he continued. "All of you know by now that it wasn't a serial killer we were dealing with last night." He gulped air. Alyson felt sorry for the man. He'd had a lot thrown at him in the last twenty-four hours.

He waved at the people sitting on podium. "They call themselves supernaturals. You know 'em by their fairy tale names. Witches, werewolves, vampires. Like everyone else in the world there's good folks and bad folks. Now, Doc Goldstein is going to speak and answer some questions." He motioned for Aaron to approach.

Instead of wearing his typical flannel and jeans, the witch was dressed in a brown suit with a forest green tie, something authoritative but non-threatening. The colors emphasized his olive complexion and brown eyes.

Aaron gave a basic overview of the International Council's rules and pointed out that last night's attack was the reason they existed. That supernaturals had coexisted with Normals for millennia without problems.

Then the questions began. Was he worried about another Salem-type witch hunt? (No.) Did any witches die during the Salem trials? (No, the executed people were all Normals.) Would someone turn into a werewolf if Logan bit them? (No.)

Finally, a teenager from the look of him stood and raised his hand. "Excuse me, Dr. Goldstein?"

"Yes, Chad?"

"I was at the front of the school w-with Dr. Zachary." The boy called Chad bobbed his head. "Are you saying them dinosaur things are werevelociraptors?"

Another woman a couple of rows behind Chad rose as well. "And what about that blond lady? She wasn't any of the things you described, Doc."

"That's because I'm Frankenstein's monster," a familiar female voice said from the back of the gymnasium.

Alyson looked over her shoulder as did the rest of the townspeople. Sam leaned against the rear wall, her arms crossed over her chest. She must have teleported into the gym while Aaron had been fielding questions. Alyson couldn't blame her one bit for skirting the truth. The townspeople were already too close to the edge.

Sam's hair was pulled into a high, tight ponytail, and she wore jeans, a t-shirt from Cher's farewell tour, boots, and a black leather coat. With the huge silver hoops that replaced the gold earrings she'd accidentally melted when she incinerated the newborn demon, she looked like a biker babe.

She pushed away from the wall. "Do you mind if I address the town?"

Aaron and Tad exchanged looks before they both nodded to Sam.

Her arms dropped to her sides, and she strode to the front of the gym. Her easy leap to the dais would leave no doubt in anyone's mind that she wasn't Normal. Aaron stepped back from the podium, and she adjusted the microphone before she started.

"For those of you who don't know me, I'm Sam Ridgeway. Once upon a time, I was a Normal like you all." She waved hand to indicate the audience. "I was kidnapped to be a guinea pig for some assholes. So I understand how freaked a lot of you may feel right now, finding out that some things are real. I've been in your shoes.

"And Chad, to answer your question, no, those weren't werevelociraptors. However, they were dinosaur demons. They recruited some vampires who were already being hunted for breaking the law. We're pretty sure we wiped out their nest, but we have teams out verifying. We want to make sure everyone in Tuttle Creek is safe, Normal and supernatural."

Alyson glanced at the teenager through the crowd. He practically glowed bright red at Sam's acknowledgement.

The woman who originally asked about the goddess stood back up. "So how many of you supernaturals really live in Tuttle Creek?"

Sam gave Aaron some space to access the microphone. "Just me, Esther, Sarah, and Logan."

"Why'd you move here?" Paula, the girl who'd been asking Roy questions last night, stood up. "I mean, Tuttle Creek is too small. Some of us were bound to find out about you sooner or later."

Everyone on the makeshift stage looked at one another. Their face muscles twitched, which meant they were discussing something telepathically. Logan stood, and Aaron and Sam backed away from the podium.

Logan cleared his throat. "First, y'all ain't as smart as yah like to think. Otherwise, Marvin wouldn't have won that pool yah had going concerning my bedroom proclivities." His grin emphasized the thick Texas charm he was dishing out.

Nearly everyone snickered, and more than a few ladies blushed as their friends teased them.

Logan sobered. "I know there's already been speculation along the grapevines. Truth is Sam wasn't the only one those assholes kidnapped and experimented on. Sarah and I were taken and experimented on, too."

Total silence fell over the crowd. Half of them were literally holding their breath.

"To be totally honest, only six of us made it out of that torture chamber alive. And we still aren't sure how many folks were abducted and died there. They tried to starve me, to see the breaking point where a wolf would lose all reason and eat another person. They tossed a little girl named Sarah Goldstein in my cage. Somehow—"

He turned and smiled at the teenage witch. "Somehow we managed to keep each other alive." He turned back to the crowd. "I can't vouch for Sam or the others, but Sarah and I are still being treated for PTSD nearly four years after we were rescued."

A collective gasp filled the huge room. Moisture filmed Alyson's vision. Admitting such vulnerability had to be killing him. Papa would sooner die than admit to something like what was done to Logan and his friends.

"Montana is neutral territory for the North American weres," Logan continued. "It was the safest place I could think of. The fact that y'all were recruiting for a doctor is the reason we settled here. Does that answer your question, Paula?"

The girl swiped at her eyes as she nodded. More than a few other women and men were sniffling, too.

Logan went back to his seat, and Aaron stepped up to the podium once again.

"We know everything that's happened in the last twenty-four hours is a lot to take in. When Sarah said she was ready to live in a dorm, Esther and I started to talk about moving back to Los Angeles—"

"Ya can't leave us! We still need you here." Abner Little was on his feet, waving his injured arm again.

The doctor smiled at his wife for a moment before addressing the crowd. "That's why I brought up the situation with Mayor Newlin and the town council a couple of months ago. We'd already put together a timeline, and we're looking for someone I would co-practice with here for three years. But it comes down to the fact that we miss the rest of our family, not to mention our parents are getting older and need a little more help."

The townspeople erupted with protests. Alyson couldn't help smiling. For all of everyone's worries about retaliation against the supernatural citizens of Tuttle Creek, the people here knew what truly mattered.

Mayor Newlin rose and held up his hands, motioning for everyone to quiet down. Once they did, he traded places at the microphone with Aaron.

"We've got two choices since we now know about supernaturals. One is getting adopted by one of the supernatural organizations on this side of the country. The Goldsteins' high priestess and Ms. Ridgeway's vampire boss have both volunteered. There's some rules we'd have to follow, but there're benefits, too."

"Wait a minute!" Abner jumped up, waving his injured arm again. "Do we have to let them vamps drink our blood?"

Tad shot Sam a pleading look.

She joined him at the podium. "For one thing, drinking human blood is illegal for vampires. In fact, it's an almost automatic death penalty." She grinned. "The other thing to consider, my boss is noted for taking in supernatural strays. Me, homeless werecoyotes, half-fairies—" She winced. "Oops. Piece of advice. Don't ever refer to the fae by the slur I just used. It can get you killed. The point being he'd welcome anyone as long as they don't cause trouble."

Tad took her place at the microphone. "The other option if we as a town feel we can't . . . handle what happened last night—" The mayor appeared distinctly uncomfortable. "We can drink a, uh, a, magick potion and forget the attack."

A rumble ran through the crowd, and Tad held up his hands for quiet again. "There's a catch. Whatever decision we make, it needs to be unanimous. The potion only blurs the memories. If some of us don't take it and accidentally mention last night's events to someone who did, then the memories can possibly come back, and we're right back to where we are now."

"No potion is going to change the fact my store's gone," Lydia yelled.

"Which is why we're taking a break from the official part of the meeting." Tad looked at his watch. "For the next thirty minutes. Talk amongst yourselves. The town council and I put together a pros and cons list. Ask questions. When time's up, we'll take the first vote."

Marvin snorted. "I already know how I'm voting," he said under his breath.

Carol leaned over and glared at him. "We've had a little more time to get used to the idea. You gotta give everyone else a chance."

A third of the crowd headed for the refreshments. Another third talked with their neighbors. The rest gathered around the podium, mainly the teens and twenty-somethings, and peppered Logan and the rest with questions.

Well, everyone except Sam. She slipped behind the chairs and jumped off the podium. No one else seemed to notice. This was Alyson's chance.

She rose. Carol raised an eyebrow, so Alyson smiled and said, "Potty break. Back in a few."

Once she cleared the row of folding chairs, she called, "Sam!"

The goddess turned and waited. Alyson dodged milling people. Something seemed to muffle all the noise in the gym when she reached Sam.

Alyson looked around, then faced the goddess who gave her a wry smile.

"I can't do crowds like I used to." Sam's attention swept across the people. "This is nothing compared to the red carpet on awards night, and—" She sighed. "Times like these I get pissed all over again at what those asshats did to me." She blinked and focused on Alyson. "Let's go outside."

Sam pushed the bar clearly marked "EMERGENCY". Yet, the alarms didn't go off. Alyson followed her outside.

Murky sunlight filtered through the low-slung clouds. Damp air brought the fresh smell of pine from the mountain. The temperature was at the sweet spot where last night's half-foot of snow wasn't melting except in the spots where salt had been spread—like the gigantic circle around the high school.

"So what's up?" Sam asked.

Alyson licked her lips, not sure where to start. "What did you do to me last night?" So much for gently broaching the subject.

The goddess frowned. "What are you talking about?"

Alyson hugged herself. "I've never acted brave. Not like I did last night. "She swallowed hard. "Alex needed the blood of a goddess and the weapon of a god to fight dino demons in Peru."

Sam smirked. "And you think I made you drink my blood?"

"No, that's not—" Alyson winced. Dammit, she was making a mess of things. "That's not what I meant."

Sam laid a hand on Alyson's shoulder. "Sweetie, I didn't do a damn thing to you. I *can't* do anything to you. Not without your permission."

Alyson stared at her in disbelief. "Yes, you can! You're a goddess!"

Sam's smirk melted into a frown. "Can you say that just a little louder? I think there's a few people in the school that didn't hear you."

"Sorry, it's just—" Alyson pushed at a clump of snow with the toe of her boot. "We couldn't have defeated . . . him. Not without a weapon of a god. And if you didn't do something to me, we still needed some kind of super weapon."

Laughter poured from Sam as she shook her head. "And what did you use to kill him?"

"A hardware store ax."

One blond eyebrow rose. "And?"

Alyson clenched her jaw. The woman could be so damn frustrating. "And what?"

"You're a documentarian. I suggest you do some research, Ms. Trib-ideaux." A brilliant grin lit Sam's face as she walked around Alyson and reached for the door handle.

"So you're not going to admit you did something to the ax."

"I can only help when I'm asked." Sam went inside. The door's pneu-matics let it close with a soft *da-snick*.

The citizens of Tuttle Creek didn't take the whole half hour to make their decision. By the time, Alyson collected herself enough to re-enter the school, they were in the process of taking the first vote. The decision to become a supernatural town was unanimous.

Maybe if the Normals in this town could change, Papa could as well. Alyson chuckled to herself. That would happen on the day there were three full moons in a month.

When she tried to join Logan and Lydia in their discussion about res-titution, they both waved her off.

"You weren't the one careless with acetylene," Lydia said. "Not to mention, you were the one who actually killed the demon. You've paid your debt."

Afterwards at the clinic, Aaron had two seconds and the energy to heal Roy's bruised ribs. When Alyson offered to drive him home, Logan overrode her.

"Sam's going with me, and we'll be meeting with Bebe and the en-forcers up at the ranch after we drop off Roy." When Alyson opened her mouth to protest, he laid a finger on her lips. "For this once, please don't argue with me. I need to know you're safe here with the Goldsteins."

She blinked and covered his hand with hers. "You suspect there's more of the half-breed demons."

"We're not sure, but we didn't want to scare the shit out of the town."

Finally, she nodded. When they left, the itch to do something, any-thing, drove her back to the Goldstein's house.

Their very empty house.

Aaron and Esther had opened the clinic since life in Tuttle Creek continued regardless of the change in perspective of its citizens. Carol, Lois from Last Buffalo, and several other business owners had cornered Sarah and were probably still peppering her with questions. Her scent hadn't indicated any distress on her part. It was almost as if last night's events had made her more confident in herself.

Alyson wished she could say the same. She made herself some tea, grabbed her laptop, and headed upstairs to Logan's room. Sam's non-answer bothered her more than she cared to admit.

She hadn't felt any different last night, other than scared out of her gourd, but she couldn't back down against the demon. Not with so many lives at stake. In the chaos of the fight at the hardware store, she had grabbed a weapon at random. Hadn't she?

She set her laptop on his desk and pulled the ax out from under his bed and unwrapped the blanket from around it. Still no corrosion on the blade. Considering the demon blood's acidic properties, Sam had to have done something to the steel if she hadn't done something to Alyson herself.

But what? It didn't glow like Alex said the Incan god's weapon had. She sniffed the blade. Plain old steel. She inhaled along the handle. Ash and lacquer.

She took it back to Logan's desk, set it beside her laptop, and booted up the machine. The research into the use of an ax for religious rituals drew her in so completely that when Logan entered the room, she nearly jumped out of her skin.

The ax caught his attention, and he frowned. "Not feeling safe in a warded house."

Alyson breathed deeply in an attempt to calm her racing heart. "No. Investigating some discrepancies in Alex's story."

Suspicion glinted in his eyes. "What do you mean?"

"Calm down. I'm not disparaging your BFF. In fact, I think Sam did something to either me or the ax, but I'm not sure what." She compared the vampire's story of killing the two dino demons in Peru with their fight last night. Then she relayed her strange conversation with the goddess this afternoon.

"Then I found this." She turned her laptop so he could see the screen. "The ax has been linked to various goddess cults, dating back nearly five thousand years. If Sam's a goddess, she could have laid a spell or something on the ax I used, right?" She shrugged. "I don't get why she'd lie about it. Or wait until I'd decapitated the demon before she showed up."

Logan straightened. "Who do you pray to?"

Alyson blinked. "Mother Wolf, but why would that matter?"

"Think about it." He crossed his arms over his chest. "Your soul is Mother Wolf's. If Sam interferes with you, even to save your life, she's going to piss off Mother Wolf. If she did help you by tapping into that ancient belief in the ax as a universal goddess symbol and charging your ax somehow, she can't admit it." He rubbed his chin. "Not without causing a war between deities. I suggest you let this one go for now, Alyson. For all our sakes. Besides, we have a bigger problem."

"A bigger problem? What could be worse than demons, rogue vampires, and angry goddesses?"

"My mother. She and Dad are in town, and they want to meet you."

# Chapter 38

Logan breathed his own little prayer to Mother Wolf. He half-expected Alyson to go ballistic over the news about his parents.

She turned the computer to face her and tapped the keys to shut down her browser. "Um, should I ask why?"

"Your dad's not happy about you leaving his pack."

A wince scrunched her features. "Please tell me he didn't do anything stupid."

Logan chuckled. "Right now, Rousseau and Augustine are acting as messengers between New Orleans and San Antonio."

Her wince turned into a scowl. "Papa can't do anything to your parents. You're not a San Antonio member. You're your own alpha."

"I'm aware of that." With everything that happened to her, the last thing he wanted was to push her into a decision.

She nodded as if coming to a conclusion. "What is my role in your new pack?"

He blinked at her unexpected response. "After everything that's happened, you want to mate?"

Her smile was a little sad and hopeful at the same time. "I won't lie. I'm attracted to you, but I'm not ready to have sex with anyone yet, much less commit to a lifetime. Not this soon. After your own experiences in Los Angeles, I would think you of all people would understand why I need some time to process everything that's happened here."

Logan smiled back. "If it helps, I know a good therapist in Billings. If you want to stick around here for a while, that is. Montana is neutral territory after all. It's the safest place to be while you recover."

She closed her laptop and nodded before she faced him again. "That sounds like a good idea. I'll have to see if Roy is willing to rent his cabin for the rest of the winter."

"He might even be willing to cut you a deal." He wasn't sure how far to push it, but he couldn't offer the guest room here without asking Aaron and Esther. Other words slipped out before he could stop them. "If you need the company—"

She opened her mouth, and he held up a hand. "If a bad blizzard comes in," he said. "Or you and Roy are struck with cabin fever, come into town. I know Esther would love to have a fellow supernatural to talk to."

"That would be good." A slight smile curved Alyson's lips. "However, I was looking in terms of another role with your pack. Like being your beta."

"My beta?"

"Your beta," she said firmly. "If you're serious about starting your own pack, that is."

"Why?"

"You're far stronger than any alpha I've ever met because of your ordeals." She ran a finger over the ax. "You played the demon with honesty." Her eyes met his. "And you kept your promise and left me the kill strike."

Nervousness hit him. Not a true anxiety attack. It had taken him enough years to recognize the difference. But he needed to know.

"I mean, why do you want to be my beta? Everything you said sounds more like hero worship. Being beta means responsibility and loyalty."

Alyson stood. "It means watching my alpha's back and working with him to build a strong pack."

"Yeah." Logan grinned. "It does, but just the two of us can't make much of a go without others."

She lifted her chin. "Then let other wolves make assumptions about our relationship. It'll help with recruiting. And if you find someone more suitable as a mate, I won't cause any problems."

"You sure about that?"

The corner of her mouth tilted upward. "Well, I'd be more than a little vexed if you didn't wait for me."

"Then I guess that leaves us with where. What about Seattle? There currently isn't a wolf pack in the city. All your city conveniences are available, and there are plenty of parks outside of the settled area."

"No." She shook her head. "The non-wolves have their own community around Puget Sound and its islands. They'll assume we've come to take over. No reason to start a fight for nothing."

"What about South Dakota? The Badlands haven't had a pack in over a century."

"It has possibilities." She smiled.

"Really?" He stared at her wondering what catch he was missing. "There aren't a lot in the way of social amenities as there are in New Orleans."

"You said you were looking for a new business challenge. Why not bring a few jobs to the area? Maybe some amenities like beignets and cherry amaretto ice cream. Besides the place doesn't matter." She held out her hand. "Just the wolves involved."

He took her warm palm in his and shook it. "Then I say we have ourselves a deal, Beta."

*Attention all werewolves: Emily and George are in the house.*

From the look on Alyson's face, she'd heard Sam's mental voice, too.

"Shall we, Ms. Tribideaux?" Logan held out his elbow.

"Certainly, Mr. Polk." She wrapped her arm around his. "If I can face dinosaur demons, I can face your mother."

"I'm holding you to that."

They both laughed as they headed downstairs to confront their first challenge as a pack.

**Augustine Coven has their hands full when rogue vampire Marcus Giovanni and his dino demon allies up the personal stakes for Tiffany. And just because she's Normal, it doesn't mean she won't make them pay in kind. Turn the page for a preview of *Sacrificed*!**

**Also, please leave a review to let other readers know what you think of this book!**

# Sacrificed

Excerpt © 2017 by Suzan Harden

# Chapter 1

Max Howell tossed ten M&Ms on the pile in the middle of the table. "See your five and raise you five, Caesar." The vampire master's left eyebrow twitched, but he said nothing. Max turned and watched the players on his other side.

Duncan held up his cards to consult with his partner sitting in his lap. "What do you think, Ellie?"

Max tried not to smile at his daughter's serious expression while she examined her uncle's hand. She'd inherited the St. James blue-black hair, but somehow ended up with the Howell blue eyes.

"Hey, that's cheating!" Alex said. His protest emphasized the Texas accent he'd kept for over a century and a half.

"You had the opportunity to obtain your own partner, Stanton." Caesar smiled over the top of his cards.

"At least Phillippa plays poker," Colin grumbled. "You should have heard the lecture I got about gambling." The last scion of the famed Fitzgerald political family scowled at his own hand.

"Auntie Anne is right. You're not very good at poker, Uncle Colin," Ellie's sweet voice piped up. She tossed twenty brown M&Ms on the pile. "Raise you by another ten, Daddy." She popped a blue one from her prodigious pile into her mouth.

Colin glared at her in mock outrage. "Did you talk Duncan into reading my mind? Because that cheating, too."

"Dude," Jake Wong drawled. "In case you hadn't noticed, two mere Normals are kicking your supernatural ass, and one of them isn't even in kindergarten yet." He tossed the requisite number of M&M's into the kitty.

Max checked his two cards again. Did the four vampires realize how obvious their tells were? Only the really crappy hands he'd drawn had kept his pile from being as big as Jake's or Ellie's.

Alex pushed his cards aside. "Too rich for me."

After a bit of grumbling, Colin folded as well.

"I'm out." Caesar laid down his hand.

Max made a show of checking his cards again. He'd played with Jake long enough to know his sister's ex was bluffing. However, his sister's husband couldn't bluff to save his life even with Ellie as his partner. "I match your bet and raise you another five."

Sure enough, Duncan whispered into Ellie's ear, and she tossed the necessary amount of M&M's into the kitty. "Raise you ten, Daddy."

Jake tossed his cards face down on the table. "Mazel tov, kid. Maybe your mom and dad will let you come to Vegas with me next weekend." He winked at Ellie.

"Can I, Daddy?" She bounced in her excitement. "Uncle Duncan and Aunt Sam will let us stay with them." She batted her big blue eyes at her poker partner. "Won't you, Uncle Duncan?"

"Of course, you may visit." He glared at Jake. "But you need to ask your mother first." Silently, Duncan mouthed over Ellie's head, "And you are not taking her on the casino floor, Wong."

That didn't mean Duncan wouldn't set up a private room for Ellie with staff to play with her. Hopefully, her presence would get Sam to . . .

Max clenched his jaw at the disturbing thoughts. To what? Relax? Rejoin the human race?

Except his baby sister wasn't human any more. And she'd become obsessed with hunting down the rest of the saurian demons who'd managed to escape the Battle of Tuttle Creek last year. Even Duncan had admitted Ellie was the only thing linking Sam to the mortal plain these days.

Max stared at the flimsy cardboard in his hand. Duncan would totally lose it if Sam simply didn't come home from one of her hunting trips someday.

"Daddy!"

Max realized with a start Ellie had been calling him more than once.

"Sorry, sweetie. Just thinking about what I should do." He tossed his matching bet on the pile. "I call."

Ellie squealed in glee. "Three kings!" She laid down her cards.

Max smiled. He may not be able to save his sister, but he could damn well make his daughter happy. He laid his full house face down. "You win, sweetie."

She clapped her hands. "Another hand."

"No. I said this was the last one for tonight." At her pout, he added, "But we can play more this weekend when we go visit Duncan and Sam." Tiffany wouldn't argue too much about a father-daughter weekend road trip. With the class load she was taking, she needed some serious study time.

"Can Uncle Jake come, too?"

Max hesitated for a moment. Jake and Sam's ancient engagement was a sore point with Duncan even though Sam was long over the stunt man turned enforcer.

"Yes, he may," Duncan said.

"Yay!" Ellie jumped off his lap and ran around the table, singing, "We're goin' to Vegas!"

Max rose and stretched, only to have Jake grab his arm and pull him aside.

"You sure this is a good idea?" Jake's brown eyes reflected Max's concern. "I was joking about Vegas. I won't come if it'll cause problems."

Max glanced at the vampires, who were studiously ignoring him and Jake. He knew damn well they could hear everything they said, but he was grateful they kept Ellie entertained while they cleared drinks and snacks so he and Jake could talk.

"Actually, yeah, it would be good if you came. Nothing against Duncan—"

"I am glad to know you bear me no ill will."

Max jerked and glared up at his brother-in-law. How could someone with his bulk and height sneak up on anyone? "I really need to put a bell on you."

Duncan's smile didn't quite reach his eyes. He turned his attention to Jake. "You are most definitely welcome to visit the Karnak. I think it would do Samantha some good."

A sick feeling filled Max's gut. Duncan wanting Jake at the hotel/casino he ran said volumes. "Are things getting worse?"

"Define 'worse.'" Duncan grimaced.

"She's been coming home, hasn't she?"

"It is not the coming home that disturbs me."

Alex joined them. "My father-in-law isn't trying to put the moves on her again, is he?"

Max leaned around the men to check on Ellie. Caesar galloped down the main hallway of his mansion with her on his back. Max shook his head. If he filmed the vampire master, and former prince of Egypt, playing horsey with his daughter, he could make a mint. He just wouldn't live long enough to enjoy it.

"No, she has made her wishes in the matter quite clear to Ares. We have not had any more issues with unwanted suitors." Duncan looked perplexed. "She has taken to playing bridge with some of the goddesses when she's home."

Max took off his glasses and cleaned them on the hem of his polo shirt to cover his own unease. He'd met some of Sam's new friends, all of them death deities from various world religions. It was creepy as hell, but what could he say when Sam was one of them? "She's not ignoring the baby zombies, is she?"

Duncan shook his head. "No, and please stop calling them 'baby zombies.' They are restored humans, and they have been for nearly five years now." Lines creased the alabaster skin of his forehead. "Frankly, they are doing better than she. And they are worried about her obsession with the Old Ones' acolytes as well."

Max put his glasses back on and rocked on his heels. "Guess we're coming out to Vegas this weekend."

As Max had figured, Ellie was out cold by the time they pulled into their Tarzana ranch house's driveway. When he lifted her out of her safety seat, her little arms automatically wrapped around his neck and baby snores filled his ear.

The living room lights weren't on. That was odd. Was Tiffany still at the university?

No, it wasn't just the main lights. Even the little antique side table lamp Grandma Neel had sent them as a wedding present was out, and he was pretty sure he'd turned it on before he and Ellie left for Caesar's for the evening.

Crap. One burnt out bulb meant tripping over whatever toys Ellie left scattered in the living room. He really didn't want set her down on the couch. If he did, she'd be wide awake, hyper about the trip to Las Vegas. Then he'd get an earful from Tiffany for allowing their daughter to stay up so late.

Maybe if he shuffled along the carpet, he'd be okay.

Max twisted the key and nudged the front door open. The hairs on the back of his neck rose before he consciously recognized the scent of sandalwood.

Vampire. Fresh vampire. Except it had been two weeks since the last time Duncan had dropped by, much less any of the rest of Augustine Coven.

The odor was followed by the equally distinctive scent of unwashed human.

Intruders.

Max pivoted back toward his Volvo, but something grabbed him from behind at the same time his daughter was ripped from his arms.

"Ellie!"

Pain exploded at the back of his head. He couldn't make his arms work. The second blow struck the side of his face, sending his glasses flying.

"Daddy!"

He struck out blindly in the direction of his daughter's terrified voice. There was a muffled grunt before a blow to his back drove him to his knees.

"Ellie!"

Her screams grew fainter. Someone was taking her away. He lashed out, but fists pounded him, boots kicked him until he couldn't take a breath. A sharp crack and his jaw broke along with a couple of teeth. More bones broke until all he felt was agony.

But it didn't match the agony in his heart. Someone took his daughter. *Ellie!*

A voice whispered through his mind. *Your daughter is ours. Make sure you remember that when your world burns.*

The fire in Max's brain consumed him until everything he'd ever been burned to ash.

**Sacrificed** is available at your favorite online retailer.

# Acknowledgements

Time has gone so fast.

To DH, aka Darling Husband, thank you for the love and support, not to mention being my guinea pig. I'll love you always.

To GK, aka Genius Kid aka my son, you were still in preschool when I started writing this series, and now you're in your last year of high school. I'm so proud of you.

To Elaina Lee of For the Muse Design, your covers are the perfect wrapping for these stories. Thank you for your creativity.

To Jaye Manus, you're always patient with my anal production values. I appreciate your skills more than you can imagine.

And to my readers, thank you for keeping this series alive through some dark times in my life. Your faith means more than you know.

# About the Author

Suzan Harden transitioned from writing information technology manuals for companies and legal articles for a law enforcement magazine to her first love, fantasy and science fiction in all their forms. She's the author of the Millersburg Magick Mysteries, the Soccer Moms of the Apocalypse series, and the Books of Apep series.

## Contact Suzan Harden

Facebook: Suzan Harden
Email: suzan@suzanharden.com
Website: www.suzanharden.com

**Sign up for Suzan's mailing list**